ABOUT TIME

ABOUT TIME

the forerunners of time travel
and temporal anomalies in
science fiction and fantasy

CHAD ARMENT, EDITOR

Washington Irving
Charles Dickens
Edgar Allan Poe
Edward Page Mitchell
Ambrose Bierce
H. G. Wells
Algernon Blackwood
and more...

COACHWHIP PUBLICATIONS
Landisville, Pennsylvania

About Time
Published 2008 Coachwhip Publications
Coachwhipbooks.com

ISBN 1-930585-55-1
ISBN-13 978-1-930585-55-3

Front cover image: Roman Krochuk (Aurora Borealis, Alaska)

Contents

Rip Van Winkle (1819)   7

Peter Rugg, the Missing Man (1824)   21

An Anachronism, or Missing One's Coach (1838)   31

A Christmas Carol in Prose (1843)   50

A Tale of the Ragged Mountains (1844)   112

An Uncommon Sort of Spectre (1879)   121

The Clock That Went Backward (1881)   129

Newton's Brain (1892)   141

John Bartine's Watch (1893)   180

The Hour-Glass (1898)   185

The New Accelerator (1901)   198

"Wireless" (1902)   210

Phantas (1910)   226

Accessory Before the Fact (1914)   239

Enoch Soames (1916)   245

Rip Van Winkle

WASHINGTON IRVING

A Posthumous Writing
of Diedrich Knickerbocker

By Woden, God of Saxons,
From whence comes Wensday, that is Wodensday,
Truth is a thing that ever I will keep
Unto thylke day in which I creep into
My sepulchre.

Cartwright

The following Tale was found among the papers of the late Diedrich Knickerbocker, an old gentleman of New York, who was very curious in the Dutch history of the province, and the manners of the descendants from its primitive settlers. His historical researches, however, did not lie so much among books as among men; for the former are lamentably scanty on his favorite topics; whereas he found the old burghers, and still more their wives, rich in that legendary lore, so invaluable to true history. Whenever, therefore, he happened upon a genuine Dutch family, snugly shut up in its low-roofed farmhouse, under a spreading sycamore, he looked upon it as a little clasped volume of black-letter, and studied it with the zeal of a book-worm.

The result of all these researches was a history of the province during the reign of the Dutch governors, which he published some years since. There have been various opinions as to the literary character of his work, and, to tell the truth, it is not a whit better than it should be. Its chief merit is its scrupulous accuracy, which indeed was a little questioned on its first appearance, but has since been completely established; and it is now admitted into all historical collections, as a book of unquestionable authority.

The old gentleman died shortly after the publication of his work, and now that he is dead and gone, it cannot do much harm to his

memory to say that his time might have been better employed in
weightier labors. He, however, was apt to ride his hobby his own way;
and though it did now and then kick up the dust a little in the eyes of
his neighbors, and grieve the spirit of some friends, for whom he felt the
truest deference and affection; yet his errors and follies are remembered "more in sorrow than in anger," and it begins to be suspected,
that he never intended to injure or offend. But however his memory may
be appreciated by critics, it is still held dear by many folks, whose good
opinion is well worth having; particularly by certain biscuit-bakers, who
have gone so far as to imprint his likeness on their new-year cakes;
and have thus given him a chance for immortality, almost equal to
the being stamped on a Waterloo Medal, or a Queen Anne's Farthing.

* * *

Whoever has made a voyage up the Hudson must remember the
Kaatskill mountains. They are a dismembered branch of the great
Appalachian family, and are seen away to the west of the river, swell-
ing up to a noble height, and lording it over the surrounding country.
Every change of season, every change of weather, indeed, every hour
of the day, produces some change in the magical hues and shapes of
these mountains, and they are regarded by all the good wives, far and
near, as perfect barometers. When the weather is fair and settled, they
are clothed in blue and purple, and print their bold outlines on the
clear evening sky, but, sometimes, when the rest of the landscape is
cloudless, they will gather a hood of gray vapors about their summits,
which, in the last rays of the setting sun, will glow and light up like a
crown of glory.

At the foot of these fairy mountains, the voyager may have descried
the light smoke curling up from a village, whose shingle-roofs gleam
among the trees, just where the blue tints of the upland melt away
into the fresh green of the nearer landscape. It is a little village of
great antiquity, having been founded by some of the Dutch colonists, in
the early times of the province, just about the beginning of the government of the good Peter Stuyvesant, (may he rest in peace!) and there were
some of the houses of the original settlers standing within a few years,
built of small yellow bricks brought from Holland, having latticed
windows and gable fronts, surmounted with weather-cocks.

In that same village, and in one of these very houses (which, to
tell the precise truth, was sadly time-worn and weather-beaten), there
lived many years since, while the country was yet a province of Great
Britain, a simple good-natured fellow of the name of Rip Van Winkle.
He was a descendant of the Van Winkles who figured so gallantly in

the chivalrous days of Peter Stuyvesant, and accompanied him to the siege of Fort Christina. He inherited, however, but little of the martial character of his ancestors. I have observed that he was a simple good-natured man; he was, moreover, a kind neighbor, and an obedient hen-pecked husband. Indeed, to the latter circumstance might be owing that meekness of spirit which gained him such universal popularity; for those men are most apt to be obsequious and conciliating abroad, who are under the discipline of shrews at home. Their tempers, doubtless, are rendered pliant and malleable in the fiery furnace of domestic tribulation; and a curtain lecture is worth all the sermons in the world for teaching the virtues of patience and long-suffering. A termagant wife may, therefore, in some respects, be considered a tolerable blessing; and if so, Rip Van Winkle was thrice blessed.

Certain it is, that he was a great favorite among all the good wives of the village, who, as usual, with the amiable sex, took his part in all family squabbles; and never failed, whenever they talked those matters over in their evening gossipings, to lay all the blame on Dame Van Winkle. The children of the village, too, would shout with joy whenever he approached. He assisted at their sports, made their playthings, taught them to fly kites and shoot marbles, and told them long stories of ghosts, witches, and Indians. Whenever he went dodging about the village, he was surrounded by a troop of them, hanging on his skirts, clambering on his back, and playing a thousand tricks on him with impunity; and not a dog would bark at him throughout the neighborhood.

The great error in Rip's composition was an insuperable aversion to all kinds of profitable labor. It could not be from the want of assiduity or perseverance; for he would sit on a wet rock, with a rod as long and heavy as a Tartar's lance, and fish all day without a murmur, even though he should not be encouraged by a single nibble. He would carry a fowling-piece on his shoulder for hours together, trudging through woods and swamps, and up hill and down dale, to shoot a few squirrels or wild pigeons. He would never refuse to assist a neighbor even in the roughest toil, and was a foremost man at all country frolics for husking Indian corn, or building stone-fences; the women of the village, too, used to employ him to run their errands, and to do such little odd jobs as their less obliging husbands would not do for them. In a word Rip was ready to attend to anybody's business but his own; but as to doing family duty, and keeping his farm in order, he found it impossible.

In fact, he declared it was of no use to work on his farm; it was the most pestilent little piece of ground in the whole country; every thing about it went wrong, and would go wrong, in spite of him. His fences were continually falling to pieces; his cow would either go astray, or get among the cabbages; weeds were sure to grow quicker in his fields than anywhere else; the rain always made a point of setting in just as he had some out-door work to do; so that though his patrimonial estate had dwindled away under his management, acre by acre, until there was little more left than a mere patch of Indian corn and potatoes, yet it was the worst conditioned farm in the neighborhood.

His children, too, were as ragged and wild as if they belonged to nobody. His son Rip, an urchin begotten in his own likeness, promised to inherit the habits, with the old clothes of his father. He was generally seen trooping like a colt at his mother's heels, equipped in a pair of his father's cast-off galligaskins, which he had much ado to hold up with one hand, as a fine lady does her train in bad weather.

Rip Van Winkle, however, was one of those happy mortals, of foolish, well-oiled dispositions, who take the world easy, eat white bread or brown, whichever can be got with least thought or trouble, and would rather starve on a penny than work for a pound. If left to himself, he would have whistled life away in perfect contentment; but his wife kept continually dinning in his ears about his idleness, his carelessness, and the ruin he was bringing on his family. Morning, noon, and night, her tongue was incessantly going, and everything he said or did was sure to produce a torrent of household eloquence. Rip had but one way of replying to all lectures of the kind, and that, by frequent use, had grown into a habit. He shrugged his shoulders, shook his head, cast up his eyes, but said nothing. This, however, always provoked a fresh volley from his wife; so that he was fain to draw off his forces, and take to the outside of the house—the only side which, in truth, belongs to a hen-pecked husband.

Rip's sole domestic adherent was his dog Wolf, who was as much hen-pecked as his master; for Dame Van Winkle regarded them as companions in idleness, and even looked upon Wolf with an evil eye, as the cause of his master's going so often astray. True it is, in all points of spirit befitting an honorable dog, he was as courageous an animal as ever scoured the woods—but what courage can withstand the ever-during and all-besetting terrors of a woman's tongue? The moment Wolf entered the house his crest fell, his tail drooped to the ground, or curled between his legs, he sneaked about with a gallows air, casting many a sidelong glance at Dame Van Winkle, and at the least flourish of a broom-stick or ladle, he would fly to the door with yelping precipitation.

Times grew worse and worse with Rip Van Winkle as years of matrimony rolled on; a tart temper never mellows with age, and a sharp tongue is the only edged tool that grows keener with constant use. For a long while he used to console himself, when driven from home, by frequenting a kind of perpetual club of the sages, philosophers, and other idle personages of the village; which held its sessions on a bench before a small inn, designated by a rubicund portrait of His Majesty George the Third. Here they used to sit in the shade through a long lazy summer's day, talking listlessly over village gossip, or telling endless sleepy stories about nothing. But it would have been worth any statesman's money to have heard the profound discussions that sometimes took place, when by chance an old newspaper fell into their hands from some passing traveller. How solemnly they would listen to the contents, as drawled out by Derrick Van Bummel, the schoolmaster, a dapper learned little man, who was not to be daunted by the most gigantic word in the dictionary; and how sagely they would deliberate upon public events some months after they had taken place.

The opinions of this junto were completely controlled by Nicholas Vedder, a patriarch of the village, and landlord of the inn, at the door of which he took his seat from morning till night, just moving sufficiently to avoid the sun and keep in the shade of a large tree; so that the neighbors could tell the hour by his movements as accurately as by a sundial. It is true he was rarely heard to speak, but smoked his pipe incessantly. His adherents, however (for every great man has his adherents), perfectly understood him, and knew how to gather his opinions. When anything that was read or related displeased him, he was observed to smoke his pipe vehemently, and to send forth short, frequent and angry puffs; but when pleased, he would inhale the smoke slowly and tranquilly, and emit it in light and placid clouds; and sometimes, taking the pipe from his mouth, and letting the fragrant vapor curl about his nose, would gravely nod his head in token of perfect approbation.

From even this stronghold the unlucky Rip was at length routed by his termagant wife, who would suddenly break in upon the tranquillity of the assemblage and call the members all to naught; nor was that august personage, Nicholas Vedder himself, sacred from the daring tongue of this terrible virago, who charged him outright with encouraging her husband in habits of idleness.

Poor Rip was at last reduced almost to despair; and his only alternative, to escape from the labor of the farm and clamor of his wife, was to take gun in hand and stroll away into the woods. Here he would sometimes seat himself at the foot of a tree, and share the contents of his wallet with Wolf, with whom he sympathized as a fellow-sufferer in persecution. "Poor Wolf," he would say, "thy mistress leads thee a dog's life of it; but never mind, my lad, whilst I live thou shalt never want a friend to stand by thee!" Wolf would wag his tail, look wistfuly in his master's face, and if dogs can feel pity I verily believe he reciprocated the sentiment with all his heart.

In a long ramble of the kind on a fine autumnal day, Rip had unconsciously scrambled to one of the highest parts of the Kaatskill mountains. He was after his favorite sport of squirrel shooting, and the still solitudes had echoed and re-echoed with the reports of his gun. Panting and fatigued, he threw himself, late in the afternoon, on a green knoll, covered with mountain herbage, that crowned the brow of a precipice. From an opening between the trees he could overlook all the lower country for many a mile of rich woodland. He saw at a distance the lordly Hudson, far, far below him, moving on its silent but majestic course, with the reflection of a purple cloud, or the sail of a lagging bark, here and there sleeping on its glassy bosom, and at last losing itself in the blue highlands.

On the other side he looked down into a deep mountain glen, wild, lonely, and shagged, the bottom filled with fragments from the impending cliffs, and scarcely lighted by the reflected rays of the setting sun. For some time Rip lay musing on this scene; evening was gradually advancing; the mountains began to throw their long blue shadows over the valleys; he saw that it would be dark long before he could reach the village, and he heaved a heavy sigh when he thought of encountering the terrors of Dame Van Winkle.

As he was about to descend, he heard a voice from a distance, hallooing, "Rip Van Winkle! Rip Van Winkle!" He looked round, but could see nothing but a crow winging its solitary flight across the mountain. He thought his fancy must have deceived him, and turned again to descend, when he heard the same cry ring through the still evening air: "Rip Van Winkle! Rip Van Winkle!"—at the same time Wolf bristled up his back, and giving a low growl, skulked to his master's side, looking fearfully down into the glen. Rip now felt a vague apprehension stealing over him; he looked anxiously in the same direction, and perceived a strange figure slowly toiling up the rocks, and bending under the weight of something he carried on his back. He was surprised to see any human being in this lonely and unfrequented place, but supposing it to be some one of the neighborhood in need of his assistance, he hastened down to yield it.

On nearer approach he was still more surprised at the singularity of the stranger's appearance. He was a short square-built old fellow, with thick bushy hair, and a grizzled beard. His dress was of the antique Dutch fashion—a cloth jerkin strapped round the waist—several pair of breeches, the outer one of ample volume, decorated with rows of buttons down the sides, and bunches at the knees. He bore on his shoulder a stout keg, that seemed full of liquor, and made signs for Rip to approach and assist him with the load. Though rather shy and distrustful of this new acquaintance, Rip complied with his usual alacrity;

and mutually relieving one another, they clambered up a narrow gully, apparently the dry bed of a mountain torrent. As they ascended, Rip every now and then heard long rolling peals, like distant thunder, that seemed to issue out of a deep ravine, or rather cleft, between lofty rocks, toward which their rugged path conducted. He paused for an instant, but supposing it to be the muttering of one of those transient thunder-showers which often take place in mountain heights, he proceeded. Passing through the ravine, they came to a hollow, like a small amphitheatre, surrounded by perpendicular precipices, over the brinks of which impending trees shot their branches, so that you only caught glimpses of the azure sky and the bright evening cloud. During the whole time Rip and his companion had labored on in silence; for though the former marvelled greatly what could be the object of carrying a keg of liquor up this wild mountain, yet there was something strange and incomprehensible about the unknown, that inspired awe and checked familiarity.

On entering the amphitheatre, new objects of wonder presented themselves. On a level spot in the centre was a company of odd-looking personages playing at nine-pins. They were dressed in a quaint outlandish fashion; some wore short doublets, others jerkins, with long knives in their belts, and most of them had enormous breeches, of similar style with that of the guide's. Their visages, too, were peculiar: one had a large beard, broad face, and small piggish eyes: the face of another seemed to consist entirely of nose, and was surmounted by a white sugar-loaf hat set off with a little red cock's tail. They all had beards, of various shapes and colors. There was one who seemed to be the commander. He was a stout old gentleman, with a weather-beaten countenance; he wore a laced doublet, broad belt and hanger, high-crowned hat and feather, red stockings, and high-heeled shoes, with roses in them. The whole group reminded Rip of the figures in an old Flemish painting, in the parlor of Dominie Van Shaick, the village parson, and which had been brought over from Holland at the time of the settlement.

What seemed particularly odd to Rip was, that though these folks were evidently amusing themselves, yet they maintained the gravest faces, the most mysterious silence, and were, withal, the most melancholy party of pleasure he had ever witnessed. Nothing interrupted the stillness of the scene but the noise of the balls, which, whenever they were rolled, echoed along the mountains like rumbling peals of thunder.

As Rip and his companion approached them, they suddenly desisted from their play, and stared at him with such fixed statue-like gaze, and such strange, uncouth, lack-lustre countenances, that his heart turned within him, and his knees smote together. His companion now emptied the contents of the keg into large flagons, and made signs to him to wait upon the company. He obeyed with fear and trembling; they quaffed the liquor in profound silence, and then returned to their game.

By degrees Rip's awe and apprehension subsided. He even ventured, when no eye was fixed upon him, to taste the beverage, which he found had much of the flavor of excellent Hollands. He was naturally a thirsty soul, and was soon tempted to repeat the draught. One taste provoked another; and he reiterated his visits to the flagon so often that at length his senses were overpowered, his eyes swam in his head, his head gradually declined, and he fell into a deep sleep.

On waking, he found himself on the green knoll whence he had first seen the old man of the glen. He rubbed his eyes—it was a bright sunny morning. The birds were hopping and twittering among the bushes, and the eagle was wheeling aloft, and breasting the pure mountain breeze. "Surely," thought Rip, "I have not slept here all night." He recalled the occurrences before he fell asleep. The strange man with a keg of liquor—the mountain ravine—the wild retreat among the rocks—the woe-begone party at ninepins—the flagon— "Oh! that flagon! that wicked flagon!" thought Rip— "what excuse shall I make to Dame Van Winkle!"

He looked round for his gun, but in place of the clean well-oiled fowling-piece, he found an old firelock lying by him, the barrel incrusted with rust, the lock falling off, and the stock worm-eaten. He now suspected that the grave roysterers of the mountain had put a trick upon him, and having dosed him with liquor, had robbed him of his gun. Wolf, too, had disappeared, but he might have strayed away after a squirrel or partridge. He whistled after him and shouted his name, but all in vain; the echoes repeated his whistle and shout, but no dog was to be seen.

He determined to revisit the scene of the last evening's gambol, and if he met with any of the party, to demand his dog and gun. As he rose to walk, he found himself stiff in the joints, and wanting in his usual activity. "These mountain beds do not agree with me," thought Rip; "and if this frolic should lay me up with a fit of the rheumatism, I shall have a blessed time with Dame Van Winkle." With some difficulty he got down into the glen: he found the gully up which he and his companion had ascended the preceding evening; but to his astonishment a mountain stream was now foaming down it, leaping from rock to rock, and filling the glen with babbling murmurs. He, however, made shift to scramble up its sides, working his toilsome way through thickets of birch, sassafras, and witch-hazel, and sometimes tripped up or entangled by the wild grapevines that twisted their coils or tendrils from tree to tree, and spread a kind of network in his path.

At length he reached to where the ravine had opened through the cliffs to the amphitheatre; but no traces of such opening remained. The rocks presented a high impenetrable wall over which the torrent came tumbling in a sheet of feathery foam, and fell into a broad deep basin, black from the shadows of the surrounding forest. Here, then, poor Rip was brought to a stand. He again called and whistled after his dog; he was only answered by the cawing of a flock of idle crows, sporting high in air about a dry tree that overhung a sunny precipice; and who, secure in their elevation, seemed to look down and scoff at the poor man's perplexities. What was to be done? the morning was passing away, and Rip felt famished for want of his breakfast. He grieved to give up his dog and gun; he dreaded to meet his wife; but it would not do to starve among the mountains. He shook his head, shouldered the rusty firelock, and, with a heart full of trouble and anxiety, turned his steps homeward.

As he approached the village he met a number of people, but none whom he knew, which somewhat surprised him, for he had thought himself acquainted with every one in the country round. Their dress, too, was of a different fashion from that to which he was accustomed. They all stared at him with equal marks of surprise, and whenever they cast their eyes upon him, invariably stroked their chins. The constant recurrence of this gesture induced Rip, involuntarily, to do the same, when to his astonishment, he found his beard had grown a foot long!

He had now entered the skirts of the village. A troop of strange children ran at his heels, hooting after him, and pointing at his gray beard. The dogs, too, not one of which he recognized for an old acquaintance, barked at him as he passed. The very village was altered; it was larger and more populous. There were rows of houses which he had never seen before, and those which had been his familiar haunts had disappeared. Strange names were over the doors—strange faces at the windows—every thing was strange. His mind now misgave him; he began to doubt whether both he and the world around him were not bewitched. Surely this was his native village, which he had left but the day before. There stood the Kaatskill mountains—there ran the silver Hudson at a distance—there was every hill and dale precisely as it had always been—Rip was sorely perplexed— "That flagon last night," thought he, "has addled my poor head sadly!"

It was with some difficulty that he found the way to his own house, which he approached with silent awe, expecting every moment to hear the shrill voice of Dame Van Winkle. He found the house gone to decay— the roof fallen in, the windows shattered, and the doors off the hinges. A half-starved dog that looked like Wolf was skulking about it. Rip called him by name, but the cur snarled, showed his teeth, and passed on. This was an unkind cut indeed— "My very dog," sighed poor Rip, "has forgotten me!"

He entered the house, which, to tell the truth, Dame Van Winkle had always kept in neat order. It was empty, forlorn, and apparently abandoned. This desolateness overcame all his connubial fears—he called loudly for his wife and children—the lonely chambers rang for a moment with his voice, and then all again was silence.

He now hurried forth, and hastened to his old resort, the village inn—but it too was gone. A large rickety wooden building stood in its place, with great gaping windows, some of them broken and mended with old hats and petticoats, and over the door was painted, "the Union Hotel, by Jonathan Doolittle." Instead of the great tree that used to shelter the quiet little Dutch inn of yore, there now was reared a tall naked pole, with something on the top that looked like a red night-cap, and from it was fluttering a flag, on which was a singular assemblage of stars and stripes—all this was strange and incomprehensible. He recognized on the sign, however, the ruby face of King George, under which he had smoked so many a peaceful pipe; but even this was singularly metamorphosed. The red coat was changed for one of blue and buff, a sword was held in the hand instead of a sceptre, the head was decorated with a cocked hat, and underneath was painted in large characters, GENERAL WASHINGTON.

There was, as usual, a crowd of folk about the door, but none that Rip recollected. The very character of the people seemed changed. There was a busy, bustling, disputatious tone about it, instead of the accustomed phlegm and drowsy tranquillity. He looked in vain for the sage Nicholas Vedder, with his broad face, double chin, and fair long pipe, uttering clouds of tobacco-smoke instead of idle speeches; or Van Bummel, the schoolmaster, doling forth the contents of an ancient newspaper. In place of these, a lean, bilious-looking fellow, with his pockets full of handbills, was haranguing vehemently about rights of citizens—elections—members of congress—liberty—Bunker's Hill—heroes of seventy-six—and other words, which were a perfect Babylonish jargon to the bewildered Van Winkle.

The appearance of Rip, with his long grizzled beard, his rusty fowling-piece, his uncouth dress, and an army of women and children at his heels, soon attracted the attention of the tavern politicians. They crowded round him, eyeing him from head to foot with great curiosity. The orator bustled up to him, and, drawing him partly aside, inquired "on which side he voted?" Rip stared in vacant stupidity. Another short but busy little fellow pulled him by the arm, and, rising on tiptoe, inquired in his ear, "Whether he was Federal or Democrat?" Rip was equally at a loss to comprehend the question; when a knowing, self-important old gentleman, in a sharp cocked hat, made his way through the crowd, putting them to the right and left with his elbows as he passed, and planting himself before Van Winkle, with one arm akimbo, the other resting on his cane, his keen eyes and sharp hat penetrating, as it were, into his very soul, demanded in an austere tone, "what brought him to the election with a gun on his shoulder, and a mob at his heels, and whether he meant to breed a riot in the village?"— "Alas! gentlemen," cried Rip, somewhat dismayed, "I am a poor quiet man, a native of the place, and a loyal subject of the king, God bless him!"

Here a general shout burst from the by-standers— "A tory! a tory! a spy! a refugee! hustle him! away with him!" It was with great difficulty that the self-important man in the cocked hat restored order; and, having assumed a tenfold austerity of brow, demanded again of the unknown culprit, what he came there for, and whom he was seeking? The poor man humbly assured him that he meant no harm, but merely came there in search of some of his neighbors, who used to keep about the tavern.

"Well—who are they?—name them."

Rip bethought himself a moment, and inquired, "Where's Nicholas Vedder?"

There was a silence for a little while, when an old man replied, in a thin piping voice, "Nicholas Vedder! why, he is dead and gone these eighteen years! There was a wooden tombstone in the church-yard that used to tell all about him, but that's rotten and gone too."

"Where's Brom Dutcher?"

"Oh, he went off to the army in the beginning of the war; some say he was killed at the storming of Stony Point—others say he was drowned in a squall at the foot of Antony's Nose. I don't know—he never came back again."

"Where's Van Bummel, the schoolmaster?"

"He went off to the wars too, was a great militia general, and is now in congress."

Rip's heart died away at hearing of these sad changes in his home and friends, and finding himself thus alone in the world. Every answer puzzled him too, by treating of such enormous lapses of time, and of matters which he could not understand: war—congress—Stony Point;—he had no courage to ask after any more friends, but cried out in despair, "Does nobody here know Rip Van Winkle?"

"Oh, Rip Van Winkle!" exclaimed two or three, "Oh, to be sure! that's Rip Van Winkle yonder, leaning against the tree."

Rip looked, and beheld a precise counterpart of himself, as he went up the mountain: apparently as lazy, and certainly as ragged. The poor fellow was now completely confounded. He doubted his own identity,

and whether he was himself or another man. In the midst of his bewilderment, the man in the cocked hat demanded who he was, and what
was his name?

"God knows," exclaimed he, at his wit's end; "I'm not myself—I'm
somebody else—that's me yonder—no—that's somebody else got into
my shoes—I was myself last night, but I fell asleep on the mountain,
and they've changed my gun, and every thing's changed, and I'm
changed, and I can't tell what's my name, or who I am!"

The by-standers began now to look at each other, nod, wink significantly, and tap their fingers against their foreheads. There was a whisper
also, about securing the gun, and keeping the old fellow from doing
mischief, at the very suggestion of which the self-important man in the
cocked hat retired with some precipitation. At this critical moment a
fresh comely woman pressed through the throng to get a peep at the
gray-bearded man. She had a chubby child in her arms, which, frightened at his looks, began to cry. "Hush, Rip," cried she, "hush, you
little fool; the old man won't hurt you." The name of the child, the air
of the mother, the tone of her voice, all awakened a train of recollections in his mind. "What is your name, my good woman?" asked he.

"Judith Gardenier."

"And your father's name?"

"Ah, poor man, Rip Van Winkle was his name, but it's twenty years
since he went away from home with his gun, and never has been heard
of since—his dog came home without him; but whether he shot himself, or was carried away by the Indians, nobody can tell. I was then
but a little girl."

Rip had but one question more to ask; but he put it with a faltering voice:

"Where's your mother?"

"Oh, she too had died but a short time since; she broke a blood-
vessel in a fit of passion at a New-England peddler."

There was a drop of comfort, at least, in this intelligence. The
honest man could contain himself no longer. He caught his daughter
and her child in his arms. "I am your father!" cried he— "Young Rip
Van Winkle once—old Rip Van Winkle now!—Does nobody know poor
Rip Van Winkle?"

All stood amazed, until an old woman, tottering out from among
the crowd, put her hand to her brow, and peering under it in his face
for a moment, exclaimed, "Sure enough! it is Rip Van Winkle—it is
himself! Welcome home again, old neighbor—Why, where have you
been these twenty long years?"

Rip's story was soon told, for the whole twenty years had been to
him but as one night. The neighbors stared when they heard it; some

were seen to wink at each other, and put their tongues in their cheeks: and the self-important man in the cocked hat, who, when the alarm was over, had returned to the field, screwed down the corners of his mouth, and shook his head—upon which there was a general shaking of the head throughout the assemblage.

It was determined, however, to take the opinion of old Peter Vanderdonk, who was seen slowly advancing up the road. He was a descendant of the historian of that name, who wrote one of the earliest accounts of the province. Peter was the most ancient inhabitant of the village, and well versed in all the wonderful events and traditions of the neighborhood. He recollected Rip at once, and corroborated his story in the most satisfactory manner. He assured the company that it was a fact, handed down from his ancestor the historian, that the Kaatskill mountains had always been haunted by strange beings. That it was affirmed that the great Hendrick Hudson, the first discoverer of the river and country, kept a kind of vigil there every twenty years, with his crew of the Half-moon; being permitted in this way to revisit the scenes of his enterprise, and keep a guardian eye upon the river, and the great city called by his name. That his father had once seen them in their old Dutch dresses playing at nine-pins in a hollow of the mountain; and that he himself had heard, one summer afternoon, the sound of their balls, like distant peals of thunder.

To make a long story short, the company broke up, and returned to the more important concerns of the election. Rip's daughter took him home to live with her; she had a snug, well-furnished house, and a stout cheery farmer for a husband, whom Rip recollected for one of the urchins that used to climb upon his back. As to Rip's son and heir, who was the ditto of himself, seen leaning against the tree, he was employed to work on the farm; but evinced an hereditary disposition to attend to anything else but his business.

Rip now resumed his old walks and habits; he soon found many of his former cronies, though all rather the worse for the wear and tear of time; and preferred making friends among the rising generation, with whom he soon grew into great favor.

Having nothing to do at home, and being arrived at that happy age when a man can be idle with impunity, he took his place once more on the bench at the inn door, and was reverenced as one of the patriarchs of the village, and a chronicle of the old times "before the war." It was some time before he could get into the regular track of gossip, or could be made to comprehend the strange events that had taken place during his torpor. How that there had been a revolutionary war—that the country had thrown off the yoke of old England— and that, instead of being a subject of his Majesty George the Third, he was now a free citizen of the United States. Rip, in fact, was no politician; the changes of states and empires made but little impression on him; but there was one species of despotism under which he had long groaned, and that was—petticoat government. Happily that was at an end; he had got his neck out of the yoke of matrimony, and could go in and out whenever he pleased, without dreading the tyranny of Dame Van Winkle. Whenever her name was mentioned, however, he shook his head, shrugged his shoulders, and cast up his eyes; which might pass either for an expression of resignation to his fate, or joy at his deliverance.

He used to tell his story to every stranger that arrived at Mr. Doolittle's hotel. He was observed, at first, to vary on some points every time he told it, which was, doubtless, owing to his having so recently awaked. It at last settled down precisely to the tale I have related, and not a man, woman, or child in the neighborhood, but knew it by heart. Some always pretended to doubt the reality of it, and insisted that Rip had been out of his head, and that this was one point on which he always remained flighty. The old Dutch inhabitants, however, almost universally gave it full credit. Even to this day they never hear a thunderstorm of a summer afternoon about the Kaatskill, but they say Hendrick Hudson and his crew are at their game of nine-pins; and it is a common wish of all hen-pecked husbands in the neighborhood, when life hangs heavy on their hands, that they might have a quieting draught out of Rip Van Winkle's flagon.

NOTE—The foregoing Tale, one would suspect, had been suggested to Mr. Knickerbocker by a little German superstition about the Emperor Frederick der Rothbart, and the Kypphauser mountain: the subjoined note, however, which he had appended to the tale, shows that it is an absolute fact, narrated with his usual fidelity:

"The story of Rip Van Winkle may seem incredible to many, but nevertheless I give it my full belief, for I know the vicinity of our old Dutch settlements to have been very subject to marvellous events and appearances. Indeed, I have heard many stranger stories than this, in the villages along the Hudson; all of which were too well authenticated to admit of a doubt. I have even talked with Rip Van Winkle myself who, when last I saw him, was a very venerable old man, and so perfectly rational and consistent on every other point, that I think no conscientious person could refuse to take this into the bargain; nay, I have seen a certificate on the subject taken before a country justice and signed with a cross, in the justice's own handwriting. The story, therefore, is beyond the possibility of doubt. D. K."

Peter Rugg, The Missing Man
WILLIAM AUSTIN

*From Jonathan Dunwell of New York,
to Mr. Herman Krauff.*

Sir,—Agreeably to my promise, I now relate to you all the particulars of the lost man and child, which I have been able to collect. It is entirely owing to the humane interest you seemed to take in the report, that I have pursued the inquiry to the following result.

You may remember that business called me to Boston in the summer of 1820. I sailed in the packet to Providence, and when I arrived there, I learned that every seat in the Stage was engaged. I was thus obliged either to wait a few hours, or accept a seat with the driver, who civilly offered me that accommodation. Accordingly, I took my seat by his side, and soon found him intelligent and communicative. When we had travelled about ten miles, the horses suddenly threw their ears on their necks, as flat as a hare's. Said the driver, "Have you a surtout with you?"

"No," said I, "why do you ask?"

"You will want one soon," said he. "Do you observe the ears of all the horses?"

"Yes," and was just about to ask the reason.

"They see the storm-breeder, and we shall see him soon."

At this moment, there was not a cloud visible in the firmament. Soon after, a small speck appeared in the road.

"There," said my companion, "comes the storm-breeder; he always leaves a Scotch mist behind him. By many a wet jacket do I remember him. I suppose the poor fellow suffers much himself, much more than is known to the world."

Presently, a man with a child beside him, with a large black horse, and a weather-beaten chair once built for a chaise body, passed in great haste, apparently at the rate of twelve miles an hour. He seemed to grasp the reins of his horse with firmness, and appeared to anticipate his speed. He seemed dejected, and looked anxiously at the passengers, particularly at the stage driver and myself. In a moment after he passed us, the horses' ears were up, and bent themselves forward so that they nearly met.

"Who is that man?" said I, "he seems in great trouble."

"Nobody knows who he is, but his person and the child are familiar to me. I have met them more than a hundred times, and have been so often asked the way to Boston, by that man, even when he was travelling directly from that town, that of late, I have refused any communication with him; and that is the reason he gave me such a fixed look."

"But does he never stop anywhere?"

"I have never known him to stop anywhere, longer than to inquire the way to Boston; and let him be where he may, he will tell you he cannot stay a moment, for he must reach Boston that night."

We were now ascending a high hill in Walpole; and as we had a fair view of the heavens, I was rather disposed to jeer the driver for thinking of his surtout, as not a cloud as big as a marble could be discerned.

"Do you look," said he, "in the direction whence the man came, that is the place to look: the storm never meets him, it follows him."

We presently approached another hill, and when at the height, the driver pointed out in an eastern direction a little black speck, about as big as a hat.

"There," said he, "is the seed-storm; we may possibly reach Polley's before it reaches us, but the wanderer and his child will go to Providence through rain, thunder and lightning."

And now the horses, as though taught by instinct, hastened with increased speed. The little black cloud came on rolling over the turnpike, and doubled and trebled itself in all directions. The appearance of this cloud attracted the notice of all the passengers; for after it had spread itself to a great bulk, it suddenly became more limited in circumference, grew more compact, dark and consolidated. And now the successive flashes of chain lightning caused the whole cloud to appear like a sort of irregular net-work, and displayed a thousand fantastic images. The driver bespoke my attention to a remarkable configuration in the cloud: He said every flash of lightning near its centre discovered to him distinctly the form of a man sitting in an open carriage drawn by a black horse. But in truth, I saw no such thing. The man's fancy was doubtless at fault. It is a very common thing for the imagination to paint for the senses, both in the visible and invisible world.

In the meantime the distant thunder gave notice of a shower at hand; and just as we reached Polley's tavern the rain poured down in torrents. It was soon over, the cloud passing in the direction of the turnpike toward Providence. In a few moments after, a respectable looking man in a chaise stopped at the door. The man and child in the chair having excited some little sympathy among the passengers, the gentleman was asked if he had observed them? He said, he had met them, that the man seemed bewildered, and inquired the way to Boston: that he was driving at great speed, as though he expected to outstrip the tempest; that the moment he had passed him, a thunder-clap broke distinctly over the man's head, and seemed to envelope both man and child, horse and carriage.

"I stopped," said the gentleman, "supposing the lightning had struck him, but the horse only seemed to loom up and increase his speed, and as well as I could judge, he travelled just as fast as the thunder cloud."

While this man was speaking, a peddler with a cart of tin merchandize came up, all dripping; and on being questioned, he said he had met that man and carriage, within a fortnight in four different states; that at each time he had inquired the way to Boston, and that a thunder shower like the present had each time, deluged him, his waggon and his wares, setting his tinpots, &c. afloat, so that he had determined to get marine insurance done for the future. But that which excited his surprise most, was the strange conduct of his horse, for that long before he could distinguish the man in the chair, his own horse stood still in the road, and flung back his ears. "In short," said the peddler, "I wish never to see that man and horse again; they do not look to me as though they belonged to this world."

This is all that I could learn at that time; and the occurrence soon after, would have become with me, "like one of those things which had never happened," had I not, as I stood recently on the door-step of Bennett's hotel in Hartford, heard a man say, "there goes Peter Rugg and his child! he looks wet and weary, and farther from Boston than ever." I was satisfied it was the same man that I had seen more than three years before; for whoever has once seen Peter Rugg can never after be deceived as to his identity.

"Peter Rugg!" said I, "and who is Peter Rugg?"

"That," said the stranger, "is more than anyone can tell exactly. He is a famous traveller, held in light esteem by all innholders, for he never stops to eat, drink, or sleep. I wonder why the government do not employ him to carry the mail."

"Aye," said a bystander, "that is a thought bright only on one side; how long would it take in that case to send a letter to Boston, for Peter has already to my knowledge been more than twenty years travelling to that place."

"But," said I, "does the man never stop any where, does he never converse with any one? I saw the same man more than three years since, near Providence; and I heard a strange story about him. Pray, sir, give me some account of this man."

"Sir," said the stranger, "those who know the most respecting that man, say the least. I have heard it asserted that heaven sometimes sets a mark on a man, either for a judgment or a trial. Under which Peter Rugg now labours, I cannot say; therefore I am rather inclined to pity, than to judge."

"You speak like a humane man," said I, "and pray if you have known him so long, I pray you will give me some account of him. Has his appearance much altered in that time?"

"Why, yes. He looks as though he never ate, drank or slept; and his child looks older than himself, and he looks like time broke off from eternity, and anxious to gain a resting place."

"And how does his horse look?" said I.

"As for his horse, he looks fatter, and gayer, and shows more animation and courage, than he did twenty years ago. The last time Rugg spoke to me, he inquired how far it was to Boston. I told him just one hundred miles.

"'Why,' said he, 'how can you deceive me so? It is cruel to mislead a traveller. I have lost my way; pray direct me the nearest way to Boston.'

"I repeated, it was one hundred miles.

"'How can you say so?' said he, 'I was told last evening it was but fifty, and I have travelled all night.'

"'But,' said I, 'you are now travelling from Boston. You must turn back.'

"'Alas,' said he, 'it is all turn back! Boston shifts with the wind, and plays all around the compass. One man tells me it is to the East, another to the West; and the guide posts too, they all point the wrong way.'

"'But will you not stop and rest,' said I 'You seem wet and weary.'

"'Yes,' said he, 'it has been foul weather since I left home.'

"'Stop then, and refresh yourself.'

"'I must not stop, I must reach home to-night if possible: though I think you must be mistaken in the distance to Boston.' He then gave the reins to his horse, which he restrained with difficulty, and disappeared in a moment. A few days afterwards, I met the man a little this side of Claremont, winding around the hills in Unity, at the rate, I believe, of twelve miles an hour."

"Is Peter Rugg his real name, or has he accidentally gained that name?"

"I know not, but presume he will not deny his name, you can ask him,—for see, he has turned his horse, and is passing this way."

In a moment, a dark-coloured, high-spirited horse approached, and would have passed without stopping, but I had resolved to speak to Peter Rugg, or whoever the man might be. Accordingly, I stepped into the street, and as the horse approached, I made a feint of stopping him. The man immediately reined in his horse. "Sir," said I, "may I be so bold as to inquire if you are not Mr. Rugg? for I think I have seen you before."

"My name is Peter Rugg," said he, "I have unfortunately lost my way; I am wet and weary, and will take it kindly of you to direct me to Boston."

"You live in Boston, do you, and in what street?"

"In Middle-street."

"When did you leave Boston?"

"I cannot tell precisely; it seems a considerable time."

"But how did you and your child become so wet? It has not rained here to-day."

"It has just rained a heavy shower up the river. But I shall not reach Boston to-night, if I tarry. Would you advise me to take the old road, or the turnpike?"

"Why, the old road is one hundred and seventeen miles, and the turnpike is ninety-seven."

"How can you say so? you impose on me; it is wrong to trifle with a traveller; you know it is but forty miles from Newburyport to Boston."

"But this is not Newburyport; this is Hartford."

"Do not deceive me, sir. Is not this town Newburyport, and the river that I have been following the Merrimac?"

"No, sir, this is Hartford, and the river, the Connecticut."

He wrung his hands and looked incredulous. "Have the rivers, too, changed their courses, as the cities have changed places? But see, the clouds are gathering in the south, and we shall have a rainy night. Ah, that fatal oath!"

He would tarry no longer, his impatient horse leaped off, his hind flanks rising like wings, he seemed to devour all before him, and to scorn all behind.

I had now, as I thought, discovered a clue to the history of Peter Rugg, and I determined, the next time my business called me to Boston, to make a further inquiry. Soon after, I was enabled to collect the following particulars from Mrs. Croft, an aged lady in Middle-street, who has resided in Boston, during the last twenty years. Her narration is this:

Just at twilight last summer, a person stopped at the door of the late Mrs. Rugg. Mrs. Croft, on coming to the door, perceived a stranger, with a child by his side, in an old weather-beaten carriage, with a black horse. The stranger asked for Mrs. Rugg, and was informed that Mrs. Rugg had died in a good old age, more than twenty years before that time.

The stranger replied, "How can you deceive me so? Do ask Mrs. Rugg to step to the door."

"Sir, I assure you Mrs. Rugg has not lived here these nineteen years; no one lives here but myself, and my name is Betsey Croft."

The stranger paused, and looked up and down the street, and said, "Though the painting is rather faded, this looks like my house."

"Yes," said the child, "that is the stone before the door, that I used to sit on to eat my bread and milk."

"But," said the stranger, "it seems to be on the wrong side of the street. Indeed, every thing here seems to be misplaced. The streets are all changed, the people are all changed, the town seems changed, and what is strangest of all, Catherine Rugg has deserted her husband and child. Pray," said the stranger, "has John Foy come home from sea? He went a long voyage, he is my kinsman. If I could see him, he could give me some account of Mrs. Rugg."

"Sir," said Mrs. Croft, "I never heard of John Foy. Where did he live?"

"Just above here, in Orange Tree Lane."

"There is no such place in this neighbourhood."

"What do you tell me! Are the streets gone? Orange Tree Lane is at the head of Hanover-street, near Pemberton's hill."

"There is no such lane now."

"Madam! You cannot be serious. But you doubtless know my brother William Rugg. He lives in Royal Exchange Lane, near King-street."

"I know of no such lane; and I am sure there is no such street as King-street, in this town."

"No such street as King-street! Why, woman! You mock me. You may as well tell me there is no King George. However, madam, you see I am wet and weary, I must find a resting place. I will go to Hart's tavern near the market."

"Which market, sir? For you seem perplexed; we have several markets."

"You know there is but one market, near the town dock."

"O, the old market, but no such man as Hart has kept there these twenty years."

Here the stranger seemed disconcerted, and uttered to himself quite audibly, "Strange mistake, how much this looks like the town of Boston! It certainly has a great resemblance to it; but I perceive my mistake now. Some other Mrs. Rugg, some other Middle-street." Then said he, "Madam, can you direct me to Boston?"

"Why, this is Boston, the city of Boston, I know of no other Boston."

"City of Boston it may be; but it is not the Boston where I live. I recollect now, I came over a bridge instead of a ferry. Pray, what bridge is that, I just came over?"

"It is Charles River Bridge."

"I perceive my mistake, there is a ferry between Boston and Charlestown, there is no bridge. Ah, I perceive my mistake, if I was in Boston my horse would carry me directly to my own door. But my horse shows by his impatience, that he is in a strange place. Absurd, that I should have mistaken this place for the old town of Boston! it is a much finer city than the town of Boston. It has been built long since Boston. I fancy Boston must lie at a distance from this city, as the good woman seems ignorant of it."

At these words his horse began to chafe, and strike the pavement with his fore feet; the stranger seemed a little bewildered, and said, 'no home tonight,' and giving the reins to his horse, passed up the street, and I saw no more of him.

It was evident that the generation to which Peter Rugg belonged had passed away.

This was all the account of Peter Rugg I could obtain from Mrs. Croft; but she directed me to an elderly man, Mr. James Felt, who lived near her, and who had kept a record of the principal occurrences for the last fifty years. At my request, she sent for him; and after I had related to him the object of my inquiry, Mr. Felt told me he had known Rugg in his youth; that his disappearance had caused some surprise; but as it sometimes happens that men run away,—sometimes to be rid of others, and sometimes to be rid of themselves;—and Rugg took his child with him, and his own horse and chair; and as it did not appear that any creditors made a stir, the occurrence soon mingled itself in the stream of oblivion; and Rugg and his child, horse and chair, were soon forgotten.

"It is true," said Mr. Felt, "sundry stories grew out of Rugg's affair, whether true or false I cannot tell; but stranger things have happened in my day, without even a newspaper notice."

"Sir," said I, "Peter Rugg is now living. I have lately seen Peter Rugg and his child, horse and chair; therefore, I pray you to relate to me all you know or ever heard of him."

"Why, my friend," said James Felt, "that Peter Rugg is now a living man, I will not deny; but that you have seen Peter Rugg and his child, is impossible, if you mean a small child, for Jenny Rugg, if living, must be at least—let me see—Boston massacre, 1770—Jenny Rugg was about ten years old. Why, sir, Jenny Rugg, if living, must be more than sixty years of age. That Peter Rugg is living, is highly probable, as he was only ten years older than myself; and I was only eighty last March; and I am as likely to live twenty years longer, as any man."

Here I perceived that Mr. Felt was in his dotage, and I despaired from gaining any intelligence from him, on which I could depend.

I took my leave of Mrs. Croft, and proceeded to my lodgings at the Marlborough Hotel.

If Peter Rugg, thought I, has been travelling since the Boston massacre, there is no reason why he should not travel to the end of time. If the present generation know little of him, the next will know less, and Peter and his child will have no hold on this world.

In the course of the evening, I related my adventure in Middle-street.

"Hah!" said one of the company, smiling, "do you really think you have seen Peter Rugg? I have heard my grandfather speak of him, as though he seriously believed his own story."

"Sir," said I, "pray let us compare your grandfather's story of Mr. Rugg, with my own."

"Peter Rugg, sir, if my grandfather was worthy of credit, once lived in Middle-street, in this city. He was a man in comfortable circumstances, had a wife and one daughter, and was generally esteemed for his sober life and manners. But unhappily, his temper, at times, was altogether ungovernable, and then, his language was terrible. In these fits of passion, if a door stood in his way, he would never do less than kick a panel through. He would sometimes throw his heels over his head, and come down on his feet, uttering oaths in a circle; and thus in a rage, he was the first who performed a somerset, and did what others have since learnt to do for merriment and money. Once, Rugg was seen to bite a ten-penny nail in halves. In those days, every body, both men and boys, wore wigs; and Peter, at these moments of violent passion, would become so profane that his wig would rise up from his head. Some said, it was on account of his terrible language. Others accounted for it in a more philosophical way, and said it was caused by the expansion of his scalp; as violent passion, we know, will swell the veins and expand the head. While these fits were on him, Rugg had no respect for heaven or earth. Except this infirmity, all agreed that Rugg was a good sort of a man; for when his fits were over, nobody was so ready to commend a placid temper as Peter.

"It was late in autumn, one morning, that Rugg, in his own chair, with a fine large bay horse, took his daughter, and proceeded to Concord. On his return, a violent storm overtook him. At dark, he stopped in Menotomy, now West Cambridge, at the door of a Mr. Cutter, a friend of his, who urged him to tarry the night. On Rugg's declining to stop, Mr. Cutter urged him vehemently. 'Why, Mr. Rugg,' said Cutter, 'the storm is overwhelming you; the night is exceeding dark; your little daughter will perish; you are in an open chair and the tempest is increasing.' 'Let the storm increase,' said Rugg, with a fearful oath, 'I will see home to-night, in spite of the last tempest! or may I never *see home!'* At these words, he gave his whip to his high spirited horse, and disappeared in a moment. But Peter Rugg did not reach home that night, nor the next; nor, when he became a missing man, could he ever be traced beyond Mr. Cutter's in Menotomy. For a long time after, on every dark and stormy night, the wife of Peter Rugg would fancy she heard the crack of a whip, and the fleet tread of a horse, and the rattling of a carriage, passing her door. The neighbours, too, heard the same noises, and some said they knew it was Rugg's horse; the tread on the pavement was perfectly familiar to them. This occurred so repeatedly, that at length the neighbours watched with lanterns, and saw the real Peter Rugg, with his own horse and chair, and child sitting beside him, pass directly before his own door, his head turning toward his house, and himself making every effort to stop his horse, but in vain. The next day, the friends of Mrs. Rugg exerted themselves to find her husband and child. They inquired at every public house and stable in town; but it did not appear that Rugg made any stay in Boston. No one, after Rugg had passed his own door, could give any account of him; though it was asserted by some that the clatter of Rugg's horse and carriage over the pavements shook the houses on both sides of the streets. And this is credible, if indeed Rugg's horse and carriage did pass on that night. For at this day, in many of the streets, a loaded truck or team in passing will shake the houses like an earthquake. However, Rugg's neighbours never afterwards watched again; some of them treated it all as a delusion, and thought no more of it. Others, of a different opinion, shook their heads, and said nothing.

"Thus Rugg, and his child, horse and chair, were soon forgotten; and probably many in the neighbourhood never heard a word on the subject.

"There was indeed a rumour, that Rugg afterwards was seen in Connecticut, between Suffield and Hartford, passing through the country, like a streak of chalk. This gave occasion to Rugg's friends to make further inquiry. But the more they inquired, the more they were baffled. If they heard of Rugg, one day in Connecticut,—the next, they heard of him winding around the hills in New-Hampshire; and soon after, a man in a chair, with a small child, exactly answering the description of Peter Rugg, would be seen in Rhode-Island, inquiring the way to Boston.

"But that which chiefly gave a colour of mystery to the story of Peter Rugg, was the affair at Charlestown bridge. The toll-gatherer asserted that sometimes, on the darkest, and most stormy nights, when no object could be discerned, about the time Rugg was missing, a horse and wheel carriage, with a noise equal to a troop, would at midnight, in utter contempt of the rates of toll, pass over the bridge.

This occurred so frequently, that the toll-gatherer resolved to attempt a discovery. Soon after, at the usual time, apparently the same horse and carriage approached the bridge from Charlestown square. The toll-gatherer, prepared, took his stand as near the middle of the bridge as he dared, with a large three-legged stool in his hand. As the appearance passed, he threw the stool at the horse, but heard nothing, except the noise of the stool skipping across the bridge. The toll-gatherer, on the next day, asserted that the stool went directly through the body of the horse: and he persisted in that belief ever after. Whether Rugg, or whoever the person was, ever passed the bridge again, the toll-gatherer would never tell—and when questioned seemed anxious to wave the subject. And thus, Peter Rugg and his child, horse and carriage, remain a mystery to this day."

This, sir, is all that I could learn of Peter Rugg in Boston.

An Anachronism, or Missing One's Coach

ANONYMOUS

Kind and credulous reader, and I wish for no other, be it known to you that I am one of those who dip into antiquarian lore, and that I am moreover like some of the same tribe, fond of long and solitary rambles on foot, in quest of the wrecks and relics of things forgotten, or forgotten by all but the family of the "Dryasdusts." Nor ought I to conceal the fact that I am (when a day's march has failed to bring me in the way of the monuments of remote ages) much given to the indulgence of splendid philosophicopoetical speculations concerning the future; thus borrowing from the time to come, entertainment for the time present, in place of that which should have been furnished me by the times that are past. Many a road-side "St. George and the Dragon," or "Robin Hood," where I have found shelter for the night, has witnessed the cheap felicity I have created for myself amid these Janus-like meditations.

During several sultry days of last August, or, if you please, of some other August, I had risen at the earliest dawn, and had held on my pilgrim path until sunset, carefully tracking the course of the Pict's wall, from the shores of Solway Firth, eastward. Toward the close of the last of these days, all my musings upon the past, as well as every bright and fair dream respecting the future had been dispelled, or had lost its wonted charm over my imagination, partly by the now overpowering sensations of bodily fatigue and mental exhaustion, and partly by the obtrusion, on every side, of objects utterly at variance with sentiment and speculation of whatever sort, and whether retrospective or anticipative; and which forbad any thing to be thought of but the bustling interests of the generation extant. Who, I ask, can be poetical, or who sublimely philosophical, within ten miles of Newcastle-upon-Tyne?

Yet let me not be thought to disparage the town and neighbourhood whence incalculable chaldrons of comfort, cookery, and gas illumination are emanating every day, and are blessing all

31

our eastern shores! This radiating, if not radiant coal mart, I entered about five o'clock in the afternoon—limping, hungry, thirsty, grimed with dust, and shorn of all sentimentality; and notwithstanding the horror I have—an instinctive horror, not to be reasoned with—of large commercial and manufacturing towns, I was now so thoroughly broken down in spirit and so footsore too, that I quietly resigned myself to the thought of spending the night at the best inn which would deign to receive a dusty pedestrian, with a wallet on his back. Thus purposing, I made a discreet choice among the caravanseries of Newcastle, lowering my pride to the dimensions of a fourth-rate hotel; and there, by assuming some airs of importance, I actually so far secured the good opinion and services of waiters, boots, and chambermaid, as to get myself renovated, in the course of two hours, and found myself a new man, or rather my own self again; that is to say, neither very *new*, nor very old; but now—shaved, dressed, cooled, rested, dined, and enlivened moreover by a sober pint of execrable sherry. In a word, by seven o'clock, I was beginning to readmit, and to dally with swarms of "fine ideas," which came crowding upon my rather fevered sensorium.

In this mood I felt it to be out of the question to remain, as a prudent man could have done, where I was, in a dusky, smoke-stained coffee-room; and in the very heart of a Babylon, like Newcastle. Although, therefore, any man in my case, would have thought he had had foot-work enough for the day, I rushed forth; yet intending nothing else but to occupy the bed I had engaged; and meaning only to muse away the twilight hour by the river's side, if I could find free space there, for a time. It happened, however, that, in limping across the market-place, on my way to the quays, I was almost run over by the impetuous "Edinburgh and Leeds Mercury," which, at the moment, swung round the corner with its reeking four. It stopped—and I stopped—and, scarcely thinking what I meant, I accosted the guard as he reached the pavement with the laconic question— "Room onside?" to which I received the not more wordy answer—

"For one, sir."

"When do you start?"

"In ten minutes, at the fullest."

"Keep a place for me in front, then."

The comparison that rushed upon my mind, at first sight of the "Mercury," between a stifling chamber in a murky inn, for the night, and the splendours of heaven, and the glories of the ensuing dawn— never better enjoyed than on the outside of a night-coach during the summer months—this instantaneous comparison, carried away all my plans, and actually seemed a dispel my bodily sensations of fatigue. I hurried back to the den within which I had thought to have gasped till morning, paid my reckoning—lavished gratuities upon waiters, boots, and chambermaid; snatched up my knapsack, and with the precipitation of a man who has scaled the walls of his prison, and in listening for pursuit, hobbled toward the great "Commercial," whence I was to start. I found that the fresh calls had not yet come out. I caught the guard by the sleeve, and telling him that I should be on the road, set forward, as if to realize the unexpected pleasure of my escape from Newcastle, or as if to exclude any possible disappointment, although, with this view, I would have been far more wise, as the event proved, to have occupied my seat on the coach, and to have endured the smutty atmosphere of the town a few minutes longer. But the suggestions of vulgar prudence contemned, I made my way, with a hurried, bobbling step through the descending streets, and over the bridge that strides the deep-dyed waters of the Tyne, thence ascending the steep opposite hill on the Durham road; from the brow of which a prospect wide (and fair, if not fouled with smoke) stretches east and west.

Perhaps a restive leader, flinging over the traces, or a lagging passenger, had delayed the Mercury so much beyond the "ten minutes" allowed me by the guard. In fact, when I reached the summit of the hill, I listened in vain for either the rattling wheels, or the bugle. In that luckless—or, shall I say lucky—moment, I descried, a little to the left, a rising ground, whence the course of the river might advantageously be seen. At the risque (almost the certainty) of losing my place, I darted toward this eminence; and finding, when I reached it, a tempting seat, upon the gnarled roots of a decayed oak, I sat down; yes, I sat; and as my sceptical reader will tell me, nodded and slept. This explanation of what follows I am, however, resolved not to admit; and yet even if this were granted, it would be not the less certain that I looked around me, as I sat with as clear a consciousness of plain reality, as I had had a while before in taking my steak at the Swan. There may, perhaps, be those who will insult me by insinuating that, worn out as I confess myself to have been, I had fallen sound asleep in my box in the coffee-room, with the last half-glass of the "execrable sherry" before me; and that the whole affair of the "Mercury" is no better than a midsummer night's dream. I shall not condescend to argue the point with any such objectors, too wise already in their own conceits; but shall go on in all simplicity to relate how that, seated in the aforesaid natural arm chair, I looked around and looked beneath, and looked in vain for the roofs, and chimneys, and spires of the dingy Newcastle—for the most entangled quays, for the spouting furnaces, for the glowing fire-heaps, at the pits' mouths, in the distance; or, in a word, for any one object indicative of recent times, or of the busy wonders of the metropolis of soot; and all which had a moment before lain outstretched before me.

In the stead of any such familiar appearances, noting the current time, the August of 1837 (or some other August of modern date,) there was, indeed, the same glowing sky, and the same general outline of country; the same winding river, yet winding in a somewhat different track, and seen only at points among overgrowing tufts of trees. But instead of the vast town and its accompaniments, I gazed upon a wild solitude; or if not a solitude, which in truth it was not, yet such comparatively. The ground about me was a rugged forest, crossed by rude paths, yet down the hill side, and in the flats beneath, I descried many small enclosures, each containing a hovel or cabin, and within which there were the indications of thrift and comfort. The distance toward the north and west was dark with wide-stretching forests, the more sullen in their aspect, as they now lay in gloomy shade, immediately beneath the dazzling expanse, whence the sun had but just sunk away.

But now—mark it, reader—what was the most surprising in this instantaneous shifting of the scene, was that I looked upon it as coolly as if it had not been surprising at all; as if it were just what I had expected, and had actually beheld a hundred times. Never in my life have I seemed more myself, more wide awake, or more calmly and familiarly conversant with things about me. I was conscious of no excitement, no poetic elevation, no wonderment, no exaggerated impressions; there was no fantastic mixing up of chimeras with ordinary realities; all within and all without was sober truth. I, who had the same afternoon entered the Swan covered with dust—I, who had a few minutes before engaged my place to Leeds, and was listening for the coach—the same real and veracious I, now stood gazing upon a scene utterly changed in aspect and objects.

In turning about, I perceived at a little distance an uncouth being— shall I call him peasant or savage—who was dragging his weary steps homeward—if, indeed, he might have a home, other than the hollow of a tree. His hatless head was matted with a mop of caroty hair, brushing his broad and naked shoulders, and almost concealing a florid Scythian-like visage, marked with the hopeless sullenness and mindless wildness, with which cruel bondage deforms the human countenance. A torn woollen jerkin, of the coarsest texture, left uncovered his shaggy bosom and brawny arms. The man, and this startled me more than even his strange appearance, passed me so near as almost to brush me with his tatters, and yet seemed no more to notice me than as if I had been a disembodied spirit. I accosted him with the question— "What place is this?" He started at the sound of my voice, but looked in an opposite direction, as if he had heard himself called from a distance, and seeing no one, went on.

Yet this question had no sooner escaped my lips, than the answer to it, like the most familiarly known fact, came to my recollection.

Where am I? where should I be, after having crossed Tina's flood—
where but on the brow of Gaetshefed; yes, Gaetshefed (Gateshead),
and close at hand must be the sacred Girvum (Janoro), and the clois-
tered retreat of the learned and venerable historian of the British and
Saxon Church!

I looked around, and although, to satisfy the strict demands of
topography, I should have had some little way to go, and far enough
to forfeit all chance of being taken up by the "Mercury;" yet, so it
was, or so it seemed, that I descried, half hid by a clump of oaks, a
pile of buildings, seemingly fresh from the mason's hand, regular in form,
but of no great extent or elevation. The main structure was surrounded
by a low, scalloped wall of uncemented stones, through which there was
access by a narrow gateway, into a court-yard or rough area, vari-
ously occupied with sheds and lumber. Behind the building, however,
I saw a much loftier wall, apparently enclosing a garden.

The edifice itself—the monastery, for such, in fact, I found it to
be—presented, in its general appearance, the combined characteris-
tics of a church, a fortress, a prison, a seignorial mansion, and a farmhouse—at least there was a something proper to each of these styles
of building, discernible in this sanctuary of piety, whose inmates,
while in the main devoting their lives to the business of piety, maintained their ground amid lawless hordes, as well by the aid of substantial defences, as by the awe of religion. Meantime, in submitting
to personal incarceration (as the spider keeps himself snug within
the leaf he has coiled), exercised lordly and lucrative jurisdiction over
the surrounding country, and in attestation of the vulgar realities that
resulted from this influence, could show stowage room enough for
provender, and livestock of all descriptions.

The main building, oblong in its general figure, rose to the height
of two stories, or I should rather say, a storey and a half; for the position of the upper windows or loops, seemed to indicate that the lofty
apartments, or halls of the ground floor, were surmounted by dwarf
chambers, or low cloisters next the roof. A circular tower sustained
each corner of the western front of the building; and these towers
were curiously annulated by bold projections in the brick-work, or
rings, at even intervals from the bases to the summits of the towers.
In fact, any one whose head was steady, might have climbed the towers,
using the belts as steps. The sides of the building were sustained and
adorned by pilasters, each of which, for chapiter displayed a several
sculpture, and each vying with its neighbour in absurdity.

On the southern side of the building, and close to the tower, at
that angle, there was a lofty massive oaken door, with narrow panels,
and broad styles, and doubly secured by heavy bars, fastening within.

This door seemed to be devoted to rare occasions, for the grass grew rank about the threshold. In advance a few feet of the other, or northern tower, stood insulated, a wreathed, slender column, surmounted by a saint—I mean the image or effigy of one; and I dare say of St. Cathbert the founder. A flight of narrow stone steps, jutting from the wall between the two towers, and secured by a slender rail, led to an open or balconied hall, or antechamber, fronted by a screen, which rested on fantastic pillons or posts. From beneath, and where I stood, one might discern the narrow apertures in the inner walls of this hall by which light and air, in parsimonious quantities, were admitted to the apartments beyond.

I approached the sacred precincts with no ordinary curiosity; and, unbidden, passed the wicket of the outer enclosure, within which I found a various assemblage of persons, and more bustle and clatter of tongues than one would expect to see and hear in so holy a place. Several groups occupied the area in front of the monastery; some were ascending and descending the flight of steps, and as many as it could fairly hold, were to be seen in the balcony, or hall, or open corridor already mentioned. These persons, some secular, some religious, far from exhibiting the demure abstraction which one thinks of as proper to a house of piety, were engaged in eager, and some of them in jocose chat, or gossip, of which the subjects were evidently not peculiarly nice or select. Excellent jests, to judge by the bursts of laughter with which they were greeted, enlivened then colloquies; and a burly monk, whose smooth cheeks bespoke a sunshine felicity within, from whatever sources derived, actually made the echoes ring from the walls of the monastery, by the peals of his mirth, while listening to a story told by a lean, raw-boned laic, who seemed to be a traveller.

At the foot of the stone steps, with one foot raised, and in attitude of impatient detention, stood a younger brother of the house, whose flowing tunic was submissively held at the lappet, by a serf, or villain, who seemed to be urging some claims of justice upon a dull ear, or reviving the recollections of a faithless memory. In the hall above, were some personages of higher rank, apparently both religious and secular—the officers of the house—and two or three franklins, whose bearing in converse with the brethren, though submissive, was not abject; and by the by, I could but notice that the fine stuffs and nice trim of some of these mortified persons, exhibited as well more solicitude as more cost, than was discernible in the dress of the best attired laic of the party. Apt commentary, thought I, upon the monastic aphorism of St. Gregory— "Quid est habitus monachi, nisi des, pectus mundi?" And here again I was reminded of another rule of the same holy father— "Ne mulieres in monasterio tuo deiticeps

qualibet occasione permittas ascendere"—for, looking upward to near
the summit of one of the before-mentioned towers, I espied, at an
opening where there were placed several large rural flower-pots, a
very pretty lass, whose flaxen hair reflected the fading glories of the
western sky, and who was busily employed aspersing the plants they
contained, with a bundle of rushes. Tell it not at Rome!

Amid these comers and goers, and merry gossips, I stood, or
glided, hither and thither, unnoticed; Or rather it seemed as if not
one of these eyes had the faculty to fix itself upon my corporeal substance; or as if, between my existence and theirs, the link of corporeal communication had slipped away. While, from the area below, I
stood peering into the dim recesses of the hall above, desirous of ascending, and yet fearing to do so, I perceived a narrow door in the furthest
corner, slowly open, and presently there appeared at the head of the
steps, a portly yet infirm figure—a reverend monk, reverend in truth—
reverend by the majesty of intelligence and personal qualities. He
firmly grasped the rail of the balustrade, in preparing to descend the
steps, and stood a few minutes to conclude a parley with an importu-
nate brother, who had followed him, as it seemed, from the door of
his cell, and who was tormenting him with some impertinent gossip.
Having courteously and yet briskly shaken off this *musquito*, the monk
worked his way, sliding down the steps, and easing his stiffened limbs by
force of his yet powerful arm. When he reached the ground, he evidently
made no little effort to edge himself through the crowd, at such a rate
as should discourage any who might essay to hold him by the sleeve.

He made his way, unassailed, athwart the court, and toward the
eastern end of the monastery, where entrance was had to the garden.
Instinctively I pressed on to follow and accost him.

Never in my days have I happened to meet an old friend on the road,
or at the corner of a street, with a more natural, easy, and undoubt-
ing impression of familiar recognition—never have I seized any one's
hand and said, "Ah! how d'ye do? how are they at home?"—never have I
looked into a well-known and smiling face, with a feeling more assured,
than that with which, while fixing my eye upon the visage before me, I
exclaimed, "the venerable Bede!"

And I had no sooner so spoken, than the old man, turning himself
a little about, and depressing the hood which muffled his ears with
his middle finger, (a characteristic action) gave me a look of reciprocal recognition, and glanced a "how d'ye do" at me. And now, strange
as it may seem, it is a fact that this interchanged greeting, as if Bede
and I had been old friends, excited in me no more surprise than I had
just before felt when the blackened roofs of Newcastle gave place to
the forest tufts, and wildness of another age.

I quickened my step; the monk slackened his, and I was soon at his side. He placed his hand, for he had the advantage of me in stature, upon my shoulder, and in easy and (may I say so?) in *wonted* chat, we entered the monastery garden together. It was a well-laboured enclosure, of ample dimensions, and seemed to be stocked with whatever a comfortable kitchen demands in the vegetable kind. We gained a bench, at the extreme corner of the garden, overhung by a gourd, and seating ourselves, enjoyed the still scene, dimly revealed by the glowing sky.

In endeavouring, as I have since done, again and again, to recover the earlier portion of the conversation which ensued, I have always felt as if a page, or a half page, of memory's record had just there been torn out; so that, although every syllable of our after discourse remains indelibly fixed in my recollection, its initial part has utterly disappeared. It must suffice then to say that, at the point where I come again into perfect possession of my consciousness, the venerable monk and I were conferring, in an easy manner, upon various points connected with his age, or with mine, and both of us having a clear understanding, and perfect recollection of the fact, that, at this same moment, he was actually living in the eighth century, and I as truly in the nineteenth; nor did this trifling difference of a thousand years or more—this *break*, as geologists would call it—this *fault* in the strata of time—trouble or perplex either of us a whit; any more than two friends are molested by the circumstance of their happening to encounter each other just as they arrive from opposite hemispheres.

"A world of things," said I, "we might talk of, which I might relate, and you be not unpleased to listen to, concerning what has happened in merry Anglo-land, these last thousand years. And a world of things, too, you might describe to me, connected with *your* age, which History, capricious, niggard as she is, has not chosen to inform us of. And I promise you that this sort of information, for which just now there is an eager demand among my contemporaries, I could bring to a good market—nay, make my fortune of it, well worked up. But we must husband our time, choice moments as they are; for whatever leisure *you* may have at command, this evening I can hardly reckon upon five minutes, for, know you, I am expecting, every instant, to be taken up by the 'Leeds Mercury.'"

"The Leeds Mercury!"

"Ah, I should have said Lhydes, and you would have understood me."

"Understood you! Heaven forbid. What then, have the people of Eborascyre, so soundly reclaimed as they are from their idolatry, and fairly consigned to the bosom of the church, have they relapsed into paganism?—have they fallen away to the horrid worship of their

Woden—their Mercury? And what is this taken up, which you say you are expecting; are you, then, on the edge of apotheosis, or of arrest by the officers of justice?"

"Neither the one nor the other; and we may better employ our flitting moments than to enter upon an explanation of the phrases which I thoughtlessly let drop. In a word, be assured that I am not just yet on my way either to the stars, or to a jail."

"Let, then, this difficulty stand over till we meet again. Meantime, and as you say you are liable to be snatched away from me every moment, allow me, before we enter upon subjects more important, to ask, in a word—pardon an old man, and a secluded author, who has had little justice done him by his contemporaries—pardon me if I ask what has become of the name and the writings of—of—the unworthy Bede?"

A flush, first of manly modesty, then of religious shame and self-condemnation, came upon the old man's clear complexion—a flush mounting to his temples, and suffusing his ample and smooth forehead with a crimson, such as the western sky was then glowing with, and with a dew too, such as was then settling upon earth, wiping his face with his sleeve, he went on before I could reply—

"Nay; I retract my unseemly question;—answer not a fool according to his folly—nil tam inglorium, quim gloriæ cupidum, deprehendi."

"Very true," I said, "but, in simple fact, if great men and great writers could only know, in their life-time, to what a mere speck their reputation would converge, as seen at the end of a thousand years (or even at the end of a hundred) upon the broad table of the public mind, I think the most naughty would receive a sufficient chastisement, so that they might very safely, nay, profitably, listen to all that might be told them of their estimation with posterity."

"Speak then, if it be so, that what you have to say will furnish a scourge for my overweening vanity."

"Know then that, in England and out of it, for a thousand years, or near it, you have been ordinarily designated as "the venerable Bede," and have been styled the light and lamp of the English Church; the star of your times; the ornament of your country; and worthy, if any one is so, of immortal fame— 'so learned (I quote the very words of pour panegyrists,) so learned that one might think you lived only for study; so pious, that one must believe you lived only for prayer.'"

"Stop, stop—more than enough."

"Oh, I must go on, or I shall have given you the poison without the antidote."

"I listen."

"Hear it then—the works of the venerable Bede, or the best of them, have gone wherever sound learning has gone, and have taken their place in all our European libraries. Moreover, in modern times, they have been given to the world in several costly editions. Let me remember, they have been printed at—"

"Printed?"

"Ay, printed; but waive the question concerning the meaning of this new-coined word—a word that has turned, and is turning the world upside down. Be satisfied, at present, to know that the learned, in all countries, have enjoyed facilities such as you never dreamed of, for making themselves acquainted with your writings, if only disposed to avail themselves of the opportunity."

"You mean to say, in plain words, that nearly all men in your modern Europe, moderately well taught, have lead the 'Historia Ecclesiastica,' and the—"

"Not quite so fast. To keep within bounds of truth, let us rather say that—taking the mass of well-informed and fairly learned men in Europe—as many as one in ten thousand might make the boast that they have just set eyes upon the cover of the Historia Ecclesiastica; and then that of those who have actually seen the book, one in a hundred might pretend to have taken it from the shelf, blown the dust from the top, and read twenty pages of it. No doubt there might be found (as one may find men with six fingers on a hand, or six toes on a foot) who have perused the venerable Bede through and through."

The old man sunk into a reverie, as I spoke, and seemed to be revolving deep thoughts. He muttered at length a vanitas vanitatum; and turned his ear to me again. That I might the more congruously fall in with his meditations, I went on sagely to observe that—

"Fame, never so bright and broad a blaze as it may be at the first, comes, at the end of a thousand years, and often long before that time, to a mere point, like the image of the glorious sun, after it has passed through a pin hole in a card. Nevertheless you should know that the venerable Bede— "the lamp of the English Church," was, soon after his decease, canonised by the holy pontiff, and that his office is still kept by the Benedictines, on the 29th day of October; by others on 27th day of May."

I had hardly uttered the word *canonised*, when the old man started as if mortally pierced, and then fell into a sort of pallid trance, or horror—a rigour fixing every limb. I hardly knew by what means I at length brought him back to calm consciousness; but even then he trembled, as one who had seen a spectre. To change the subject, and by the means of an easy transition, I went on:

"And yet, let me tell you, that how small a portion soever of the light and warmth that is enjoyed by us moderns may fairly be attributed to the influence of the writings of the venerable Bede, it is quite true, and you ought to know it, that a very large amount of both—I mean of the light and warmth actually diffused among the people of England, in the nineteenth century—emanates, year after year, from the immediate neighbourhood of this very monastery. Yes, most true it is that the rich and the poor, the learned and the simple, daily and nightly rejoice in the radiance which is shed from this luminous district—ay, one might justly call this Gateshead, and its surrounding territory the lamp and hearth of England."

"Blessed St. Cuthbert," exclaimed the good man, "my father and good intercessor; blessed St. Cuthbert, founder and patron of this house—be it so then—(and I am well content that it should be so)—be it so, that the labours of thy unworthy son have fallen almost fruitless to the ground, or have failed from the eyes of men; yet has it not been the same with thine own: no; for it seems that this sacred foundation, the cherished work of thy piety and wisdom, has not only braved the storms and revolutions of a thousand years, but has continued, from age to age, to send forth those who have enlightened all the land! Immortal and thrice happy Saint Cuthbert!—I will henceforward be proud only of having known and followed thee!"

It grieved me to find that the old man had so far become the dupe of my *double entendre*, and was beguiled to utter an encomium of his patron so poorly borne out by facts. I had not, however, the heart to disabuse him by telling him of the hundreds of thousands of chaldrons of "the best Walls-end," that every year drop down the Tyne.

"More of this," said he, "anon; but now, in few words, tell me what has been the fate of our seven kingdoms?"

"To be melted into one—to be ravaged, and trodden in the dust, by host after host of foreign marauders, avenging the Britons, whom the Saxons drove from their homes; then to be conquered again by a fierce despot, who would not leave a rush burning after sunset, any where between Gwaede and Michaelstowe, except in his own castles. Thenceforward, England has bowed to foreign dynasties."

"Alas, then! no doubt, this fair island, which was taking a place of honour, at last, among the nations, has fallen, and lost all glory and all power!"

"This fair island, conquered four times over, distracted by civil broils, and by contests for the crown, shaken by mighty revolutions, this rent and convulsed island, is now acknowledged queen of the sea, and mistress too of a foreign empire, more extensive than those of Assyria, Macedonia, and Rome, piled one on the other."

"Ah, I seen then she has given birth to giants; tell me the names of your modern Sesostris, Cyrus, Alexander, Cæsar, who, singly or in series, have vanquished the world?"

"I cannot; we have had our mighty spirits, and might boast a name even now, which a thousand years will not blot from the page of history; but in plain truth, England, sovereign as she is of many lands, has not seen a warrior prince on her throne these last five hundred years."

"Well, then, her polity must be of the most despotic kind, and such as leaves an uncontrolled power with the monarch."

"No democracy the sun has ever shone upon, has allowed more scope to personal liberty, or granted much more influence to the people, in limiting the sovereign authority. The royal prerogative, in England, is the prerogative of the lion in his cage, who looks to his keeper for every bone he gnaws, and who must rise, and show himself, and roar, whenever poked."

"Has one English king in ten died in his bed?"

"Not one in ten has died out of it; and one only has actually been trampled on by the populace."

"The kings of England then have been demi-gods, or archangels."

"Most of them have given sufficient proof of their earthly origin, and at this moment the empire of England, in the height of her power, giving law to hundreds of millions of men—men of all complexions—this empire is swayed by a young and fair hand, ay, and the heart that throbs at its wrist, beats, I do not doubt, as tranquilly as does any other heart that heaves a soft bosom, among the peerless beauties of her court."

"Well, then, I divine the enigma. You must owe this wide-stretched power, and this peace, to the universal supremacy of the church. Yes, so it must be, that the rightful and paternal authority of the successors of St. Peter has at length been bowed to by all nations; and, therefore, it is that a child—a fair girl, may rule a hemisphere, because the eyes of all men we devoutly fixed upon the claims of St. Peter; is it not so?"

"I must not conceal the truth; the chair of St. Peter is as much thought of by the people of England, or by the nations she governs, as is the cushion on which the king of Persia reposes his corpulence; or if, in fact, it be reverently regarded by any, it is just by those whom she finds it the most difficult to manage. But I wish I could spare you this. Yet let me add that, in fact, the diffusion of sentiments of reason, justice, and benevolence, in modern times, does render many things practicable, in the business of government, which, centuries ago, could not have been attempted."

"Ah! the bright idea that opens on my dim sight!—a vast empire tranquilly swayed—a fair and gentle maiden, the angel of order and symbol of goodness! How potent, then, must have become those controlling sentiments of reason, justice, and benevolence, which you speak of; none in your time trenches upon the rights of another. You know of no slavery; you have no prisons; no penal laws. It is some hundred years since last the nations of Europe have confronted each other, sword in hand?"

"Alas! it is little more than twenty years ago that some two hundred thousand men, English, Saxons, Germans, Franks, met in a field of that Tungrian Belgium, where a sixth part of them fattened the soil with their blood."

"I pray you, friend, find some themes of discourse less fraught with paradoxes than these you have touched; for, although a propounder of riddles finds ready listeners among the young and curious, whose wits are keen, this sort of amusement is annoying to dull age."

"All I have told you is naked truth, but need I remind a man so sagacious, that the faits of one age, seen apart from their causes, and out of their connexion, are always riddles to the men of another age. But I change my course at your request, and an easy transition from our last topic leads me to mention a marvellous invention and improvement—mark the word *improvement*—of modern times. I mean a mode of abbreviating the work of slaughter on a battle field, or of killing men by hundreds at a time, instead of tens. Imagine, then, two opposing hosts, no longer, as heretofore, hurling sticks and stones at each other like boys at play, but vomiting death—pouring forth bolts and fire, more fatal than the lenient thunder and lightning of heaven; yes, hurling hurricanes of sulphur and smoke, and hail-stones of lead and iron at each other, with a roar louder than a hundred cataracts, and sweeping down ranks of men, or thinning solid squadrons—think, I say, of heads and limbs flying in all directions, like the fruit and boughs of a tempest-torn orchard."

"And do the nations practise war at this rate? Europe then has become a solitude; and this is why an extended empire may be so easily governed, because, in fact, kings rule over herds of deer, not men— over forests and swamps and deserts, not populous provinces;—confess the truth."

'The truth then is that, spite of our wars, dealing in death wholesale, population has so swollen in most of the European kingdoms, and especially in England, that the tide of life has burst its dikes and rolled itself over, as a vast deluge, upon newly discovered continents; and the human inundation runs on, year after year, in a stream full and strong, from east to west just as once it flowed from north to south."

"New continents? a word to satisfy my curiosity. How many? Twenty?"

"Two; or you may call them one, just as we call the panniers swung on a mule's back two, or one."

"Of what sort; and where?"

"The one, a rugged waste of dark forests, bluff mountains, trackless swamps, icy deserts, blast-troubled lakes; yet fertile enough in patches. The other, except in patches, fat, prolific, inexhaustible; its bowels teeming with gold, silver, diamonds."

"Have these continents then fallen as inheritances to the nations of Europe? and if so, to which among them; but no doubt it is England that has snatched the realm of gold and diamonds:—Hence her extent of empire."

"Nay, it is England that has snatched the rugged prize, leaving her neighbours to impoverish and enslave themselves with mountains of wealth. England's sons, driven from her bosom, and seeking a home where they might find one, in an unenvied wilderness, are now rearing an empire as great as her own. Do you not know that it is not the precious metals themselves, but the inducements to acquire them, that enrich a people?"

"I know it; yet one is apt to be child enough to mistake gold for wealth. But where are these new worlds?"

"Where *you* might well have guessed them to be; when you told the ignorance of your times that this earth of ours is a ball, why did you not send some of your bold Saxon adventurers to seek what you might have been sure was somewhere to be found, another continent?"

"Because the most simple and probable truth, advanced hypothetically, startles and shocks even those who have sagacity enough to descry it, while it horribly frightens and scandalizes the vulgar. Let us now call together the fraternity of this religious house, and, then, on some ridiculous evidence, I will assure them that the other side of the world is sprawled over by a red dragon, measuring five thousand miles from his snout to the tip of his tail; all but one or two, I wager you, will swallow the fable with open mouths—the red dragon will go down with them as glib as an oyster. But let me show solid reason for believing that our western ocean washes the shores of another continent, and Bede, if not so happy as to be consigned to his cloister for life, with a keeper, would be condemned, and, likely enough, burnt as a sorcerer or heretic."

"Things go rather better with us now-a-days; the vulgar is still the vulgar; but it has learned to be guided a little by those who know better than itself. Reason, in our times, has won so many triumphs in the eyes of the people, that she has gained credit enough with them to make them know their place."

"But how is it that these new continents of the western hemisphere are reached from our shores? Are they joined by a tongue of land?"

"They are reached as certainly, and one may say as easily, as Tyna's mouth is reached by the fisherman's boat that drops down with the ebb of tide. Each vessel is securely led on its way across the pathless ocean, and far remote from any land—a distance of two thousand five hundred miles, by—"

"By an angel?"

"By—a needle!"

"Oh, oh, then the people of Europe, how can I doubt it, and not least the English, if they have not lapsed into paganism, have horribly addicted themselves to the black art. What you speak of is sheer magic; a dealing with—"

"Well, say so if you please; and, in truth, if we are speaking of the English, and most especially of the people of this northern part of the island, I hardly know how they could wash themselves entirely clean of such an imputation. If you were just now to visit almost any of the great towns north of the Humber, I fear you would think that, among this busy and curious race, all the arts are black; and much you might see that is more amazing than any thing which magic has attempted or pretended."

"Good friend, my spirit fails me speak of things ordinary and intelligible. With all its strange doings, and dark dealings, is England wealthy?"

"Beyond example—almost beyond calculation—what would you say if I were to tell you that her own sons have lent her a sum, out of their private pockets—out of their savings, so great that any one is laughed at as a fool, who talks of its ever being repaid—a sum large enough to have bought Europe—lands, houses, slaves, jewels, treasures, such as it was in your time, four times over; and yet, this loan, that can never be paid, frets nobody—not the borrower—not the lender."

"Whence has flowed this deluge of riches, if the western mountains of gold are in the keeping of others?"

"I will tell you by a sample. We send our ships fourteen thousand mile for some pods of cotton: when we get them, we work them up into stuffs of various texture and dye. We return them whence they came—a fourteen thousand miles, and sell them to the very people who gathered the raw material, at so vile a price, that none can drive us from the market; and yet it is out of the profits of this trade that we get rich as princes."

"At this rate then, and if it be so easy to cram your bags, you can have no poor left among you."

"No, if you will first except a few millions of paupers, maintained at the public cost, and a few millions more left to starve, or near it. Yet do not think us hard-hearted. We build palaces for our poor; ay, it would turn the head of the mightiest of your Saxons to be made the master of an edifice, such as you may find scores of now-a-days, wherein our abjects find a refuge, and remain:—until they learn that houseless want is more tolerable than such entertainment."

"Who, then, grasps and enjoys the vast profits of your spinning, and weaving, and grinding?"

"Be sure that the looms and the wheels do not get more than just so much oil as keeps them from catching fire; and, unluckily, the weaver, the spinner, and the grinder, have come to be looked upon, by our knowing folks, as nothing better than the cogs and cranks of the machinery, and, therefore, it is deemed a folly and a waste to pour into their hands or hearts, a drop more of the oil of gladness than what is absolutely necessary to keep them agoing."

"Why do you not make laws to enforce a more equitable division of profits?"

"We mean to do so, when we find that statutes prohibitory of east winds, blights, and cold summers, take effect, and better the seasons."

"Here then are your governments ruling, as you say, vast empires, as pleasantly as a dainty lass manages her well-bitted palfrey, and yet unable to secure the rights of nature, and a crust to the poor."

"Our governments, it is true, can do little; nevertheless man, in modern times, has vastly extended his power over—"

"Over his passions and selfishness?—over invisible beings and evil demons?"

"Over neither; but over nature."

"What then; you turn the course of the planets?"

"No; but yet we can bring them as near to the eye as if we could bend them some millions of miles from their spheres, or could ourselves walk the skies."

"Can you command the winds?"

"No; but we often outrun them—on land; and on the ocean, force a passage in the very teeth of a hurricane."

"Tell me plainly by what new-mastered giant force?

"By the potency of a boiling kettle; you have the naked fact. Yes, and if you will be my companion this evening, I will show you, flitting athwart the bogs and moors of Cealclythe, a long caravan of people and merchandize—such a company as crawls across the deserts of Arabia; yes, flitting away, and leaving the western gales to lag behind; all, all, by the boiling of a kettle!"

"Friend, abuse not so largely my simplicity."

"Venerable man, trust me no more if I fail to make good what I have affirmed. I will give you proof anon. But take from me, meanwhile, the general rule, that whatever in your wonted musings in this monastery garden, you may have thought of as likely to come about, *that* has not come about; while whatever, had it been roundly mentioned to you, you would have scouted as grossly absurd and incredible (as you are now fain to reject my report) *this* has actually realized itself, and is now reckoned among the most familiar and ordinary of ordinary things."

"Is all this then the fruit of a new dispensation of miracles; or of the subjugation of etherial tribes to the will of man, or of the bestowment upon human nature of unthought of faculties?"

"Neither the first, the second, nor the third hypothesis meets the case. Man, individually, or abstractedly, is nothing more, or more potent now, than he was in the days of Tubalcain. But he has learned to use his faculties in a better manner; or, shall I say, to attempt only what comes within the range of his powers; whereas, heretofore, men of intelligence have spurned what they knew, or might easily have known; while they spent their forces in the endeavour to know and to do, what is inscrutable, or unavailing, or impracticable. I should, however, add that we moderns have owed much to what we must call accidents, or discoveries of such a kind that we much rather wonder at the dulness of our Predecessors in not having seen what is so obvious, than admire our own wit in seeing it now. And, while we thank God, who has at length granted this or that boon to man, we tremble and are perplexed equally by the thought of that mysterious Providence, which so long hid from the eyes of men things they might as well have descried before the world was five centuries old."

"Thank God always, my son, for what he is pleased to afford us—unworthy of the least of his favours; nor question him ever concerning what he thinks fit to withhold. All such questioning ends in asking, why a worm should not have been a man—a man a seraph—a seraph a god; and thence we come to the enigma, why there should be any thing in the universe but God himself. Let us return to our discursive talk."

"Well, then, I just now saw you surrounded by franklins and lords of the soil; can they all write their names?"

"Scarcely one."

"What do they then when they are parties to a grant or covenant?"

"Use a stamp, and most of them carry such set in rings on their fingers, as ornaments."

"Those fingers then carry, in embryo, the principle or element of the greatest of all modern or ancient inventions—an invention which has already changed everything, as one may say, except the colours of the sky, and which is yet only beginning to show the extent of the powers it involves—nothing so simple in itself, if we think of it mechanically—nothing so wonderful in its energies, and yet the chief wonderment is—that it had not been thought of and practised centuries before.

Comparing the two contrivances, one might have thought that the art of printing should have preceded the construction of a loom, by a thousand years."

"And what is this mystery, the art of printing?"

"An art which makes it so easy a thing to multiply books, that they have become the vilest of commodities, and thus reach the hands of many who often cannot muster pence for a dinner."

"Then, no doubt all men of your times have become knowing?"

"Many more than have become wise; and yet the absolutely ignorant among us are many more is absolute number than the entire population of the heptarchy."

"Stop friend; before you relate any more wonders, please to give me the upshot of the matter; are you and your contemporaries of the nineteenth century, happier and better men than we of the eighth? or are you wiser to any good purpose?"

"Your question admits not of a round and categorical answer; but must be replied to disjunctively. I say, then, without a doubt, that many of my time are incomparably more knowing, and to better purpose, than were *any* of yours. Many also, I think I may say, among us, are better than any, saving a very few among you, and multitudes—thousands of the nineteenth century, are more firmly and ordinarily happy, than any but a small class of the eighth; and yet, nor can I cloak the fact—the wretched, the ignorant, and the vicious, are absolutely twenty times as many in my age as in yours."

"Where then is the gain of your astounding improvements?"

"Instead of attempting an answer to your question, I will merely put you in mind of the fact, which is a law of the human system, that, although nations may remain thousands of years in the same state of barbarism, or semi-barbarism, yet when once the development of reason actually commences, on it goes, and must go, whether the consequences be good or ill; nothing stops the process, which we must call *improvement*; nothing but the national overthrow or social destruction of the people among whom it is going on. The *cui bono* question, therefore, may be met by a *cui bono*, as to the inquiry itself. To what good purpose shall we ask concerning the ultimate benefit of the improvements which follow the development of mind, seeing that the process is inevitable, the yeast, once mixed in the lump, *will* work."

"Shall I look out for a host of Scandinavians, a northern besom, by whose aid your modern arts may be swept away, and mankind be restored to a happy ignorance?"

"You may do so, if you please. But beside that we are pretty well prepared to meet them on our shores, the remedy would not be efficacious—the arts have more than one sanctuary in the world. Sink the British islands in the sea—overrun or overturn Europe—the arts still live. The press too, of which I have spoken, immortalizes the philosophy, literature, and arts of modern nations."

"Is there room to hope, then, that such other improvements may yet take place, as will render your philosophy and your arts really beneficial to the mass of mankind; and such as can secure a moderate portion of comfort and enjoyment to the many?"

"Yes, I think so—only let—But what is this hubbub without?"

Before I could get a reply, the gate of the monastery garden burst open, and a dozen or more of the fraternity, pressing one over the other, and bawling in cracked voices, spread themselves over the garden. Missing their revered master from his place in the refectory, at the usual hour, and fearing that harm had come to him, all were in movement in quest of him. I started up, and hardly knowing how I might be handled among these scared good fellows, several of whom I saw had bludgeons in their hands, I looked wildly about me for some other exit than the garden gate. I rushed forward, I knew not whither, and reaching the wall, with a convulsed effort, scaled it; and instantly beheld, not the wild scene that had lately been before my eyes, but the high Durham road, shrouded in dust, through which I dimly descried, just beyond call, the Leeds Mercury, whisking away, and leaving me mulct of my fare, and in doubt whether to take the chances of the road, or to make my way back, and ashamed, to the Swan in Newcastle.

A Christmas Carol In Prose, Being a Ghost Story of Christmas

Charles Dickens

PREFACE

I have endeavoured in this Ghostly little book, to raise the Ghost of an Idea, which shall not put my readers out of humour with themselves, with each other, with the season, or with me. May it haunt their houses pleasantly, and no one wish to lay it.

Their faithful Friend and Servant,

C. D.

December, 1843.

Stave One
Marley's Ghost

Marley was dead: to begin with. There is no doubt whatever about that. The register of his burial was signed by the clergyman, the clerk, the undertaker, and the chief mourner. Scrooge signed it: and Scrooge's name was good upon 'Change, for anything he chose to put his hand to. Old Marley was as dead as a door-nail.

Mind! I don't mean to say that I know, of my own knowledge, what there is particularly dead about a door-nail. I might have been inclined, myself, to regard a coffin-nail as the deadest piece of ironmongery in the trade. But the wisdom of our ancestors is in the simile; and my unhallowed hands shall not disturb it, or the Country's done for. You will therefore permit me to repeat, emphatically, that Marley was as dead as a door-nail.

Scrooge knew he was dead? Of course he did. How could it be otherwise? Scrooge and he were partners for I don't know how many years. Scrooge was his sole executor, his sole administrator, his sole assign, his sole residuary legatee, his sole friend, and sole mourner. And even Scrooge was not so dreadfully cut up by the sad event, but that he was an excellent man of business on the very day of the funeral, and solemnised it with an undoubted bargain.

The mention of Marley's funeral brings me back to the point I started from. There is no doubt that Marley was dead. This must be distinctly understood, or nothing wonderful can come of the story I am going to relate. If we were not perfectly convinced that Hamlet's Father died before the play began, there would be nothing more remarkable in his taking a stroll at night, in an easterly wind, upon his own ramparts, than there would be in any other middle-aged gentleman rashly turning out after dark in a breezy spot—say Saint Paul's Churchyard for instance—literally to astonish his son's weak mind.

Scrooge never painted out Old Marley's name. There it stood, years afterwards, above the warehouse door: Scrooge and Marley. The firm was known as Scrooge and Marley. Sometimes people new to the business called Scrooge Scrooge, and sometimes Marley, but he answered to both names. It was all the same to him.

Oh! But he was a tight-fisted hand at the grindstone, Scrooge! a squeezing, wrenching, grasping, scraping, clutching, covetous, old sinner! Hard and sharp as flint, from which no steel had ever struck out generous fire; secret, and self-contained, and solitary as an oyster. The cold within him froze his old features, nipped his pointed nose, shrivelled his cheek, stiffened his gait; made his eyes red, his thin lips blue; and spoke out shrewdly in his grating voice. A frosty rime was on his head, and on his eyebrows, and his wiry chin. He carried his own low temperature always about with him; he iced his office in the dog-days; and didn't thaw it one degree at Christmas.

External heat and cold had little influence on Scrooge. No warmth could warm, no wintry weather chill him. No wind that blew was bitterer than he, no falling snow was more intent upon its purpose, no pelting rain less open to entreaty. Foul weather didn't know where to have him. The heaviest rain, and snow, and hail, and sleet, could boast of the advantage over him in only one respect. They often "came down" handsomely, and Scrooge never did.

Nobody ever stopped him in the street to say, with gladsome looks, "My dear Scrooge, how are you? When will you come to see me?" No beggars implored him to bestow a trifle, no children asked him what it was o'clock, no man or woman ever once in all his life inquired the way to such and such a place, of Scrooge. Even the blind men's dogs appeared to know him; and when they saw him coming on, would tug their owners into doorways and up courts; and then would wag their tails as though they said, "No eye at all is better than an evil eye, dark master!"

But what did Scrooge care! It was the very thing he liked. To edge his way along the crowded paths of life, warning all human sympathy to keep its distance, was what the knowing ones call "nuts" to Scrooge.

Once upon a time—of all the good days in the year, on Christmas Eve—old Scrooge sat busy in his counting-house. It was cold, bleak, biting weather: foggy withal: and he could hear the people in the court outside, go wheezing up and down, beating their hands upon their breasts, and stamping their feet upon the pavement stones to warm them. The city clocks had only just gone three, but it was quite dark already—it had not been light all day—and candles were flaring in the windows of the neighbouring offices, like ruddy smears upon the palpable brown air. The fog came pouring in at every chink and key-hole, and was so dense without, that although the court was of the narrowest, the houses opposite were mere phantoms. To see the dingy cloud come drooping down, obscuring everything, one might have thought that Nature lived hard by, and was brewing on a large scale.

The door of Scrooge's counting-house was open that he might keep his eye upon his clerk, who in a dismal little cell beyond, a sort of tank, was copying letters. Scrooge had a very small fire, but the clerk's fire was so very much smaller that it looked like one coal. But he couldn't replenish it, for Scrooge kept the coal-box in his own room; and so surely as the clerk came in with the shovel, the master predicted that it would be necessary for them to part. Wherefore the clerk put on his white comforter, and tried to warm himself at the candle; in which effort, not being a man of a strong imagination, he failed.

"A merry Christmas, uncle! God save you!" cried a cheerful voice. It was the voice of Scrooge's nephew, who came upon him so quickly that this was the first intimation he had of his approach.

"Bah!" said Scrooge, "Humbug!"

He had so heated himself with rapid walking in the fog and frost, this nephew of Scrooge's, that he was all in a glow; his face was ruddy and handsome; his eyes sparkled, and his breath smoked again.

"Christmas a humbug, uncle!" said Scrooge's nephew. "You don't mean that, I am sure?"

"I do," said Scrooge. "Merry Christmas! What right have you to be merry? What reason have you to be merry? You're poor enough."

"Come, then," returned the nephew gaily. "What right have you to be dismal? What reason have you to be morose? You're rich enough."

Scrooge having no better answer ready on the spur of the moment, said, "Bah!" again; and followed it up with "Humbug."

"Don't be cross, uncle!" said the nephew.

"What else can I be," returned the uncle, "when I live in such a world of fools as this? Merry Christmas! Out upon merry Christmas! What's Christmas time to you but a time for paying bills without money; a time for finding yourself a year older, but not an hour richer;

a time for balancing your books and having every item in 'em through a round dozen of months presented dead against you? If I could work my will," said Scrooge indignantly, "every idiot who goes about with 'Merry Christmas' on his lips, should be boiled with his own pudding, and buried with a stake of holly through his heart. He should!"

"Uncle!" pleaded the nephew.

"Nephew!" returned the uncle sternly, "keep Christmas in your own way, and let me keep it in mine."

"Keep it!" repeated Scrooge's nephew. "But you don't keep it."

"Let me leave it alone, then," said Scrooge. "Much good may it do you! Much good it has ever done you!"

"There are many things from which I might have derived good, by which I have not profited, I dare say," returned the nephew. "Christmas among the rest. But I am sure I have always thought of Christmas time, when it has come round—apart from the veneration due to its sacred name and origin, if anything belonging to it can be apart from that—as a good time; a kind, forgiving, charitable, pleasant time; the only time I know of, in the long calendar of the year, when men and women seem by one consent to open their shut-up hearts freely, and to think of people below them as if they really were fellow-passengers to the grave, and not another race of creatures bound on other journeys. And therefore, uncle, though it has never put a scrap of gold or silver in my pocket, I believe that it *has* done me good, and *will* do me good; and I say, God bless it!"

The clerk in the Tank involuntarily applauded. Becoming immediately sensible of the impropriety, he poked the fire, and extinguished the last frail spark for ever.

"Let me hear another sound from *you*," said Scrooge, "and you'll keep your Christmas by losing your situation! You're quite a powerful speaker, sir," he added, turning to his nephew. "I wonder you don't go into Parliament."

"Don't be angry, uncle. Come! Dine with us to-morrow."

Scrooge said that he would see him—yes, indeed he did. He went the whole length of the expression, and said that he would see him in that extremity first.

"But why?" cried Scrooge's nephew. "Why?"

"Why did you get married?" said Scrooge.

"Because I fell in love."

"Because you fell in love!" growled Scrooge, as if that were the only one thing in the world more ridiculous than a merry Christmas. "Good afternoon!"

"Nay, uncle, but you never came to see me before that happened. Why give it as a reason for not coming now?"

"Good afternoon," said Scrooge.

"I want nothing from you; I ask nothing of you; why cannot we be friends?"

"Good afternoon," said Scrooge.

"I am sorry, with all my heart, to find you so resolute. We have never had any quarrel, to which I have been a party. But I have made the trial in homage to Christmas, and I'll keep my Christmas humour to the last. So A Merry Christmas, uncle!"

"Good afternoon!" said Scrooge.

"And A Happy New Year!"

"Good afternoon!" said Scrooge.

His nephew left the room without an angry word, notwithstanding. He stopped at the outer door to bestow the greetings of the season on the clerk, who, cold as he was, was warmer than Scrooge; for he returned them cordially.

"There's another fellow," muttered Scrooge; who overheard him: "my clerk, with fifteen shillings a week, and a wife and family, talking about a merry Christmas. I'll retire to Bedlam."

This lunatic, in letting Scrooge's nephew out, had let two other people in. They were portly gentlemen, pleasant to behold, and now stood, with their hats off, in Scrooge's office. They had books and papers in their hands, and bowed to him.

"Scrooge and Marley's, I believe," said one of the gentlemen, referring to his list. "Have I the pleasure of addressing Mr. Scrooge, or Mr. Marley?"

"Mr. Marley has been dead these seven years," Scrooge replied. "He died seven years ago, this very night."

"We have no doubt his liberality is well represented by his surviving partner," said the gentleman, presenting his credentials.

It certainly was; for they had been two kindred spirits. At the ominous word "liberality," Scrooge frowned, and shook his head, and handed the credentials back.

"At this festive season of the year, Mr. Scrooge," said the gentleman, taking up a pen, "it is more than usually desirable that we should make some slight provision for the Poor and destitute, who suffer greatly at the present time. Many thousands are in want of common necessaries; hundreds of thousands are in want of common comforts, sir."

"Are there no prisons?" asked Scrooge.

"Plenty of prisons," said the gentleman, laying down the pen again.

"And the Union workhouses?" demanded Scrooge. "Are they still in operation?"

"They are. Still," returned the gentleman, "I wish I could say they were not."

"The Treadmill and the Poor Law are in full vigour, then?" said Scrooge.

"Both very busy, sir."

"Oh! I was afraid, from what you said at first, that something had occurred to stop them in their useful course," said Scrooge. "I'm very glad to hear it."

"Under the impression that they scarcely furnish Christian cheer of mind or body to the multitude," returned the gentleman, "a few of us are endeavouring to raise a fund to buy the Poor some meat and drink, and means of warmth. We choose this time, because it is a time, of all others, when Want is keenly felt, and Abundance rejoices. What shall I put you down for?"

"Nothing!" Scrooge replied.

"You wish to be anonymous?"

"I wish to be left alone," said Scrooge. "Since you ask me what I wish, gentlemen, that is my answer. I don't make merry myself at Christmas and I can't afford to make idle people merry. I help to support the establishments I have mentioned—they cost enough; and those who are badly off must go there."

"Many can't go there; and many would rather die."

"If they would rather die," said Scrooge, "they had better do it, and decrease the surplus population. Besides—excuse me—I don't know that."

"But you might know it," observed the gentleman.

"It's not my business," Scrooge returned. "It's enough for a man to understand his own business, and not to interfere with other people's. Mine occupies me constantly. Good afternoon, gentlemen!"

Seeing clearly that it would be useless to pursue their point, the gentlemen withdrew. Scrooge resumed his labours with an improved opinion of himself, and in a more facetious temper than was usual with him.

Meanwhile the fog and darkness thickened so, that people ran about with flaring links, proffering their services to go before horses in carriages, and conduct them on their way. The ancient tower of a church, whose gruff old bell was always peeping slily down at Scrooge out of a Gothic window in the wall, became invisible, and struck the hours and quarters in the clouds, with tremulous vibrations afterwards as if its teeth were chattering in its frozen head up there. The cold became intense. In the main street, at the corner of the court, some labourers were repairing the gas-pipes, and had lighted a great fire in a brazier, round which a party of ragged men and boys were gathered: warming their hands and winking their eyes before the blaze in rapture. The water-plug being left in solitude, its overflowings sullenly congealed,

and turned to misanthropic ice. The brightness of the shops where
holly sprigs and berries crackled in the lamp heat of the windows,
made pale faces ruddy as they passed. Poulterers' and grocers' trades
became a splendid joke: a glorious pageant, with which it was next to
impossible to believe that such dull principles as bargain and sale had
anything to do. The Lord Mayor, in the stronghold of the mighty Mansion House, gave orders to his fifty cooks and butlers to keep Christmas
as a Lord Mayor's household should; and even the little tailor, whom
he had fined five shillings on the previous Monday for being drunk
and bloodthirsty in the streets, stirred up to-morrow's pudding in his
garret, while his lean wife and the baby sallied out to buy the beef.

Foggier yet, and colder. Piercing, searching, biting cold. If the
good Saint Dunstan had but nipped the Evil Spirit's nose with a touch
of such weather as that, instead of using his familiar weapons, then
indeed he would have roared to lusty purpose. The owner of one scant
young nose, gnawed and mumbled by the hungry cold as bones are
gnawed by dogs, stooped down at Scrooge's keyhole to regale him with
a Christmas carol: but at the first sound of

"God bless you, merry gentleman!
May nothing you dismay!"

Scrooge seized the ruler with such energy of action, that the singer
fled in terror, leaving the keyhole to the fog and even more congenial
frost.

At length the hour of shutting up the counting-house arrived. With
an ill-will Scrooge dismounted from his stool, and tacitly admitted
the fact to the expectant clerk in the Tank, who instantly snuffed his
candle out, and put on his hat.

"You'll want all day to-morrow, I suppose?" said Scrooge.

"If quite convenient, sir."

"It's not convenient," said Scrooge, "and it's not fair. If I was to
stop half-a-crown for it, you'd think yourself ill-used, I'll be bound?"

The clerk smiled faintly.

"And yet," said Scrooge, "you don't think me ill-used, when I pay
a day's wages for no work."

The clerk observed that it was only once a year.

"A poor excuse for picking a man's pocket every twenty-fifth of
December!" said Scrooge, buttoning his great-coat to the chin. "But I
suppose you must have the whole day. Be here all the earlier next
morning."

The clerk promised that he would; and Scrooge walked out with a
growl. The office was closed in a twinkling, and the clerk, with the

long ends of his white comforter dangling below his waist (for he boasted no great-coat), went down a slide on Cornhill, at the end of a lane of boys, twenty times, in honour of its being Christmas Eve, and then ran home to Camden Town as hard as he could pelt, to play at blindman's-buff.

Scrooge took his melancholy dinner in his usual melancholy tavern; and having read all the newspapers, and beguiled the rest of the evening with his banker's-book, went home to bed. He lived in chambers which had once belonged to his deceased partner. They were a gloomy suite of rooms, in a lowering pile of building up a yard, where it had so little business to be, that one could scarcely help fancying it must have run there when it was a young house, playing at hide-and-seek with other houses, and forgotten the way out again. It was old enough now, and dreary enough, for nobody lived in it but Scrooge, the other rooms being all let out as offices. The yard was so dark that even Scrooge, who knew its every stone, was fain to grope with his hands. The fog and frost so hung about the black old gateway of the house, that it seemed as if the Genius of the Weather sat in mournful meditation on the threshold.

Now, it is a fact, that there was nothing at all particular about the knocker on the door, except that it was very large. It is also a fact, that Scrooge had seen it, night and morning, during his whole residence in that place; also that Scrooge had as little of what is called fancy about him as any man in the city of London, even including—which is a bold word—the corporation, aldermen, and livery. Let it also be borne in mind that Scrooge had not bestowed one thought on Marley, since his last mention of his seven years' dead partner that afternoon. And then let any man explain to me, if he can, how it happened that Scrooge, having his key in the lock of the door, saw in the knocker, without its undergoing any intermediate process of change—not a knocker, but Marley's face.

Marley's face. It was not in impenetrable shadow as the other objects in the yard were, but had a dismal light about it, like a bad lobster in a dark cellar. It was not angry or ferocious, but looked at Scrooge as Marley used to look: with ghostly spectacles turned up on its ghostly forehead. The hair was curiously stirred, as if by breath or hot air; and, though the eyes were wide open, they were perfectly motionless. That, and its livid colour, made it horrible; but its horror seemed to be in spite of the face and beyond its control, rather than a part of its own expression.

As Scrooge looked fixedly at this phenomenon, it was a knocker again.

To say that he was not startled, or that his blood was not conscious of a terrible sensation to which it had been a stranger from infancy, would be untrue. But he put his hand upon the key he had relinquished, turned it sturdily, walked in, and lighted his candle.

He *did* pause, with a moment's irresolution, before he shut the door; and he did look cautiously behind it first, as if he half expected to be terrified with the sight of Marley's pigtail sticking out into the hall. But there was nothing on the back of the door, except the screws and nuts that held the knocker on, so he said "Pooh, pooh!" and closed it with a bang.

The sound resounded through the house like thunder. Every room above, and every cask in the wine-merchant's cellars below, appeared to have a separate peal of echoes of its own. Scrooge was not a man to be frightened by echoes. He fastened the door, and walked across the hall, and up the stairs; slowly too: trimming his candle as he went.

You may talk vaguely about driving a coach-and-six up a good old flight of stairs, or through a bad young Act of Parliament; but I mean to say you might have got a hearse up that staircase, and taken it broadwise, with the splinter-bar towards the wall and the door towards the balustrades: and done it easy. There was plenty of width for that, and room to spare; which is perhaps the reason why Scrooge thought he saw a locomotive hearse going on before him in the gloom. Half-a-dozen gas-lamps out of the street wouldn't have lighted the entry too well, so you may suppose that it was pretty dark with Scrooge's dip.

Up Scrooge went, not caring a button for that. Darkness is cheap, and Scrooge liked it. But before he shut his heavy door, he walked through his rooms to see that all was right. He had just enough recollection of the face to desire to do that.

Sitting-room, bedroom, lumber-room. All as they should be. Nobody under the table, nobody under the sofa; a small fire in the grate; spoon and basin ready; and the little saucepan of gruel (Scrooge had a cold in his head) upon the hob. Nobody under the bed; nobody in the closet; nobody in his dressing-gown, which was hanging up in a suspicious attitude against the wall. Lumber-room as usual. Old fire-guard, old shoes, two fish-baskets, washing-stand on three legs, and a poker.

Quite satisfied, he closed his door, and locked himself in; double-locked himself in, which was not his custom. Thus secured against surprise, he took off his cravat; put on his dressing-gown and slippers, and his nightcap; and sat down before the fire to take his gruel.

It was a very low fire indeed; nothing on such a bitter night. He was obliged to sit close to it, and brood over it, before he could extract the least sensation of warmth from such a handful of fuel. The fireplace was an old one, built by some Dutch merchant long ago, and paved all round with quaint Dutch tiles, designed to illustrate the

Scriptures. There were Cains and Abels, Pharaoh's daughters; Queens of Sheba, Angelic messengers descending through the air on clouds like feather-beds, Abrahams, Belshazzars, Apostles putting off to sea in butter-boats, hundreds of figures to attract his thoughts; and yet that face of Marley, seven years dead, came like the ancient Prophet's rod, and swallowed up the whole. If each smooth tile had been a blank at first, with power to shape some picture on its surface from the disjointed fragments of his thoughts, there would have been a copy of old Marley's head on every one.

"Humbug!" said Scrooge; and walked across the room.

After several turns, he sat down again. As he threw his head back in the chair, his glance happened to rest upon a bell, a disused bell, that hung in the room, and communicated for some purpose now forgotten with a chamber in the highest story of the building. It was with great astonishment, and with a strange, inexplicable dread, that as he looked, he saw this bell begin to swing. It swung so softly in the outset that it scarcely made a sound; but soon it rang out loudly, and so did every bell in the house.

This might have lasted half a minute, or a minute, but it seemed an hour. The bells ceased as they had begun, together. They were succeeded by a clanking noise, deep down below; as if some person were dragging a heavy chain over the casks in the wine-merchant's cellar. Scrooge then remembered to have heard that ghosts in haunted houses were described as dragging chains.

The cellar-door flew open with a booming sound, and then he heard the noise much louder, on the floors below; then coming up the stairs; then coming straight towards his door.

"It's humbug still!" said Scrooge. "I won't believe it."

His colour changed though, when, without a pause, it came on through the heavy door, and passed into the room before his eyes. Upon its coming in, the dying flame leaped up, as though it cried, "I know him; Marley's Ghost!" and fell again.

The same face: the very same. Marley in his pigtail, usual waistcoat, tights and boots; the tassels on the latter bristling, like his pigtail, and his coat-skirts, and the hair upon his head. The chain he drew was clasped about his middle. It was long, and wound about him like a tail; and it was made (for Scrooge observed it closely) of cash-boxes, keys, padlocks, ledgers, deeds, and heavy purses wrought in steel. His body was transparent; so that Scrooge, observing him, and looking through his waistcoat, could see the two buttons on his coat behind.

Scrooge had often heard it said that Marley had no bowels, but he had never believed it until now.

No, nor did he believe it even now. Though he looked the phantom through and through, and saw it standing before him; though he felt the chilling influence of its death-cold eyes; and marked the very texture of the folded kerchief bound about its head and chin, which wrapper he had not observed before; he was still incredulous, and fought against his senses.

"How now!" said Scrooge, caustic and cold as ever. "What do you want with me?"

"Much!"—Marley's voice, no doubt about it.

"Who are you?"

"Ask me who I *was*."

"Who *were* you then?" said Scrooge, raising his voice. "You're particular, for a shade." He was going to say "*to* a shade," but substituted this, as more appropriate.

"In life I was your partner, Jacob Marley."

"Can you—can you sit down?" asked Scrooge, looking doubtfully at him.

"I can."

"Do it, then."

Scrooge asked the question, because he didn't know whether a ghost so transparent might find himself in a condition to take a chair; and felt that in the event of its being impossible, it might involve the necessity of an embarrassing explanation. But the ghost sat down on the opposite side of the fireplace, as if he were quite used to it.

"You don't believe in me," observed the Ghost.

"I don't," said Scrooge.

"What evidence would you have of my reality beyond that of your senses?"

"I don't know," said Scrooge.

"Why do you doubt your senses?"

"Because," said Scrooge, "a little thing affects them. A slight disorder of the stomach makes them cheats. You may be an undigested bit of beef, a blot of mustard, a crumb of cheese, a fragment of an underdone potato. There's more of gravy than of grave about you, whatever you are!"

Scrooge was not much in the habit of cracking jokes, nor did he feel, in his heart, by any means waggish then. The truth is, that he tried to be smart, as a means of distracting his own attention, and keeping down his terror; for the spectre's voice disturbed the very marrow in his bones.

To sit, staring at those fixed glazed eyes, in silence for a moment, would play, Scrooge felt, the very deuce with him. There was something very awful, too, in the spectre's being provided with an infernal atmosphere of its own. Scrooge could not feel it himself, but this was clearly the case; for though the Ghost sat perfectly motionless, its hair, and skirts, and tassels, were still agitated as by the hot vapour from an oven.

"You see this toothpick?" said Scrooge, returning quickly to the charge, for the reason just assigned; and wishing, though it were only for a second, to divert the vision's stony gaze from himself.

"I do," replied the Ghost.

"You are not looking at it," said Scrooge.

"But I see it," said the Ghost, "notwithstanding."

"Well!" returned Scrooge, "I have but to swallow this, and be for the rest of my days persecuted by a legion of goblins, all of my own creation. Humbug, I tell you! humbug!"

At this the spirit raised a frightful cry, and shook its chain with such a dismal and appalling noise, that Scrooge held on tight to his chair, to save himself from falling in a swoon. But how much greater was his horror, when the phantom taking off the bandage round its head, as if it were too warm to wear indoors, its lower jaw dropped down upon its breast!

Scrooge fell upon his knees, and clasped his hands before his face.

"Mercy!" he said. "Dreadful apparition, why do you trouble me?"

"Man of the worldly mind!" replied the Ghost, "do you believe in me or not?"

"I do," said Scrooge. "I must. But why do spirits walk the earth, and why do they come to me?"

"It is required of every man," the Ghost returned, "that the spirit within him should walk abroad among his fellowmen, and travel far and wide; and if that spirit goes not forth in life, it is condemned to do so after death. It is doomed to wander through the world—oh, woe is me!—and witness what it cannot share, but might have shared on earth, and turned to happiness!"

Again the spectre raised a cry, and shook its chain and wrung its shadowy hands.

"You are fettered," said Scrooge, trembling. "Tell me why?"

"I wear the chain I forged in life," replied the Ghost. "I made it link by link, and yard by yard; I girded it on of my own free will, and of my own free will I wore it. Is its pattern strange to *you*?"

Scrooge trembled more and more.

"Or would you know," pursued the Ghost, "the weight and length of the strong coil you bear yourself? It was full as heavy and as long as this, seven Christmas Eves ago. You have laboured on it, since. It is a ponderous chain!"

Scrooge glanced about him on the floor, in the expectation of finding himself surrounded by some fifty or sixty fathoms of iron cable: but he could see nothing.

"Jacob," he said, imploringly. "Old Jacob Marley, tell me more. Speak comfort to me, Jacob!"

"I have none to give," the Ghost replied. "It comes from other regions, Ebenezer Scrooge, and is conveyed by other ministers, to other kinds of men. Nor can I tell you what I would. A very little more is all permitted to me. I cannot rest, I cannot stay, I cannot linger anywhere. My spirit never walked beyond our counting-house—mark me!—in life my spirit never roved beyond the narrow limits of our money-changing hole; and weary journeys lie before me!"

It was a habit with Scrooge, whenever he became thoughtful, to put his hands in his breeches pockets. Pondering on what the Ghost had said, he did so now, but without lifting up his eyes, or getting off his knees.

"You must have been very slow about it, Jacob," Scrooge observed, in a business-like manner, though with humility and deference.

"Slow!" the Ghost repeated.

"Seven years dead," mused Scrooge. "And travelling all the time!"

"The whole time," said the Ghost. "No rest, no peace. Incessant torture of remorse."

"You travel fast?" said Scrooge.

"On the wings of the wind," replied the Ghost.

"You might have got over a great quantity of ground in seven years," said Scrooge.

The Ghost, on hearing this, set up another cry, and clanked its chain so hideously in the dead silence of the night, that the Ward would have been justified in indicting it for a nuisance.

"Oh! captive, bound, and double-ironed," cried the phantom, "not to know, that ages of incessant labour by immortal creatures, for this earth must pass into eternity before the good of which it is susceptible is all developed. Not to know that any Christian spirit working kindly in its little sphere, whatever it may be, will find its mortal life too short for its vast means of usefulness. Not to know that no space of regret can make amends for one life's opportunity misused! Yet such was I! Oh! such was I!"

"But you were always a good man of business, Jacob," faltered Scrooge, who now began to apply this to himself.

"Business!" cried the Ghost, wringing its hands again. "Mankind was my business. The common welfare was my business; charity, mercy, forbearance, and benevolence, were, all, my business. The dealings of my trade were but a drop of water in the comprehensive ocean of my business!"

It held up its chain at arm's length, as if that were the cause of all its unavailing grief, and flung it heavily upon the ground again.

"At this time of the rolling year," the spectre said, "I suffer most. Why did I walk through crowds of fellow-beings with my eyes turned down, and never raise them to that blessed Star which led the Wise Men to a poor abode! Were there no poor homes to which its light would have conducted *me*!"

Scrooge was very much dismayed to hear the spectre going on at this rate, and began to quake exceedingly.

"Hear me!" cried the Ghost. "My time is nearly gone."

"I will," said Scrooge. "But don't be hard upon me! Don't be flowery, Jacob! Pray!"

"How it is that I appear before you in a shape that you can see, I may not tell. I have sat invisible beside you many and many a day."

It was not an agreeable idea. Scrooge shivered, and wiped the perspiration from his brow.

"That is no light part of my penance," pursued the Ghost. "I am here to-night to warn you, that you have yet a chance and hope of escaping my fate. A chance and hope of my procuring, Ebenezer."

"You were always a good friend to me," said Scrooge. "Thank'ee!"

"You will be haunted," resumed the Ghost, "by Three Spirits."

Scrooge's countenance fell almost as low as the Ghost's had done.

"Is that the chance and hope you mentioned, Jacob?" he demanded, in a faltering voice.

"It is."

"I—I think I'd rather not," said Scrooge.

"Without their visits," said the Ghost, "you cannot hope to shun the path I tread. Expect the first to-morrow, when the bell tolls One."

"Couldn't I take 'em all at once, and have it over, Jacob?" hinted Scrooge.

"Expect the second on the next night at the same hour. The third upon the next night when the last stroke of Twelve has ceased to vibrate. Look to see me no more; and look that, for your own sake, you remember what has passed between us!"

When it had said these words, the spectre took its wrapper from the table, and bound it round its head, as before. Scrooge knew this, by the smart sound its teeth made, when the jaws were brought together by the bandage. He ventured to raise his eyes again, and found his supernatural visitor confronting him in an erect attitude, with its chain wound over and about its arm.

The apparition walked backward from him; and at every step it took, the window raised itself a little, so that when the spectre reached it, it was wide open.

It beckoned Scrooge to approach, which he did. When they were within two paces of each other, Marley's Ghost held up its hand, warning him to come no nearer. Scrooge stopped.

Not so much in obedience, as in surprise and fear: for on the raising of the hand, he became sensible of confused noises in the air; incoherent sounds of lamentation and regret; wailings inexpressibly sorrowful and self-accusatory. The spectre, after listening for a moment, joined in the mournful dirge; and floated out upon the bleak, dark night.

Scrooge followed to the window: desperate in his curiosity. He looked out.

The air was filled with phantoms, wandering hither and thither in restless haste, and moaning as they went. Every one of them wore chains like Marley's Ghost; some few (they might be guilty governments) were linked together; none were free. Many had been personally known to Scrooge in their lives. He had been quite familiar with one old ghost, in a white waistcoat, with a monstrous iron safe attached to its ankle, who cried piteously at being unable to assist a wretched woman with an infant, whom it saw below, upon a door-step. The misery with them all was, clearly, that they sought to interfere, for good, in human matters, and had lost the power for ever.

Whether these creatures faded into mist, or mist enshrouded them, he could not tell. But they and their spirit voices faded together; and the night became as it had been when he walked home.

Scrooge closed the window, and examined the door by which the Ghost had entered. It was double-locked, as he had locked it with his own hands, and the bolts were undisturbed. He tried to say "Humbug!" but stopped at the first syllable. And being, from the emotion he had undergone, or the fatigues of the day, or his glimpse of the Invisible World, or the dull conversation of the Ghost, or the lateness of the hour, much in need of repose; went straight to bed, without undressing, and fell asleep upon the instant.

STAVE TWO
The First of the Three Spirits

When Scrooge awoke, it was so dark, that looking out of bed, he could scarcely distinguish the transparent window from the opaque walls of his chamber. He was endeavouring to pierce the darkness with his ferret eyes, when the chimes of a neighbouring church struck the four quarters. So he listened for the hour.

To his great astonishment the heavy bell went on from six to seven, and from seven to eight, and regularly up to twelve; then stopped. Twelve! It was past two when he went to bed. The clock was wrong. An icicle must have got into the works. Twelve!

He touched the spring of his repeater, to correct this most preposterous clock. Its rapid little pulse beat twelve: and stopped.

"Why, it isn't possible," said Scrooge, "that I can have slept through a whole day and far into another night. It isn't possible that anything has happened to the sun, and this is twelve at noon!"

The idea being an alarming one, he scrambled out of bed, and groped his way to the window. He was obliged to rub the frost off with the sleeve of his dressing-gown before he could see anything; and could see very little then. All he could make out was, that it was still very foggy and extremely cold, and that there was no noise of people running to and fro, and making a great stir, as there unquestionably would have been if night had beaten off bright day, and taken possession of the world. This was a great relief, because "three days after sight of this First of Exchange pay to Mr. Ebenezer Scrooge or his order," and so forth, would have become a mere United States' security if there were no days to count by.

Scrooge went to bed again, and thought, and thought, and thought it over and over and over, and could make nothing of it. The more he thought, the more perplexed he was; and the more he endeavoured not to think, the more he thought.

Marley's Ghost bothered him exceedingly. Every time he resolved within himself, after mature inquiry, that it was all a dream, his mind flew back again, like a strong spring released, to its first position, and presented the same problem to be worked all through, "Was it a dream or not?"

Scrooge lay in this state until the chime had gone three quarters more, when he remembered, on a sudden, that the Ghost had warned him of a visitation when the bell tolled one. He resolved to lie awake until the hour was passed; and, considering that he could no more go to sleep than go to Heaven, this was perhaps the wisest resolution in his power.

The quarter was so long, that he was more than once convinced he must have sunk into a doze unconsciously, and missed the clock. At length it broke upon his listening ear.

"Ding, dong!"

"A quarter past," said Scrooge, counting.

"Ding, dong!"

"Half-past!" said Scrooge.

"Ding, dong!"

"A quarter to it," said Scrooge.

"Ding, dong!"

"The hour itself," said Scrooge, triumphantly, "and nothing else!"

He spoke before the hour bell sounded, which it now did with a deep, dull, hollow, melancholy One. Light flashed up in the room upon the instant, and the curtains of his bed were drawn.

The curtains of his bed were drawn aside, I tell you, by a hand. Not the curtains at his feet, nor the curtains at his back, but those to which his face was addressed. The curtains of his bed were drawn aside; and Scrooge, starting up into a half-recumbent attitude, found himself face to face with the unearthly visitor who drew them: as close to it as I am now to you, and I am standing in the spirit at your elbow.

It was a strange figure—like a child: yet not so like a child as like an old man, viewed through some supernatural medium, which gave him the appearance of having receded from the view, and being diminished to a child's proportions. Its hair, which hung about its neck and down its back, was white as if with age; and yet the face had not a wrinkle in it, and the tenderest bloom was on the skin. The arms were very long and muscular; the hands the same, as if its hold were of uncommon strength. Its legs and feet, most delicately formed, were, like those upper members, bare. It wore a tunic of the purest white; and round its waist was bound a lustrous belt, the sheen of which was beautiful. It held a branch of fresh green holly in its hand; and, in singular contradiction of that wintry emblem, had its dress trimmed with summer flowers. But the strangest thing about it was, that from the crown of its head there sprung a bright clear jet of light, by which all this was visible; and which was doubtless the occasion of its using, in its duller moments, a great extinguisher for a cap, which it now held under its arm.

Even this, though, when Scrooge looked at it with increasing steadiness, was *not* its strangest quality. For as its belt sparkled and glittered now in one part and now in another, and what was light one instant, at another time was dark, so the figure itself fluctuated in its distinctness: being now a thing with one arm, now with one leg, now with twenty legs, now a pair of legs without a head, now a head without a body: of which dissolving parts, no outline would be visible in the dense gloom wherein they melted away. And in the very wonder of this, it would be itself again; distinct and clear as ever.

"Are you the Spirit, sir, whose coming was foretold to me?" asked Scrooge.

"I am!"

The voice was soft and gentle. Singularly low, as if instead of being so close beside him, it were at a distance.

"Who, and what are you?" Scrooge demanded.

"I am the Ghost of Christmas Past."

"Long Past?" inquired Scrooge: observant of its dwarfish stature.

"No. Your past."

Perhaps, Scrooge could not have told anybody why, if anybody could have asked him; but he had a special desire to see the Spirit in his cap; and begged him to be covered.

"What!" exclaimed the Ghost, "would you so soon put out, with worldly hands, the light I give? Is it not enough that you are one of those whose passions made this cap, and force me through whole trains of years to wear it low upon my brow!"

Scrooge reverently disclaimed all intention to offend or any knowledge of having wilfully "bonneted" the Spirit at any period of his life. He then made bold to inquire what business brought him there.

"Your welfare!" said the Ghost.

Scrooge expressed himself much obliged, but could not help thinking that a night of unbroken rest would have been more conducive to that end. The Spirit must have heard him thinking, for it said immediately:

"Your reclamation, then. Take heed!"

It put out its strong hand as it spoke, and clasped him gently by the arm.

"Rise! and walk with me!"

It would have been in vain for Scrooge to plead that the weather and the hour were not adapted to pedestrian purposes; that bed was warm, and the thermometer a long way below freezing; that he was clad but lightly in his slippers, dressing-gown, and nightcap; and that he had a cold upon him at that time. The grasp, though gentle as a woman's hand, was not to be resisted. He rose: but finding that the Spirit made towards the window, clasped his robe in supplication.

"I am a mortal," Scrooge remonstrated, "and liable to fall."

"Bear but a touch of my hand *there*," said the Spirit, laying it upon his heart, "and you shall be upheld in more than this!"

As the words were spoken, they passed through the wall, and stood upon an open country road, with fields on either hand. The city had entirely vanished. Not a vestige of it was to be seen. The darkness and the mist had vanished with it, for it was a clear, cold, winter day, with snow upon the ground.

"Good Heaven!" said Scrooge, clasping his hands together, as he looked about him. "I was bred in this place. I was a boy here!"

The Spirit gazed upon him mildly. Its gentle touch, though it had been light and instantaneous, appeared still present to the old man's sense of feeling. He was conscious of a thousand odours floating in the air, each one connected with a thousand thoughts, and hopes, and joys, and cares long, long, forgotten!

"Your lip is trembling," said the Ghost. "And what is that upon your cheek?"

Scrooge muttered, with an unusual catching in his voice, that it was a pimple; and begged the Ghost to lead him where he would.

"You recollect the way?" inquired the Spirit.

"Remember it!" cried Scrooge with fervour; "I could walk it blindfold."

"Strange to have forgotten it for so many years!" observed the Ghost. "Let us go on."

They walked along the road, Scrooge recognising every gate, and post, and tree; until a little market-town appeared in the distance, with its bridge, its church, and winding river. Some shaggy ponies now were seen trotting towards them with boys upon their backs, who called to other boys in country gigs and carts, driven by farmers. All these boys were in great spirits, and shouted to each other, until the broad fields were so full of merry music, that the crisp air laughed to hear it!

"These are but shadows of the things that have been," said the Ghost. "They have no consciousness of us."

The jocund travellers came on; and as they came, Scrooge knew and named them every one. Why was he rejoiced beyond all bounds to see them! Why did his cold eye glisten, and his heart leap up as they went past! Why was he filled with gladness when he heard them give each other Merry Christmas, as they parted at cross-roads and bye-ways, for their several homes! What was merry Christmas to Scrooge? Out upon merry Christmas! What good had it ever done to him?

"The school is not quite deserted," said the Ghost. "A solitary child, neglected by his friends, is left there still."

Scrooge said he knew it. And he sobbed.

They left the high-road, by a well-remembered lane, and soon approached a mansion of dull red brick, with a little weathercock-surmounted cupola, on the roof, and a bell hanging in it. It was a large house, but one of broken fortunes; for the spacious offices were little used, their walls were damp and mossy, their windows broken, and their gates decayed. Fowls clucked and strutted in the stables; and the coach-houses and sheds were over-run with grass. Nor was it more retentive of its ancient state, within; for entering the dreary hall, and glancing through the open doors of many rooms, they found them poorly furnished, cold, and vast. There was an earthy savour in the air, a chilly bareness in the place, which associated itself somehow with too much getting up by candle-light, and not too much to eat.

They went, the Ghost and Scrooge, across the hall, to a door at the back of the house. It opened before them, and disclosed a long, bare, melancholy room, made barer still by lines of plain deal forms and desks. At one of these a lonely boy was reading near a feeble fire; and Scrooge sat down upon a form, and wept to see his poor forgotten self as he used to be.

Not a latent echo in the house, not a squeak and scuffle from the mice behind the panelling, not a drip from the half-thawed waterspout in the dull yard behind, not a sigh among the leafless boughs of one despondent poplar, not the idle swinging of an empty store-house door, no, not a clicking in the fire, but fell upon the heart of Scrooge with a softening influence, and gave a freer passage to his tears.

The Spirit touched him on the arm, and pointed to his younger self, intent upon his reading. Suddenly a man, in foreign garments: wonderfully real and distinct to look at: stood outside the window, with an axe stuck in his belt, and leading by the bridle an ass laden with wood.

"Why, it's Ali Baba!" Scrooge exclaimed in ecstasy. "It's dear old honest Ali Baba! Yes, yes, I know! One Christmas time, when yonder solitary child was left here all alone, he *did* come, for the first time, just like that. Poor boy! And Valentine," said Scrooge, "and his wild brother, Orson; there they go! And what's his name, who was put down in his drawers, asleep, at the Gate of Damascus; don't you see him! And the Sultan's Groom turned upside down by the Genii; there he is upon his head! Serve him right. I'm glad of it. What business had *he* to be married to the Princess!"

To hear Scrooge expending all the earnestness of his nature on such subjects, in a most extraordinary voice between laughing and crying; and to see his heightened and excited face; would have been a surprise to his business friends in the city, indeed.

"There's the Parrot!" cried Scrooge. "Green body and yellow tail, with a thing like a lettuce growing out of the top of his head; there he is! Poor Robin Crusoe, he called him, when he came home again after sailing round the island. 'Poor Robin Crusoe, where have you been, Robin Crusoe?' The man thought he was dreaming, but he wasn't. It was the Parrot, you know. There goes Friday, running for his life to the little creek! Halloa! Hoop! Halloo!"

Then, with a rapidity of transition very foreign to his usual character, he said, in pity for his former self, "Poor boy!" and cried again.

"I wish," Scrooge muttered, putting his hand in his pocket, and looking about him, after drying his eyes with his cuff: "but it's too late now."

"What is the matter?" asked the Spirit.

"Nothing," said Scrooge. "Nothing. There was a boy singing a Christmas Carol at my door last night. I should like to have given him something: that's all."

The Ghost smiled thoughtfully, and waved its hand: saying as it did so, "Let us see another Christmas!"

Scrooge's former self grew larger at the words, and the room became a little darker and more dirty. The panels shrunk, the windows cracked; fragments of plaster fell out of the ceiling, and the naked laths were shown instead; but how all this was brought about, Scrooge knew no more than you do. He only knew that it was quite correct; that everything had happened so; that there he was, alone again, when all the other boys had gone home for the jolly holidays.

He was not reading now, but walking up and down despairingly. Scrooge looked at the Ghost, and with a mournful shaking of his head, glanced anxiously towards the door.

It opened; and a little girl, much younger than the boy, came darting in, and putting her arms about his neck, and often kissing him, addressed him as her "Dear, dear brother."

"I have come to bring you home, dear brother!" said the child, clapping her tiny hands, and bending down to laugh. "To bring you home, home, home!"

"Home, little Fan?" returned the boy.

"Yes!" said the child, brimful of glee. "Home, for good and all. Home, for ever and ever. Father is so much kinder than he used to be, that home's like Heaven! He spoke so gently to me one dear night when I was going to bed, that I was not afraid to ask him once more if you might come home; and he said Yes, you should; and sent me in a coach to bring you. And you're to be a man!" said the child, opening her eyes, "and are never to come back here; but first, we're to be together all the Christmas long, and have the merriest time in all the world."

"You are quite a woman, little Fan!" exclaimed the boy.

She clapped her hands and laughed, and tried to touch his head; but being too little, laughed again, and stood on tiptoe to embrace him. Then she began to drag him, in her childish eagerness, towards the door; and he, nothing loth to go, accompanied her.

A terrible voice in the hall cried, "Bring down Master Scrooge's box, there!" and in the hall appeared the schoolmaster himself, who glared on Master Scrooge with a ferocious condescension, and threw him into a dreadful state of mind by shaking hands with him. He then conveyed him and his sister into the veriest old well of a shivering best-parlour that ever was seen, where the maps upon the wall, and the celestial and terrestrial globes in the windows, were waxy with cold. Here he produced a decanter of curiously light wine, and a block of curiously heavy cake, and administered instalments of those dainties to the young people: at the same time, sending out a meagre servant to offer a glass of "something" to the postboy, who answered that he thanked the gentleman, but if it was the same tap as he had tasted before, he had rather not. Master Scrooge's trunk being by this time tied on to the top of the chaise, the children bade the schoolmaster good-bye right willingly; and getting into it, drove gaily down the garden-sweep: the quick wheels dashing the hoar-frost and snow from off the dark leaves of the evergreens like spray.

"Always a delicate creature, whom a breath might have withered," said the Ghost. "But she had a large heart!"

"So she had," cried Scrooge. "You're right. I will not gainsay it, Spirit. God forbid!"

"She died a woman," said the Ghost, "and had, as I think, children."

"One child," Scrooge returned.

"True," said the Ghost. "Your nephew!"

Scrooge seemed uneasy in his mind; and answered briefly, "Yes."

Although they had but that moment left the school behind them, they were now in the busy thoroughfares of a city, where shadowy passengers passed and repassed; where shadowy carts and coaches battled for the way, and all the strife and tumult of a real city were. It was made plain enough, by the dressing of the shops, that here too it was Christmas time again; but it was evening, and the streets were lighted up.

The Ghost stopped at a certain warehouse door, and asked Scrooge if he knew it.

"Know it!" said Scrooge. "Was I apprenticed here!"

They went in. At sight of an old gentleman in a Welsh wig, sitting behind such a high desk, that if he had been two inches taller he must have knocked his head against the ceiling, Scrooge cried in great excitement:

"Why, it's old Fezziwig! Bless his heart; it's Fezziwig alive again!"

Old Fezziwig laid down his pen, and looked up at the clock, which pointed to the hour of seven. He rubbed his hands; adjusted his capacious waistcoat; laughed all over himself, from his shoes to his organ of benevolence; and called out in a comfortable, oily, rich, fat, jovial voice:

"Yo ho, there! Ebenezer! Dick!"

Scrooge's former self, now grown a young man, came briskly in, accompanied by his fellow-'prentice.

"Dick Wilkins, to be sure!" said Scrooge to the Ghost. "Bless me, yes. There he is. He was very much attached to me, was Dick. Poor Dick! Dear, dear!"

"Yo ho, my boys!" said Fezziwig. "No more work to-night. Christmas Eve, Dick. Christmas, Ebenezer! Let's have the shutters up," cried old Fezziwig, with a sharp clap of his hands, "before a man can say Jack Robinson!"

You wouldn't believe how those two fellows went at it! They charged into the street with the shutters—one, two, three—had 'em up in their places—four, five, six—barred 'em and pinned 'em—seven, eight, nine—and came back before you could have got to twelve, panting like race-horses.

"Hilli-ho!" cried old Fezziwig, skipping down from the high desk, with wonderful agility. "Clear away, my lads, and let's have lots of room here! Hilli-ho, Dick! Chirrup, Ebenezer!"

Clear away! There was nothing they wouldn't have cleared away, or couldn't have cleared away, with old Fezziwig looking on. It was done in a minute. Every movable was packed off, as if it were dismissed from public life for evermore; the floor was swept and watered, the lamps were trimmed, fuel was heaped upon the fire; and the warehouse was as snug, and warm, and dry, and bright a ball-room, as you would desire to see upon a winter's night.

In came a fiddler with a music-book, and went up to the lofty desk, and made an orchestra of it, and tuned like fifty stomach-aches. In came Mrs. Fezziwig, one vast substantial smile. In came the three Miss Fezziwigs, beaming and lovable. In came the six young followers whose hearts they broke. In came all the young men and women employed in the business. In came the housemaid, with her cousin, the baker. In came the cook, with her brother's particular friend, the milkman. In came the boy from over the way, who was suspected of not having board enough from his master; trying to hide himself behind the girl from next door but one, who was proved to have had her ears pulled by her mistress. In they all came, one after another; some shyly, some boldly, some gracefully, some awkwardly, some pushing, some pulling; in they all came, anyhow and everyhow. Away they all went, twenty couple at once; hands half round and back again the other way; down the middle and up again; round and round in various stages of affectionate grouping; old top couple always turning up in the wrong place; new top couple starting off again, as soon as they got there; all top couples at last, and not a bottom one to help them! When this result was brought about, old Fezziwig, clapping his hands to stop the dance, cried out, "Well done!" and the fiddler plunged his hot face into a pot of porter, especially provided for that purpose. But scorning rest, upon his reappearance, he instantly began again, though there were no dancers yet, as if the other fiddler had been carried home, exhausted, on a shutter, and he were a bran-new man resolved to beat him out of sight, or perish.

There were more dances, and there were forfeits, and more dances, and there was cake, and there was negus, and there was a great piece of Cold Roast, and there was a great piece of Cold Boiled, and there were mince-pies, and plenty of beer. But the great effect of the evening came after the Roast and Boiled, when the fiddler (an artful dog, mind!

The sort of man who knew his business better than you or I could have told it him!) struck up "Sir Roger de Coverley." Then old Fezziwig stood out to dance with Mrs. Fezziwig. Top couple, too; with a good stiff piece of work cut out for them; three or four and twenty pair of partners; people who were not to be trifled with; people who *would* dance, and had no notion of walking.

But if they had been twice as many—ah, four times—old Fezziwig would have been a match for them, and so would Mrs. Fezziwig. As to *her*, she was worthy to be his partner in every sense of the term. If that's not high praise, tell me higher, and I'll use it. A positive light appeared to issue from Fezziwig's calves. They shone in every part of the dance like moons. You couldn't have predicted, at any given time, what would have become of them next. And when old Fezziwig and Mrs. Fezziwig had gone all through the dance; advance and retire, both hands to your partner, bow and curtsey, corkscrew, thread-the-needle, and back again to your place; Fezziwig "cut"—cut so deftly, that he appeared to wink with his legs, and came upon his feet again without a stagger.

When the clock struck eleven, this domestic ball broke up. Mr. and Mrs. Fezziwig took their stations, one on either side of the door, and shaking hands with every person individually as he or she went out, wished him or her a Merry Christmas. When everybody had retired but the two 'prentices, they did the same to them; and thus the cheerful voices died away, and the lads were left to their beds; which were under a counter in the back-shop.

During the whole of this time, Scrooge had acted like a man out of his wits. His heart and soul were in the scene, and with his former self. He corroborated everything, remembered everything, enjoyed everything, and underwent the strangest agitation. It was not until now, when the bright faces of his former self and Dick were turned from them, that he remembered the Ghost, and became conscious that it was looking full upon him, while the light upon its head burnt very clear.

"A small matter," said the Ghost, "to make these silly folks so full of gratitude."

"Small!" echoed Scrooge.

The Spirit signed to him to listen to the two apprentices, who were pouring out their hearts in praise of Fezziwig: and when he had done so, said,

"Why! Is it not? He has spent but a few pounds of your mortal money: three or four perhaps. Is that so much that he deserves this praise?"

"It isn't that," said Scrooge, heated by the remark, and speaking unconsciously like his former, not his latter, self. "It isn't that, Spirit.

He has the power to render us happy or unhappy; to make our service light or burdensome; a pleasure or a toil. Say that his power lies in words and looks; in things so slight and insignificant that it is impossible to add and count 'em up: what then? The happiness he gives, is quite as great as if it cost a fortune."

He felt the Spirit's glance, and stopped.

"What is the matter?" asked the Ghost.

"Nothing particular," said Scrooge.

"Something, I think?" the Ghost insisted.

"No," said Scrooge, "No. I should like to be able to say a word or two to my clerk just now. That's all."

His former self turned down the lamps as he gave utterance to the wish; and Scrooge and the Ghost again stood side by side in the open air.

"My time grows short," observed the Spirit. "Quick!"

This was not addressed to Scrooge, or to any one whom he could see, but it produced an immediate effect. For again Scrooge saw himself. He was older now; a man in the prime of life. His face had not the harsh and rigid lines of later years; but it had begun to wear the signs of care and avarice. There was an eager, greedy, restless motion in the eye, which showed the passion that had taken root, and where the shadow of the growing tree would fall.

He was not alone, but sat by the side of a fair young girl in a mourning-dress: in whose eyes there were tears, which sparkled in the light that shone out of the Ghost of Christmas Past.

"It matters little," she said, softly. "To you, very little. Another idol has displaced me; and if it can cheer and comfort you in time to come, as I would have tried to do, I have no just cause to grieve."

"What Idol has displaced you?" he rejoined.

"A golden one."

"This is the even-handed dealing of the world!" he said. "There is nothing on which it is so hard as poverty; and there is nothing it professes to condemn with such severity as the pursuit of wealth!"

"You fear the world too much," she answered, gently. "All your other hopes have merged into the hope of being beyond the chance of its sordid reproach. I have seen your nobler aspirations fall off one by one, until the master-passion, Gain, engrosses you. Have I not?"

"What then?" he retorted. "Even if I have grown so much wiser, what then? I am not changed towards you."

She shook her head.

"Am I?"

"Our contract is an old one. It was made when we were both poor and content to be so, until, in good season, we could improve our worldly fortune by our patient industry. You are changed. When it was made, you were another man."

"I was a boy," he said impatiently.

"Your own feeling tells you that you were not what you are," she returned. "I am. That which promised happiness when we were one in heart, is fraught with misery now that we are two. How often and how keenly I have thought of this, I will not say. It is enough that I *have* thought of it, and can release you."

"Have I ever sought release?"

"In words. No. Never."

"In what, then?"

"In a changed nature; in an altered spirit; in another atmosphere of life; another Hope as its great end. In everything that made my love of any worth or value in your sight. If this had never been between us," said the girl, looking mildly, but with steadiness, upon him; "tell me, would you seek me out and try to win me now? Ah, no!"

He seemed to yield to the justice of this supposition, in spite of himself. But he said with a struggle, "You think not."

"I would gladly think otherwise if I could," she answered, "Heaven knows! When I have learned a Truth like this, I know how strong and irresistible it must be. But if you were free to-day, to-morrow, yester-day, can even I believe that you would choose a dowerless girl—you who, in your very confidence with her, weigh everything by Gain: or, choosing her, if for a moment you were false enough to your one guiding principle to do so, do I not know that your repentance and regret would surely follow? I do; and I release you. With a full heart, for the love of him you once were."

He was about to speak; but with her head turned from him, she resumed.

"You may—the memory of what is past half makes me hope you will—have pain in this. A very, very brief time, and you will dismiss the recol-lection of it, gladly, as an unprofitable dream, from which it happened well that you awoke. May you be happy in the life you have chosen!"

She left him, and they parted.

"Spirit!" said Scrooge, "show me no more! Conduct me home. Why do you delight to torture me?"

"One shadow more!" exclaimed the Ghost.

"No more!" cried Scrooge. "No more. I don't wish to see it. Show me no more!"

But the relentless Ghost pinioned him in both his arms, and forced him to observe what happened next.

They were in another scene and place; a room, not very large or handsome, but full of comfort. Near to the winter fire sat a beautiful young girl, so like that last that Scrooge believed it was the same, until he saw *her*, now a comely matron, sitting opposite her daughter. The noise in this room was perfectly tumultuous, for there were more children there, than Scrooge in his agitated state of mind could count; and, unlike the celebrated herd in the poem, they were not forty children conducting themselves like one, but every child was conducting itself like forty. The consequences were uproarious beyond belief; but no one seemed to care; on the contrary, the mother and daughter laughed heartily, and enjoyed it very much; and the latter, soon beginning to mingle in the sports, got pillaged by the young brigands most ruthlessly. What would I not have given to be one of them! Though I never could have been so rude, no, no! I wouldn't for the wealth of all the world have crushed that braided hair, and torn it down; and for the precious little shoe, I wouldn't have plucked it off, God bless my soul! to save my life. As to measuring her waist in sport, as they did, bold young brood, I couldn't have done it; I should have expected my arm to have grown round it for a punishment, and never come straight again. And yet I should have dearly liked, I own, to have touched her lips; to have questioned her, that she might have opened them; to have looked upon the lashes of her downcast eyes, and never raised a blush; to have let loose waves of hair, an inch of which would be a keepsake beyond price: in short, I should have liked, I do confess, to have had the lightest licence of a child, and yet to have been man enough to know its value.

But now a knocking at the door was heard, and such a rush immediately ensued that she with laughing face and plundered dress was borne towards it the centre of a flushed and boisterous group, just in time to greet the father, who came home attended by a man laden with Christmas toys and presents. Then the shouting and the struggling, and the onslaught that was made on the defenceless porter! The scaling him with chairs for ladders to dive into his pockets, despoil him of brown-paper parcels, hold on tight by his cravat, hug him round his neck, pommel his back, and kick his legs in irrepressible affection! The shouts of wonder and delight with which the development of every package was received! The terrible announcement that the baby had been taken in the act of putting a doll's frying-pan into his mouth, and was more than suspected of having swallowed a fictitious turkey, glued on a wooden platter! The immense relief of finding this a false alarm! The joy, and gratitude, and ecstasy! They are all indescribable alike. It is enough that by degrees the children and their emotions got out of the parlour, and by one stair at a time, up to the top of the house; where they went to bed, and so subsided.

And now Scrooge looked on more attentively than ever, when the master of the house, having his daughter leaning fondly on him, sat down with her and her mother at his own fireside; and when he thought that such another creature, quite as graceful and as full of promise, might have called him father, and been a spring-time in the haggard winter of his life, his sight grew very dim indeed.

"Belle," said the husband, turning to his wife with a smile, "I saw an old friend of yours this afternoon."

"Who was it?"

"Guess!"

"How can I? Tut, don't I know?" she added in the same breath, laughing as he laughed. "Mr. Scrooge."

"Mr. Scrooge it was. I passed his office window; and as it was not shut up, and he had a candle inside, I could scarcely help seeing him. His partner lies upon the point of death, I hear; and there he sat alone. Quite alone in the world, I do believe."

"Spirit!" said Scrooge in a broken voice, "remove me from this place."

"I told you these were shadows of the things that have been," said the Ghost. "That they are what they are, do not blame me!"

"Remove me!" Scrooge exclaimed, "I cannot bear it!"

He turned upon the Ghost, and seeing that it looked upon him with a face, in which in some strange way there were fragments of all the faces it had shown him, wrestled with it.

"Leave me! Take me back. Haunt me no longer!"

In the struggle, if that can be called a struggle in which the Ghost with no visible resistance on its own part was undisturbed by any effort of its adversary, Scrooge observed that its light was burning high and bright; and dimly connecting that with its influence over him, he seized the extinguisher-cap, and by a sudden action pressed it down upon its head.

The Spirit dropped beneath it, so that the extinguisher covered its whole form; but though Scrooge pressed it down with all his force, he could not hide the light: which streamed from under it, in an unbroken flood upon the ground.

He was conscious of being exhausted, and overcome by an irresistible drowsiness; and, further, of being in his own bedroom. He gave the cap a parting squeeze, in which his hand relaxed; and had barely time to reel to bed, before he sank into a heavy sleep.

STAVE THREE
The Second of the Three Spirits

Awaking in the middle of a prodigiously tough snore, and sitting up in bed to get his thoughts together, Scrooge had no occasion to be told that the bell was again upon the stroke of One. He felt that he was restored to consciousness in the right nick of time, for the especial

purpose of holding a conference with the second messenger des-
patched to him through Jacob Marley's intervention. But finding that
he turned uncomfortably cold when he began to wonder which of his
curtains this new spectre would draw back, he put them every one
aside with his own hands; and lying down again, established a sharp
look-out all round the bed. For he wished to challenge the Spirit on the
moment of its appearance, and did not wish to be taken by surprise,
and made nervous.

Gentlemen of the free-and-easy sort, who plume themselves on
being acquainted with a move or two, and being usually equal to the
time-of-day, express the wide range of their capacity for adventure
by observing that they are good for anything from pitch-and-toss to
manslaughter; between which opposite extremes, no doubt, there lies a
tolerably wide and comprehensive range of subjects. Without venturing for Scrooge quite as hardily as this, I don't mind calling on you to
believe that he was ready for a good broad field of strange appearances, and that nothing between a baby and rhinoceros would have
astonished him very much.

Now, being prepared for almost anything, he was not by any means
prepared for nothing; and, consequently, when the Bell struck One,
and no shape appeared, he was taken with a violent fit of trembling.
Five minutes, ten minutes, a quarter of an hour went by, yet nothing
came. All this time, he lay upon his bed, the very core and centre of a
blaze of ruddy light, which streamed upon it when the clock pro-
claimed the hour; and which, being only light, was more alarming
than a dozen ghosts, as he was powerless to make out what it meant,
or would be at; and was sometimes apprehensive that he might be at
that very moment an interesting case of spontaneous combustion,
without having the consolation of knowing it. At last, however, he
began to think—as you or I would have thought at first; for it is always
the person not in the predicament who knows what ought to have been
done in it, and would unquestionably have done it too—at last, I say,
he began to think that the source and secret of this ghostly light might
be in the adjoining room, from whence, on further tracing it, it seemed
to shine. This idea taking full possession of his mind, he got up softly
and shuffled in his slippers to the door.

The moment Scrooge's hand was on the lock, a strange voice called
him by his name, and bade him enter. He obeyed.

It was his own room. There was no doubt about that. But it had
undergone a surprising transformation. The walls and ceiling were
so hung with living green, that it looked a perfect grove; from every
part of which, bright gleaming berries glistened. The crisp leaves of
holly, mistletoe, and ivy reflected back the light, as if so many little

mirrors had been scattered there; and such a mighty blaze went roaring up the chimney, as that dull petrification of a hearth had never known in Scrooge's time, or Marley's, or for many and many a winter season gone. Heaped up on the floor, to form a kind of throne, were turkeys, geese, game, poultry, brawn, great joints of meat, sucking-pigs, long wreaths of sausages, mince-pies, plum-puddings, barrels of oysters, red-hot chestnuts, cherry-cheeked apples, juicy oranges, luscious pears, immense twelfth-cakes, and seething bowls of punch, that made the chamber dim with their delicious steam. In easy state upon this couch, there sat a jolly Giant, glorious to see; who bore a glowing torch, in shape not unlike Plenty's horn, and held it up, high up, to shed its light on Scrooge, as he came peeping round the door.

"Come in!" exclaimed the Ghost. "Come in! and know me better, man!"

Scrooge entered timidly, and hung his head before this Spirit. He was not the dogged Scrooge he had been; and though the Spirit's eyes were clear and kind, he did not like to meet them.

"I am the Ghost of Christmas Present," said the Spirit. "Look upon me!"

Scrooge reverently did so. It was clothed in one simple green robe, or mantle, bordered with white fur. This garment hung so loosely on the figure, that its capacious breast was bare, as if disdaining to be warded or concealed by any artifice. Its feet, observable beneath the ample folds of the garment, were also bare; and on its head it wore no other covering than a holly wreath, set here and there with shining icicles. Its dark brown curls were long and free; free as its genial face, its sparkling eye, its open hand, its cheery voice, its unconstrained demeanour, and its joyful air. Girded round its middle was an antique scabbard; but no sword was in it, and the ancient sheath was eaten up with rust.

"You have never seen the like of me before!" exclaimed the Spirit.

"Never," Scrooge made answer to it.

"Have never walked forth with the younger members of my family; meaning (for I am very young) my elder brothers born in these later years?" pursued the Phantom.

"I don't think I have," said Scrooge. "I am afraid I have not. Have you had many brothers, Spirit?"

"More than eighteen hundred," said the Ghost.

"A tremendous family to provide for!" muttered Scrooge.

The Ghost of Christmas Present rose.

"Spirit," said Scrooge submissively, "conduct me where you will. I went forth last night on compulsion, and I learnt a lesson which is working now. To-night, if you have aught to teach me, let me profit by it."

"Touch my robe!"

Scrooge did as he was told, and held it fast.

Holly, mistletoe, red berries, ivy, turkeys, geese, game, poultry, brawn, meat, pigs, sausages, oysters, pies, puddings, fruit, and punch, all vanished instantly. So did the room, the fire, the ruddy glow, the hour of night, and they stood in the city streets on Christmas morning, where (for the weather was severe) the people made a rough, but brisk and not unpleasant kind of music, in scraping the snow from the pavement in front of their dwellings, and from the tops of their houses, whence it was mad delight to the boys to see it come plumping down into the road below, and splitting into artificial little snow-storms.

The house fronts looked black enough, and the windows blacker, contrasting with the smooth white sheet of snow upon the roofs, and with the dirtier snow upon the ground; which last deposit had been ploughed up in deep furrows by the heavy wheels of carts and waggons; furrows that crossed and re-crossed each other hundreds of times where the great streets branched off; and made intricate channels, hard to trace in the thick yellow mud and icy water. The sky was gloomy, and the shortest streets were choked up with a dingy mist, half thawed, half frozen, whose heavier particles descended in a shower of sooty atoms, as if all the chimneys in Great Britain had, by one consent, caught fire, and were blazing away to their dear hearts' content. There was nothing very cheerful in the climate or the town, and yet was there an air of cheerfulness abroad that the clearest summer air and brightest summer sun might have endeavoured to diffuse in vain.

For, the people who were shovelling away on the housetops were jovial and full of glee; calling out to one another from the parapets, and now and then exchanging a facetious snowball—better-natured missile far than many a wordy jest—laughing heartily if it went right and not less heartily if it went wrong. The poulterers' shops were still half open, and the fruiterers' were radiant in their glory. There were great, round, pot-bellied baskets of chestnuts, shaped like the waist-coats of jolly old gentlemen, lolling at the doors, and tumbling out into the street in their apoplectic opulence. There were ruddy, brown-faced, broad-girthed Spanish Onions, shining in the fatness of their growth like Spanish Friars, and winking from their shelves in wanton slyness at the girls as they went by, and glanced demurely at the hung-up mistletoe. There were pears and apples, clustered high in blooming pyramids; there were bunches of grapes, made, in the shopkeepers' benevolence to dangle from conspicuous hooks, that people's mouths might water gratis as they passed; there were piles of filberts, mossy and brown, recalling, in their fragrance, ancient walks among the woods, and pleasant shufflings ankle deep through withered leaves; there were Norfolk Biffins, squat and swarthy, setting off the yellow of the oranges and lemons, and, in the great compactness of their juicy persons, urgently entreating and beseeching to be carried home in paper bags and eaten after dinner. The very gold and silver fish, set forth among these choice fruits in a bowl, though members of a dull and stagnant-blooded race, appeared to know that there was something going on; and, to a fish, went gasping round and round their little world in slow and passionless excitement.

The Grocers'! oh, the Grocers'! nearly closed, with perhaps two shutters down, or one; but through those gaps such glimpses! It was not alone that the scales descending on the counter made a merry sound, or that the twine and roller parted company so briskly, or that the canisters were rattled up and down like juggling tricks, or even that the blended scents of tea and coffee were so grateful to the nose, or even that the raisins were so plentiful and rare, the almonds so extremely white, the sticks of cinnamon so long and straight, the other spices so delicious, the candied fruits so caked and spotted with molten sugar as to make the coldest lookers-on feel faint and subsequently bilious. Nor was it that the figs were moist and pulpy, or that the French plums blushed in modest tartness from their highly-decorated boxes, or that everything was good to eat and in its Christmas dress; but the customers were all so hurried and so eager in the hopeful promise of the day, that they tumbled up against each other at the door, crashing their wicker baskets wildly, and left their purchases upon the counter, and came running back to fetch them, and committed hundreds of the like mistakes, in the best humour possible; while the Grocer and his people were so frank and fresh that the polished hearts with which they fastened their aprons behind might have been their own, worn outside for general inspection, and for Christmas daws to peck at if they chose.

But soon the steeples called good people all, to church and chapel, and away they came, flocking through the streets in their best clothes, and with their gayest faces. And at the same time there emerged from scores of bye-streets, lanes, and nameless turnings, innumerable people, carrying their dinners to the bakers' shops. The sight of these poor revellers appeared to interest the Spirit very much, for he stood with Scrooge beside him in a baker's doorway, and taking off the covers as their bearers passed, sprinkled incense on their dinners from his torch. And it was a very uncommon kind of torch, for once or twice when there were angry words between some dinner-carriers who had jostled each other, he shed a few drops of water on them from it, and their good humour was restored directly. For they said, it was a shame to quarrel upon Christmas Day. And so it was! God love it, so it was!

In time the bells ceased, and the bakers were shut up; and yet there was a genial shadowing forth of all these dinners and the progress of their cooking, in the thawed blotch of wet above each baker's oven; where the pavement smoked as if its stones were cooking too.

"Is there a peculiar flavour in what you sprinkle from your torch?" asked Scrooge.

"There is. My own."

"Would it apply to any kind of dinner on this day?" asked Scrooge.

"To any kindly given. To a poor one most."

"Why to a poor one most?" asked Scrooge.

"Because it needs it most."

"Spirit," said Scrooge, after a moment's thought, "I wonder you, of all the beings in the many worlds about us, should desire to cramp these people's opportunities of innocent enjoyment."

"I!" cried the Spirit.

"You would deprive them of their means of dining every seventh day, often the only day on which they can be said to dine at all," said Scrooge. "Wouldn't you?"

"I!" cried the Spirit.

"You seek to close these places on the Seventh Day?" said Scrooge. "And it comes to the same thing."

"*I* seek!" exclaimed the Spirit.

"Forgive me if I am wrong. It has been done in your name, or at least in that of your family," said Scrooge.

"There are some upon this earth of yours," returned the Spirit, "who lay claim to know us, and who do their deeds of passion, pride, ill-will, hatred, envy, bigotry, and selfishness in our name, who are as strange to us and all our kith and kin, as if they had never lived. Remember that, and charge their doings on themselves, not us."

Scrooge promised that he would; and they went on, invisible, as they had been before, into the suburbs of the town. It was a remarkable quality of the Ghost (which Scrooge had observed at the baker's), that notwithstanding his gigantic size, he could accommodate himself to any place with ease; and that he stood beneath a low roof quite as gracefully and like a supernatural creature, as it was possible he could have done in any lofty hall.

And perhaps it was the pleasure the good Spirit had in showing off this power of his, or else it was his own kind, generous, hearty nature, and his sympathy with all poor men, that led him straight to Scrooge's clerk's; for there he went, and took Scrooge with him, holding to his robe; and on the threshold of the door the Spirit smiled, and stopped to bless Bob Cratchit's dwelling with the sprinkling of his torch. Think of that! Bob had but fifteen "Bob" a-week himself; he pocketed on Saturdays but fifteen copies of his Christian name; and yet the Ghost of Christmas Present blessed his four-roomed house!

Then up rose Mrs. Cratchit, Cratchit's wife, dressed out but poorly in a twice-turned gown, but brave in ribbons, which are cheap and make a goodly show for sixpence; and she laid the cloth, assisted by Belinda Cratchit, second of her daughters, also brave in ribbons; while Master Peter Cratchit plunged a fork into the saucepan of potatoes, and getting the corners of his monstrous shirt collar (Bob's private property, conferred upon his son and heir in honour of the day) into his mouth, rejoiced to find himself so gallantly attired, and yearned to show his linen in the fashionable Parks. And now two smaller Cratchits, boy and girl, came tearing in, screaming that outside the baker's they had smelt the goose, and known it for their own; and basking in luxurious thoughts of sage and onion, these young Cratchits danced about the table, and exalted Master Peter Cratchit to the skies, while he (not proud, although his collars nearly choked him) blew the fire, until the slow potatoes bubbling up, knocked loudly at the saucepan-lid to be let out and peeled.

"What has ever got your precious father then?" said Mrs. Cratchit. "And your brother, Tiny Tim! And Martha warn't as late last Christmas Day by half-an-hour?"

"Here's Martha, mother!" said a girl, appearing as she spoke.

"Here's Martha, mother!" cried the two young Cratchits. "Hurrah! There's *such* a goose, Martha!"

"Why, bless your heart alive, my dear, how late you are!" said Mrs. Cratchit, kissing her a dozen times, and taking off her shawl and bonnet for her with officious zeal.

"We'd a deal of work to finish up last night," replied the girl, "and had to clear away this morning, mother!"

"Well! Never mind so long as you are come," said Mrs. Cratchit. "Sit ye down before the fire, my dear, and have a warm, Lord bless ye!"

"No, no! There's father coming," cried the two young Cratchits, who were everywhere at once. "Hide, Martha, hide!"

So Martha hid herself, and in came little Bob, the father, with at least three feet of comforter exclusive of the fringe, hanging down before him; and his threadbare clothes darned up and brushed, to look seasonable; and Tiny Tim upon his shoulder. Alas for Tiny Tim, he bore a little crutch, and had his limbs supported by an iron frame!

"Why, where's our Martha?" cried Bob Cratchit, looking round.

"Not coming," said Mrs. Cratchit.

"Not coming!" said Bob, with a sudden declension in his high spirits; for he had been Tim's blood horse all the way from church, and had come home rampant. "Not coming upon Christmas Day!"

Martha didn't like to see him disappointed, if it were only in joke; so she came out prematurely from behind the closet door, and ran into his arms, while the two young Cratchits hustled Tiny Tim, and bore him off into the wash-house, that he might hear the pudding singing in the copper.

"And how did little Tim behave?" asked Mrs. Cratchit, when she had rallied Bob on his credulity, and Bob had hugged his daughter to his heart's content.

"As good as gold," said Bob, "and better. Somehow he gets thoughtful, sitting by himself so much, and thinks the strangest things you ever heard. He told me, coming home, that he hoped the people saw him in the church, because he was a cripple, and it might be pleasant to them to remember upon Christmas Day, who made lame beggars walk, and blind men see."

Bob's voice was tremulous when he told them this, and trembled more when he said that Tiny Tim was growing strong and hearty.

His active little crutch was heard upon the floor, and back came Tiny Tim before another word was spoken, escorted by his brother and sister to his stool before the fire; and while Bob, turning up his cuffs—as if, poor fellow, they were capable of being made more shabby—compounded some hot mixture in a jug with gin and lemons, and stirred it round and round and put it on the hob to simmer; Master Peter, and the two ubiquitous young Cratchits went to fetch the goose, with which they soon returned in high procession.

Such a bustle ensued that you might have thought a goose the rarest of all birds; a feathered phenomenon, to which a black swan was a matter of course—and in truth it was something very like it in that house. Mrs. Cratchit made the gravy (ready beforehand in a little saucepan) hissing hot; Master Peter mashed the potatoes with incredible vigour; Miss Belinda sweetened up the apple-sauce; Martha dusted the hot plates; Bob took Tiny Tim beside him in a tiny corner at the table; the two young Cratchits set chairs for everybody, not forgetting themselves, and mounting guard upon their posts, crammed spoons into their mouths, lest they should shriek for goose before their turn came to be helped. At last the dishes were set on, and grace was said. It was succeeded by a breathless pause, as Mrs. Cratchit, looking slowly all along the carving-knife, prepared to plunge it in the breast; but when she did, and when the long expected gush of stuffing issued forth, one murmur of delight arose all round the board, and even Tiny Tim, excited by the two young Cratchits, beat on the table with the handle of his knife, and feebly cried Hurrah!

There never was such a goose. Bob said he didn't believe there ever was such a goose cooked. Its tenderness and flavour, size and cheapness, were the themes of universal admiration. Eked out by apple-sauce and mashed potatoes, it was a sufficient dinner for the whole family; indeed, as Mrs. Cratchit said with great delight (surveying one small atom of a bone upon the dish), they hadn't ate it all at last! Yet every one had had enough, and the youngest Cratchits in particular, were steeped in sage and onion to the eyebrows! But now, the plates being changed by Miss Belinda, Mrs. Cratchit left the room alone—too nervous to bear witnesses—to take the pudding up and bring it in.

Suppose it should not be done enough! Suppose it should break in turning out! Suppose somebody should have got over the wall of the back-yard, and stolen it, while they were merry with the goose—a supposition at which the two young Cratchits became livid! All sorts of horrors were supposed.

Hallo! A great deal of steam! The pudding was out of the copper. A smell like a washing-day! That was the cloth. A smell like an eating-house and a pastrycook's next door to each other, with a laundress's next door to that! That was the pudding! In half a minute Mrs. Cratchit entered—flushed, but smiling proudly—with the pudding, like a speckled cannon-ball, so hard and firm, blazing in half of half-a-quartern of ignited brandy, and bedight with Christmas holly stuck into the top.

Oh, a wonderful pudding! Bob Cratchit said, and calmly too, that he regarded it as the greatest success achieved by Mrs. Cratchit since their marriage. Mrs. Cratchit said that now the weight was off her mind, she would confess she had had her doubts about the quantity of flour. Everybody had something to say about it, but nobody said or thought it was at all a small pudding for a large family. It would have been flat heresy to do so. Any Cratchit would have blushed to hint at such a thing.

At last the dinner was all done, the cloth was cleared, the hearth swept, and the fire made up. The compound in the jug being tasted, and considered perfect, apples and oranges were put upon the table, and a shovel-full of chestnuts on the fire. Then all the Cratchit family drew round the hearth, in what Bob Cratchit called a circle, meaning half a one; and at Bob Cratchit's elbow stood the family display of glass. Two tumblers, and a custard-cup without a handle.

These held the hot stuff from the jug, however, as well as golden goblets would have done; and Bob served it out with beaming looks, while the chestnuts on the fire sputtered and cracked noisily. Then Bob proposed:

"A Merry Christmas to us all, my dears. God bless us!"

Which all the family re-echoed.

"God bless us every one!" said Tiny Tim, the last of all.

He sat very close to his father's side upon his little stool. Bob held his withered little hand in his, as if he loved the child, and wished to keep him by his side, and dreaded that he might be taken from him.

"Spirit," said Scrooge, with an interest he had never felt before, "tell me if Tiny Tim will live."

"I see a vacant seat," replied the Ghost, "in the poor chimney-corner, and a crutch without an owner, carefully preserved. If these shadows remain unaltered by the Future, the child will die."

"No, no," said Scrooge. "Oh, no, kind Spirit! say he will be spared."

"If these shadows remain unaltered by the Future, none other of my race," returned the Ghost, "will find him here. What then? If he be like to die, he had better do it, and decrease the surplus population."

Scrooge hung his head to hear his own words quoted by the Spirit, and was overcome with penitence and grief.

"Man," said the Ghost, "if man you be in heart, not adamant, forbear that wicked cant until you have discovered What the surplus is, and Where it is. Will you decide what men shall live, what men shall die? It may be, that in the sight of Heaven, you are more worthless and less fit to live than millions like this poor man's child. Oh God! to hear the Insect on the leaf pronouncing on the too much life among his hungry brothers in the dust!"

Scrooge bent before the Ghost's rebuke, and trembling cast his eyes upon the ground. But he raised them speedily, on hearing his own name.

"Mr. Scrooge!" said Bob; "I'll give you Mr. Scrooge, the Founder of the Feast!"

"The Founder of the Feast indeed!" cried Mrs. Cratchit, reddening. "I wish I had him here. I'd give him a piece of my mind to feast upon, and I hope he'd have a good appetite for it."

"My dear," said Bob, "the children! Christmas Day."

"It should be Christmas Day, I am sure," said she, "on which one drinks the health of such an odious, stingy, hard, unfeeling man as Mr. Scrooge. You know he is, Robert! Nobody knows it better than you do, poor fellow!"

"My dear," was Bob's mild answer, "Christmas Day."

"I'll drink his health for your sake and the Day's," said Mrs. Cratchit, "not for his. Long life to him! A merry Christmas and a happy new year! He'll be very merry and very happy, I have no doubt!"

The children drank the toast after her. It was the first of their proceedings which had no heartiness. Tiny Tim drank it last of all, but he didn't care twopence for it. Scrooge was the Ogre of the family. The mention of his name cast a dark shadow on the party, which was not dispelled for full five minutes.

After it had passed away, they were ten times merrier than before, from the mere relief of Scrooge the Baleful being done with. Bob Cratchit told them how he had a situation in his eye for Master Peter, which would bring in, if obtained, full five-and-sixpence weekly. The two young Cratchits laughed tremendously at the idea of Peter's being a man of business; and Peter himself looked thoughtfully at the fire from between his collars, as if he were deliberating what particular investments he should favour when he came into the receipt of that bewildering income. Martha, who was a poor apprentice at a milliner's, then told them what kind of work she had to do, and how many hours she worked at a stretch, and how she meant to lie abed to-morrow morning for a good long rest; to-morrow being a holiday she passed at home. Also how she had seen a countess and a lord some days before, and how the lord "was much about as tall as Peter;" at which Peter pulled up his collars so high that you couldn't have seen his head if you had been there. All this time the chestnuts and the jug went round and round; and by-and-bye they had a song, about a lost child travelling in the snow, from Tiny Tim, who had a plaintive little voice, and sang it very well indeed.

There was nothing of high mark in this. They were not a handsome family; they were not well dressed; their shoes were far from being water-proof; their clothes were scanty; and Peter might have known, and very likely did, the inside of a pawnbroker's. But, they were happy, grateful, pleased with one another, and contented with the time; and when they faded, and looked happier yet in the bright sprinklings of the Spirit's torch at parting, Scrooge had his eye upon them, and especially on Tiny Tim, until the last.

By this time it was getting dark, and snowing pretty heavily; and as Scrooge and the Spirit went along the streets, the brightness of the roaring fires in kitchens, parlours, and all sorts of rooms, was wonderful. Here, the flickering of the blaze showed preparations for a cosy dinner, with hot plates baking through and through before the fire, and deep red curtains, ready to be drawn to shut out cold and darkness. There all the children of the house were running out into the snow to meet their married sisters, brothers, cousins, uncles, aunts, and be the first to greet them. Here, again, were shadows on the window-blind of guests assembling; and there a group of handsome girls, all hooded and fur-booted, and all chattering at once, tripped lightly off to some near neighbour's house; where, woe upon the single man who saw them enter—artful witches, well they knew it—in a glow!

But, if you had judged from the numbers of people on their way to friendly gatherings, you might have thought that no one was at home to give them welcome when they got there, instead of every house expecting company, and piling up its fires half-chimney high. Blessings on it, how the Ghost exulted! How it bared its breadth of breast, and opened its capacious palm, and floated on, outpouring, with a generous hand, its bright and harmless mirth on everything within its reach! The very lamplighter, who ran on before, dotting the dusky street with specks of light, and who was dressed to spend the evening somewhere, laughed out loudly as the Spirit passed, though little kenned the lamplighter that he had any company but Christmas!

And now, without a word of warning from the Ghost, they stood upon a bleak and desert moor, where monstrous masses of rude stone were cast about, as though it were the burial-place of giants; and water spread itself wheresoever it listed, or would have done so, but for the frost that held it prisoner; and nothing grew but moss and furze, and coarse rank grass. Down in the west the setting sun had left a streak of fiery red, which glared upon the desolation for an instant, like a sullen eye, and frowning lower, lower, lower yet, was lost in the thick gloom of darkest night.

"What place is this?" asked Scrooge.

"A place where Miners live, who labour in the bowels of the earth," returned the Spirit. "But they know me. See!"

A light shone from the window of a hut, and swiftly they advanced towards it. Passing through the wall of mud and stone, they found a cheerful company assembled round a glowing fire. An old, old man and woman, with their children and their children's children, and another generation beyond that, all decked out gaily in their holiday attire. The old man, in a voice that seldom rose above the howling of the wind upon the barren waste, was singing them a Christmas song— it had been a very old song when he was a boy—and from time to time they all joined in the chorus. So surely as they raised their voices, the old man got quite blithe and loud; and so surely as they stopped, his vigour sank again.

The Spirit did not tarry here, but bade Scrooge hold his robe, and passing on above the moor, sped—whither? Not to sea? To sea. To Scrooge's horror, looking back, he saw the last of the land, a frightful range of rocks, behind them; and his ears were deafened by the thundering of water, as it rolled and roared, and raged among the dreadful caverns it had worn, and fiercely tried to undermine the earth.

Built upon a dismal reef of sunken rocks, some league or so from shore, on which the waters chafed and dashed, the wild year through, there stood a solitary lighthouse. Great heaps of sea-weed clung to its base, and storm-birds—born of the wind one might suppose, as sea-weed of the water—rose and fell about it, like the waves they skimmed.

But even here, two men who watched the light had made a fire, that through the loophole in the thick stone wall shed out a ray of brightness on the awful sea. Joining their horny hands over the rough table at which they sat, they wished each other Merry Christmas in their can of grog; and one of them: the elder, too, with his face all damaged and scarred with hard weather, as the figure-head of an old ship might be: struck up a sturdy song that was like a Gale in itself.

Again the Ghost sped on, above the black and heaving sea—on, on—until, being far away, as he told Scrooge, from any shore, they lighted on a ship. They stood beside the helmsman at the wheel, the look-out in the bow, the officers who had the watch; dark, ghostly figures in their several stations; but every man among them hummed a Christmas tune, or had a Christmas thought, or spoke below his breath to his companion of some bygone Christmas Day, with home-ward hopes belonging to it. And every man on board, waking or sleeping, good or bad, had had a kinder word for another on that day than on any day in the year; and had shared to some extent in its festivities; and had remembered those he cared for at a distance, and had known that they delighted to remember him.

It was a great surprise to Scrooge, while listening to the moaning of the wind, and thinking what a solemn thing it was to move on through the lonely darkness over an unknown abyss, whose depths were secrets as profound as Death: it was a great surprise to Scrooge, while thus engaged, to hear a hearty laugh. It was a much greater surprise to Scrooge to recognise it as his own nephew's and to find himself in a bright, dry, gleaming room, with the Spirit standing smiling by his side, and looking at that same nephew with approving affability!

"Ha, ha!" laughed Scrooge's nephew. "Ha, ha, ha!"

If you should happen, by any unlikely chance, to know a man more blest in a laugh than Scrooge's nephew, all I can say is, I should like to know him too. Introduce him to me, and I'll cultivate his acquaintance.

It is a fair, even-handed, noble adjustment of things, that while there is infection in disease and sorrow, there is nothing in the world so irresistibly contagious as laughter and good-humour. When Scrooge's nephew laughed in this way: holding his sides, rolling his head, and twisting his face into the most extravagant contortions: Scrooge's niece, by marriage, laughed as heartily as he. And their assembled friends being not a bit behindhand, roared out lustily.

"Ha, ha! Ha, ha, ha, ha!"

"He said that Christmas was a humbug, as I live!" cried Scrooge's nephew. "He believed it too!"

"More shame for him, Fred!" said Scrooge's niece, indignantly. Bless those women; they never do anything by halves. They are always in earnest.

She was very pretty: exceedingly pretty. With a dimpled, surprised-looking, capital face; a ripe little mouth, that seemed made to be kissed—as no doubt it was; all kinds of good little dots about her chin, that melted into one another when she laughed; and the sunniest pair of eyes you ever saw in any little creature's head. Altogether she was what you would have called provoking, you know; but satisfactory, too. Oh, perfectly satisfactory.

"He's a comical old fellow," said Scrooge's nephew, "that's the truth: and not so pleasant as he might be. However, his offences carry their own punishment, and I have nothing to say against him."

"I'm sure he is very rich, Fred," hinted Scrooge's niece. "At least you always tell *me* so."

"What of that, my dear!" said Scrooge's nephew. "His wealth is of no use to him. He don't do any good with it. He don't make himself comfortable with it. He hasn't the satisfaction of thinking—ha, ha, ha!—that he is ever going to benefit US with it."

"I have no patience with him," observed Scrooge's niece. Scrooge's niece's sisters, and all the other ladies, expressed the same opinion.

"Oh, I have!" said Scrooge's nephew. "I am sorry for him; I couldn't be angry with him if I tried. Who suffers by his ill whims! Himself, always. Here, he takes it into his head to dislike us, and he won't come and dine with us. What's the consequence? He don't lose much of a dinner."

"Indeed, I think he loses a very good dinner," interrupted Scrooge's niece. Everybody else said the same, and they must be allowed to have been competent judges, because they had just had dinner; and, with the dessert upon the table, were clustered round the fire, by lamplight.

"Well! I'm very glad to hear it," said Scrooge's nephew, "because I haven't great faith in these young housekeepers. What do *you* say, Topper?"

Topper had clearly got his eye upon one of Scrooge's niece's sisters, for he answered that a bachelor was a wretched outcast, who had no right to express an opinion on the subject. Whereat Scrooge's niece's sister—the plump one with the lace tucker: not the one with the roses—blushed.

"Do go on, Fred," said Scrooge's niece, clapping her hands. "He never finishes what he begins to say! He is such a ridiculous fellow!"

Scrooge's nephew revelled in another laugh, and as it was impossible to keep the infection off; though the plump sister tried hard to do it with aromatic vinegar; his example was unanimously followed.

"I was only going to say," said Scrooge's nephew, "that the consequence of his taking a dislike to us, and not making merry with us, is,
as I think, that he loses some pleasant moments, which could do him
no harm. I am sure he loses pleasanter companions than he can find
in his own thoughts, either in his mouldy old office, or his dusty chambers. I mean to give him the same chance every year, whether he likes
it or not, for I pity him. He may rail at Christmas till he dies, but he
can't help thinking better of it—I defy him—if he finds me going there,
in good temper, year after year, and saying Uncle Scrooge, how are
you? If it only puts him in the vein to leave his poor clerk fifty pounds,
that's something; and I think I shook him yesterday."

It was their turn to laugh now at the notion of his shaking Scrooge.
But being thoroughly good-natured, and not much caring what they
laughed at, so that they laughed at any rate, he encouraged them in
their merriment, and passed the bottle joyously.

After tea, they had some music. For they were a musical family,
and knew what they were about, when they sung a Glee or Catch, I
can assure you: especially Topper, who could growl away in the bass
like a good one, and never swell the large veins in his forehead, or get
red in the face over it. Scrooge's niece played well upon the harp; and
played among other tunes a simple little air (a mere nothing: you
might learn to whistle it in two minutes), which had been familiar to
the child who fetched Scrooge from the boarding-school, as he had
been reminded by the Ghost of Christmas Past. When this strain of
music sounded, all the things that Ghost had shown him, came upon
his mind; he softened more and more; and thought that if he could
have listened to it often, years ago, he might have cultivated the
kindnesses of life for his own happiness with his own hands, without
resorting to the sexton's spade that buried Jacob Marley.

But they didn't devote the whole evening to music. After a while
they played at forfeits; for it is good to be children sometimes, and
never better than at Christmas, when its mighty Founder was a child
himself. Stop! There was first a game at blind-man's buff. Of course
there was. And I no more believe Topper was really blind than I believe
he had eyes in his boots. My opinion is, that it was a done thing between him and Scrooge's nephew; and that the Ghost of Christmas
Present knew it. The way he went after that plump sister in the lace
tucker, was an outrage on the credulity of human nature. Knocking
down the fire-irons, tumbling over the chairs, bumping against the
piano, smothering himself among the curtains, wherever she went,
there went he! He always knew where the plump sister was. He
wouldn't catch anybody else. If you had fallen up against him (as some of
them did), on purpose, he would have made a feint of endeavouring

to seize you, which would have been an affront to your understanding, and would instantly have sidled off in the direction of the plump
sister. She often cried out that it wasn't fair; and it really was not.
But when at last, he caught her; when, in spite of all her silken
rustlings, and her rapid flutterings past him, he got her into a corner
whence there was no escape; then his conduct was the most execrable.
For his pretending not to know her; his pretending that it was necessary
to touch her head-dress, and further to assure himself of her identity
by pressing a certain ring upon her finger, and a certain chain about
her neck; was vile, monstrous! No doubt she told him her opinion of
it, when, another blind-man being in office, they were so very confidential together, behind the curtains.

Scrooge's niece was not one of the blind-man's buff party, but was
made comfortable with a large chair and a footstool, in a snug corner,
where the Ghost and Scrooge were close behind her. But she joined
in the forfeits, and loved her love to admiration with all the letters of
the alphabet. Likewise at the game of How, When, and Where, she
was very great, and to the secret joy of Scrooge's nephew, beat her
sisters hollow: though they were sharp girls too, as Topper could have
told you. There might have been twenty people there, young and old,
but they all played, and so did Scrooge; for wholly forgetting in the
interest he had in what was going on, that his voice made no sound in
their ears, he sometimes came out with his guess quite loud, and very
often guessed quite right, too; for the sharpest needle, best
Whitechapel, warranted not to cut in the eye, was not sharper than
Scrooge; blunt as he took it in his head to be.

The Ghost was greatly pleased to find him in this mood, and looked
upon him with such favour, that he begged like a boy to be allowed to
stay until the guests departed. But this the Spirit said could not be
done.

"Here is a new game," said Scrooge. "One half hour, Spirit, only
one!"

It was a Game called Yes and No, where Scrooge's nephew had to
think of something, and the rest must find out what; he only answering
to their questions yes or no, as the case was. The brisk fire of questioning to which he was exposed, elicited from him that he was thinking
of an animal, a live animal, rather a disagreeable animal, a savage
animal, an animal that growled and grunted sometimes, and talked
sometimes, and lived in London, and walked about the streets, and
wasn't made a show of, and wasn't led by anybody, and didn't live in
a menagerie, and was never killed in a market, and was not a horse,
or an ass, or a cow, or a bull, or a tiger, or a dog, or a pig, or a cat, or
a bear. At every fresh question that was put to him, this nephew burst

into a fresh roar of laughter; and was so inexpressibly tickled, that he was obliged to get up off the sofa and stamp. At last the plump sister, falling into a similar state, cried out:

"I have found it out! I know what it is, Fred! I know what it is!"

"What is it?" cried Fred.

"It's your Uncle Scro-o-o-o-oge!"

Which it certainly was. Admiration was the universal sentiment, though some objected that the reply to "Is it a bear?" ought to have been "Yes;" inasmuch as an answer in the negative was sufficient to have diverted their thoughts from Mr. Scrooge, supposing they had ever had any tendency that way.

"He has given us plenty of merriment, I am sure," said Fred, "and it would be ungrateful not to drink his health. Here is a glass of mulled wine ready to our hand at the moment; and I say, 'Uncle Scrooge!' "

"Well! Uncle Scrooge!" they cried.

"A Merry Christmas and a Happy New Year to the old man, whatever he is!" said Scrooge's nephew. "He wouldn't take it from me, but may he have it, nevertheless. Uncle Scrooge!"

Uncle Scrooge had imperceptibly become so gay and light of heart, that he would have pledged the unconscious company in return, and thanked them in an inaudible speech, if the Ghost had given him time. But the whole scene passed off in the breath of the last word spoken by his nephew; and he and the Spirit were again upon their travels.

Much they saw, and far they went, and many homes they visited, but always with a happy end. The Spirit stood beside sick beds, and they were cheerful; on foreign lands, and they were close at home; by struggling men, and they were patient in their greater hope; by poverty, and it was rich. In almshouse, hospital, and jail, in misery's every refuge, where vain man in his little brief authority had not made fast the door, and barred the Spirit out, he left his blessing, and taught Scrooge his precepts.

It was a long night, if it were only a night; but Scrooge had his doubts of this, because the Christmas Holidays appeared to be condensed into the space of time they passed together. It was strange, too, that while Scrooge remained unaltered in his outward form, the Ghost grew older, clearly older. Scrooge had observed this change, but never spoke of it, until they left a children's Twelfth Night party, when, looking at the Spirit as they stood together in an open place, he noticed that its hair was grey.

"Are spirits' lives so short?" asked Scrooge.

"My life upon this globe, is very brief," replied the Ghost. "It ends to-night."

"To-night!" cried Scrooge.

"To-night at midnight. Hark! The time is drawing near."

The chimes were ringing the three quarters past eleven at that moment.

"Forgive me if I am not justified in what I ask," said Scrooge, looking intently at the Spirit's robe, "but I see something strange, and not belonging to yourself, protruding from your skirts. Is it a foot or a claw?"

"It might be a claw, for the flesh there is upon it," was the Spirit's sorrowful reply. "Look here."

From the foldings of its robe, it brought two children; wretched, abject, frightful, hideous, miserable. They knelt down at its feet, and clung upon the outside of its garment.

"Oh, Man! look here. Look, look, down here!" exclaimed the Ghost.

They were a boy and girl. Yellow, meagre, ragged, scowling, wolfish; but prostrate, too, in their humility. Where graceful youth should have filled their features out, and touched them with its freshest tints, a stale and shrivelled hand, like that of age, had pinched, and twisted them, and pulled them into shreds. Where angels might have sat enthroned, devils lurked, and glared out menacing. No change, no degradation, no perversion of humanity, in any grade, through all the mysteries of wonderful creation, has monsters half so horrible and dread.

Scrooge started back, appalled. Having them shown to him in this way, he tried to say they were fine children, but the words choked themselves, rather than be parties to a lie of such enormous magnitude.

"Spirit! are they yours?" Scrooge could say no more.

"They are Man's," said the Spirit, looking down upon them. "And they cling to me, appealing from their fathers. This boy is Ignorance. This girl is Want. Beware them both, and all of their degree, but most of all beware this boy, for on his brow I see that written which is Doom, unless the writing be erased. Deny it!" cried the Spirit, stretching out its hand towards the city. "Slander those who tell it ye! Admit it for your factious purposes, and make it worse. And bide the end!"

"Have they no refuge or resource?" cried Scrooge.

"Are there no prisons?" said the Spirit, turning on him for the last time with his own words. "Are there no workhouses?"

The bell struck twelve.

Scrooge looked about him for the Ghost, and saw it not. As the last stroke ceased to vibrate, he remembered the prediction of old Jacob Marley, and lifting up his eyes, beheld a solemn Phantom, draped and hooded, coming, like a mist along the ground, towards him.

The Last of the Spirits

The Phantom slowly, gravely, silently, approached. When it came near him, Scrooge bent down upon his knee; for in the very air through which this Spirit moved it seemed to scatter gloom and mystery.

It was shrouded in a deep black garment, which concealed its head, its face, its form, and left nothing of it visible save one outstretched hand. But for this it would have been difficult to detach its figure from the night, and separate it from the darkness by which it was surrounded.

He felt that it was tall and stately when it came beside him, and that its mysterious presence filled him with a solemn dread. He knew no more, for the Spirit neither spoke nor moved.

"I am in the presence of the Ghost of Christmas Yet To Come?" said Scrooge.

The Spirit answered not, but pointed onward with its hand.

"You are about to show me shadows of the things that have not happened, but will happen in the time before us," Scrooge pursued. "Is that so, Spirit?"

The upper portion of the garment was contracted for an instant in its folds, as if the Spirit had inclined its head. That was the only answer he received.

Although well used to ghostly company by this time, Scrooge feared the silent shape so much that his legs trembled beneath him, and he found that he could hardly stand when he prepared to follow it. The Spirit paused a moment, as observing his condition, and giving him time to recover.

But Scrooge was all the worse for this. It thrilled him with a vague uncertain horror, to know that behind the dusky shroud, there were ghostly eyes intently fixed upon him, while he, though he stretched his own to the utmost, could see nothing but a spectral hand and one great heap of black.

"Ghost of the Future!" he exclaimed, "I fear you more than any spectre I have seen. But as I know your purpose is to do me good, and as I hope to live to be another man from what I was, I am prepared to bear you company, and do it with a thankful heart. Will you not speak to me?"

It gave him no reply. The hand was pointed straight before them.

"Lead on!" said Scrooge. "Lead on! The night is waning fast, and it is precious time to me, I know. Lead on, Spirit!"

The Phantom moved away as it had come towards him. Scrooge followed in the shadow of its dress, which bore him up, he thought, and carried him along.

They scarcely seemed to enter the city; for the city rather seemed to spring up about them, and encompass them of its own act. But there they were, in the heart of it; on 'Change, amongst the merchants; who hurried up and down, and chinked the money in their pockets, and conversed in groups, and looked at their watches, and trifled thoughtfully with their great gold seals; and so forth, as Scrooge had seen them often.

The Spirit stopped beside one little knot of business men. Observing that the hand was pointed to them, Scrooge advanced to listen to their talk.

"No," said a great fat man with a monstrous chin, "I don't know much about it, either way. I only know he's dead."

"When did he die?" inquired another.

"Last night, I believe."

"Why, what was the matter with him?" asked a third, taking a vast quantity of snuff out of a very large snuff-box. "I thought he'd never die."

"God knows," said the first, with a yawn.

"What has he done with his money?" asked a red-faced gentleman with a pendulous excrescence on the end of his nose, that shook like the gills of a turkey-cock.

"I haven't heard," said the man with the large chin, yawning again. "Left it to his company, perhaps. He hasn't left it to *me*. That's all I know."

This pleasantry was received with a general laugh.

"It's likely to be a very cheap funeral," said the same speaker; "for upon my life I don't know of anybody to go to it. Suppose we make up a party and volunteer?"

"I don't mind going if a lunch is provided," observed the gentleman with the excrescence on his nose. "But I must be fed, if I make one."

Another laugh.

"Well, I am the most disinterested among you, after all," said the first speaker, "for I never wear black gloves, and I never eat lunch. But I'll offer to go, if anybody else will. When I come to think of it, I'm not at all sure that I wasn't his most particular friend; for we used to stop and speak whenever we met. Bye, bye!"

Speakers and listeners strolled away, and mixed with other groups. Scrooge knew the men, and looked towards the Spirit for an explanation.

The Phantom glided on into a street. Its finger pointed to two persons meeting. Scrooge listened again, thinking that the explanation might lie here.

He knew these men, also, perfectly. They were men of business: very wealthy, and of great importance. He had made a point always of standing well in their esteem: in a business point of view, that is; strictly in a business point of view.

"How are you?" said one.

"How are you?" returned the other.

"Well!" said the first. "Old Scratch has got his own at last, hey?"

"So I am told," returned the second. "Cold, isn't it?"

"Seasonable for Christmas time. You're not a skater, I suppose?"

"No. No. Something else to think of. Good morning!"

Not another word. That was their meeting, their conversation, and their parting.

Scrooge was at first inclined to be surprised that the Spirit should attach importance to conversations apparently so trivial; but feeling assured that they must have some hidden purpose, he set himself to consider what it was likely to be. They could scarcely be supposed to have any bearing on the death of Jacob, his old partner, for that was Past, and this Ghost's province was the Future. Nor could he think of any one immediately connected with himself, to whom he could apply them. But nothing doubting that to whomsoever they applied they had some latent moral for his own improvement, he resolved to treasure up every word he heard, and everything he saw; and especially to observe the shadow of himself when it appeared. For he had an expectation that the conduct of his future self would give him the clue he missed, and would render the solution of these riddles easy.

He looked about in that very place for his own image; but another man stood in his accustomed corner, and though the clock pointed to his usual time of day for being there, he saw no likeness of himself among the multitudes that poured in through the Porch. It gave him little surprise, however; for he had been revolving in his mind a change of life, and thought and hoped he saw his new-born resolutions carried out in this.

Quiet and dark, beside him stood the Phantom, with its outstretched hand. When he roused himself from his thoughtful quest, he fancied from the turn of the hand, and its situation in reference to himself, that the Unseen Eyes were looking at him keenly. It made him shudder, and feel very cold.

They left the busy scene, and went into an obscure part of the town, where Scrooge had never penetrated before, although he recognised its situation, and its bad repute. The ways were foul and narrow; the shops and houses wretched; the people half-naked, drunken, slipshod, ugly. Alleys and archways, like so many cesspools, disgorged their offences of smell, and dirt, and life, upon the straggling streets; and the whole quarter reeked with crime, with filth, and misery.

Far in this den of infamous resort, there was a low-browed, beetling shop, below a pent-house roof, where iron, old rags, bottles, bones, and greasy offal, were bought. Upon the floor within, were piled

up heaps of rusty keys, nails, chains, hinges, files, scales, weights,
and refuse iron of all kinds. Secrets that few would like to scrutinise
were bred and hidden in mountains of unseemly rags, masses of cor-
rupted fat, and sepulchres of bones. Sitting in among the wares he
dealt in, by a charcoal stove, made of old bricks, was a grey-haired
rascal, nearly seventy years of age; who had screened himself from
the cold air without, by a frousy curtaining of miscellaneous tatters, hung
upon a line; and smoked his pipe in all the luxury of calm retirement.

Scrooge and the Phantom came into the presence of this man, just
as a woman with a heavy bundle slunk into the shop. But she had
scarcely entered, when another woman, similarly laden, came in too;
and she was closely followed by a man in faded black, who was no
less startled by the sight of them, than they had been upon the recognition of each other. After a short period of blank astonishment, in
which the old man with the pipe had joined them, they all three burst
into a laugh.

"Let the charwoman alone to be the first!" cried she who had entered
first. "Let the laundress alone to be the second; and let the
undertaker's man alone to be the third. Look here, old Joe, here's a
chance! If we haven't all three met here without meaning it!"

"You couldn't have met in a better place," said old Joe, removing
his pipe from his mouth. "Come into the parlour. You were made free
of it long ago, you know; and the other two an't strangers. Stop till I
shut the door of the shop. Ah! How it skreeks! There an't such a rusty
bit of metal in the place as its own hinges, I believe; and I'm sure
there's no such old bones here, as mine. Ha, ha! We're all suitable to
our calling, we're well matched. Come into the parlour. Come into
the parlour."

The parlour was the space behind the screen of rags. The old man
raked the fire together with an old stair-rod, and having trimmed his
smoky lamp (for it was night), with the stem of his pipe, put it in his
mouth again.

While he did this, the woman who had already spoken threw her
bundle on the floor, and sat down in a flaunting manner on a stool;
crossing her elbows on her knees, and looking with a bold defiance at
the other two.

"What odds then! What odds, Mrs. Dilber?" said the woman. "Every
person has a right to take care of themselves. *He* always did."

"That's true, indeed!" said the laundress. "No man more so."

"Why then, don't stand staring as if you was afraid, woman; who's
the wiser? We're not going to pick holes in each other's coats, I suppose?"

"No, indeed!" said Mrs. Dilber and the man together. "We should
hope not."

"Very well, then!" cried the woman. "That's enough. Who's the worse for the loss of a few things like these? Not a dead man, I suppose."

"No, indeed," said Mrs. Dilber, laughing.

"If he wanted to keep 'em after he was dead, a wicked old screw," pursued the woman, "why wasn't he natural in his lifetime? If he had been, he'd have had somebody to look after him when he was struck with Death, instead of lying gasping out his last there, alone by himself."

"It's the truest word that ever was spoke," said Mrs. Dilber. "It's a judgment on him."

"I wish it was a little heavier judgment," replied the woman; "and it should have been, you may depend upon it, if I could have laid my hands on anything else. Open that bundle, old Joe, and let me know the value of it. Speak out plain. I'm not afraid to be the first, nor afraid for them to see it. We know pretty well that we were helping ourselves, before we met here, I believe. It's no sin. Open the bundle, Joe."

But the gallantry of her friends would not allow of this; and the man in faded black, mounting the breach first, produced *his* plunder. It was not extensive. A seal or two, a pencil-case, a pair of sleeve-buttons, and a brooch of no great value, were all. They were severally examined and appraised by old Joe, who chalked the sums he was disposed to give for each, upon the wall, and added them up into a total when he found there was nothing more to come.

"That's your account," said Joe, "and I wouldn't give another sixpence, if I was to be boiled for not doing it. Who's next?"

Mrs. Dilber was next. Sheets and towels, a little wearing apparel, two old-fashioned silver teaspoons, a pair of sugar-tongs, and a few boots. Her account was stated on the wall in the same manner.

"I always give too much to ladies. It's a weakness of mine, and that's the way I ruin myself," said old Joe. "That's your account. If you asked me for another penny, and made it an open question, I'd repent of being so liberal and knock off half-a-crown."

"And now undo *my* bundle, Joe," said the first woman.

Joe went down on his knees for the greater convenience of opening it, and having unfastened a great many knots, dragged out a large and heavy roll of some dark stuff.

"What do you call this?" said Joe. "Bed-curtains!"

"Ah!" returned the woman, laughing and leaning forward on her crossed arms. "Bed-curtains!"

"You don't mean to say you took 'em down, rings and all, with him lying there?" said Joe.

"Yes I do," replied the woman. "Why not?"

"You were born to make your fortune," said Joe, "and you'll certainly do it."

"I certainly shan't hold my hand, when I can get anything in it by reaching it out, for the sake of such a man as He was, I promise you, Joe," returned the woman coolly. "Don't drop that oil upon the blankets, now."

"His blankets?" asked Joe.

"Whose else's do you think?" replied the woman. "He isn't likely to take cold without 'em, I dare say."

"I hope he didn't die of anything catching? Eh?" said old Joe, stopping in his work, and looking up.

"Don't you be afraid of that," returned the woman. "I an't so fond of his company that I'd loiter about him for such things, if he did. Ah! you may look through that shirt till your eyes ache; but you won't find a hole in it, nor a threadbare place. It's the best he had, and a fine one too. They'd have wasted it, if it hadn't been for me."

"What do you call wasting of it?" asked old Joe.

"Putting it on him to be buried in, to be sure," replied the woman with a laugh. "Somebody was fool enough to do it, but I took it off again. If calico an't good enough for such a purpose, it isn't good enough for anything. It's quite as becoming to the body. He can't look uglier than he did in that one."

Scrooge listened to this dialogue in horror. As they sat grouped about their spoil, in the scanty light afforded by the old man's lamp, he viewed them with a detestation and disgust, which could hardly have been greater, though they had been obscene demons, marketing the corpse itself.

"Ha, ha!" laughed the same woman, when old Joe, producing a flannel bag with money in it, told out their several gains upon the ground. "This is the end of it, you see! He frightened every one away from him when he was alive, to profit us when he was dead! Ha, ha, ha!"

"Spirit!" said Scrooge, shuddering from head to foot. "I see, I see. The case of this unhappy man might be my own. My life tends that way, now. Merciful Heaven, what is this!"

He recoiled in terror, for the scene had changed, and now he almost touched a bed: a bare, uncurtained bed: on which, beneath a ragged sheet, there lay a something covered up, which, though it was dumb, announced itself in awful language.

The room was very dark, too dark to be observed with any accuracy, though Scrooge glanced round it in obedience to a secret impulse, anxious to know what kind of room it was. A pale light, rising in the outer air, fell straight upon the bed; and on it, plundered and bereft, unwatched, unwept, uncared for, was the body of this man.

Scrooge glanced towards the Phantom. Its steady hand was pointed to the head. The cover was so carelessly adjusted that the slightest raising of it, the motion of a finger upon Scrooge's part, would have disclosed the face. He thought of it, felt how easy it would be to do, and longed to do it; but had no more power to withdraw the veil than to dismiss the spectre at his side.

Oh cold, cold, rigid, dreadful Death, set up thine altar here, and dress it with such terrors as thou hast at thy command: for this is thy dominion! But of the loved, revered, and honoured head, thou canst not turn one hair to thy dread purposes, or make one feature odious. It is not that the hand is heavy and will fall down when released; it is not that the heart and pulse are still; but that the hand was open, generous, and true; the heart brave, warm, and tender; and the pulse a man's. Strike, Shadow, strike! And see his good deeds springing from the wound, to sow the world with life immortal!

No voice pronounced these words in Scrooge's ears, and yet he heard them when he looked upon the bed. He thought, if this man could be raised up now, what would be his foremost thoughts? Avarice, hard-dealing, griping cares? They have brought him to a rich end, truly!

He lay, in the dark empty house, with not a man, a woman, or a child, to say that he was kind to me in this or that, and for the memory of one kind word I will be kind to him. A cat was tearing at the door, and there was a sound of gnawing rats beneath the hearth-stone. What *they* wanted in the room of death, and why they were so restless and disturbed, Scrooge did not dare to think.

"Spirit!" he said, "this is a fearful place. In leaving it, I shall not leave its lesson, trust me. Let us go!"

Still the Ghost pointed with an unmoved finger to the head.

"I understand you," Scrooge returned, "and I would do it, if I could. But I have not the power, Spirit. I have not the power."

Again it seemed to look upon him.

"If there is any person in the town, who feels emotion caused by this man's death," said Scrooge quite agonised, "show that person to me, Spirit, I beseech you!"

The Phantom spread its dark robe before him for a moment, like a wing; and withdrawing it, revealed a room by daylight, where a mother and her children were.

She was expecting some one, and with anxious eagerness; for she walked up and down the room; started at every sound; looked out from the window; glanced at the clock; tried, but in vain, to work with her needle; and could hardly bear the voices of the children in their play.

At length the long-expected knock was heard. She hurried to the door, and met her husband; a man whose face was careworn and depressed, though he was young. There was a remarkable expression in it now; a kind of serious delight of which he felt ashamed, and which he struggled to repress.

He sat down to the dinner that had been hoarding for him by the fire; and when she asked him faintly what news (which was not until after a long silence), he appeared embarrassed how to answer.

"Is it good?" she said, "or bad?"—to help him.

"Bad," he answered.

"We are quite ruined?"

"No. There is hope yet, Caroline."

"If *he* relents," she said, amazed, "there is! Nothing is past hope, if such a miracle has happened."

"He is past relenting," said her husband. "He is dead."

She was a mild and patient creature if her face spoke truth; but she was thankful in her soul to hear it, and she said so, with clasped hands. She prayed forgiveness the next moment, and was sorry; but the first was the emotion of her heart.

"What the half-drunken woman whom I told you of last night, said to me, when I tried to see him and obtain a week's delay; and what I thought was a mere excuse to avoid me; turns out to have been quite true. He was not only very ill, but dying, then."

"To whom will our debt be transferred?"

"I don't know. But before that time we shall be ready with the money; and even though we were not, it would be a bad fortune indeed to find so merciless a creditor in his successor. We may sleep to-night with light hearts, Caroline!"

Yes. Soften it as they would, their hearts were lighter. The children's faces, hushed and clustered round to hear what they so little understood, were brighter; and it was a happier house for this man's death! The only emotion that the Ghost could show him, caused by the event, was one of pleasure.

"Let me see some tenderness connected with a death," said Scrooge; "or that dark chamber, Spirit, which we left just now, will be for ever present to me."

The Ghost conducted him through several streets familiar to his feet; and as they went along, Scrooge looked here and there to find himself, but nowhere was he to be seen. They entered poor Bob Cratchit's house; the dwelling he had visited before; and found the mother and the children seated round the fire.

Quiet. Very quiet. The noisy little Cratchits were as still as statues in one corner, and sat looking up at Peter, who had a book before him. The mother and her daughters were engaged in sewing. But surely they were very quiet!

" 'And He took a child, and set him in the midst of them.' "

Where had Scrooge heard those words? He had not dreamed them. The boy must have read them out, as he and the Spirit crossed the threshold. Why did he not go on?

The mother laid her work upon the table, and put her hand up to her face.

"The colour hurts my eyes," she said.

The colour? Ah, poor Tiny Tim!

"They're better now again," said Cratchit's wife. "It makes them weak by candle-light; and I wouldn't show weak eyes to your father when he comes home, for the world. It must be near his time."

"Past it rather," Peter answered, shutting up his book. "But I think he has walked a little slower than he used, these few last evenings, mother."

They were very quiet again. At last she said, and in a steady, cheerful voice, that only faltered once:

"I have known him walk with—I have known him walk with Tiny Tim upon his shoulder, very fast indeed."

"And so have I," cried Peter. "Often."

"And so have I," exclaimed another. So had all.

"But he was very light to carry," she resumed, intent upon her work, "and his father loved him so, that it was no trouble: no trouble. And there is your father at the door!"

She hurried out to meet him; and little Bob in his comforter—he had need of it, poor fellow—came in. His tea was ready for him on the hob, and they all tried who should help him to it most. Then the two young Cratchits got upon his knees and laid, each child a little cheek, against his face, as if they said, "Don't mind it, father. Don't be grieved!"

Bob was very cheerful with them, and spoke pleasantly to all the family. He looked at the work upon the table, and praised the industry and speed of Mrs. Cratchit and the girls. They would be done long before Sunday, he said.

"Sunday! You went to-day, then, Robert?" said his wife.

"Yes, my dear," returned Bob. "I wish you could have gone. It would have done you good to see how green a place it is. But you'll see it often. I promised him that I would walk there on a Sunday. My little, little child!" cried Bob. "My little child!"

He broke down all at once. He couldn't help it. If he could have helped it, he and his child would have been farther apart perhaps than they were.

He left the room, and went up-stairs into the room above, which was lighted cheerfully, and hung with Christmas. There was a chair set close beside the child, and there were signs of some one having been there, lately. Poor Bob sat down in it, and when he had thought a little and composed himself, he kissed the little face. He was reconciled to what had happened, and went down again quite happy.

They drew about the fire, and talked; the girls and mother working still. Bob told them of the extraordinary kindness of Mr. Scrooge's nephew, whom he had scarcely seen but once, and who, meeting him in the street that day, and seeing that he looked a little— "just a little down you know," said Bob, inquired what had happened to distress him. "On which," said Bob, "for he is the pleasantest-spoken gentleman you ever heard, I told him. 'I am heartily sorry for it, Mr. Cratchit,' he said, 'and heartily sorry for your good wife.' By the bye, how he ever knew *that*, I don't know."

"Knew what, my dear?"

"Why, that you were a good wife," replied Bob.

"Everybody knows that!" said Peter.

"Very well observed, my boy!" cried Bob. "I hope they do. 'Heartily sorry,' he said, 'for your good wife. If I can be of service to you in any way,' he said, giving me his card, 'that's where I live. Pray come to me.' Now, it wasn't," cried Bob, "for the sake of anything he might be able to do for us, so much as for his kind way, that this was quite delightful. It really seemed as if he had known our Tiny Tim, and felt with us."

"I'm sure he's a good soul!" said Mrs. Cratchit.

"You would be surer of it, my dear," returned Bob, "if you saw and spoke to him. I shouldn't be at all surprised—mark what I say!— if he got Peter a better situation."

"Only hear that, Peter," said Mrs. Cratchit.

"And then," cried one of the girls, "Peter will be keeping company with some one, and setting up for himself."

"Get along with you!" retorted Peter, grinning.

"It's just as likely as not," said Bob, "one of these days; though there's plenty of time for that, my dear. But however and whenever we part from one another, I am sure we shall none of us forget poor Tiny Tim—shall we—or this first parting that there was among us?"

"Never, father!" cried they all.

"And I know," said Bob, "I know, my dears, that when we recollect how patient and how mild he was; although he was a little, little child; we shall not quarrel easily among ourselves, and forget poor Tiny Tim in doing it."

"No, never, father!" they all cried again.

"I am very happy," said little Bob, "I am very happy!"

Mrs. Cratchit kissed him, his daughters kissed him, the two young Cratchits kissed him, and Peter and himself shook hands. Spirit of Tiny Tim, thy childish essence was from God!

"Spectre," said Scrooge, "something informs me that our parting moment is at hand. I know it, but I know not how. Tell me what man that was whom we saw lying dead?"

The Ghost of Christmas Yet To Come conveyed him, as before—though at a different time, he thought: indeed, there seemed no order in these latter visions, save that they were in the Future—into the resorts of business men, but showed him not himself. Indeed, the Spirit did not stay for anything, but went straight on, as to the end just now desired, until besought by Scrooge to tarry for a moment.

"This court," said Scrooge, "through which we hurry now, is where my place of occupation is, and has been for a length of time. I see the house. Let me behold what I shall be, in days to come!"

The Spirit stopped; the hand was pointed elsewhere.

"The house is yonder," Scrooge exclaimed. "Why do you point away?"

The inexorable finger underwent no change.

Scrooge hastened to the window of his office, and looked in. It was an office still, but not his. The furniture was not the same, and the figure in the chair was not himself. The Phantom pointed as before.

He joined it once again, and wondering why and whither he had gone, accompanied it until they reached an iron gate. He paused to look round before entering.

A churchyard. Here, then; the wretched man whose name he had now to learn, lay underneath the ground. It was a worthy place. Walled in by houses; overrun by grass and weeds, the growth of vegetation's death, not life; choked up with too much burying; fat with repleted appetite. A worthy place!

The Spirit stood among the graves, and pointed down to One. He advanced towards it trembling. The Phantom was exactly as it had been, but he dreaded that he saw new meaning in its solemn shape.

"Before I draw nearer to that stone to which you point," said Scrooge, "answer me one question. Are these the shadows of the things that Will be, or are they shadows of things that May be, only?"

Still the Ghost pointed downward to the grave by which it stood.

"Men's courses will foreshadow certain ends, to which, if persevered in, they must lead," said Scrooge. "But if the courses be departed from, the ends will change. Say it is thus with what you show me!"

The Spirit was immovable as ever.

Scrooge crept towards it, trembling as he went; and following the finger, read upon the stone of the neglected grave his own name, EBENEZER SCROOGE.

"Am *I* that man who lay upon the bed?" he cried, upon his knees.

The finger pointed from the grave to him, and back again.

"No, Spirit! Oh no, no!"

The finger still was there.

"Spirit!" he cried, tight clutching at its robe, "hear me! I am not the man I was. I will not be the man I must have been but for this intercourse. Why show me this, if I am past all hope!"

For the first time the hand appeared to shake.

"Good Spirit," he pursued, as down upon the ground he fell before it: "Your nature intercedes for me, and pities me. Assure me that I yet may change these shadows you have shown me, by an altered life!"

The kind hand trembled.

"I will honour Christmas in my heart, and try to keep it all the year. I will live in the Past, the Present, and the Future. The Spirits of all Three shall strive within me. I will not shut out the lessons that they teach. Oh, tell me I may sponge away the writing on this stone!"

In his agony, he caught the spectral hand. It sought to free itself, but he was strong in his entreaty, and detained it. The Spirit, stronger yet, repulsed him.

Holding up his hands in a last prayer to have his fate reversed, he saw an alteration in the Phantom's hood and dress. It shrunk, collapsed, and dwindled down into a bedpost.

STAVE FIVE
The End of It

Yes! and the bedpost was his own. The bed was his own, the room was his own. Best and happiest of all, the Time before him was his own, to make amends in!

"I will live in the Past, the Present, and the Future!" Scrooge repeated, as he scrambled out of bed. "The Spirits of all Three shall strive within me. Oh Jacob Marley! Heaven, and the Christmas Time be praised for this! I say it on my knees, old Jacob; on my knees!"

He was so fluttered and so glowing with his good intentions, that his broken voice would scarcely answer to his call. He had been sobbing violently in his conflict with the Spirit, and his face was wet with tears.

"They are not torn down," cried Scrooge, folding one of his bed-curtains in his arms, "they are not torn down, rings and all. They are here—I am here—the shadows of the things that would have been, may be dispelled. They will be. I know they will!"

His hands were busy with his garments all this time; turning them inside out, putting them on upside down, tearing them, mislaying them, making them parties to every kind of extravagance.

"I don't know what to do!" cried Scrooge, laughing and crying in the same breath; and making a perfect Laocoön of himself with his stockings. "I am as light as a feather, I am as happy as an angel, I am as merry as a schoolboy. I am as giddy as a drunken man. A merry

Christmas to everybody! A happy New Year to all the world. Hallo here! Whoop! Hallo!"

He had frisked into the sitting-room, and was now standing there: perfectly winded.

"There's the saucepan that the gruel was in!" cried Scrooge, starting off again, and going round the fireplace. "There's the door, by which the Ghost of Jacob Marley entered! There's the corner where the Ghost of Christmas Present, sat! There's the window where I saw the wandering Spirits! It's all right, it's all true, it all happened. Ha ha ha!"

Really, for a man who had been out of practice for so many years, it was a splendid laugh, a most illustrious laugh. The father of a long, long line of brilliant laughs!

"I don't know what day of the month it is!" said Scrooge. "I don't know how long I've been among the Spirits. I don't know anything. I'm quite a baby. Never mind. I don't care. I'd rather be a baby. Hallo! Whoop! Hallo here!"

He was checked in his transports by the churches ringing out the lustiest peals he had ever heard. Clash, clang, hammer; ding, dong, bell. Bell, dong, ding; hammer, clang, clash! Oh, glorious, glorious!

Running to the window, he opened it, and put out his head. No fog, no mist; clear, bright, jovial, stirring, cold; cold, piping for the blood to dance to; Golden sunlight; Heavenly sky; sweet fresh air; merry bells. Oh, glorious! Glorious!

"What's to-day!" cried Scrooge, calling downward to a boy in Sunday clothes, who perhaps had loitered in to look about him.

"Eh?" returned the boy, with all his might of wonder.

"What's to-day, my fine fellow?" said Scrooge.

"To-day!" replied the boy. "Why, CHRISTMAS DAY."

"It's Christmas Day!" said Scrooge to himself. "I haven't missed it. The Spirits have done it all in one night. They can do anything they like. Of course they can. Of course they can. Hallo, my fine fellow!"

"Hallo!" returned the boy.

"Do you know the Poulterer's, in the next street but one, at the corner?" Scrooge inquired.

"I should hope I did," replied the lad.

"An intelligent boy!" said Scrooge. "A remarkable boy! Do you know whether they've sold the prize Turkey that was hanging up there?—Not the little prize Turkey: the big one?"

"What, the one as big as me?" returned the boy.

"What a delightful boy!" said Scrooge. "It's a pleasure to talk to him. Yes, my buck!"

"It's hanging there now," replied the boy.

"Is it?" said Scrooge. "Go and buy it."

"Walk-*er*!" exclaimed the boy.

"No, no," said Scrooge, "I am in earnest. Go and buy it, and tell 'em to bring it here, that I may give them the direction where to take it. Come back with the man, and I'll give you a shilling. Come back with him in less than five minutes and I'll give you half-a-crown!"

The boy was off like a shot. He must have had a steady hand at a trigger who could have got a shot off half so fast.

"I'll send it to Bob Cratchit's!" whispered Scrooge, rubbing his hands, and splitting with a laugh. "He sha'n't know who sends it. It's twice the size of Tiny Tim. Joe Miller never made such a joke as sending it to Bob's will be!"

The hand in which he wrote the address was not a steady one, but write it he did, somehow, and went down-stairs to open the street door, ready for the coming of the poulterer's man. As he stood there, waiting his arrival, the knocker caught his eye.

"I shall love it, as long as I live!" cried Scrooge, patting it with his hand. "I scarcely ever looked at it before. What an honest expression it has in its face! It's a wonderful knocker!—Here's the Turkey! Hallo! Whoop! How are you! Merry Christmas!"

It *was* a Turkey! He never could have stood upon his legs, that bird. He would have snapped 'em short off in a minute, like sticks of sealing-wax.

"Why, it's impossible to carry that to Camden Town," said Scrooge. "You must have a cab."

The chuckle with which he said this, and the chuckle with which he paid for the Turkey, and the chuckle with which he paid for the cab, and the chuckle with which he recompensed the boy, were only to be exceeded by the chuckle with which he sat down breathless in his chair again, and chuckled till he cried.

Shaving was not an easy task, for his hand continued to shake very much; and shaving requires attention, even when you don't dance while you are at it. But if he had cut the end of his nose off, he would have put a piece of sticking-plaister over it, and been quite satisfied.

He dressed himself "all in his best," and at last got out into the streets. The people were by this time pouring forth, as he had seen them with the Ghost of Christmas Present; and walking with his hands behind him, Scrooge regarded every one with a delighted smile. He looked so irresistibly pleasant, in a word, that three or four good-humoured fellows said, "Good morning, sir! A merry Christmas to you!" And Scrooge said often afterwards, that of all the blithe sounds he had ever heard, those were the blithest in his ears.

He had not gone far, when coming on towards him he beheld the portly gentleman, who had walked into his counting-house the day before, and said, "Scrooge and Marley's, I believe?" It sent a pang across his heart to think how this old gentleman would look upon him when they met; but he knew what path lay straight before him, and he took it.

"My dear sir," said Scrooge, quickening his pace, and taking the old gentleman by both his hands. "How do you do? I hope you succeeded yesterday. It was very kind of you. A merry Christmas to you, sir!"

"Mr. Scrooge?"

"Yes," said Scrooge. "That is my name, and I fear it may not be pleasant to you. Allow me to ask your pardon. And will you have the goodness"—here Scrooge whispered in his ear.

"Lord bless me!" cried the gentleman, as if his breath were taken away. "My dear Mr. Scrooge, are you serious?"

"If you please," said Scrooge. "Not a farthing less. A great many back-payments are included in it, I assure you. Will you do me that favour?"

"My dear sir," said the other, shaking hands with him. "I don't know what to say to such munifi—"

"Don't say anything, please," retorted Scrooge. "Come and see me. Will you come and see me?"

"I will!" cried the old gentleman. And it was clear he meant to do it.

"Thank'ee," said Scrooge. "I am much obliged to you. I thank you fifty times. Bless you!"

He went to church, and walked about the streets, and watched the people hurrying to and fro, and patted children on the head, and questioned beggars, and looked down into the kitchens of houses, and up to the windows, and found that everything could yield him pleasure. He had never dreamed that any walk—that anything—could give him so much happiness. In the afternoon he turned his steps towards his nephew's house.

He passed the door a dozen times, before he had the courage to go up and knock. But he made a dash, and did it:

"Is your master at home, my dear?" said Scrooge to the girl. Nice girl! Very.

"Yes, sir."

"Where is he, my love?" said Scrooge.

"He's in the dining-room, sir, along with mistress. I'll show you up-stairs, if you please."

"Thank'ee. He knows me," said Scrooge, with his hand already on the dining-room lock. "I'll go in here, my dear."

He turned it gently, and sidled his face in, round the door. They were looking at the table (which was spread out in great array); for these young housekeepers are always nervous on such points, and like to see that everything is right.

"Fred!" said Scrooge.

Dear heart alive, how his niece by marriage started! Scrooge had forgotten, for the moment, about her sitting in the corner with the footstool, or he wouldn't have done it, on any account.

"Why bless my soul!" cried Fred, "who's that?"

"It's I. Your uncle Scrooge. I have come to dinner. Will you let me in, Fred?"

Let him in! It is a mercy he didn't shake his arm off. He was at home in five minutes. Nothing could be heartier. His niece looked just the same. So did Topper when *he* came. So did the plump sister when *she* came. So did every one when *they* came. Wonderful party, wonderful games, wonderful unanimity, won-der-ful happiness!

But he was early at the office next morning. Oh, he was early there. If he could only be there first, and catch Bob Cratchit coming late! That was the thing he had set his heart upon.

And he did it; yes, he did! The clock struck nine. No Bob. A quarter past. No Bob. He was full eighteen minutes and a half behind his time. Scrooge sat with his door wide open, that he might see him come into the Tank.

His hat was off, before he opened the door; his comforter too. He was on his stool in a jiffy; driving away with his pen, as if he were trying to overtake nine o'clock.

"Hallo!" growled Scrooge, in his accustomed voice, as near as he could feign it. "What do you mean by coming here at this time of day?"

"I am very sorry, sir," said Bob. "I *am* behind my time."

"You are?" repeated Scrooge. "Yes. I think you are. Step this way, sir, if you please."

"It's only once a year, sir," pleaded Bob, appearing from the Tank. "It shall not be repeated. I was making rather merry yesterday, sir."

"Now, I'll tell you what, my friend," said Scrooge, "I am not going to stand this sort of thing any longer. And therefore," he continued, leaping from his stool, and giving Bob such a dig in the waistcoat that he staggered back into the Tank again; "and therefore I am about to raise your salary!"

Bob trembled, and got a little nearer to the ruler. He had a momentary idea of knocking Scrooge down with it, holding him, and calling to the people in the court for help and a strait-waistcoat.

"A merry Christmas, Bob!" said Scrooge, with an earnestness that could not be mistaken, as he clapped him on the back. "A merrier Christmas, Bob, my good fellow, than I have given you, for many a year! I'll raise your salary, and endeavour to assist your struggling family, and we will discuss your affairs this very afternoon, over a Christmas bowl of smoking bishop, Bob! Make up the fires, and buy another coal-scuttle before you dot another i, Bob Cratchit!"

Scrooge was better than his word. He did it all, and infinitely more; and to Tiny Tim, who did *not* die, he was a second father. He became as good a friend, as good a master, and as good a man, as the good old city knew, or any other good old city, town, or borough, in the good old world. Some people laughed to see the alteration in him, but he let them laugh, and little heeded them; for he was wise enough to know that nothing ever happened on this globe, for good, at which some people did not have their fill of laughter in the outset; and knowing that such as these would be blind anyway, he thought it quite as well that they should wrinkle up their eyes in grins, as have the malady in less attractive forms. His own heart laughed: and that was quite enough for him.

He had no further intercourse with Spirits, but lived upon the Total Abstinence Principle, ever afterwards; and it was always said of him, that he knew how to keep Christmas well, if any man alive possessed the knowledge. May that be truly said of us, and all of us! And so, as Tiny Tim observed, God bless Us, Every One!

A Tale of the Ragged Mountains

Edgar Allan Poe

During the fall of the year 1827, while residing near Charlottesville, Virginia, I casually made the acquaintance of Mr. Augustus Bedloe. This young gentleman was remarkable in every respect, and excited in me a profound interest and curiosity. I found it impossible to comprehend him either in his moral or his physical relations. Of his family I could obtain no satisfactory account. Whence he came, I never ascertained. Even about his age—although I call him a young gentleman—there was something which perplexed me in no little degree. He certainly *seemed* young—and he made a point of speaking about his youth—yet there were moments when I should have had little trouble in imagining him a hundred years of age. But in no regard was he more peculiar than in his personal appearance. He was singularly tall and thin. He stooped much. His limbs were exceedingly long and emaciated. His forehead was broad and low. His complexion was absolutely bloodless. His mouth was large and flexible, and his teeth were more wildly uneven, although sound, than I had ever before seen teeth in a human head. The expression of his smile, however, was by no means unpleasing, as might be supposed: but it had no variation whatever. It was one of profound melancholy—of a phaseless and unceasing gloom. His eyes were abnormally large, and round like those of a cat. The pupils, too, upon any accession or diminution of light, underwent contraction or dilation, just such as is observed in the feline tribe. In moments of excitement the orbs grew bright to a degree almost inconceivable; seeming to emit luminous rays, not of a reflected but of an intrinsic lustre, as does a candle or the sun; yet their ordinary condition was to totally vapid, filmy, and dull, as to convey the idea of the eyes of a long-interred corpse.

These peculiarities of person appeared to cause him much annoyance, and he was continually alluding to them in a sort of half explanatory, half apologetic strain, which, when I first heard it, impressed me very painfully. I soon, however, grew accustomed to it, and my uneasiness wore off. It seemed to be his design rather to insinuate than directly to assert that, physically, he had not always been what he was—that a long series of neuralgic attacks had reduced him from a condition of more than usual personal beauty, to that which I saw. For many years past he had been attended by a physician, named Templeton—an old gentleman, perhaps seventy years of age—whom he had first encountered at Saratoga, and from whose attention, while there, he either received, or fancied that he received, great benefit. The result was that Bedloe, who was wealthy, had made an arrangement with Dr Templeton, by which the latter, in consideration of a liberal annual allowance, had consented to devote his time and medical experience exclusively to the care of the invalid.

Doctor Templeton had been a traveller in his younger days, and at Paris had become a convert, in great measure, to the doctrine of Mesmer. It was altogether by means of magnetic remedies that he had succeeded in alleviating the acute pains of his patient; and this success had very naturally inspired the latter with a certain degree of confidence in the opinions from which the remedies had been educed. The doctor, however, like all enthusiasts, had struggled hard to make a thorough convert of his pupil, and finally so far gained his point as to induce the sufferer to submit to numerous experiments. By a frequent repetition of these, a result had arisen, which of late days has become so common as to attract little or no attention, but which, at the period of which I write, had very rarely been known in America. I mean to say, that between Dr Templeton and Bedloe there had grown up, little by little, a very distinct and strongly-marked *rapport*, or magnetic relation. I am not prepared to assert, however, that this *rapport* extended beyond the limits of the simple sleep-producing power; but this power itself had attained great intensity. At the first attempt to induce the magnetic somnolency, the mesmerist entirely failed. In the fifth or sixth he succeeded very partially, and after long-continued effort. Only at the twelfth was the triumph complete. After this the will of the patient succumbed rapidly to that of the physician, so that, when I first became acquainted with the two, sleep was brought about almost instantaneously by the mere volition of the operator, even when the invalid was unaware of his presence. It is only now, in the year 1845, when similar miracles are witnessed daily by thousands, that I dare venture to record this apparent impossibility as a matter of serious fact.

The temperature of Bedloe was in the highest degree sensitive, excitable, enthusiastic. His imagination was singularly vigorous and creative; and no doubt it derived additional force from the habitual use of morphine, which he swallowed in great quantity, and without which he would have found it impossible to exist. It was his practice

to take a very large dose of it immediately after breakfast each morning,—or, rather, immediately after a cup of strong coffee, for he ate
nothing in the forenoon,—and then set forth alone, or attended only
by a dog, upon a long ramble among the chain of wild and dreary hills
that lie westward and southward of Charlottesville, and are there dignified by the title of the Ragged Mountains.

Upon a dim, warm, misty day, toward the close of November, and
during the strange *interregnum* of the seasons which in America is
termed the Indian summer, Mr. Bedloe departed as usual for the hills.
The day passed, and still he did not return.

About eight o'clock at night, having become seriously alarmed at
his protracted absence, we were about setting out in search of him,
when he unexpectedly made his appearance, in health no worse than
usual, and in rather more than ordinary spirits. The account which
he gave of his expedition, and of the events which had detained him,
was a singular one indeed.

"You will remember," said he, "that it was about nine in the morning when I left Charlottesville. I bent my steps immediately to the
mountains, and, about ten, entered a gorge which was entirely new
to me. I followed the windings of this pass with much interest. The
scenery which presented itself on all sides, although scarcely entitled
to be called grand, had about it an indescribable and to me a delicious
aspect of dreary desolation. The solitude seemed absolutely virgin. I could
not help believing that the green sods and the grey rocks upon which
I trod had been trodden never before by the foot of a human being.
So entirely secluded, and in fact inaccessible, except through a series of
accidents, is the entrance of the ravine, that it is by no means impossible that I was the first adventurer—the very first and sole adventurer who had ever penetrated its recesses.

"The thick and peculiar mist, or smoke, which distinguishes the
Indian summer, and which now hung heavily over all objects, served,
no doubt, to deepen the vague impressions which these objects created. So dense was this pleasant fog that I could at no time see more
than a dozen yards of the path before me. This path was excessively
sinuous, and as the sun could not be seen, I soon lost all idea of the
direction in which I journeyed. In the meantime the morphine had
its customary effect—that of enduing all the external world with an
intensity of interest. In the quivering of a leaf—in the hue of a blade
of grass—in the shape of a trefoil—in the humming of a bee—in the
gleaming of a dew-drop—in the breathing of the wind—in the faint
odours that came from the forest—there came a whole universe of suggestion—a gay and motley train of rhapsodical and immethodical
thought.

"Busied in this, I walked on for several hours, during which the mist deepened around me to so great an extent that at length I was reduced to an absolute groping of the way. And now an indescribable uneasiness possessed me—a species of nervous hesitation and tremor. I feared to tread, lest I should be precipitated into some abyss. I remembered, too, strange stories told about these Ragged Hills, and of the uncouth and fierce races of men who tenanted their groves and caverns. A thousand vague fancies oppressed and disconcerted me—fancies the more distressing because vague. Very suddenly my attention was arrested by the loud beating of a drum.

"My amazement was, of course, extreme. A drum in these hills was a thing unknown. I could not have been more surprised at the sound of the trump of the Archangel. But a new and still more astounding source of interest and perplexity arose. There came a wild rattling or jingling sound, as if of a bunch of large keys, and upon the instant a dusky-visaged and half-naked man rushed past me with a shriek. He came so close to my person that I felt his hot breath upon my face. He bore in one hand an instrument composed of an assemblage of steel rings, and shook them vigorously as he ran. Scarcely had he disappeared in the mist, before, panting after him, with open mouth and glaring eyes, there darted a huge beast. I could not be mistaken in its character. It was a hyena.

"The sight of this monster rather relieved than heightened my terrors—for I now made sure that I dreamed, and endeavoured to arouse myself to waking consciousness. I stepped boldly and briskly forward. I rubbed my eyes. I called aloud. I pinched my limbs. A small spring of water presented itself to my view, and here, stooping, I bathed my hands and my head and neck. This seemed to dissipate the equivocal sensations which had hitherto annoyed me. I arose, as I thought, a new man, and proceeded steadily and complacently on my unknown way.

"At length, quite overcome by exertion, and by a certain oppressive closeness of the atmosphere, I seated myself beneath a tree. Presently there came a feeble gleam of sunshine, and the shadow of the leaves of the tree fell faintly but definitely upon the grass. At this shadow I gazed wonderingly for many minutes. Its character stupefied me with astonishment. I looked upward. The tree was a palm.

"I now rose hurriedly, and in a state of fearful agitation—for the fancy that I dreamed would serve me no longer. I saw—I felt that I had perfect command of my senses—and these senses now brought to my soul a world of novel and singular sensation. The heat became all at once intolerable. A strange odour loaded the breeze. A low, continuous murmur, like that arising from a full, but gently flowing river,

came to my ears, intermingled with the peculiar hum of multitudi-
nous human voices.

"While I listened in an extremity of astonishment which I need
not attempt to describe, a strong and brief gust of wind bore off the
incumbent fog as if by the wand of an enchanter.

"I found myself at the foot of a high mountain, and looking down
into a vast plain, through which wound a majestic river. On the margin
of this river stood an Eastern-looking city, such as we read of in the
Arabian Tales, but of a character even more singular than any there
described. From my position, which was far above the level of the town, I
could perceive its every nook and corner, as if delineated on a map. The
streets seemed innumerable, and crossed each other irregularly in all
directions, but were rather long winding alleys than streets, and absolutely swarmed with inhabitants. The houses were wildly picturesque.
On every hand was a wilderness of balconies, of verandas, of minarets, of shrines, and fantastically carved oriels. Bazaars abounded;
and there were displayed rich wares in infinite variety and profusion—
silks, muslins, the most dazzling cutlery, the most magnificent jewels and
gems. Besides these things, were seen, on all sides, banners and
palanquins, litters with stately dames close-veiled, elephants gor-
geously caparisoned, idols grotesquely hewn, drums, banners, and
gongs, spears, silver and gilded maces. And amid the crowd, and the
clamour, and the general intricacy and confusion—amid the million
of black and yellow men, turbaned and robed, and of flowing beard,
there roamed a countless multitude of holy filleted bulls, while vast
legions of the filthy but sacred ape clambered, chattering and shrieking,
about the cornices of the mosques, or clung to the minarets and oriels.
From the swarming streets to the banks of the river, there descended
innumerable flights of steps leading to bathing places, while the river
itself seemed to force a passage with difficulty through the vast fleets
of deeply burdened ships that far and wide encountered its surface.
Beyond the limits of the city arose, in frequent majestic groups, the
palm and the cocoa, with other gigantic and weird trees of vast age;
and here and there might be seen a field of rice, the thatched hut of a
peasant, a tank, a stray temple, a gipsy camp, or a solitary graceful
maiden taking her way, with a pitcher upon her head, to the banks of
the magnificent river.

"You will say now, of course, that I dreamed; but not so. What I
saw—what I heard—what I felt—what I thought—had about it nothing of the unmistakable idiosyncrasy of the dream. All was rigorously
self-consistent. At first, doubting that I was really awake, I entered
into a series of tests, which soon convinced me that I really was. Now
when one dreams, and, in the dream, suspects that he dreams, the

suspicion *never fails to confirm itself*, and the sleeper is almost immediately aroused. Thus Novalis errs not in saying that 'we are near waking when we dream that we dream.' Had the vision occurred to me as I describe it, without my suspecting it as a dream, then a dream it might absolutely have been, but, occurring as it did, and suspected and tested as it was, I am forced to class it among other phenomena."

"In this I am not sure that you are wrong," observed Dr Templeton, "but proceed. You arose and descended into the city."

"I arose," continued Bedloe, regarding the Doctor with an air of profound astonishment, "I arose as you say, and descended into the city. On my way I fell in with an immense populace, crowding through every avenue, all in the same direction, and exhibiting in every action the wildest excitement. Very suddenly, and by some inconceivable impulse, I became intensely imbued with personal interest in what was going on. I seemed to feel that I had an important part to play, without exactly understanding what it was. Against the crowd which environed me, however, I experienced a deep sentiment of animosity. I shrank from amid them, and, swiftly, by a circuitous path, reached and entered the city. Here all was the wildest tumult and contention. A small party of men, clad in garments half Indian, half European, and officered by gentlemen in a uniform partly British, were engaged, at great odds, with the swarming rabble of the allies. I joined the weaker party, arming myself with the weapons of a fallen officer, and fighting I knew not whom with the nervous ferocity of despair. We were soon overpowered by numbers, and driven to seek refuge in a species of kiosk. Here we barricaded ourselves, and, for the present, were secure. From a loop-hole near the summit of the kiosk, I perceived a vast crowd, in furious agitation, surrounding and assaulting a gay palace that overhung the river. Presently, from an upper window of this palace, there descended an effeminate-looking person, by means of a string made of the turbans of his attendants. A boat was at hand in which he escaped to the opposite bank of the river.

"And now a new object took possession of my soul. I spoke a few hurried but energetic words to my companions, and, having succeeded in gaining over a few of them to my purpose, made a frantic sally from the kiosk. We rushed amid the crowd that surrounded it. They retreated, at first, before us. They rallied, fought madly, and retreated again. In the meantime we were borne far from the kiosk, and became bewildered and entangled among the narrow streets of tall, overhanging houses, into the recesses of which the sun had never been able to shine. The rabble pressed impetuously upon us, harassing us with their spears, and overwhelming us with flights of arrows. These latter were very remarkable, and resembled in some respects the writhing creese of the Malay. They were made to imitate the body of a creeping serpent, and were long and black, with a poisoned barb. One of them struck me upon the right temple. I reeled and fell. An instantaneous and dreadful sickness seized me. I struggled—I gasped—I died."

"You will hardly persist *now*," said I, smiling, "that the whole of your adventure was not a dream. You are not prepared to maintain that you are dead?"

When I said these words, I of course expected some lively sally from Bedloe in reply; but, to my astonishment, he hesitated, trembled, became fearfully pallid, and remained silent. I looked towards Templeton. He was erect and rigid in his chair—his teeth chattered, and his eyes were staring from their sockets. "Proceed!" he at length said hoarsely to Bedloe.

"For many minutes," continued the latter, "my sole sentiment—my sole feeling—was that of darkness and nonentity, with the consciousness of death. At length there seemed to pass a violent and sudden shock through my soul, as if of electricity. With it came the sense of elasticity and of light. This latter I felt—not saw. In an instant I seemed to rise from the ground. But I had no bodily, no visible, audible, or palpable presence. The crowd had departed. The tumult had ceased. The city was in comparative repose. Beneath me lay my corpse, with the arrow in my temple, the whole head greatly swollen and disfigured. But all these things I felt—not saw. I took interest in nothing. Even the corpse seemed a matter in which I had no concern. Volition I had none, but appeared to be impelled into motion, and flitted buoyantly out of the city, retracing the circuitous path by which I had entered it. When I had attained that point of the ravine in the mountains at which I had encountered the hyena, I again experienced a shock as of a galvanic battery; the sense of weight, of volition, of substance, returned. I became my original self, and bent my step eagerly homeward—but the past had not lost the vividness of the real—and not now, even for an instant, can I compel my understanding to regard it as a dream."

"Nor was it," said Templeton, with an air of deep solemnity, "yet it would be difficult to say how otherwise it should be termed. Let us suppose only, that the soul of the man of to-day is upon the verge of some stupendous psychal discoveries. Let us content ourselves with this supposition. For the rest I have some explanation to make. Here is a water-colour drawing, which I should have shown you before, but which an accountable sentiment of horror has hitherto prevented me from showing."

We looked at the picture which he presented. I saw nothing in it of an extraordinary character; but its effect upon Bedloe was prodigious. He nearly fainted as he gazed. And yet it was but a miniature portrait—a miraculously accurate one, to be sure—of his own very remarkable features. At least this was my thought as I regarded it.

"You will perceive," said Templeton, "the date of this picture—it is here, scarcely visible, in this corner—1780. In this year was the portrait taken. It is the likeness of a dead friend—a Mr. Oldeb—to whom I became much attached at Calcutta, during the administration of Warren Hastings. I was then only twenty years old. When I first saw you, Mr. Bedloe, at Saratoga, it was the miraculous similarity which existed between yourself and the painting which induced me to accost you, to seek your friendship, and to bring about those arrangements which resulted in my becoming your constant companion. In accomplishing this point, I was urged partly, and perhaps principally, by a regretful memory of the deceased, but also, in part, by an uneasy, and not altogether horrorless curiosity respecting yourself.

"In your detail of the vision which presented itself to you amid the hills, you have described, with the minutest accuracy, the Indian city of Benares, upon the Holy River. The riots, the combat, the massacre, were the actual events of the insurrection of Cheyte Sing, which took place in 1780, when Hastings was put in imminent peril of his life. The man escaping by the string of turbans was Cheyte Sing himself. The party in the kiosk were sepoys and British officers, headed by Hastings. Of this party I was one, and did all I could do to prevent the rash and fatal sally of the officer who fell, in the crowded alleys, by the poisoned arrow of a Bengalee. That officer was my dearest friend. It was Oldeb. You will perceive by these manuscripts" (here the speaker produced a note-book in which several pages appeared to have been freshly written), "that at the very period in which you fancied these things amid the hills I was engaged in detailing them upon paper here at home."

In about a week after this conversation, the following paragraphs appeared in a Charlottesville paper:

"We have the painful duty of announcing the death of Mr. Augustus Bedlo, a gentleman whose amiable manners and many virtues have long endeared him to the citizens of Charlottesville.

"Mr B., for some years past, has been subject to neuralgia, which has often threatened to terminate fatally; but this can be regarded only as the mediate cause of his decease. The proximate cause was one of especial singularity. In an excursion to the Ragged Mountains, a few days since, a slight cold and fever were contracted, attended with great determination of blood to the head. To relieve this, Dr. Templeton resorted to topical bleeding. Leeches were applied to the temples. In a fearfully brief period the patient died, when it appeared that, in the jar containing the leeches, had been introduced, by accident, one of the venomous vermicular sangsues which are now and then found in the neighbouring ponds. This creature fastened itself upon a small artery in the right temple. Its close resemblance to the medicinal leech caused the mistake to be overlooked until too late.

"N.B.—The poisonous sangsue of Charlottesville may always be distinguished from the medicinal leech by its blackness, and especially by its writhing or vermicular motions, which very nearly resemble those of a snake."

I was speaking with the editor of the paper in question, upon the topic of this remarkable accident, when it occurred to me to as how it happened that the name of the deceased had been given as Bedlo.

"I presume," said I, "you have authority for this spelling, but I have always supposed the name to be written with an e at the end."

"Authority?—no," he replied. 'It is a mere typographical error. The name is Bedlo with an *e*, all the world over, and I never knew it to be spelt otherwise in my life."

"Then," said I mutteringly, as I turned upon my heel, "then indeed has it come to pass that one truth is stranger than any fiction—for Bedlo, without the e, what is it but Oldeb conversed? And this man tells me it is a typographical error."

An Uncommon Sort of Spectre
EDWARD PAGE MITCHELL

I

The ancient castle of Weinstein, on the upper Rhine, was, as everybody knows, inhabited in the autumn of 1352 by the powerful Baron Kalbsbraten, better known in those parts as Old Twenty Flasks, a sobriquet derived from his reputed daily capacity for the product of the vineyard. The baron had many other admirable qualities. He was a genial, whole-souled, public-spirited gentleman, and robbed, murdered, burned, pillaged, and drove up the steep sides of the Weinstein his neighbors' cattle, wives, and sisters, with a hearty bonhomie that won for him the unaffected esteem of his contemporaries.

One evening the good baron sat alone in the great hall of Weinstein, in a particularly happy mood. He had dined well, as was his habit, and twenty empty bottles stood before him in a row upon the table, like a train of delightful memories of the recent past. But the baron had another reason to be satisfied with himself and with the world. The consciousness that he had that day become a parent lit up his countenance with a tender glow that mere wine cannot impart.

"What ho! Without! Hi! Seneschal!" he presently shouted, in a tone that made the twenty empty bottles ring as if they were musical glasses, while a score of suits of his ancestors' armor hanging around the walls gave out in accompaniment a deep metallic bass. The seneschal was speedily at his side.

"Seneschal," said Old Twenty Flasks, "you gave me to understand that the baroness was doing finely?"

"I am told," replied the seneschal, "that her ladyship is doing as well as could be expected."

The baron mused in silence for a moment, absently regarding the empty bottles. "You also gave me to understand," he continued, "that there were—"

"Four," said the seneschal, gravely. "I am credibly informed that there are four, all boys."

"That," exclaimed the baron, with a glow of honest pride, bringing a brawny fist down upon the table— "That, in these days, when the abominable doctrines of Malthus are gaining ground among the upper classes, is what I call creditable—creditable, by Saint Christopher. If I do say it!" His eyes rested again upon the empty bottles. "I think, Seneschal," he added, after a brief pause, "that under the circumstances we may venture—"

"Nothing could be more eminently proper," rejoined the seneschal. "I will fetch another flask forthwith, and of the best. What says Your Excellency to the vintage of 1304, the year of the comet?"

"But," hesitated the baron, toying with his mustache, "I understood you to say that there were four of 'em—four boys?"

"True, my lord," replied the seneschal, snatching the idea with the readiness of a well-trained domestic. "I will fetch four more flasks."

As the excellent retainer deposited four fresh bottles upon the table within the radius of the baron's reach, he casually remarked, "A pious old man, a traveler, is in the castle yard, my lord, seeking shelter and a supper. He comes from beyond the Alps, and fares toward Cologne."

"I presume," said the baron, with an air of indifference, "that he has been duly searched for plunder."

"He passed this morning," replied the retainer, "through the domain of your well-born cousin, Count Conrad of Schwinkenfels. Your lordship will readily understand that he has nothing now save a few beggarly Swiss coins of copper."

"My worthy cousin Conrad!" exclaimed the baron, affectionately. "It is the one great misfortune of my life that I live to the leeward of Schwinkenfels. But you relieved the pious man of his copper?"

"My lord," said the seneschal, with an apologetic smile, "it was not worth the taking."

"Now by my soul," roared the baron, "you exasperate me! Coin, and not worth the taking! Perhaps not for its intrinsic value, but you should have cleaned him out as a matter of principle, you fool!"

The seneschal hung his head and muttered an explanation. At the same time he opened the twenty-first bottle.

"Never," continued the baron, less violently but still severely, "if you value my esteem and your own paltry skin, suffer yourself to be swerved a hair's breadth from principle by the apparent insignificance of the loot. A conscientious attention to details is one of the fundamental elements of a prosperous career—in fact, it underlies all political economy."

The withdrawal of the cork from the twenty-second bottle emphasized this statement.

"However," the baron went on, somewhat mollified, "this is not a day on which I can consistently make a fuss over a trifle. Four, and all boys! This is a glorious day for Weinstein. Open the two remaining flasks, Seneschal, and show the pious stranger in. I fain would amuse myself with him."

II

Viewed through the baron's twenty-odd bottles, the stranger appeared to be an aged man—eighty years, if a day. He wore a shabby gray cloak and carried a palmer's staff, and seemed an innocuous old fellow, cast in too commonplace a mold to furnish even a few minutes' diversion. The baron regretted sending for him, but being a person of unfailing politeness, when not upon the rampage, he bade his guest be seated and filled him a beaker of the comet wine.

After an obeisance, profound yet not servile, the pilgrim took the glass and critically tasted the wine. He held the beaker up athwart the light with trembling hand, and then tasted again. The trial seemed to afford him great satisfaction, and he stroked his long white beard.

"Perhaps you are a connoisseur. It pleases your palate, eh?" said the baron, winking at the full-length portrait of one of his ancestors.

"Proper well," replied the pilgrim, "though it is a trifle syrupy from too long keeping. By the bouquet and the tint, I should pronounce it of the vintage of 1304, grown on the steep slope south southeast of the castle, in the fork of the two pathways that lead to under the hill. The sun's rays reflected from the turret give a peculiar excellence to the growth of that particular spot. But your rascally varlets have shelved the bottle on the wrong side of the cellar. It should have been put on the dry side, near where your doughty grandsire Sigismund von Weinstein, the Hairy Handed, walled up his third wife in preparation for a fourth."

The baron regarded his guest with a look of amazement. "Upon my life!" said he, "but you appear to be familiar with the ins and outs of this establishment."

"If I do," rejoined the stranger, composedly sipping his wine, "'tis no more than natural, for I lived more than sixty years under this roof and know its every leak. I happen to be a Von Weinstein myself."

The baron crossed himself and pulled his chair a little further away from the bottles and the stranger.

"Oh no," said the pilgrim, laughing; "quiet your fears. I am aware that every well-regulated castle has an ancestral ghost, but my flesh and blood are honest. I was lord of Weinstein till I went, twelve years ago, to study metaphysics in the Arabic schools, and the cursed scriveners wrote me out of the estate. Why, I know this hall from infancy!

Yonder is the fireplace at which I used to warm my baby toes. There
is the identical suit of armor into which I crawled when a boy of six
and hid till my sainted mother—heaven rest her!—nigh died of fright.
It seems but yesterday. There on the wall hangs the sharp two-handed
sword of our ancestor, Franz, the One-Eared, with which I cut off the
mustaches of my tipsy sire as he sat muddled over his twentieth bottle.
There is the very casque—but perhaps these reminiscences weary you.
You must pardon the garrulity of an old man who has come to revisit
the home of his childhood and prime."

The baron pressed his hand to his forehead. "I have lived in this
castle myself for half a century," said he, "and am tolerably familiar
with the history of my immediate progenitors. But I can't say that I
ever had the pleasure of your acquaintance. However, permit me to
fill your glass."

"It is good wine," said the pilgrim, holding out his glass. "Except,
perhaps, the vintage of 1392, when the grapes—"

The baron stared at his guest. "The grapes of 1392," said he dryly,
"lack forty years of ripening. You are aged, my friend, and your mind
wanders."

"Excuse me, worthy host," calmly replied the pilgrim. "The vintage
of 1392 has been forty years cellared. You have no memory for dates."

"What call you this year?" demanded the baron.

"By the almanacs, and the stars, and precedent, and common consent, it is the year of grace 1433."

"By my soul and hope of salvation," ejaculated the baron, "it is
the year of grace 1352."

"There is evidently a misunderstanding somewhere," remarked the
venerable stranger. "I was born here in the year 1352, the year the
Turks invaded Europe."

"No Turk has invaded Europe, thanks be to heaven," replied Old
Twenty Flasks, recovering his self-control. "You are either a magician or an imposter. In either case I shall order you drawn and quartered as soon as we have finished this bottle. Pray proceed with your
very interesting reminiscences, and do not spare the wine."

"I never practice magic," quietly replied the pilgrim, "and as to
being an imposter, scan well my face. Don't you recognize the family
nose, thick, short, and generously colored? How about the three lateral
and two diagonal wrinkles on my brow? I see them there on yours.
Are not my chaps Weinstein chaps? Look closely. I court investigation."

"You do look damnably like us," the baron admitted.

"I was the youngest," the stranger went on, "of quadruplets. My
three brothers were puny, sickly things, and did not long survive their
birth. As a child I was the idol of my poor father, who had some traits

worthy of respectful mention, guzzling old toper and unconscionable thief though he was."

The baron winced.

"They used to call him Old Twenty Flasks. It is my candid opinion, based on memory, that Old Forty Flasks would have been nearer the truth."

"It's a lie!" shouted the baron, "I rarely exceeded twenty bottles."

"And as for his standing in the community," the pilgrim went on, without taking heed of the interruption, "it must be confessed that nothing could be worse. He was the terror of honest folk for miles around. Property rights were extremely insecure in this neighborhood, for the rapacity of my lamented parent knew no bounds. Yet nobody dared to complain aloud, for lives were not much safer than sheep or ducats. How the people hated his shadow, and roundly cursed him behind his back! I remember well that, when I was about fourteen—it must have been in '66, the year the Grand Turk occupied Adrianople— tall Hugo, the miller, called me up to him, and said: 'Boy, thou has a right pretty nose.' 'It is a pretty nose, Hugo,' said I, straightening up. 'Is it on firm and strong?' asked Hugo, with a sneer. 'Firm enough, and strong enough, I dare say,' I answered; 'but why ask such a fool's question?' 'Well, well, boy,' said Hugo, turning away, gook sharp with thine eyes after thy nose when thy father is unoccupied, for he has just that conscience to steal the nose off his son's face in lack of better plunder.'"

"By St. Christopher!" roared the baron, "tall Hugo, the miller, shall pay for this. I always suspected him. By St. Christopher's burden, I'll break every bone in his villainous body."

"'Twould be an ignoble vengeance," replied the pilgrim, quietly, "for tall Hugo has been in his grave these sixty years."

"True," said the baron, putting both hands to his head, and gazing at his guest with a look of utter helplessness. "I forget that it is now next century—that is to say, if you be not a spectre."

"You will excuse me, my respected parent," returned the pilgrim, "if I subject your hypothesis to the test of logic, for it touches me upon a very tender spot, impugning, as it does, my physical verity and my status as an actual individualized ego. Now, what is our relative position? You acknowledge the date of my birth to have been the year of grace 1352. That is a matter in which your memory is not likely to be at fault. On the other hand, with a strange inconsistency, you maintain, in the face of almanacs, chronologies, and the march of events, that it is still the year of grace 1352. Were you one of the seven sleepers, your hallucination [to use no harsher term] might be pardoned, but you are neither a sleeper nor a saint. Now, every one of the eighty

years that are packed away in the carpet bag of my experience pro-
tests against your extraordinary error. It is I who have a prima facie
right to question your physical existence, not you mine. Did you ever
hear of a ghost, spectre, wraith, apparition, eldolon, or spook coming
out of the future to haunt, annoy, or frighten individuals of an earlier
generation?"

The baron was obliged to admit that he never had.

"But you have heard of instances where apparitions, ghosts,
spooks, call them what you will, have invaded the present from out
the limbo of the past?"

The baron crossed himself a second time and peered anxiously
into the dark corners of the apartment. "If you are a genuine Von
Weinstein," he whispered, "you already know that this castle is over-
run with spectres of that sort. It is difficult to move about after nightfall without tumbling over half a dozen of them."

"Then," said the placid logician, "you surrender your case. You
commit what, my revered preceptor in dialectics, the learned Arabian
Ben Dusty, used to style syllogistic suicide. For you allow that, while
ghosts out of the future are unheard of, ghosts from the past are not
infrequently encountered. Now I submit to you as a man, this propo-
sition: That it is infinitely more probable that you are a ghost than
that I am one!"

The baron turned very red. "Is this filial," he demanded, "to deny
the flesh and blood of your own father?"

"Is it paternal," retorted the pilgrim, not losing his composure,
"to insinuate the unrealness of the son of your own begetting?"

"By all the saints!" growled the baron, growing still redder, "this
question shall be settled, and speedily. Halloo, there, Seneschal!" He
called again and again, but in vain.

"Spare your lungs," calmly suggested the pilgrim. "The best-
trained domestic in the world will not stir from beneath the sod for
all your shouting."

Twenty Flasks sank back helplessly in his chair. He tried to speak,
but his tongue and throat repudiated their functions. They only
gurgled.

"That is right," said his guest, approvingly. "Conduct yourself as
befits a venerable and respectable ghost from the last century. A well-
behaved apparition neither blusters nor is violent. You can well afford
to be peaceable in your deportment now; you were turbulent enough
before your death."

"My death?" gasped the baron.

"Excuse me," apologized the pilgrim, "for referring to that unpleasant event."

"My death!" stammered the baron, his hair standing on end. "I should like to hear the particulars."

"I was hardly more than fifteen at the time," said the pilgrim musingly; "but I shall never forget the most trifling circumstances of the great popular arising that put an end to my worthy sire's career. Exasperated beyond endurance by your outrageous crimes, the people for miles around at last rose in a body, and, led by my old friend tall Hugo, the miller, flocked to Schwinkenfels and appealed to your cousin, Count Conrad, for protection against yourself, their natural protector. Von Schwinkenfels heard their complaints with great gravity. He replied that he had long watched your abominable actions with distress and consternation; that he had frequently remonstrated with you, but in vain; that he regarded you as the scourge of the neighborhood; that your castle was full of blood-stained treasure and shamefully acquired booty; and that he now regarded it as the personal duty of himself, the conservator of lawful order and good morals, to march against Weinstein and exterminate you for the common good."

"The hypocritical pirate!" exclaimed Twenty Flasks.

"Which he proceeded to do," continued the pilgrim, "supported not only by his retainers but by your own. I must say that you made a sturdy defense. Had not your rascally seneschal sold you out to Schwinkenfels and let down the drawbridge one evening when you were as usual fuddling your brains with your twenty bottles, perhaps Conrad never would have gained an entrance, and my young eyes would have been spared the horrid task of watching the body of my venerated parent dangling at the end of a rope from the topmost turret of the northwest tower."

The baron buried his face in his hands and began to cry like a baby. "They hanged me, did they?" he faltered.

"I am afraid no other construction can be put on it," said the pilgrim. "It was the inevitable termination of such a career as yours had been. They hanged you, they strangled you, they choked you to death with a rope; and the unanimous verdict of the community was Justifiable Homicide. You weep! Behold, Father, I also weep for the shame of the house of Von Weinstein! Come to my arms."

Father and son clasped each other in a long, affectionate embrace and mingled their tears over the disgrace of Weinstein. When the baron recovered from his emotion he found himself alone with his conscience and twenty-four empty bottles. The pilgrim had disappeared.

III

Meanwhile, in the apartments consecrated to the offices of maternity, all had been confusion, turmoil, and distress. In four huge armchairs sat four experienced matrons, each holding in her lap a pillow of swan's-down. On each pillow had reposed an infinitesimal fraction of humanity, recently added to the sum total of Von Weinstein. One experienced matron had dozed over her charge; when she awoke the pillow in her lap was unoccupied. An immediate census taken by the alarmed attendants disclosed the startling fact that, although there were still four armchairs, and four sage women, and four pillows of swan's-down, there were but three infants. The seneschal, as an expert in mathematics and accounts, was hastily summoned from below. His reckoning merely confirmed the appalling suspicion. One of the quadruplets was gone.

Prompt measures were taken in this fearful emergency. The corners of the rooms were ransacked in vain. Piles of bedclothing and baskets of linen were searched through and through. The hunt extended to other parts of the castle. The seneschal even sent out trusted and discreet retainers on horseback to scour the surrounding country. They returned with downcast countenances; no trace of the lost Von Weinstein had been found.

During one terrible hour the wails of the three neglected infants mingled with the screams of the hysterical mother, to whom the attention of the four sage women was exclusively directed. At the end of the hour her ladyship had sufficiently recovered to implore her attendants to make a last, though hopeless count. On three pillows lay three babies howling lustily in unison. On the fourth pillow reposed a fourth infant, with a mysterious smile upon his face, but cheeks that bore traces of recent tears.

The Clock That Went Backward
Edward Page Mitchell

I.

A row of Lombardy poplars stood in front of my great-aunt Gertrude's house, on the bank of the Sheepscot River. In personal appearance my aunt was surprisingly like one of those trees. She had the look of hopeless anemia that distinguishes them from fuller blooded sorts. She was tall, severe in outline, and extremely thin. Her habiliments clung to her. I am sure that had the gods found occasion to impose upon her the fate of Daphne she would have taken her place easily and naturally in the dismal row, as melancholy a poplar as the rest.

Some of my earliest recollections are of this venerable relative. Alive and dead she bore an important part in the events I am about to recount: events which I believe to be without parallel in the experience of mankind.

During our periodical visits of duty to Aunt Gertrude in Maine, my cousin Harry and myself were accustomed to speculate much on her age. Was she sixty, or was she six score? We had no precise information; she might have been either. The old lady was surrounded by old-fashioned things. She seemed to live altogether in the past. In her short half-hours of communicativeness, over her second cup of tea, or on the piazza where the poplars sent slim shadows directly toward the east, she used to tell us stories of her alleged ancestors. I say alleged, because we never fully believed that she had ancestors.

A genealogy is a stupid thing. Here is Aunt Gertrude's, reduced to its simplest forms:

Her great-great-grandmother (1599-1642) was a woman of Holland who married a Puritan refugee, and sailed from Leyden to Plymouth in the ship Ann in the year of our Lord 1632. This Pilgrim mother had a daughter, Aunt Gertrude's great-grandmother (1640-1718). She came to the Eastern District of Massachusetts in the early part of the last century, and was carried off by the Indians in the Penobscot wars.

Her daughter (1680-1776) lived to see these colonies free and independent, and contributed to the population of the coming republic
not less than nineteen stalwart sons and comely daughters. One of
the latter (1735-1802) married a Wiscasset skipper engaged in the
West India trade, with whom she sailed. She was twice wrecked at
sea—once on what is now Seguin Island and once on San Salvador. It
was on San Salvador that Aunt Gertrude was born.

We got to be very tired of hearing this family history. Perhaps it
was the constant repetition and the merciless persistency with which
the above dates were driven into our young ears that made us skep-
tics. As I have said, we took little stock in Aunt Gertrude's ancestors.
They seemed highly improbable. In our private opinion the great-
grandmothers and grandmothers and so forth were pure myths, and
Aunt Gertrude herself was the principal in all the adventures attributed to them, having lasted from century to century while generations of contemporaries went the way of all flesh.

On the first landing of the square stairway of the mansion loomed
a tall Dutch clock. The case was more than eight feet high, of a dark
red wood, not mahogany, and it was curiously inlaid with silver. No
common piece of furniture was this. About a hundred years ago there
flourished in the town of Brunswick a horologist named Cary, an indus-
trious and accomplished workman. Few well-to-do houses on that part
of the coast lacked a Cary timepiece. But Aunt Gertrude's clock had
marked the hours and minutes of two full centuries before the
Brunswick artisan was born. It was running when William the Taciturn
pierced the dikes to relieve Leyden. The name of the maker, Jan
Lipperdam, and the date, 1572, were still legible in broad black letters
and figures reaching quite across the dial. Cary's masterpieces were
plebeian and recent beside this ancient aristocrat. The jolly Dutch
moon, made to exhibit the phases over a landscape of windmills and
polders, was cunningly painted. A skilled hand had carved the grim
ornament at the top, a death's head transfixed by a two-edged sword.
Like all timepieces of the sixteenth century, it had no pendulum. A
simple Van Wyck escapement governed the descent of the weights to
the bottom of the tall case.

But these weights never moved. Year after year, when Harry and
I returned to Maine, we found the hands of the old clock pointing to
the quarter past three, as they had pointed when we first saw them.
The fat moon hung perpetually in the third quarter, as motionless as
the death's head above. There was a mystery about the silenced movement and the paralyzed hands. Aunt Gertrude told us that the works
had never performed their functions since a bolt of lightning entered
the clock; and she showed us a black hole in the side of the case near

the top, with a yawning rift that extended downward for several feet. This explanation failed to satisfy us. It did not account for the sharpness of her refusal when we proposed to bring over the watchmaker from the village, or for her singular agitation once when she found Harry on a stepladder, with a borrowed key in his hand, about to test for himself the clock's suspended vitality.

One August night, after we had grown out of boyhood, I was awakened by a noise in the hallway. I shook my cousin. "Somebody's in the house," I whispered.

We crept out of our room and on to the stairs. A dim light came from below. We held breath and noiselessly descended to the second landing. Harry clutched my arm. He pointed down over the banisters, at the same time drawing me back into the shadow.

We saw a strange thing.

Aunt Gertrude stood on a chair in front of the old clock, as spectral in her white nightgown and white nightcap as one of the poplars when covered with snow. It chanced that the floor creaked slightly under our feet. She turned with a sudden movement, peering intently into the darkness, and holding a candle high toward us, so that the light was full upon her pale face. She looked many years older than when I bade her good night. For a few minutes she was motionless, except in the trembling arm that held aloft the candle. Then, evidently reassured, she placed the light upon a shelf and turned again to the clock.

We now saw the old lady take a key from behind the face and proceed to wind up the weights. We could hear her breath, quick and short. She rested a band on either side of the case and held her face close to the dial, as if subjecting it to anxious scrutiny. In this attitude she remained for a long time. We heard her utter a sigh of relief, and she half turned toward us for a moment. I shall never forget the expression of wild joy that transfigured her features then.

The hands of the clock were moving; they were moving backward.

Aunt Gertrude put both arms around the clock and pressed her withered cheek against it. She kissed it repeatedly. She caressed it in a hundred ways, as if it had been a living and beloved thing. She fondled it and talked to it, using words which we could hear but could not understand. The hands continued to move backward.

Then she started back with a sudden cry. The clock had stopped. We saw her tall body swaying for an instant on the chair. She stretched out her arms in a convulsive gesture of terror and despair, wrenched the minute hand to its old place at a quarter past three, and fell heavily to the floor.

II

Aunt Gertrude's will left me her bank and gas stocks, real estate, railroad bonds, and city sevens, and gave Harry the clock. We thought at the time that this was a very unequal division, the more surprising because my cousin had always seemed to be the favorite. Half in seriousness we made a thorough examination of the ancient timepiece, sounding its wooden case for secret drawers, and even probing the not complicated works with a knitting needle to ascertain if our whimsical relative had bestowed there some codicil or other document changing the aspect of affairs. We discovered nothing.

There was testamentary provision for our education at the University of Leyden. We left the military school in which we had learned a little of the theory of war, and a good deal of the art of standing with our noses over our heels, and took ship without delay. The clock went with us. Before many months it was established in a corner of a room in the Breede Straat.

The fabric of Jan Lipperdam's ingenuity, thus restored to its native air, continued to tell the hour of quarter past three with its old fidelity. The author of the clock had been under the sod for nearly three hundred years. The combined skill of his successors in the craft at Leyden could make it go neither forward nor backward.

We readily picked up enough Dutch to make ourselves understood by the townspeople, the professors, and such of our eight hundred and odd fellow students as came into intercourse. This language, which looks so hard at first, is only a sort of polarized English. Puzzle over it a little while and it jumps into your comprehension like one of those simple cryptograms made by running together all the words of a sentence and then dividing in the wrong places.

The language acquired and the newness of our surroundings worn off, we settled into tolerably regular pursuits. Harry devoted himself with some assiduity to the study of sociology, with especial reference to the round-faced and not unkind maidens of Leyden. I went in for the higher metaphysics.

Outside of our respective studies, we had a common ground of unfailing interest. To our astonishment, we found that not one in twenty of the faculty or students knew or cared a sliver about the glorious history of the town, or even about the circumstances under which the university itself was founded by the Prince of Orange. In marked contrast with the general indifference was the enthusiasm of Professor Van Stopp, my chosen guide through the cloudiness of speculative philosophy.

This distinguished Hegelian was a tobacco-dried little old man, with a skullcap over features that reminded me strangely of Aunt Gertrude's. Had he been her own brother the facial resemblance could not have been closer. I told him so once, when we were together in the Stadthuis looking at the portrait of the hero of the siege, the Burgomaster Van der Werf. The professor laughed. "I will show you what is even a more extraordinary coincidence," said he; and, leading the way across the hall to the great picture of the siege, by Warmers, he pointed out the figure of a burgher participating in the defense. It was true. Van Stopp might have been the burgher's son; the burgher might have been Aunt Gertrude's father.

The professor seemed to be fond of us. We often went to his rooms in an old house in the Rapenburg Straat, one of the few houses remaining that antedate 1574. He would walk with us through the beautiful suburbs of the city, over straight roads lined with poplars that carried us back to the bank of the Sheepscot in our minds. He took us to the top of the ruined Roman tower in the center of the town, and from the same battlements from which anxious eyes three centuries ago had watched the slow approach of Admiral Boisot's fleet over the submerged polders, he pointed out the great dike of the Landscheiding, which was cut that the oceans might bring Boisot's Zealanders to raise the leaguer and feed the starving. He showed us the headquarters of the Spaniard Valdez at Leyderdorp, and told us how heaven sent a violent northwest wind on the night of the first of October, piling up the water deep where it had been shallow and sweeping the fleet on between Zoeterwoude and Zwieten up to the very walls of the fort at Lammen, the last stronghold of the besiegers and the last obstacle in the way of succor to the famishing inhabitants. Then he showed us where, on the very night before the retreat of the besieging army, a huge breach was made in the wall of Leyden, near the Cow Gate, by the Walloons from Lammen.

"Why!" cried Harry, catching fire from the eloquence of the professor's narrative, "that was the decisive moment of the siege."

The professor said nothing. He stood with his arms folded, looking intently into my cousin's eyes.

"For," continued Harry, "had that point not been watched, or had defense failed and the breach been carried by the night assault from Lammen, the town would have been burned and the people massacred under the eyes of Admiral Boisot and the fleet of relief. Who defended the breach?"

Van Stopp replied very slowly, as if weighing every word:

"History records the explosion of the mine under the city wall on the last night of the siege; it does not tell the story of the defense or give the defender's name. Yet no man that ever lived had a more tremendous charge than fate entrusted to this unknown hero. Was it chance that sent him to meet that unexpected danger? Consider some of the consequences had he failed. The fall of Leyden would have destroyed the last hope of the Prince of Orange and of the free states. The tyranny of Philip would have been reestablished. The birth of religious liberty and of self-government by the people would have been postponed, who knows for how many centuries? Who knows that there would or could have been a republic of the United States of America had there been no United Netherlands? Our University, which has given to the world Grotius, Scaliger, Arminius, and Descartes, was founded upon this hero's successful defense of the breach. We owe to him our presence here today. Nay, you owe to him your very existence. Your ancestors were of Leyden; between their lives and the butchers outside the walls he stood that night."

The little professor towered before us, a giant of enthusiasm and patriotism. Harry's eyes glistened and his cheeks reddened.

"Go home, boys," said Van Stopp, "and thank God that while the burghers of Leyden were straining their gaze toward Zoeterwoude and the fleet, there was one pair of vigilant eyes and one stout heart at the town wall just beyond the Cow Gate!"

III

The rain was splashing against the windows one evening in the autumn of our third year at Leyden, when Professor Van Stopp honored us with a visit in the Breede Straat. Never had I seen the old gentleman in such spirits. He talked incessantly. The gossip of the town, the news of Europe, science, poetry, philosophy, were in turn touched upon and treated with the same high and good humor. I sought to draw him out on Hegel, with whose chapter on the complexity and interdependency of things I was just then struggling.

"You do not grasp the return of the Itself into Itself through its Otherself?" he said smiling. "Well, you will, sometime."

Harry was silent and preoccupied. His taciturnity gradually affected even the professor. The conversation flagged, and we sat a long while without a word. Now and then there was a flash of lightning succeeded by distant thunder.

"Your clock does not go," suddenly remarked the professor. "Does it ever go?"

"Never since we can remember," I replied. "That is, only once, and then it went backward. It was when Aunt Gertrude—"

Here I caught a warning glance from Harry. I laughed and stammered, "The clock is old and useless. It cannot be made to go."

"Only backward?" said the professor, calmly, and not appearing to notice my embarrassment. "Well, and why should not a clock go backward? Why should not Time itself turn and retrace its course?"

He seemed to be waiting for an answer. I had none to give.

"I thought you Hegelian enough," he continued, "to admit that every condition includes its own contradiction. Time is a condition, not an essential. Viewed from the Absolute, the sequence by which future follows present and present follows past is purely arbitrary. Yesterday, today, tomorrow; there is no reason in the nature of things why the order should not be tomorrow, today, yesterday."

A sharper peal of thunder interrupted the professor's speculations.

"The day is made by the planet's revolution on its axis from west to east. I fancy you can conceive conditions under which it might turn from east to west, unwinding, as it were, the revolutions of past ages. Is it so much more difficult to imagine Time unwinding itself; Time on the ebb, instead of on the flow; the past unfolding as the future recedes; the centuries countermarching; the course of events proceeding toward the Beginning and not, as now, toward the End?"

"But," I interposed, "we know that as far as we are concerned the—"

"We know!" exclaimed Van Stopp, with growing scorn. "Your intelligence has no wings. You follow in the trail of Compte and his slimy brood of creepers and crawlers. You speak with amazing assurance of your position in the universe. You seem to think that your wretched little individuality has a firm foothold in the Absolute. Yet you go to bed tonight and dream into existence men, women, children, beasts of the past or of the future. How do you know that at this moment you yourself, with all your conceit of nineteenth-century thought, are anything more than a creature of a dream of the future, dreamed, let us say, by some philosopher of the sixteenth century? How do you know that you are anything more than a creature of a dream of the past, dreamed by some Hegelian of the twenty-sixth century? How do you know, boy, that you will not vanish into the sixteenth century or 2060 the moment the dreamer awakes?"

There was no replying to this, for it was sound metaphysics. Harry yawned. I got up and went to the window. Professor Van Stopp approached the clock.

"Ah, my children," said he, "there is no fixed progress of human events. Past, present, and future are woven together in one inextricable mesh. Who shall say that this old clock is not right to go backward?"

A crash of thunder shook the house. The storm was over our heads.

When the blinding glare had passed away, Professor Van Stopp was standing upon a chair before the tall timepiece. His face looked more than ever like Aunt Gertrude's. He stood as she had stood in that last quarter of an hour when we saw her wind the clock.

The same thought struck Harry and myself.

"Hold!" we cried, as he began to wind the works. "It may be death if you—"

The professor's sallow features shone with the strange enthusiasm that had transformed Aunt Gertrude's.

"True," he said, "it may be death; but it may be the awakening. Past, present, future; all woven together! The shuttle goes to and fro, forward and back—"

He had wound the clock. The hands were whirling around the dial from right to left with inconceivable rapidity. In this whirl we ourselves seemed to be borne along. Eternities seemed to contract into minutes while lifetimes were thrown off at every tick. Van Stopp, both arms outstretched, was reeling in his chair. The house shook again under a tremendous peal of thunder. At the same instant a ball of fire, leaving a wake of sulphurous vapor and filling the room with dazzling light, passed over our heads and smote the clock. Van Stopp was prostrated. The hands ceased to revolve.

IV

The roar of the thunder sounded like heavy cannonading. The lightning's blaze appeared as the steady light of a conflagration. With our hands over our eyes, Harry and I rushed out into the night.

Under a red sky people were hurrying toward the Stadthuis. Flames in the direction of the Roman tower told us that the heart of the town was afire. The faces of those we saw were haggard and emaciated. From every side we caught disjointed phrases of complaint or despair. "Horseflesh at ten schillings the pound," said one, "and bread at sixteen schillings." "Bread indeed!" an old woman retorted: "It's eight weeks gone since I have seen a crumb." "My little grandchild, the lame one, went last night." "Do you know what Gekke Betje, the washerwoman, did? She was starving. Her babe died, and she and her man—"

A louder cannon burst cut short this revelation. We made our way on toward the citadel of the town, passing a few soldiers here and there and many burghers with grim faces under their broad-brimmed felt hats.

"There is bread plenty yonder where the gunpowder is, and full pardon, too. Valdez shot another amnesty over the walls this morning."

An excited crowd immediately surrounded the speaker. "But the fleet!" they cried.

"The fleet is grounded fast on the Greenway polder. Boisot may turn his one eye seaward for a wind till famine and pestilence have carried off every mother's son of ye, and his ark will not be a rope's length nearer. Death by plague, death by starvation, death by fire and musketry— that is what the burgomaster offers us in return for glory for himself and kingdom for Orange."

"He asks us," said a sturdy citizen, "to hold out only twenty-four hours longer, and to pray meanwhile for an ocean wind."

"Ah, yes!" sneered the first speaker. "Pray on. There is bread enough locked in Pieter Adriaanszoon van der Werf's cellar. I warrant you that is what gives him so wonderful a stomach for resisting the Most Catholic King."

A young girl, with braided yellow hair, pressed through the crowd and confronted the malcontent. "Good people," said the maiden, "do not listen to him. He is a traitor with a Spanish heart. I am Pieter's daughter. We have no bread. We ate malt cakes and rapeseed like the rest of you till that was gone. Then we stripped the green leaves from the lime trees and willows in our garden and ate them. We have eaten even the thistles and weeds that grew between the stones by the canal. The coward lies."

Nevertheless, the insinuation had its effect. The throng, now become a mob, surged off in the direction of the burgomaster's house. One ruffian raised his hand to strike the girl out of the way. In a wink the cur was under the feet of his fellows, and Harry, panting and glowing, stood at the maiden's side, shouting defiance in good English at the backs of the rapidly retreating crowd.

With the utmost frankness she put both her arms around Harry's neck and kissed him.

"Thank you," she said. "You are a hearty lad. My name is Gertruyd van der Wert."

Harry was fumbling in his vocabulary for the proper Dutch phrases, but the girl would not stay for compliments. "They mean mischief to my father"; and she hurried us through several exceedingly narrow streets into a three-cornered market place dominated by a church with two spires. "There he is," she exclaimed, "on the steps of St. Pancras."

There was a tumult in the market place. The conflagration raging beyond the church and the voices of the Spanish and Walloon cannon outside of the walls were less angry than the roar of this multitude of desperate men clamoring for the bread that a single word from their leader's lips would bring them. "Surrender to the King!" they cried, "or we will send your dead body to Lammen as Leyden's token of submission."

One tall man, taller by half a head than any of the burghers confronting him, and so dark of complexion that we wondered how he could be the father of Gertruyd, heard the threat in silence. When the burgomaster spoke, the mob listened in spite of themselves.

"What is it you ask, my friends? That we break our vow and surrender Leyden to the Spaniards? That is to devote ourselves to a fate
far more horrible than starvation. I have to keep the oath! Kill me, if
you will have it so. I can die only once, whether by your hands, by the
enemy's, or by the hand of God. Let us starve, if we must, welcoming
starvation because it comes before dishonor. Your menaces do not
move me; my life is at your disposal. Here, take my sword, thrust it
into my breast, and divide my flesh among you to appease your hunger.
So long as I remain alive expect no surrender."

There was silence again while the mob wavered. Then there were
mutterings around us. Above these rang out the clear voice of the girl
whose hand Harry still held—unnecessarily, it seemed to me.

"Do you not feel the sea wind? It has come at last. To the tower!
And the first man there will see by moonlight the full white sails of
the prince's ships."

For several hours I scoured the streets of the town, seeking in vain
my cousin and his companion; the sudden movement of the crowd
toward the Roman tower had separated us. On every side I saw evidences of the terrible chastisement that had brought this stout-
hearted people to the verge of despair. A man with hungry eyes chased
a lean rat along the bank of the canal. A young mother, with two dead
babes in her arms, sat in a doorway to which they bore the bodies of
her husband and father, just killed at the walls. In the middle of a
deserted street I passed unburied corpses in a pile twice as high as
my head. The pestilence had been there—kinder than the Spaniard,
because it held out no treacherous promises while it dealt its blows.

Toward morning the wind increased to a gale. There was no sleep
in Leyden, no more talk of surrender, no longer any thought or care
about defense. These words were on the lips of everybody I met: "Daylight will bring the fleet!"

Did daylight bring the fleet? History says so, but I was not a witness. I know only that before dawn the gale culminated in a violent
thunderstorm, and that at the same time a muffled explosion, heavier
than the thunder, shook the town. I was in the crowd that watched
from the Roman Mound for the first signs of the approaching relief.
The concussion shook hope out of every face. "Their mine has reached
the wall!" But where? I pressed forward until I found the burgomaster,
who was standing among the rest. "Quick!" I whispered. "It is beyond
the Cow Gate, and this side of the Tower of Burgundy." He gave me a
searching glance, and then strode away, without making any attempt
to quiet the general panic. I followed close at his heels.

It was a tight run of nearly half a mile to the rampart in question.
When we reached the Cow Gate this is what we saw:

A great gap, where the wall had been, opening to the swampy fields beyond: in the moat, outside and below, a confusion of upturned faces, belonging to men who struggled like demons to achieve the breach, and who now gained a few feet and now were forced back; on the shattered rampart a handful of soldiers and burghers forming a living wall where masonry had failed; perhaps a double handful of women and girls, serving stones to the defenders and boiling water in buckets, besides pitch and oil and unslaked lime, and some of them quoiting tarred and burning hoops over the necks of the Spaniards in the moat; my cousin Harry leading and directing the men; the burgomaster's daughter Gertruyd encouraging and inspiring the women.

But what attracted my attention more than anything else was the frantic activity of a little figure in black, who, with a huge ladle, was showering molten lead on the heads of the assailing party. As he turned to the bonfire and kettle which supplied him with ammunition, his features came into the full light. I gave a cry of surprise: the ladler of molten lead was Professor Van Stopp.

The burgomaster Van der Werf turned at my sudden exclamation. "Who is that?" I said. "The man at the kettle?"

"That," replied Van der Werf, "is the brother of my wife, the clockmaker Jan Lipperdam."

The affair at the breach was over almost before we had had time to grasp the situation. The Spaniards, who had overthrown the wall of brick and stone, found the living wall impregnable. They could not even maintain their position in the moat; they were driven off into the darkness. Now I felt a sharp pain in my left arm. Some stray missile must have hit me while we watched the fight.

"Who has done this thing?" demanded the burgomaster. "Who is it that has kept watch on today while the rest of us were straining fools' eyes toward tomorrow?"

Gertruyd van der Werf came forward proudly, leading my cousin. "My father," said the girl, "he has saved my life."

"That is much to me," said the burgomaster, "but it is not all. He has saved Leyden and he has saved Holland."

I was becoming dizzy. The faces around me seemed unreal. Why were we here with these people? Why did the thunder and lightning forever continue? Why did the clockmaker, Jan Lipperdam, turn always toward me the face of Professor Van Stopp? "Harry!" I said, "come back to our rooms."

But though he grasped my hand warmly his other hand still held that of the girl, and he did not move. Then nausea overcame me. My head swam, and the breach and its defenders faded from sight.

V

Three days later I sat with one arm bandaged in my accustomed seat in Van Stopp's lecture room. The place beside me was vacant.

"We hear much," said the Hegelian professor, reading from a note-book in his usual dry, hurried tone, "of the influence of the sixteenth century upon the nineteenth. No philosopher, as far as I am aware, has studied the influence of the nineteenth century upon the sixteenth. If cause produces effect, does effect never induce cause? Does the law of heredity, unlike all other laws of this universe of mind and matter, operate in one direction only? Does the descendant owe everything to the ancestor, and the ancestor nothing to the descendant? Does destiny, which may seize upon our existence, and for its own pur-poses bear us far into the future, never carry us back into the past?"

I went back to my rooms in the Breede Straat, where my only com-panion was the silent clock.

Newton's Brain

Jakub Arbes

(TR. Josef Jiri Král)

I want to tell an amusing story and yet begin at a grave. It is cynical; but I hope that after a few words of explanation even tender souls will forgive me.

Severe and implacable Science has robbed many of us of the sweetest dream of life; her cruel hand has torn asunder that veil which has covered the destiny of living beings after death, and a dreadful, but more or less clear, perspective opens to every one who trusts to her proofs, instead of to old traditional, though pleasant, prejudices.

Why, then, should we lament at the grave of a man who believed—nay, what is more, who was convinced—that all that blesses or grieves us ends with death? Why mourn the death of a man who disliked sorrow?

The man of whom I speak had been a friend of mine from his early youth, and died—or, more correctly, was killed—in the battle of Königgrätz, as an officer of Prince Konstantin's regiment. A Prussian sabre cut his skull in two.

His father was manager of Prince Kinský's garden. We were remote relations; and although my friend's family was quite rich, while mine was poor, we lived in most intimate friendship for almost twenty years. We played together in childhood and studied together in boyhood.

Our life and studies were as peculiar as our inclinations. At first we busied ourselves with everything that came into our hands: we examined, analyzed, and discussed whatever chance would bring us. Our debates were lively—nay, impassioned. But the exchange of strange, often eccentric opinions was pleasing and tempting; and there was not a single day, perhaps, that we did not debate something seemingly beyond solution. This thoughtless, desultory study naturally had no practical ends; but it developed our dialectics and inflamed our fancy, which often performed real wonders in the world of the *bizarre*.

To the no small grief of our fathers, neither I nor my friend was very proficient at school.

141

In our "private" studies, however,—that is, in those sciences which we loved above all,—we excelled all our fellow-students. Nature had endowed me with ugliness and my friend with beauty, and our inclinations were similarly dissimilar: I liked dry and tiresome mathematics, whereas he preferred the fresh and noble natural sciences. But we were so far from a true scientific course that I really do not know whether I should not regard all we studied then as mere play.

There was, however, some definite end in my friend's studies. He studied mainly physics, chemistry, mechanics, and a few kindred branches,—but all with a view to *escamotage*. God knows when and where he conceived the idea of having special talents for *escamotage*; but from that time nothing interested him unless it had some connection with his hobby. In all his doings he aimed at acquiring skill in that playful pseudo-science, as he called it; and from his favorite sciences he picked out only what was related to it.

His father knew nothing about it, for he worked in secret. I was his only confidential friend, and it was in my room that the most varied experiments were performed. Every single penny that he could earn or get he turned toward buying magical tools, or books on *escamotage*; all of which he deposited in my room. In a few years there were so many curious instruments and appliances heaped within this narrow precinct that it looked very much like the study of a mediaeval alchemist.

Pursuing his hobby with zeal, my friend made such rapid progress in *escamotage* as showed that he was really very gifted. But the more he prospered in it the more his passion grew; and thus it often happened that while I was busy figuring out how high, under certain conditions, a balloon of a certain weight filled with one or another gas must rise, only a few feet from me my friend was repeating for the thousandth time a trifling experiment—how, at a moment's notice, to throw a given card out of a pack.

Oftentimes he would experiment in my absence, and then surprise me with many a clever piece of work. His labors were never superficial, and he despised common jugglery. His secret lay in aptly combining various mechanical, chemical, and physical effects. Statics and dynamics, optics with its branches, acoustics, magnetism, electricity, synthetical and analytical chemistry,—all these and in part other sciences also, as astronomy, anatomy, physiology, were mastered by him with an unusual earnestness in the course of seven or eight years; but all with a view to *escamotage*.

He bought every book or pamphlet, no matter how trifling, which dealt with *escamotage* or kindred matters, as magic, alchemy, astrology, magnetism, and somnambulism, mystics, chiromancy, and the like. His library, which, like his instruments, he kept in my room, was an odd collection. Beside books of actual value, works of famous *savants* like Newton, Linné, Locke, Leibnitz, Bacon, Arago, Wolf, Lavoisier, Cartesius, Brown, Mohs, Cuvier, Humboldt, etc., you might see books of unknown or forgotten pseudo-scientists and charlatans; e.g., "Ten Books on the Secrets of Nature," by Paracelsus Bombastus, published in Strasburg in 1570; or Mehnu's "Mirror of Alchemy;" Bockmann's "Archives of Magnetism and Somnambulism;" Cagliostro's "Adventures;" Commiers's "Les Oracles des Sybilles," published about a hundred years ago; Crusius's work on Schroepfer's art of summoning spirits; Wincer's "Demonology," and many other like works. But the clear mind of my friend was elevated above that enormous mass of men's errors. He studied those strange books rather from curiosity than for use, although he was well aware that knowledge of such mental aberrations might assist him in strengthening natural delusions.

His work was not only thorough, but also independent. He not only learned known experiments, but invented new ones, and through systematical efforts endeavored to place his pseudo-science upon a broad and secure basis. No wonder, then, that later his performances surpassed all expectations. His elegant appearance, his eloquence, a light and even sarcastic wit, and a technical skill acquired through many years' training served him well in the most difficult experiments. As evidence of his skill, I shall mention a few out of many hundreds of more or less familiar experiments which I have myself seen: swallowing burning tar and stones, drawing threads and ribbons out of one's mouth, thrusting a knife into one's breast, are mostly feats of obsolete jugglery; but he knew how to perform these and other tricks so well that he could rival the most famous magician.

At the wedding feast of one of my relatives he once performed an original and pretty experiment: we were seated at a long table, in the centre of a spacious hall. There were about twelve persons in all. The bride was sitting at the head of the table, the bridegroom beside her, then the bridesmaid and the groomsman. I sat opposite the bridesmaid; my friend was at the other end of the table, about nine feet from the bride. We were in gay spirits. The menu was excellent, and joke and jest soon ruled the field of talk. When the feast was near its end a large deep dish of boiled crabs was served and placed before the bride. But she either did not fancy that dish or was too mindful of etiquette; for she asked the groom to pass it on. He obeyed, and the dish passed from hand to hand until it came, though nearly empty, back to the bride. Only small crabs were left, and seeing that the groom had not yet been served, the bride was about to pick out for him one or two of the best that were left; she bowed her head a little, looked over the dish with her pretty blue eyes, and seized the largest crab. But hardly had she put it on the groom's plate when she shrieked in terror and pushed back from the table: from the plate there looked at her a loathsome toad.

"What's that?" the bridegroom cried out, and stabbed the creature with his fork. The toad leaped from the plate upon the table in front of the bride. All the guests showed surprise; but my friend, quietly sitting at the other end of the table, said, "Why do you stab the little unfortunate?" Then he arose and touched the toad, which leaped over the bride's head toward the door.

The bridegroom jumped from his seat, and with one foot trod upon it. To the amazement of all it moaned in a human voice, "Alas, now I am dead!" The groom stepped back, my friend stooped to the floor and, instead of a toad, picked up a snow-white glove. Taking the bride's handkerchief, he wrapped the glove in it, and, placing the handkerchief before the bride, he murmured, like the famous Bosco, the magic Italian formula, "*Spiriti miei, ubbidite!*" And when one of the guests had unfolded the handkerchief he found there a pair of choice gold ear-rings—my friend's gift to the bride.

To prove the death of a sparrow, pigeon, hare, mole, or some other little animal, and then with a penknife cautiously to take out its brain from the skull, replace it with a perfumed piece of cotton, and then to order the animal slowly to wake up to life as though it were reviving from a swoon, and afterward to jump up and fly or flee away, is a feat of *escamotage* well enough known; but my friend would perform it in so many ways that it interested even those spectators who had many times seen like experiments.

I should need a thick book to exhaust his repertory; but from the few examples I have mentioned it will be seen that he could honorably compete with the most skilful conjurors. His main efforts, however, were directed toward summoning spirits. His apparatus and the means he employed were concealed even from me. Once he told me if I wished to see any historical personage that he would call him. I named Napoleon I.

Several nights had passed, but Napoleon did not put in an appearance; once, however, after I had forgotten the promise of my friend, I was awakened from sleep by a gentle tapping at my door. Rising, I rubbed my eyes; but as the tapping was repeated I asked, "Who is there?" No one answered; the door quietly opened, and in stepped, with a grave gait, Napoleon I., just as I had oftentimes seen him pictured,—in a gray coat, white breeches, with high riding-boots and the historical three-cornered hat. Silently he walked to the window, and

back to the door. I wanted to address the vision, but did not; and as a
curiosity I must confess that to this day I do not know *why* I did not.

I did not see more experiments of this kind. Whenever I wished
anything like it my friend always referred me to some later time when
he would have all the necessary apparatus and be better skilled. Sometimes he told me that he was engaged in constructing automatons,
with the aid of which he expected to perform real "miracles," and delude entire companies of *savants* and scientists. He intended to invite a
considerable number of friends and lovers of this kind of amusement,
and to perform experiments of the most complicated and intricate
kinds. He assured me that I would really be surprised; and, taking all
I saw into account, I could readily judge that he would fulfil his word.

We lived and studied thus for several years. Our study—many-
sided at first, afterward one-sided—was not fruitless. Shortly before
1860 our records were so low that we had to stay another year in the
same class. We stayed; and at the end of the year we failed again, and
next year we failed the third time. The father of my friend, who often
jokingly threatened to apprentice his son to a cobbler if he continued
to fail, finally lost all patience, and, in a family conference, it was
decreed that the best thing for him to do would be to become a soldier. He did not object, and a short time afterward called on me
dressed in the uniform of a cadet of the foot regiment of Prince
Konstantin of Russia.

" Well, what are *you* doing?" he inquired, shaking hands with me.

"I am going to be a carpenter."

"Forever?"

"I do not know; I am practising now, or, in other words, I am entered
as an apprentice, although I have not yet had an axe in my hands."

"And probably you never will have one," laughed the young can-
didate of a bloody trade.

"Maybe," I replied; "and probably your hands will never touch any
of your magic tools any more!"

"Far from it! I have just come to rid you of this rubbish. Why, you
can hardly move here!"

"Very well. But where shall we put it?"

"To-morrow I shall send several boxes; you will help me to pack them.
I shall have them secretly delivered in the cellars of the Prince's castle;
and should I ever—when I feel lonesome in Trieste or Pesth, or some
Catholic village of the Tyrol, you know—well, then I shall write to you,
and you will look up the necessary instruments and send them to me."

I promised to do so. The next day we filled no less than five large
boxes with books, apparatus, and other magicians' trash. On the following day the boxes were carried away. We saw each other several more

times; but two or three weeks afterward he was ordered to leave for Königgrätz, the seat of his regiment. From then on I was lonely. My friend did not write, nor did I; and thus our formerly indissoluble friendship ended with mutual, though only seeming, indifference.

Two years later—I believe it was in January or February of 1866—my friend sent me a letter. He told me various incidents of his life, recalled the "folly" of his studies, and, asking me to reply soon, concluded thus:

Do you know the phrase "Let pleasure live"? If you do not, you would learn to know it in its full extent if you were an officer of the same regiment with me. I should never ask for jollier comrades or a more pleasant life. Only sometimes,—sometimes only, understand,—when the last days of the month have come and the salary has gone, I feel rather melancholy. Several times I thought how I might prevent this, but never ventured to follow my wishes, and therefore I beg you now, write me if you know of any one who would be as crazy now as I was years ago. Possibly he might purchase either all or a part at least of my tools and instruments, which I have stored in the cellars of Prince Kinský's villa.

I did not expect such a conclusion of the letter. Knowing his passion for his favorite pursuit, I could not believe that he had freed himself altogether from it; and thinking that this was either a momentary fancy or an *escamoteur's* attempt to deceive me, I simply replied that I knew of no one who would buy that which he offered for sale.

A partial proof, at least, that I was not mistaken was his second letter. He declared that after all his endeavors to forsake and forget his folly, *escamotage*, he could not but try if he could rid himself of his passion by selling his apparatus; but that as soon as he sent the letter he felt sorry for having written it, and he added that even in case a purchaser had been found he would not have sold his instruments. In times of leisure, he wrote, he always thought of constructing his automatons; and he assured me that if his exhibition of them should ever take place it would be magnificent.

Shortly before the Austro-Prussian war was declared, I received one more letter from my friend—the last one. It was again written in a gay, almost frivolous tone. I give here the following passage:

In a few days, perhaps, we shall be ordered to go to the battlefield. Pity your unhappy friend. Without any apparatus, cards, mirrors, tinctures, and other necessaries, he will have to murmur, "*Spiriti miei, ubbidite!*" and the "spirits," always obedient, will, mayhap, for the first time refuse obedience. In the midst of a rain of bullets a small piece of lead is more powerful than magic *formulæ*, and my sword and my revolver will, perhaps, make many a one familiar with the mysterious truth that no human power can. Eh! why fall into sentimentality? Sooner or later each of us will learn, as have those innumerable millions of creatures who have preceded us, whether life ends with death. Why this useless philosophizing? When the last fierce struggle shall come, I shall, perhaps, mournfully beg, "*Spiriti miei, ubbidite!*" or, it may be, I shall not think of my "*spiriti*" at all.

Yet there is one thing I beg of you: should I get killed, don't mourn! Call our old friends together, and then think of me with cups of wine in your hands. If you grant this request, you may be sure that, even after that, I shall once more at least call on you.

Reading the last lines I smiled as we smile at a paradox.

From then on I heard nothing more of my friend until after the battle of Königgrätz. Just before the complete stoppage of the mails I received the following letter:

Dear Sir: A young officer, a first lieutenant of the Königgrätz regiment, has to-day been brought to our town. He is severely wounded,—his skull is cut in two,—and he is constantly beside himself. He was found this morning, about an hour's journey hence, in a gorge, whither he seems to have crawled after being wounded. His identity has not yet been established; but I hope it will be either to-day or to-morrow. In a letter found in his pocket I found your address, and send you this sad news so that you may inform his relatives and friends.

Respectfully yours,
P. Vojta Nosal,
Parson, Nechanice.

Travelling through regions occupied by the Prussian army was neither easy nor pleasant; still, I decided at once to leave for Nechanice. I wrote a note to my friend's father, and enclosing the Parson's letter sent it by a messenger; then, without waiting for a reply, I took a train for Kolin, and thence proceeded to Nechanice in a coach.

I arrived at two o'clock in the morning. Prussian guards stopped the coach before the town. I told them where I was going, and a soldier was ordered to accompany me to the Parsonage. In a few minutes the coach stopped before the Parson's house; I rang the bell, a man opened the gate, heard the reason for my coming, and went to announce me to the Parson, just come back from tending a Saxon officer who lay dying in the church with other wounded soldiers. The Parson welcomed me politely, and, rejecting as politely my excuse for disturbing him so late, he led me to the upper floor, where he had his drawing-room and several other rooms arranged to receive the wounded. "His name has not yet been ascertained," the Parson said, as he opened the door; "but I hope you will recognize him."

We entered. The room was half dark. Along the walls there lay about twenty soldiers on improvised beds on the floor; several bedsteads bearing those severely wounded stood near the windows. The Parson led me to one of these, and silently raised the light. The head of the wounded man was surrounded with ice. I looked into his pale face, and at once recognized my friend. He was still beside himself: there he lay motionless, with his eyes half shut, and his heavy breath was the only sign of life.

"It is three days now," the Parson whispered, "since he was brought hither, and the physicians give up all hope. They recommend quiet, ice, and quinine."

I was going to speak to my friend; but seeing his hard struggle I turned away, and we left the room. In the hall I thanked the Parson for his kindness, and was about to go; but he courteously invited me to be his guest at least until the next morning. Being tired to death, I gladly accepted the invitation, and stepped with my host into a large room on the ground floor.

"Do you know anything particular about my friend's accident, reverend sir?" I asked, as we were seated at a large table.

"In the terrible confusion that has reigned here for several days," the Parson answered, "it was impossible to obtain any certain information; for as yet we know nothing more about the dreadful battle of the third of July than a few details we learned from those slightly wounded. The regiment of your friend took part in the battle of Jicín, where it was severed. One division retreated to Smirice; the other, the stronger of the two, turned southward, and was then joined to the first army corps. On the third of July this division was among the reserves of the first army corps, and it appears to have been sent to the aid of those fighting near Probluz about four o'clock in the afternoon; and in this skirmish your friend was wounded. Judging from the wound itself, he must have been struck with a sabre just as he was stooping down for something; for the upper part of the skull is almost wholly split off. His wound is a deadly one, and all the surgeons who have inspected the wound are wondering not a little that he is still alive."

Hardly had he said this when the door opened. In came one of the men who attended the wounded, and whispered something to the Parson. The sad look of the priest caused me involuntarily to ask:

"Is he dead?"

"Dead," the Parson sadly repeated.

Once more we went into the drawing-room. My friend lay on his bed, uncovered. His youthful face, once so handsome, wore an expression unutterably painful.

"He must be buried this morning," the Parson remarked. I stepped close to the bed and touched my friend's hand. It was ice-cold. Tears filled my eyes. I turned away, and, being unable to speak, went downstairs with the Parson. The first dawn of day was already pouring in through the windows. Leaving me in the first room, the Parson went to his bedroom. I lay down, dressed, upon a sofa, but could not fall asleep. About two hours later the yard was full of men. I arose, and walking about the room awaited the funeral in feverish excitement.

After nine o'clock all soldiers that died of their wounds during the night were buried. I escorted my friend on his last journey, I saw how he was let down into the grave, and with a broken heart I returned to Prague.

Now, after many years have passed, after I have seen so many times how mercilessly Death often rages among the living, how suddenly his icy breath overtakes even vigorous persons,—now I can bear even my friend's death more easily, in accordance with his wishes and views, as a welcome deliverance from the griefs and woes with which so-called Providence has so liberally overwhelmed mortals. At that time, however, I was young—that is, at an age when the death of a beloved friend deeply affects even a person less sensitive than I was, and therefore it is no wonder that this death was a crushing blow.

At first it seemed to me impossible that he should be really dead. But when, at times, I recalled all the details, when I reminded myself of the truth that the grave never gives up its prey, when I reflected that I could never, never see my friend any more, that for me and for everybody else he was forever lost,—I felt an inexpressible bitterness. And yet, whenever I thought of him, the words of his last letter always came to my mind: "Should I get killed, don't mourn! Call our old friends together, and then think of me with cups of wine in your hands."

I held it to be my duty to fulfil even this last wish of his; but at first I was prevented by grief, and later by studies, which I renewed with double zest. Yet all mental toil could not obliterate his memory, or drive away the thought that I was violating our friendship in not fulfilling his request.

Nearly four months had passed since his death, and the autumn had already come, when I determined to perform his last wish. Toward the end of October I invited all our old comrades and some acquaintances to come in the evening to a small inn in the Maltá Strana, renowned for its wine, where in the past we had spent many an hour in merriment. But when I went there, I found that out of the twelve invited friends there had come—not a single one.

I sat sadly down, ordered a bottle of Bohemian wine, and betook myself to thinking. The tavern was empty, and so I could think uninterruptedly; and I thought of friendship, faithfulness, life, death, and God knows of what else. My thoughts and recollections were gloomy, bitter, painful. No wonder that one of the most vivid was the memory of my friend. His image still was vivid enough in my mind, though not as vivid as when I left Nechanice four months ago. It was losing its vividness, and the thought that sometime it would vanish altogether, and that after some years I should probably be unable to recall a single feature of his face, caused my soul great bitterness.

"Never!"— for the first time in my life did I understand the deep and fearful meaning of that simple word that is so often spoken every day. Never to see a beloved face; never to touch a dear hand—never—never!

The longer I meditated upon the meaning of that fatal little word, the more hopeless were the thoughts which swarmed in my head. But what gave birth to those dark thoughts was not so much the circumstances under which they originated as my own mental fatigue. For I had lately studied so earnestly that I had hardly left my room for two weeks. He who knows from experience how a long mental strain exhausts a man will understand my condition. For several months I had studied chiefly optics and mathematics as applied to astronomy; but my studies did not progress as I wished, and in my soul there was that chaos which precludes a clear comprehension of the more important principles of science.

No wonder that I oftener sought a glass than usual; no wonder that I left the tavern sooner than I had intended, and that, when I returned to my room, I felt more tired than when I left. I sat upon a chair near my writing-desk, took a book out of the case at random, opened it, and began reading. I had hardly glanced over half a page when I pushed the book aside, and resting my head on both my hands went on thinking, and by and by began to slumber.

All of a sudden I heard the hollow rattling of a carriage. I lifted my head and listened. A dead stillness was around me; only now and then I heard the moan of the autumnal wind. The rattling sound came nearer and nearer, until the carriage stopped, it seemed, in front of the house where I dwelt. I wanted to rise and look from the window, but being tired I overcame my curiosity and remained seated. I heard how some one rang the janitor's bell, and how the door opened and was closed.

No one lived in the house who would come home in a carriage; but the sound of voices, especially the janitor's voice, showed that the comer was one who had a right to enter. In a few moments drowsiness overcame me again. I cannot say how long I dozed, but I was awakened by a gentle tapping at the chamber door. Again I lifted up my head and listened. A lamp was burning on the table before me, only faintly illuminating my study with its yellowish light; all around was as still as the grave.

But what is that? Again I heard a distinct knocking at the door.

"Come in!" I said with a feeble voice.

The door opened quietly, and in the dusk I saw the tall figure of a man. I was about ten steps from him, and could not distinguish his features nor his dress.

"Who are you, and what do you wish so late?" I addressed the figure that stood motionless at the door. Without answering, the man opened wide the door, and the yellowish glitter of the lamp fell upon his face. I cried out in amazement; I tried to jump up, but my legs were too heavy. There he stood at the door. It was—my friend!

For a few moments the silence was unbroken. Not uttering a word, he stood motionless, while I could not turn my eyes away from him. His face was deadly pale; but the clear blue eyes were sparkling with life, and a light, kindly smile played about his lips.

"Good evening," he said, after a while, and stepped forward a little. Hearing the clatter of a sabre, I noticed that he was dressed as a military officer.

"Why! are you not dead?" I asked, astonished.

"How can I be dead, and stand before you?" he replied, with his clear, agreeable voice.

"Am I asleep or awake?" I uttered, forcedly. "Did I not see you dying and dead—at Nechanice—with your skull cut in two?"

"Possibly you saw me, and possibly you saw some one else," was the answer of my unexpected guest; "but now you see me standing before you safe and alive—there can be no doubt. Here is my hand!"

I hesitated a moment, but finally shook hands with him, and I found that his hand was not cold, but as warm as formerly.

"You complied with my last request," my friend continued, "and I have kept my word; I have come to see you."

"But how is all this possible?" I inquired diffidently.

"It is all very simple," he answered; "but please allow me to sit down, and I shall briefly tell you everything, for I have no time to lose."

Silently I drew a chair nearer, and my friend sat down by me.

"Well?" I asked.

"Doubtless you saw only an officer who looked like me when you were at Nechanice. It was First Lieutenant Jiruš, who was seriously wounded in the battle of Probluz and died at Nechanice, as I learned afterward. The mistake was possible only because he resembled me, that's all."

"But how was it possible that my letter to you was found on him?"

"That is very simple, too. A few hours before the battle a greater part of our regiment was lying in reserve in a small grove. The troops were ready for battle; the officers were walking from one company to another, or stood in groups talking. You must not think that the light military heart is particularly grave before battle. Jokes are perpetrated even in the hottest fight—the more so while the soldiers are impatiently waiting for a signal to march or to fire. I well remember that I was not in good humor that day, and to escape *ennui* I took out your letter and read it a second time. By chance First Lieutenant Jiruš came unnoticed behind me, and thinking that I was reading a love-letter he snatched it in jest from my hands, intending to read it aloud to my colleagues; but at the same moment we were ordered to march out. Jiruš put the letter into his pocket and hastened to his company; while I drew my sabre and stepped into line. A moment later a fierce shooting followed, and we thought of nothing but the enemy. You know the end of the fight: I was captured, and have just returned from Königsberg, where I have been vexed with *ennui*."

"But why, at least, did you not write me a card?" I asked, when he finished.

"A mere whim," he answered quietly. "And besides, I followed your example, and wearied myself with mathematical and astronomical studies."

"But what brings you here so late? When did you come?" I asked urgently, being almost fully convinced that he was alive and well.

"I arrived this evening; but even yesterday our friends knew that I was coming, so they failed to go to the tavern where you invited them. You are the only one whom I did not inform, in order to surprise you the more. I come now to invite you to a banquet which my father gives in the castle of Prince Kinský, in celebration of my safe return. At the same time I must tell you that I shall give there the great performance in *escamotage* which, as you know, I have been preparing for years. My automatons and other apparatus are all in the best order, and I hope to interest all the guests."

Everything I had just heard and seen showed that my friend, supposed to be dead, had really come to see me, and that his passion for *escamotage* was unabated.

"But why is the banquet given this very day? Can it not be postponed?" I asked, after a while.

"What an idea!" said he. "My father gives the entertainment with the consent of Prince Kinský, who has invited many guests. Look, the castle is all illuminated!"

Then he stepped to the window, from which a part of Kinský's villa could be seen, and rolled up the curtain. All the windows of the palace were, indeed, lighted.

"The banquet has already begun, about an hour ago," he went on; "my performance will begin later, and for this reason I came to inform you. Come, if you like. But excuse me; you will have to come by foot alone. I must leave in haste and without you, purely for an *escamoteur's* reasons, of course. Will you come, then?"

"I will," I said, rising.

He arose quickly, shook hands, and left. I heard his steps, heard the door open and close, and then a carriage rattling along the street. I listened, listened until the sound died away.

All I had just witnessed was so strange, in spite of all explanation, that for a time I remained sitting motionless, unable to collect myself. Distrust soon arose in me. Being alone, and seeing nothing changed about me, I was ready to believe it all a dream; but the Prince Kinský's illuminated palace, which I saw from my window, confirmed the opinion that I was really awake, and that I was able, nay, obliged, to perform my friend's request.

I shall never forget the sensation I felt after his departure. I felt as happy as a man who was unexpectedly freed from some dreadful vision that had haunted him a long time. I felt an unusual briskness and strength. Without any long deliberation I put on an overcoat, took my hat, and left the room. I went slowly downstairs, knocked at the janitor's window, had the door opened, and walked into the street.

It was a clear autumn night. The pensive moon, lightly veiled in thin mist, hovered above Petrín, and in its silvery beams the moist pavement glittered like the surface of a lake curled by a gentle breeze. Now and then I felt the breath of a cold north wind. As the wind was blowing directly against my face, I hastened my pace, and in about a quarter of an hour I stood before the grated entrance of the Kinský park. The main gate and the side doors were wide open; and an old porter, an old acquaintance of mine, dressed in a fur coat, as though it were midwinter, was impatiently walking up and down.

"Are there many guests to-night?" I asked the porter.

"Yes, sir," he murmured in answer.

"Is it long since the celebration began?"

"Possibly; but I am not sure. About half an hour ago Frederic, the young gentleman, rode out and has just returned."

"What do they celebrate?"

"I do not know; but the young gentleman whom they thought dead came back, and undoubtedly it is in his honor."

"Really?" I whispered unwillingly; and now was I first fully convinced that all I had shortly before witnessed in my study was no delusion, but reality.

"I may go upstairs, may I?" I asked formally, knowing beforehand that the old porter would let me in, even if he had an express order not to admit any uninvited guest.

"Why, you are in the first place on my list of guests," he answered.

"Good-by, then," I said, and walked up the broad gravel drive.

The cold of the autumnal nights had left evident traces of its implacable destructive power in the park. The leaves of trees and bushes were yellow, and had mostly fallen. Here and there a tree stretched out perfectly bare branches. The dead silence of the night was broken only now and then by a blast of the cold north wind. I hurried on and soon saw the palace, about five hundred paces before me.

All the windows were lighted; in front of the villa I saw dark figures coming and going, and farther on stood a long row of carriages. A little later I heard low sounds of music, evidently coming from the villa. What kind of music it was I could not exactly tell; but it seemed to be rather melancholy, sad as a funeral march.

In a few moments, however, the music became silent, and I heard nothing but the scraping of the gravel under my feet. I hastened still more. The nearer I came to the palace the fewer dark personages I saw before it, and when I finally stopped directly in front of the villa all was as still and quiet as if the palace had been uninhabited. At some other time this would have seemed strange to me; but now, remembering that I was coming to a special celebration, given in honor of an *escamoteur* who, after many years of study, desired to surprise his guests with an extraordinary performance, I did not wonder even when on entering the foyer I found myself in utter darkness. I only looked back on hearing the clapping of a large door; but I judged that all this was done only to strengthen the effect.

I stopped and waited to see what would happen next; but deep silence and darkness reigned all around. After some time, after my eyes, coming suddenly from moonlight into darkness, had become adapted to the dark, I noticed a streak of light a few paces before me. Coming nearer, I found that it was due to the moonlight penetrating through the half-open door from an adjoining room.

I opened the door wide and entered. The room was vacant and without any furniture; and though I had not been in the castle for a long time I recollected that that room used to serve as an antechamber to the corridor leading to the main hall, where all greater banquets were usually held. I also remembered that this was the usual way to the main hall whenever a person did not wish to enter through the chief entrance. Knowing which way to go, I stepped to the window, through which the moonlight was pouring in, and near which there was a secret tapestried door leading to the corridor. Without any difficulty I found a small knob in the wall,—a secret spring,—and pressing the knob I opened the door, as I had often done in the past.

I saw before me a long vaulted corridor devoid of all ornaments. The moon shone faintly in through some windows, and there was light enough to enable one to see that the corridor was empty. The moonlight was so sharply reflected from the snowy walls and partly from the floor, paved with smooth, alternately white and black diamond-shaped stones, that I could tell every cloud that passed over the moon.

I entered the corridor; but to my astonishment a peculiar cold blew on me, as though it were open at the other end. I went on through it until I came to a point where it joined another corridor at a right angle.

This second corridor was empty, too. I went through that, and coming to a third corridor I thought I came to the entrance to the main hall. But in place of the door through which I had in past years so often entered the hall unnoticed, I found merely a bare wall. I went on, therefore, to the corner; but here I discovered a fourth corridor, forming a right angle with the third.

Doubtless during the few years since I had visited the palace many changes had taken place. The location of the corridors must have been altered, and the entrance to the hall destroyed or removed. I went through the fourth corridor, but found no door, no exit. At the same time I discovered that the corridors through which I had gone formed a rectangular parallelogram. Thus, from the fourth corridor I passed into the first. Judging by the light, I thought I was in the corridor which I entered from the antechamber; but I could not find the door again through which I came, and which had been mysteriously shut behind me. For several minutes I searched for a door in the walls, but in vain. I wondered how all this was possible, and finally I became convinced that I was in a series of corridors from which there could be no escape until my friend should think it best to utter his magical *"Efetta!"*

I must confess that I was surprised by this introduction into these arts. To entice a man in the night from his home, under a pretext that he is to come to a banquet, to lead him into a palace, let him enter through an open gate, and then decoy him into a labyrinth of corridors,—this was as difficult an experiment as it was original.

"Well, let us wait till the adroit magician thinks fit to release us from the prison," was my resolution; and I quietly walked up and down the four corridors until I found myself again at the point whence I had started. At times I would stop and listen; but I heard nothing but the wind, which finally became silent, and a mysterious stillness, interrupted only by the hollow echo of my steps, overspread the corridors.

At first I was perfectly quiet; but after about half an hour had passed I began to be a little impatient. Several times I shouted my friend's name; but in answer I merely heard an echo of my own voice.

Walking through the corridors at a constantly growing pace, I warmed myself a little; I felt the cold the more acutely when I slackened my pace or stopped. I had to walk faster and faster. In the true sense of the word I ran through all the corridors, stopping at that point where I supposed the door was by which I had entered. For a while I searched for the door; but the cold drove me on. My anxiety increased. It seemed to me that I had been wandering through the corridors fully three hours. Every minute was almost an hour to me. I stamped, clapped, and shouted; but the stillness was unbroken. And whenever I stopped, the mysterious cold forced me on. Again I ran; I felt that my blood boiled—that the sweat was running down my face; but a mysterious power urged me on. I saw nothing before me but a dark corridor, seemingly growing narrower, and I began to doubt whether all this were real. But immediately I remembered that I saw the castle illuminated, that I spoke to the porter, and heard the music; in a word, that all this must be a reality, ... and yet I could not comprehend why I heard only the hollow echo of my own steps and words, as though I were in an uninhabited palace. "Thus," I thought, "thus fares a man who, staggering from one error into another, is in vain looking for firm ground; thus arises the chaos of divergent notions and ideas which usually precedes that awful state of mind known as—insanity."

This thought suddenly arose in my mind, and instantly made my blood rise to my head. An involuntary cry escaped me; I tottered; my heavy legs ceased moving; I fell to the floor. Darkness spread over my soul.

But lo! what is that?

Does it not seem to me as though I were listening to gentle sounds of music, and as though a clear stream of light had flitted before me? I rub my eyes and try to get up. In a few moments I succeed.

I see that I am standing in an arched corridor; there is a door, only half shut, in front of me, and a stream of light comes in through the opening. I really hear music. I advance staggering toward the door.

Through the opening I look into a brightly illuminated hall. But my eyes are so dim that I cannot distinguish anything in the hall. But my consciousness is returning. I try to advance, but I stagger again, and have to lean against the wall. In that position I remain about five minutes; then I open the door a little more and glance into the hall.

I then first became fully satisfied that I was standing at the secret door so well known to me, and that the music I heard was coming from the hall, where I saw a considerable number of guests. But how it could have happened that I had wandered for about three hours, as it seemed to me, in the simplest labyrinth of four corridors forming a regular parallelogram, that I had been unable to find the door which was so near,—this I could not explain. At that time, however, I did not trouble myself about solving the enigma; my unusual excitement had not yet ceased, and I was curious, too, to learn who was in the hall and what would happen next. Putting off my overcoat and throwing aside my hat, I slipped through the door and remained standing on the sill, leaning against the doorposts.

The large, high hall was splendidly decorated, and illuminated with numberless lights, so that a person could find a grain of poppy-seed on the floor. The first look convinced me that there was a large and rare company assembled, but a company of men only.

There may have been about two hundred persons in the hall. They sat at tables which were so arranged in a half-circle that a person could easily walk around each table, and from each one could see a black curtain, reaching from the ceiling to the floor, and dividing off a part of the hall. A number of servants were waiting on the guests; others were busy bringing the most varied meats and drinks on silver plates. I was unable to discover where the band of music was placed, but I heard distinctly the soft sounds of a melancholy piece. The band was undoubtedly either in a recess or in some adjoining room. The hall was full of a gentle noise; I heard the murmur of the guests and the half-stifled calls of the lackeys; but to me all this was one unintelligible rustle, as when a distant waterfall disturbs the silence of the night.

No one seemed to notice me at first, and I was at full liberty to observe the guests. Though I did not know, except by name, a great many of the prominent citizens of Prague, yet I soon found out that the company assembled was a choice one.

Recollecting that the Kinskýs were cooperating with the father of my friend, I was not surprised to see a number of noblemen at one or two of the tables. I recognized one of the Princes Lobkovic, two Waldštýns, a Count of Thurn and Taxis, two Kaunices, the old Count Hanuš, of Kolovrat, the Rohans, etc.,—noblemen nearly all of whom had frequently been guests of the Kinskýs in the past. All these, and others whose names I did not know, were seated at one end of the half-circle of tables.

Neither was I surprised to find, at the opposite end of the half-circle, Prince Schwarzenberg, the Archbishop of Prague, two canons, the Abbot of Strahov, the generals of the Knights of the Cross and of the Maltese order, the Provost of Vyšehrad, and other ecclesiastical dignitaries; at the next table I saw the parsons of St. Nicholas and of Smíchov, and several other divines whom I did not know.

Next to the tables of the noblemen there were two or three tables where civil and military officers, Bohemian and German deputies, and governmental and city officials of various sorts were sitting. Then followed other guests, whom I classed as *savants* and university professors; for I had recognized some of my former teachers among them.

In the Bohemian literary world I knew—at that time—only Pfleger, who was related to my friend, and our beloved poet, Neruda, who had been my teacher and my friend's. Both of them, and many others, I found among the guests, engaged in lively discourse.

Our friends who failed to come to the inn when I invited them were also present, and sat at a table near by that of the men of letters.

I might perhaps have recognized many other prominent personages had I not been interrupted in my observations: one of the lackeys, passing by, stopped before me. I recognized an old acquaintance of my early years, when I used to be almost an everyday guest in the castle or in the park.

"Come at last!" he said, in a low voice; and his gray, deep-set little eyes glittered with a peculiar flame. "I must instantly announce that you have arrived. Please step down into the hall, and take a seat at the middle table." He pointed to the table where our friends were seated.

"Why at that table, exactly?" I asked.

"Because it has been so ordered," answered the poor fellow, who had been doing nothing else during all his life but obeying orders.

"But why?"

"I do not know, and I need not know. But it cannot be otherwise. Look how the guests are seated: There noblemen sit in a group; opposite them are the divines; here are the officials, and so forth. 'Each to his fellows,' was our motto. Thus there are seated in separate groups the physicians, lawyers, philosophers, architects, sculptors, actors, opera singers, painters, musicians, authors, and so on; even the people that have no calling are seated together."

"But why all this? No such ceremonies have ever been observed here," I remarked.

"They *were* not, that is true; this time, however, it has been so ordered," the lackey retorted. "Please," he added, in the pleading tone in which only a nobleman's servant knows how to beg without expressing his request in words. While speaking, he pointed again to the table where my friends were sitting.

"Well, I shall obey the order and take my seat accordingly, to spare you trouble," I said, softened, and walked to the table assigned me, while the lackey went through the hall and quickly disappeared through the main entrance.

The guests paid little or no attention to me. Some turned their heads; others glanced at me; but not having seen me coming in by the main door, they probably thought that I had left the table before and was now returning. Some shook hands with me; others greeted me with a kind smile or a bow of the head.

But before I sat down the gentle music had changed into a deafening *fanfare*. A few moments later the flourish ceased, a greater part of the lights were turned out, and as the black curtain was being drawn we heard a sonorous voice saying:

"The performance begins!"

The eyes of all present were fixed upon the curtain. When the curtain was fully drawn I beheld a platform covered with a black cloth. On the platform stood a low catafalque, supporting a metallic coffin. Around the coffin there was a multitude of beautiful exotic flowers. Large candles were burning on both sides of the coffin. At its head there lay a large laurel-wreath; farther down was an officer's hat and sabre; and at the foot, in front, was this simple epitaph:

FREDERIC WÜNSCHER,
Imp. Royal First Lieutenant.
Born on the 7th of July, 1841.
Died on the 7th of July, 1866.

There was a general surprise.

A stillness so great that the least whisper could have been easily heard spread over the hall. After a few moments the silence was broken by sad, touching voices singing the well-known "Salve Regina," seemingly coming from afar, perhaps from some of the adjoining rooms.

No one spoke a word as long as the singing lasted. Even after the singing ceased and a dead stillness filled the hall again, no one moved or stirred. Doubtless for the moment there was no one in the hall except myself who was conscious that all this was nothing more than an original opening of an *escamoteur's* performance.

The Archbishop rose first of all; evidently he was the most impatient. But at the same moment the lid of the coffin flew up with a din, and remained hanging in the air between the floor and the ceiling, just as they say the lid is hovering above Mohammed's coffin.

In the uncovered coffin I saw a dead body in the uniform of a military officer. Standing too far off, however, I could not distinctly see the features of the face.

The hall was still buried in silence.

First, after several minutes, one of the guests arose at the table where the physicians and men of science were seated. I at once recognized the expressive face of Dr. Sperlich, of Smíchov.

"Let us examine the body," he said, and walked briskly to the catafalque. His colleagues followed. Then the engineers and the architects arose, then others; the philosophers and the divines were the last. In a few moments the catafalque was surrounded by nearly all the guests. Only a few of the physicians stood close to the coffin—all the others looked on from a safe distance; hence it was not difficult for me to get near. Standing at the head of the corpse, I fastened my eyes upon the pale, set face.

It was the same face which I had seen at Nechanice after the battle of Königgrätz. Its likeness to the face of my friend was so striking that after looking awhile at the cold features I could not help believing that I saw his dead body.

Dr. Sperlich passed his hand over the forehead of the corpse, felt the pulse, unbuttoned the white jacket and the shirt, and declared that it really was an embalmed corpse that was lying in the coffin. Some of those standing nearest followed his example to test the truth of his words, and no one doubted it. I too put my hand upon the forehead; it was ice-cold. Bowing nearer to the face, I did not notice the least breath. The hand, too, was cold, and the half-uncovered bosom showed unmistakable signs of death.

In order to prove beyond any doubt that the body in the coffin was lifeless, Dr. Sperlich drew out a pocket-knife and thrust it into the chest of the corpse. The body was moved by the thrust, but otherwise remained unchanged. The guests could not comprehend this in any way. There was an exchange of opinion among some; others returned to their places. In five or six minutes there were not more than twenty persons remaining by the coffin. About to go back to my place, I looked once more at the corpse's face.

The rosy leaflet of an exotic plant lay on the rigid lips, and just as I fixed my eyes upon the face the leaflet shivered as though a feeble breath had touched it. I looked at the face more fixedly, and noticed that the eyebrows seemed to be trembling, and again the breast looked as though it had moved. At once I grasped the corpse's hand to see if my eyes were not deceived. The hand was no longer ice-cold, but warm; and it seemed to me as though its warmth were increasing. I was about to call Dr. Sperlich's attention to the sudden change, but before I could do so the eyes of the corpse slowly opened and closed again. A slight cry escaped my lips. Some of those standing nearest came still nearer; but in a moment all stepped back in amazement. The corpse moved, or rather shook convulsively, as though an electrical current had suddenly gone through it; and I distinctly perceived the symptoms of returning animal life.

About three minutes later the head moved, then both hands, and in a few moments the whole body was in motion. The corpse sat up with difficulty and remained awhile in that position; then it fell back into the coffin, then rose and sat up again. The surprise of those present grew into awe. Whatever may have been the effect of the unexpected occurrence upon this or that one of the guests, it was certain that there was no one who was not amazed in the highest degree. Evidently no one thought that the performance of an *escamoteur* would be opened in such an original way. All eagerly wondered what would come next.

After the corpse sat up in the coffin, a general silence prevailed. Not a finger stirred; all eyes were bent upon the wonderful automaton which the experts had just pronounced to be an embalmed corpse.

And now the corpse gave further signs of life! True, it sat motionless for some time, but its eyes glistened. Then it moved its head, and looked around as though it were seeking some one; then it nodded as if satisfied; a light smile passed over its face; the mouth opened and spoke: "*De mortuis nil nisi bene!*"

How strange! All that had been going on before the eyes of the guests until now failed to elicit one single word of admiration or surprise. The sound of the human voice drew out the first response, and stormy applause rang through the hall, accompanied by shouts of "Bravo!" "Well done!"

At the same time all the lights went out suddenly; utter darkness filled the hall. A few moments later, however, the lights were lighted again; but instead of the catafalque, the coffin, and the animated corpse, there appeared before our eyes a simple writing-desk and a chair, and behind the desk there stood my friend in an elegant black dress.

Again a long roar of applause filled the hall, and everybody shouted, "Very good!" or "Bravo!"

After the stormy manifestations of approval had subsided, my friend addressed the guests:

"You will excuse, gentlemen, this unusual way of opening my performance; but as I have begun, so shall I finish it; only between the acts permit me to say a few words which may interest some of you. You see a man before you whose brain is not his own, but—another's."

Then with his right hand my friend grasped the top of his head, and, as easily as if he were taking off his cap, he took off the upper part of his skull, and holding it awhile in his hand advanced a few steps to the foreground.

"Nearly all that I am going to tell you now will seem improbable," he said, "but any of the *savants* present may convince himself of its truth. Allow me!"

Stepping down into the half-circle of guests, he seated himself on a chair and continued:

"Let some one who knows anatomy and physiology examine my brain!"

At these words, some of the guests at the professors' table arose, surrounded my friend, and began to examine. One of them undertook an oral explanation:

"Truly, so it is! We really see the skull pared off and the surface of the brain. The surface shows quite normal convolutions. Under a microscope some of them might, perhaps, show some differences in size and form, but now we can only see a common surface. We see plainly also the well-known gray matter, composed of nerve-cells and deposited all along the surface in small convolutions; and, for the benefit of laymen, I add that modern physiologists designate this gray matter as the seat of consciousness, thought, talent, and recollection. More I do not pretend to say."

"It will be my turn now," my friend remarked, as he put the skull on his head and slowly walked back to his desk.

"The brain which one of my esteemed guests has just examined," said my friend, opening his preliminary explanations, "is not, as I have mentioned, my own, but another's. I borrowed it for the same purpose for which millions of others have for ages been borrowing the most precious results of the activity of other people's brains—their ideas; for it is easier to think with another's brain, to boast of another man's ideas, and to benefit thus oneself and others, than to hammer out an idea in one's own brain. I had long been thinking which brain would be the most suitable, and finally I decided to try the brain of a man whom the whole civilized world classes among its most acute thinkers. I knew that the brain of that man was preserved in the British Museum; by stratagem I succeeded in securing this invaluable treasure; and when, after the battle of Königgrätz, the longed-for opportunity came, and my own skull was cut off by a sabre, I replaced my brain with that of Newton."

"That is an impossibility!" was shouted at the table of the physicians, anatomists, and physiologists.

"An absurdity!" said the lawyers.

"Nonsense!" concluded the philosophers.

"A godless blasphemy!" sounded indignantly from the theologians' table.

This many-sided expression of displeasure failed to embarrass my friend. He must have expected it; and he went on quietly:

"I beg your pardon, my esteemed friends. Every one judges after his own fashion; every one perceives, qualifies, and names various conceptions and objects in the way he has learned and acquired, and as he likes. Different opinions and different names do not change the things themselves in the least; they remain such as they are in fact."

This sophistical turn apparently allayed the resentment of most of the guests, but convinced no one. Accordingly it was not surprising to hear new shouts from among the crowd:

"A proof! We want a conclusive proof."

"A conclusive proof"—my friend resumed his talk— "is something that I am unable to offer at this moment, just as none of us can furnish unanswerable proofs of the most ingenious hypothesis of all ages—Newton's law of universal gravitation. I must, therefore, ask my honored guests to accept my views, as those often do who, disregarding proof, rely always on their own conviction, so-called.

"Let us suppose, my honored guests, that my brain has really been supplanted by the brain of Newton.

"I suppose," my friend continued, "that every one of us will concede that the human brain has always been made of the same material, that ages ago it was composed of the same parts, that its actions were governed by the same laws, that its surface was composed of the same convolutions, and that ages ago, even, there was deposited in these convolutions that wonderful gray matter, surrounded with white matter and composed of nerve-cells, which modern physiologists designate as the seat of thought, reason, judgment, and talent. The chief organ of thinking and of talent is, therefore, the same. But what are its functions? Why do they differ so substantially from the working of that same organ in the past? Why is it that there do not arise in the brains of our age thoughts like those that originated in the brains of Homer, Sophocles, Æschylus, Euripides, Aristophanes, Shakespeare, Cervantes, Dante, Milton, Petrarch, Tasso, Calderon, Molière, Voltaire, Rousseau, and others? Where are the brains which gave birth to the wonderful works which have been left to us by Michael Angelo, Rafael Sanzio, Rubens, Titian, Murillo, Leonardo da Vinci, Van Dyke, Rembrandt, Hogarth, Salvator Rosa, Ostade, Ruysdael, or even by our own Škreta and Brandl? Where are the brains to be found to-day which marked the long array of ingenious sculptors beginning with Phidias, Skopas, and Praxiteles? Where are the brains which constructed plans

of magnificent domes, palaces, pantheons? Where are the brains of
Mozart, Beethoven, Haydn? Where are the brains of the Garricks,
Keans, Talmas, Rachels? And if we live in the age of progress, what
shows that progress?

"The object of my discourse will be plainly seen after my final experiment.

"The mysterious gray matter of the human brain, which our physiologists look upon as the source of thought and the home of mental
abilities, still remains the same in substance. Ideas spring from it,
and human talents are hidden in it. For this reason, notwithstanding
all the difference of ideas and faculties, the unknown laws which govern
this mysterious process remain forever the same; in a word, logic is
one and eternal. Who knows whether the brain of some farmer, me-
chanic, servant, or slave, long forgotten, if shaped under the same
circumstances, laboring in the same direction, under like conditions,
as the brain of Newton,—who knows whether that brain would not
have reached the same conclusions, or perhaps grander results, and
much sooner, than the brain of Newton?"

"No one will dispute a sentence so conditioned," came from an
unknown voice at the authors' table.

"Why, then, that absurd worship of the so-called geniuses, when
it is known that the same conditions under which this or that celebrated deed or work was done exist with thousands of others who do
not even attempt performance?"

"Bravo!" "Bravo!" the noblemen applauded.

"But why, too, that still more absurd worship of men without any
talent who have become famous only through the genius of others,
hired and paid?"

There was heard a suppressed murmur of disapproval from the
table of the noblemen and officials; but my friend went on:

"Why worship one's own genius, one's own deeds, one's own age?
Why those eternal eulogies on the age of enlightenment and progress,
when we are still so far from the true universal enlightenment, when
we know that all that the human mind has achieved in the course of ages
may be abused? Is not a modern workingman, attending a machine,
still the same slave as ever? Is his life any more pleasant, safer, or
happier than it used to be? Do we not know that all the sciences, from
mathematics (the queen) down to the last, often charlatanical pseudo-
science,—do we not know that all achievements, old and new, are alike
employed in the mutual killing of men? The progress of modern strat-
egy and military tactics shows that all newly discovered means of communication are used to convey large armies in the shortest time to
places where they may engage in reciprocal slaughter. Mathematics,

chemistry, optics, mechanics, and a series of other sciences furnish their latest and best productions to sub-serve that purpose. Ay, even history, dealing with mere facts, and pedagogy, pointing to models, have oftentimes the same object. What is the model heroism of which the historian speaks, what this modern drill,—these army orders,— but the refined means which stimulate human souls to a passionate, furious, and often useless battle?"

The military men fell in line with, "Don't insult your vocation!" and from the rear a deep voice asked:

"How is all this connected with the experiment?"

"Very simply," my friend replied. "My experiment is based on a scientific hypothesis."

"Well, why don't you take up your experiment?" the same unknown voice suggested.

"Go on with the lecture!" came from the tables to the right.

"No, no! The experiment! We want the experiment!" came from the left.

"Speak, speak!" urged the centre.

Such a noise and din arose in the hall that for a time not a word could be understood. Strange as it may seem, persons whose profession led them to frequent public speechmaking—the divines, legislators, and professors—showed the greatest impatience in calling for the experiment; whereas people who seldom tried to deliver a lecture in public—such as artists, architects, soldiers, etc.—evinced an especial willingness to listen to my friend's rhapsodical discourse.

"My esteemed guests are separated into two camps," he began, after the noise had subsided a little. "As a wretched artist, desiring to please all who appreciate my art, I cannot at present satisfy either party, for I do not know which possesses the keener appreciation of my performance. There remains nothing for me but to satisfy both; therefore I ask your permission to finish my talk, and then the experiment shall immediately follow."

"Very well!" all cried on the right, on the left, and in the centre; and my friend resumed:

"The modern man's proud boast of progress is really pitiable. It seems that a moment's success, often questionable, of some ingenious head dazzles a thousand others with a false vision of an amazing progress; and yet man's powerlessness appears daily in a more and more intensive light. Early in our youth our teachers told us that the human sight was feebler than that of the eagle or the falcon; that man's hearing, smell, touch, and other senses were duller than those of many animals. Man has known this long; hence his dreadful chase after some means to sharpen his senses. He strengthened them artificially, to be the more convinced how powerless, miserable, and wretched a being he is. He took a dissecting-knife, found and classified his organs, endeavored to find out their functions, established their importance and necessity, and became convinced that the life of the master of all creation, created 'in God's own image,' did not and does not substantially differ from the life of the most subordinate creatures. He has traced the operations of his mind; but the boundary line between good and evil he has not yet defined exactly. He has penetrated deeply into the universe, and has endeavored to ascertain the laws of the world; but he has been unable to repel the awful truth that merciless death and oblivion are awaiting him. Be born, live, and suffer; then perish, crumble into atoms, and vanish forever—such is the horrible prospective which the progress of science opens to man. To feign ignorance, to console oneself with illusions and Utopian fiction, does not help any, and is cowardly. Yet how do we regard human life in view of this horrible truth? Do we put a just value upon it? Which of us can step forward and show that a single life he has destroyed ever revived? Still we look on at fearful mutual murders—quick by means of force, or slow by means of enervating toil and suffering."

My friend paused as though he were going to rest for a time. Not the least whisper disturbed the dead stillness. It was evident that the speaker tried to suppress his thoughts rather than give them free play; and for this very reason his discourse made a favorable impression upon those present.

After a few moments he proceeded:

"Neither I nor anybody else could return life to a dead body. All my art is based on quickness; and in everything I rely upon the relative slowness of thought. It is generally supposed that there is nothing faster than thought. This is a mistaken notion. Figures—those cold, merciless, but most sincere friends of reasoning—have proved the contrary. It has been ascertained that compared with the velocity of light and electricity the velocity of thought is astonishingly small. If I touch the skin of an adult's leg, it takes no less than about one-third of a second before the sensation is reported by the spinal cord to the brain—the central organ of consciousness; whereas in the same time light will travel over more than fourteen thousand geographical miles; electricity, conducted by a copper wire, nearly thirty-one thousand miles. Just as slowly as the sensation of touch passes through the spine, every notion evidently passes through the brain."

Again he paused.

I must confess that up to this time I had no idea what kind of an experiment he was going to perform. His disconnected talk excited my curiosity; but mentally I had already joined those who asked for an immediate performance of the experiment. Notwithstanding this, I was unwilling to interrupt, and so kept silence.

"Along with all his other knowledge the modern man also knows how to declaim beautifully upon immortality, although he realizes too well that his final, inevitable lot is oblivion. Truly he has ever been and is endeavoring with all his power to save a picture of himself or a scene for his descendants; but art in all its phases has proved unable to do more than preserve a mere shadow of a picture—a shadow that fades and vanishes until it disappears entirely and forever, just like the original. I have been thinking about it several years; and aided by all the discoveries of science that were accessible to me I have become able to present vividly to human eyes any scene that existed hundreds or even thousands of years ago."

"What?" "What?" was heard on all sides.

Curiosity, which my friend evidently aimed to awaken by his speech, was universal. But he went on:

"If before the invention of glass and the telescope anybody should have appeared before a learned body of men like the present, and claimed that by means of certain instruments it would sometime become possible to look out over distances of many miles, even to study heavenly bodies, his story surely would have been listened to with distrust even by the most profound thinker of the time. The same would have happened if before the invention of the steam-engine or the telegraph any one should have claimed that a journey of several months might be made in a few hours, or that one might in a moment's time hear from a person hundreds of miles away. To-day we should compassionately smile at the sceptics; yet I am sure that I shall not be believed if I make an analogous assertion before my experiment is finished. For I have succeeded in discovering an alloy out of which a tool may be made which excels the most perfect microscopes and telescopes of to-day, although it looks just like ordinary eyeglasses. These eyeglasses enable a person clearly to distinguish things at enormous distances—a *milliard* of miles, for example."

"That is impossible!" "A fairy tale!" came from various parts of the hall.

"Considering what I have said," my friend continued, "I had to expect that I should not be believed. It is the same as if half a thousand years ago I should have asserted what has since been conclusively proved—that the earth moves around the sun. I am not at all surprised, therefore, that my esteemed guests think it impossible that I should have invented a better instrument than all our telescopes, and an incredibly simple one at that. But this is not all. For I have made another invention more improbable than the first. In truth, it is no new invention, for it has been known for ages; but its application is wholly modern. Its simplicity will surprise every one; but he who recalls the fact that the results of all human thinking may be summed up in a few words, who knows that the apparent chaos of the universe and all its millions of natural forces are governed by one law,—he will at least understand how for a given purpose we may use the resultant of only a few forces. I have succeeded in inventing, or utilizing rather, a precious motor that has been known for ages—a motor whose velocity exceeds that of light—ay, even that of electricity."

"A Utopian idea!" some of the guests exclaimed.

"Yet I shall prove it," my friend went on, "for I have constructed a machine to test the effects of this wonderful force; the machine, ready for the most daring experiments, is here, and any one may convince himself of the truth of my words."

My friend looked up. I noticed that a large regular triangle was hanging in the air where the metallic coffin-lid had been before. One corner of the triangle pointed to the ceiling; the opposite side was in a horizontal position. The triangle was so large that two persons could comfortably stand in it. I could not tell of what material it was made. It looked as though it were made of bright, strong wire; all three sides glittered as if rays of light were reflected from a smooth wire.

Before I could examine the machine from afar, my friend simply beckoned, and the triangle instantly slipped down upon the table. And look! First now I noticed that at its two lower corners there were hanging two glittering objects which I failed to see before. My friend put both of these upon the table and said:

"Let any one who wants to convince himself come forward and examine my apparatus."

The guests surrounded the table. I too, being exceedingly curious, hastened forward and struggled to get as near as possible to the table, so that I could view the instruments closely. I saw two pairs of eyeglasses, seemingly common glass. I looked through them, but found nothing peculiar. They seemed to be common unpolished glass. The triangular instrument was more peculiar. What from a distance seemed to be a bright thick wire was an unknown, thin, cobwebby matter, as tough as a wire and glittering; its resemblance to a thick wire was evidently an optical delusion. I, and many of the guests, examined the machine with our own eyes and our own touch.

A few minutes later my friend politely asked the guests to resume their seats. Then he proceeded:

"By way of introduction I shall give a few well-known facts concerning the velocity of light. The speed of my machine will then be better understood. As is well known, the velocity of light is computed to be more than forty-two thousand geographical miles a second. A ray of moonlight, therefore, reaches the earth in about a second and a half; sunlight arrives in about eight minutes. The light of Neptune, the farthest-known planet, needs nearly three hours to reach the earth. The nearest fixed star is four billion miles distant from us; it takes no less than three thousand two hundred years before we see its light. The distance of the fixed stars of the twelfth magnitude, according to Struve, is about five billion miles, and their light comes to us in four thousand years. And Rosse's gigantic telescope discovered stars so remote that their light reaches us only in about thirty million years. Accordingly the so-called universe must be at least thirty million years old. All this is well known, however. I merely state it to prove my assertion. If by means of polished glasses we are enabled to view bodies so distant, why should we not, by means of a far more perfect instrument, look, say, from a fixed star of the twelfth magnitude at the earth and see everything as distinctly as a naked eye sees even minute objects at a distance of ten or twelve inches?"

"Humbug!" burst from some one in the rear.

A light smile passed over my friend's face; so smiles a man who is sure of victory.

"Any one may doubt all I have said until I prove its truth," he went on. "But certainly every one will admit that if it were possible for us in one hour to make a journey of five billion miles from a star of the twelfth magnitude to our earth, and were our eyes strengthened as I have mentioned, we could in as short a time view scenes from the whole of mankind's history, beginning with the first man down to this very moment. This, too, every one will admit: that if the traveller desired to view a scene longer, he would have to fly with the same velocity and in the same direction as light does. Now, if we should soar up from this hall and fly with the velocity of light, we should see continually the very scene that is now before our eyes. But if we should suddenly be transferred to a point distant a little over 3,225,000,000 miles from the earth, and should then speed on with the velocity of light, the earth would appear to us as it looked twenty-four hours ago. If we should then suddenly advance ten, a hundred, or a thousand times as far, we should see what had happened on earth ten, a hundred, or a thousand days ago, and so on. The course of our flight of course would not be direct or arbitrary: it would be a gigantic cycloid, so as to follow not only the earth's rotation around its axis, but also its course around the sun. Of all the scenes that have taken place on the face of the globe, not a single one has been lost, but images of all are being preserved in the great mirror of the universe. By means of enormous speed all these images may be traced, looked at, and examined at will. I have invented the instruments necessary for this journey, and although they may surprise everybody by their unparalleled simplicity, they have been so often successfully tested that I can tonight invite any one of the company to undertake with me an expedition into the universe."

Loud laughter, expressive partly of distrust, partly of ridicule, shook the hall. "A Utopian scheme!" "A hypothesis!" "Nonsense!" Such and similar cries came from various parts of the room. After the laughter had somewhat subsided, the same grumbler in the rear who had interrupted my friend shortly before remarked:

"Jules Verne is ahead of you, for he undertook a like journey to the moon."

A light smile again passed over my friend's face.

"You are right," he said, "but only partly so; for even Jules Verne was not the first to undertake so adventurous a journey. Edgar Allan Poe went on a like journey about a quarter of a century before him; and so did one Cyrano de Bergerac in the seventeenth century. The course of the journey is the same, but the means and the object are different. All of those who have undertaken the journey before have employed complicated apparatus, and have intended to amuse and to instruct; but I use the simplest means, and the object of my journey is"—

"We don't care what it is!" the morose guest in the rear interjected. "We want proof that such an excursion is feasible!"

"I shall furnish the proof immediately," my friend answered. "Let any one who chooses take a slip of paper and write down what event of history he wants to see; then let a delegate be chosen who shall undertake the journey with me as a manager of the machine."

My friend gave a sign with his hand, and the machine flew up several times, and again slipped noiselessly down upon the table. Its movements were so rapid that it was impossible to count them. This showed that the machine was really something wonderful.

Thereupon there was a moderate commotion in the hall. Some of the guests, served with small slips of paper by the valets, wrote what events they wished to see; others stood in groups and talked; while my friend quietly waited at his table until all should be ready.

Like the rest, I too was fully convinced that a real performance of this fantastic excursion into the universe could not even be thought of; yet I was eager to see how my friend would proceed. Positive that the experiment could not be performed save by means of an optical delusion, I was the more curious to see how he would delude the senses of so choice a company, and whether he would succeed in deceiving me too.

After the notes had been written and put on the table, he resumed:

"You will please choose your delegate. The journey is a daring one; your delegate will stand in the triangle with me, and so we shall start up."

"Why should we choose? Let us give preference to volunteers," said the Archbishop.

"Who will volunteer?" asked my friend. No one replied. The silence of the grave prevailed.

"Now you have the opportunity to examine the whole thing with your own senses," I said to myself; and as my friend repeated his question I rose and slowly walked to his table. A placid smile passed across his lips as he saw that I was the volunteer; and when I came to his desk he said:

"My esteemed guests, the gentleman who is willing to go on the excursion is a friend of mine. If I do not wish to be considered a charlatan who performs his experiments with the aid of his secret allies, I cannot then accept his services unless you expressly declare that you accept him as your delegate."

All fastened their searching eyes on me; it seemed to me as though each guest tried to read in my face whether I deserved to be trusted. Then some one in the centre suggested:

"We cannot do otherwise, as no one else has applied. After all, the main thing is proof; and our delegate must prove the trustworthiness of his report."

"Exactly so! " came from the tables to the right.

"We are satisfied," came from the left.

"I am willing," I said, with some hesitation, "to furnish not only a faithful account of what I shall see, but also proof—if possible."

"First of all," my friend resumed, "permit me to arrange the papers chronologically."

Then he began to arrange them rapidly. Standing close to his table, I could in many cases easily read what was written on this or that slip. There were over four hundred slips. Evidently many wrote more than one note. He showed such skill in arranging them that it took him only about five minutes.

"The first event," he then said to the guests, "which, according to the written notes, is to be seen anew, happened one hundred and nineteen days ago. If, therefore, we wish once more to see it as it is mirrored in the universe, we must first make a long journey, such as light has made in one hundred and nineteen days; then we shall for a moment regard the scene. If we wish to look longer, we must speed on with the velocity of light. In this case our first task will be to get ahead of the light. As light travels over 42,000 miles in a second, it makes

2,520,000 miles in a minute, about 3,629,000,000 miles in a day, and more than 431,851,000,000 miles in one hundred and nineteen days. With my machine we shall reach that distance in a moment, and then we shall fly on, either with the velocity of light or a little faster, in a gigantic spiral answering to the rotation of the earth both around its axis and around the sun."

He pushed the table a little forward, and his triangle slid down to the ground without any noise. Then he put on a pair of the wonderful spectacles and entered the triangle. I followed his example.

Silence prevailed in the hall. No one stirred; evidently every one expected with eagerness what would follow. Suddenly it occurred to me that it would be impossible to break through the ceiling with the machine. I looked up toward the ceiling, and lo! I saw a large round aperture, through which I saw the sky and some groups of stars. Before I asked for an explanation of this strange change, which I had not noticed before, I heard a clear clink, as though some one had struck a silvery bell; and instantly it seemed to me that we were flying up. I say expressly that it *seemed* to me; for the scene in the hall was constantly before me.

"Do we fly, or do we not?" I inquired of my friend, who, holding the guests' notes in one hand, was managing the machine with the other.

"We do fly," was his answer. "We have only the velocity of light now, and consequently you see the same scene you saw before we started. In a few seconds I shall so direct the machine that we shall suddenly find ourselves 431,851,000,000 miles away from the earth, whereupon we shall fly for some time with the velocity of light merely."

"All right," I said.

The scene before me grew misty. Soon I saw nothing but gray dusk passing into darkness, until there was impenetrable darkness before me.

"How is it that I do not see anything? " I inquire of my friend.

"We are as far from the earth," says my friend, "as light has travelled in one hundred and nineteen days. From a distance of more than 431,851,000,000 miles you see now the region where the event happened one hundred and nineteen days ago in the night. We fly on with the velocity of light. A light pressure on the mainspring of my machine will, however, suffice to make us fly faster, and so the whole scene will gradually develop before your eyes."

I do not answer, for in the same moment it seems to me that darkness is changing into twilight with a reddish coloring. Now flames flash through the dusk, and now the landscape emerges. I see at first only indistinct outlines of mountains, woods, rivers, cities, and villages. Soon everything looks clearer. I distinguish single fields, highways, farms, and houses; I see entire villages ablaze, and innumerable lesser lights scattered all over the region like will-o'-the-wisps. The scene grows still more distinct. I notice how dark shadows are hurrying in a wild disorder along the highways and over the fields. Soon I perceive that the shadows are numberless living beings. I recognize horsemen and wagons and foot-soldiers. I see how in some places groups or streams of men are fleeing in disorder, how in others they form immovable crowds. All this I see in the twilight of a summer night. The landscape gradually becomes more distinct. Near the burning villages I see swarms of men. Then I recognize the groups as camps of larger and smaller divisions of soldiery, or stations where the wounded are being cared for. I see places strewn with dead horses and men, with overturned wagons and cannons, and distinguish single individuals— some digging graves, others spying about, others, again, picking up the fallen men and carrying them to the camp-fires or to the graves.

In another moment I have a perfect bird's-eye view of an evening-clad landscape with a battlefield after battle. The scene extends several miles in width and length. Nearly a hundred towns and villages are before me, and I seem to recognize some of them. But the strange image does not remain unchanged. The longer I look at it the brighter it becomes, and I see everything clearly as though I were looking down from a tower. It is a panorama of a battle, but the scenes follow one another in reversed order—from the end of the fight to its beginning. Thus I see successively images of soldiers fleeing and pursuing, then fighting, and later preparing for battle. Now there is a daring and bloody attack of a few regiments against a firm position of the enemy; then a wild combat of single regiments of horsemen, manoeuvres of the infantry, movements of the artillery. At times I see only clouds of white smoke with occasional flashes of fire. The silence of the grave is spread over the entire scene. I do not hear the thunder of cannons, the rattle of drums and the clang of trumpets, the clashing of arms and the moans of the wounded. I see a vivid and horrible, but noise-less scene. Gradually the scene of a terrible battle is changing into a milder one, until I see a peaceful region in the lustre of the golden rays of a summer sun.

How strange! It took less time to survey the whole scene than it takes to read this description. The skill with which my friend had deluded my eyes was indeed surprising, and I fully believed that his other experiments would be equally successful.

"I think I have seen an image of the battle of Königgrätz," I said to my friend, who, standing silently by me in the triangle, was engineering the machine.

"You are right," he replied; "now you will see all the battles of the Seven Days' war in a reverse order. I shall assist you with short explanations so that you can have more time to look."

"I am satisfied," I said, waiting quietly for what would follow. I did not have to wait long. The image of the peaceful region began to darken, and in a few seconds I had utter darkness before me again. I had hardly noticed the change when darkness began to yield to twilight, twilight to daylight, and I saw another battle—the battle of Königinhof. Then followed in rapid succession the battles of Trutnov, Skalice, Náchod, Jicin, Podol, and many skirmishes and smaller engagements of the Austro-Prussian war.

"No less than 45,000 men were killed in seven days," remarked my friend.

"On!" I exclaimed; and in a moment the scene was changed. Again I saw scenes of battles from the Polish revolution and the Schleswig-Holstein war. Then followed the terrible battle of Pueblo, and scenes from the French invasion of Mexico; further on the internecine battle of Fredericksburg and a series of battles and skirmishes of the American Civil war.

"The South American wars," my friend said, "took 519,000, the North American war 381,000, lives."

"On!" I urged; and in a moment I saw the battle of Aspremonte, the capture of Palermo, the slaughters of Solferino, Magenta, and a number of smaller battles; then scenes of dread and shame from the Hindoo revolution and equally bloody events of the Crimean war, from the last frightful attack on Sebastopol to the murderous battles of Balaklava and Inkerman.

"No less than 785,000 men was the cost of the Crimean war," my friend commented coolly.

"On, on!" I exclaimed; and instantly there was passing before my eyes scenes of street barricades following Napoleon's *coup d'état*, and scenes of dread and cruelty from the stormy years of 1849 and 1848, in a wonderful mass, and all in reversed chronological order.

The battlefields were scattered all, over Europe. I saw the camp at Vilagos, the defeats of the Magyars, the bombardment of Pesth, scenes from the Paris revolution of June, the capture of Ofen by the Magyars, the defeats of the Italians, and scenes from the Milan revolution.

I was going to speak; but my friend silenced me with a motion of his hand.

Other defeats of the Magyars followed; then the taking and the siege of Vienna, scenes from the Viennese revolution of October, from the Prague uprising of June and the bombardment of Prague by Windischgrätz, defeats of the Italians, scenes from the Paris revolution of February, and the stormy scenes from the revolutionary movements in Italy.

"And is it possible to count the victims of all these wars and battles?" my friend asked, when these images had disappeared and for a short time I beheld only quiet scenes of peace.

"Let us go on!" I urge, and soon I gaze upon scenes from the Polish revolution of 1846, and after a pause various scenes from the uprising of republicans in Paris, Toulon, and Grenoble in 1834, the capture of Warsaw by the Russian army in 1831, the Dresden tumults, and the battle of Ostrolenka.

While looking at this horrible fratricidal battle of the Slavs, I asked: "How far are we from the earth?"

"About 46,000,000,000 miles," was his answer.

Thereupon I saw scenes from the Parisian revolution of July, the taking of Erivan by Paskievich, and the bloody battle of Missolonghi; then followed various scenes from the wars of independence on the Balkan Peninsula.

After a long pause again I saw a terrible battle.

"How far are we from the earth now? " I inquired.

"About 68,000,000,000 miles," said my friend; "you have just seen the battle of Waterloo."

While my friend was continuing his short explanations, I viewed the three days' carnage of Leipzig, the battles of Montmartre and Kulm, the remnant of the French army crossing the Berezina, the conflagration of Moscow, the battle of Borodino, the battle of Aspern, scenes from the revolutions of Peru and Mexico, and again scenes from Napoleon's wars—the slaughter of Austerlitz and the magnificent naval battle of Trafalgar.

"Is it possible to tell the number of the victims of the ambition of one despot—Napoleon?" my friend asked.

I did not answer.

We sped on. I saw the taking of Prague by Suvarov; the fratricidal battle of Maciejovice, where Kosciusko fell down wounded with the exclamation, "*Finis Poloniæ!*" Then came the bloody scenes of the great French revolution, of the Polish insurrection, of the wars with the Turks; scenes from the American war of Independence; scenes from the Seven Years' war; a series of scenes from the fierce Northern war between the Russians and the Swedes; the battle of Narva; scenes from the Spanish war of Succession; the defeat of the Turks at Vienna by the Polish king Sobieski; and wars of the French with the Spanish and Dutch. I saw the battle of Dunbar, where Cromwell gained victory, and a series of battles down to that of Marston Moor, where ten thousand Royalists were killed. Intermixed with these battles were scenes from the Swedish invasion of Bohemia; then followed scenes of brutality from the Thirty Years' war; and finally the beheading of

Bohemian patriots at Prague, and the battle of the White Mountain, of 1620, where the independence of Bohemia was crushed forever.

"How far are we from the earth now?" I inquired.

"About 325,000,000,000 miles," my friend answered; adding, "But let us speed on—the hour is passing." And in a moment we rushed on. Again I saw a series of horrible and bloody scenes—the massacre of the Huguenots, the religious wars of France, the dire deeds of the Duke of Alva, the peasants' uprisings. Then followed scenes of slaughter from Peru, Mexico, and other American countries to which European avarice brought destruction.

"On, on!" I exclaimed impatiently.

After a short pause I saw Mathias Corvinus defeated by the Bohemians, the Tartars by the Russians, and the fanatical German crusaders conquered by the Hussites. Then followed the fratricidal battle of Lipany, where the Taborites were defeated by their Bohemian brethren in 1434, the bloody victories of the Hussites, the camp of •i•ka, and the hero himself dying at Pribyslav in 1424.

Grief overcame my heart for a time, but again I saw numerous victories of the Taborites under •i•ka's leadership, and, after a short pause, the horrible spectacle of Huss dying at the stake at Constance in 1415.

I could hardly catch sight of the images of all these scenes in flight before me or listen to my friend's instructive remarks; the blood began to rush to my head.

"How far are we now?" I inquired.

"About 598,000,000,000 miles," was the quiet reply. "We have flown through a distance of about four hundred and fifty-one years. We have to travel a trifle of about 6,000,000,000,000 miles farther in order to reach the spheres of stars of the twelfth magnitude, whose light needs more than four thousand years to reach the earth."

"And is it possible to make this journey in an arbitrarily short time?" I asked, without thinking that I could not even imagine the enormous distance.

"Certainly," my friend replied.

"But tell me, please, what wonderful motor is it that moves our machine so rapidly through the universe."

"Later! Later!" he answers. "I must manage the machine. The least fault would make us lose our balance, and we should fall."

"Whither?" I ask.

"Do I know?"

"Let us rush on, then, as fast as we can!"

"If we are to finish our excursion in an hour, we must confine ourselves to a few more important views."

"Speed on, speed on!" I urge him.

Again I see a wonderful, but horrible panorama of strife. The scenes change rapidly, but each is very distinct. And lo! this time images of battles and skirmishes are intermingled with other scenes; but in all of them there is some struggle in which the brutality of man's nature is triumphing, in which sheer force or fraud and deception are gaining the victory over natural weakness or guilelessness.

Suddenly I notice that while the scene is changing we are in darkness longer than usual.

"What's the matter? " I ask impatiently.

"I direct the machine so that you may see the final scene. We are farther than the stars of the twelfth magnitude, in spheres whose light reaches the earth in about six thousand years. This time, however, we shall change our mode of observation. When we reach the point of view I shall stop the machine, only allowing it to rotate so that the scene will develop before your eye in the natural, not in the reversed, order."

Soon a few bright rays pierce the darkness; then it changes into a gray fog, and the fog grows thinner and thinner. The dark contour of a wild, desolate land rises from the fog. Then I see a bare, stony plain, with a dense fir forest and a high mountain range in the background. A sultry, oppressive dusk, such as usually precedes a storm, overspreads the landscape; and only now and then the sun's rays pierce the dense clouds. Close to the forest, near a cave,

I see a young woman with three children. Two of them cling to their mother in fear; the third, a babe in arms, looks into its mother's eyes with a smile of happiness on its childish lips. But the pale face of the mother shows inexpressible fear and dread. Her eyes are fastened upon the dark thicket of the forest; her naked body is shivering; and while pressing the naked babe to her bosom with her left hand she stretches the right protectingly toward the other two naked children.

Suddenly a tall young man rushes out of the forest, carrying a doe on his shoulders. Another, stronger, rushes after him; a brutal fury blazes in his idiotic face. Both are naked. The first throws down the deer and courageously faces the other, who pursues him with a club in his hand. A duel ensues. The woman watches with deadly anxiety. It is a desperate fight for life. The first man falls; the stronger has broken his skull. The woman flies in despair, pressing the babe to her bosom. Both children follow her into the darkness of the forest.

I feel the blood running wildly in my veins, rushing to my brain, and vertigo seizing me. I try to speak, but fail. My friend forestalls me:

"You have just seen the first struggle of the first of men. We are at the end of our excursion. From beginning to end you saw nothing but continual strife—a mutual killing and slaughter of the most perfect of beings. This struggle has been going on since the beginning of the world. In the course of several thousand years men tried to persuade themselves that the world was governed by the principle of love and humanity; but they find that they have been deceiving themselves. They have learned to know that a merciless and dreadful God has condemned to destruction everything that he has created weak and powerless. After thousands of years they recognize that life is but an everlasting struggle for mere existence. Men have been striving for power and glory, coveting riches, hugging their souls in the sweet embrace of sentimentality. The cold reason of Newton, fully penetrating the nothingness and perversion of men's endeavors, frightened and terrified them. They dreaded the cold, but truthful figures with which he measured the universe; the unmerciful consequences of his ice-cold, but indisputable calculations; and lo! to-day mankind stands before the throne of the Darwinian god—a horrible god of force and power. Certain people have fought this god for years; but the purpose of the fight is only to put the dethroned gloomy god of religious fanaticism upon the throne of the god of force and power. But the fight against the Darwinian god is unequal. Should the whole world undertake the war, he cannot be dethroned. The throne of this god can be undermined only by principles of humanity."

My friend paused. His words thundered like the stern sentence of a just and austere judge. But I could not see his face; for we were in utter darkness. I kept silence. Suddenly my friend began again:

"What is that? Our machine is shaking—we have lost our balance! We sink!"

My friend's doleful voice so frightened me that my heart grew cold.

"Drop the machine!" my friend exclaimed. "One of us must sacrifice himself, else both of us will perish."

I did not answer; I could not. I only felt that my senses were failing.

"Leave, or I shall push you down!" my friend insisted again.

"Tell me the name of your motor, at least," I pleaded. At the same time I felt that the machine was overturned. We fell rapidly headlong; I dropped.

It seemed to me as though I heard my friend's wild laughter and these words:

"Good-by forever! My motor is known to all the world. It is the ever-creating—Fancy."

The voice sounded hollow; I could hardly hear the last words, for I lost consciousness.

Any one who has fallen asleep at an open window in autumn, and awakens suddenly, knows the peculiar sensation of chilliness which accompanies the awakening. A like chill thrilled me when I noticed the glimmering dawn, the faint rays pouring through the half-open window into my lone room.

I looked around in surprise, and my first thought was: "Was it a reality, a delusion, or a dream?" But my senses were so dull that they could not answer the question. I remember only that it occurred to me at once that Dr. Sperlich, who announced the death of my friend in the Kinskýs' villa, had been dead for years, and that in the castle itself there never were any such corridors as those through which I had wandered. I remember, too, that I was sitting at my desk, on which an astronomical book lay open that I must have been reading before I fell asleep.

I recall no more. I became unconscious again. I did not wake up for some time.

Then I lay on my bed, and my dear old mother was kneeling by me. I opened my eyes and looked into her sincere, wrinkled face, and a feeling of inexpressible bliss thrilled my soul.

"Oh! my dear child, what were you doing? They ran for me and told me you were unconscious. This is the third day."

"The third day?"

"The third," my mother repeated. "The physician came here several times every day, and advised rest and quiet. He said something about signs of—insanity."

A clear thought flashed through my clouded mind. I shivered.

"And he said you must stop your studies for some time." My mother rose and lightly kissed my brow.

I followed the doctor's advice and stopped studying for some time; but the haunting thoughts return now after years.

John Bartine's Watch

Ambrose Bierce

A Story by a Physician

"The exact time? Good God! my friend, why do you insist? One would think—but what does it matter; it is easily bedtime—isn't that near enough? But, here, if you must set your watch, take mine and see for yourself."

With that he detached his watch—a tremendously heavy, old-fashioned one—from the chain, and handed it to me; then turned away, and walking across the room to a shelf of books, began an examination of their backs. His agitation and evident distress surprised me; they appeared reasonless. Having set my watch by his, I stepped over to where he stood and said, "Thank you."

As he took his timepiece and reattached it to the guard I observed that his hands were unsteady. With a tact upon which I greatly prided myself, I sauntered carelessly to the sideboard and took some brandy and water; then, begging his pardon for my thoughtlessness, asked him to have some and went back to my seat by the fire, leaving him to help himself, as was our custom. He did so and presently joined me at the hearth, as tranquil as ever.

This odd little incident occurred in my apartment, where John Bartine was passing an evening. We had dined together at the club, had come home in a cab and—in short, everything had been done in the most prosaic way; and why John Bartine should break in upon the natural and established order of things to make himself spectacular with a display of emotion, apparently for his own entertainment, I could nowise understand. The more I thought of it, while his brilliant conversational gifts were commending themselves to my inattention, the more curious I grew, and of course had no difficulty in persuading myself that my curiosity was friendly solicitude. That is the disguise that curiosity usually assumes to evade resentment. So I ruined one of the finest sentences of his disregarded monologue by cutting it short without ceremony.

"John Bartine," I said, "you must try to forgive me if I am wrong, but with the light that I have at present I cannot concede your right to go all to pieces when asked the time o' night. I cannot admit that it is proper to experience a mysterious reluctance to look your own watch in the face and to cherish in my presence, without explanation, painful emotions which are denied to me, and which are none of my business."

To this ridiculous speech Bartine made no immediate reply, but sat looking gravely into the fire. Fearing that I had offended I was about to apologize and beg him to think no more about the matter, when looking me calmly in the eyes he said:

"My dear fellow, the levity of your manner does not at all disguise the hideous impudence of your demand; but happily I had already decided to tell you what you wish to know, and no manifestation of your unworthiness to hear it shall alter my decision. Be good enough to give me your attention and you shall hear all about the matter.

"This watch," he said, "had been in my family for three generations before it fell to me. Its original owner, for whom it was made, was my great-grandfather, Bramwell Olcott Bartine, a wealthy planter of Colonial Virginia, and as stanch a Tory as ever lay awake nights contriving new kinds of maledictions for the head of Mr. Washington, and new methods of aiding and abetting good King George. One day this worthy gentleman had the deep misfortune to perform for his cause a service of capital importance which was not recognized as legitimate by those who suffered its disadvantages. It does not matter what it was, but among its minor consequences was my excellent ancestor's arrest one night in his own house by a party of Mr. Washington's rebels. He was permitted to say farewell to his weeping family, and was then marched away into the darkness which swallowed him up forever. Not the slenderest clew to his fate was ever found. After the war the most diligent inquiry and the offer of large rewards failed to turn up any of his captors or any fact concerning his disappearance. He had disappeared, and that was all."

Something in Bartine's manner that was not in his words—I hardly knew what it was—prompted me to ask:

"What is your view of the matter—of the justice of it?"

"My view of it," he flamed out, bringing his clenched hand down upon the table as if he had been in a public house dicing with blackguards— "my view of it is that it was a characteristically dastardly assassination by that damned traitor, Washington, and his ragamuffin rebels!"

For some minutes nothing was said: Bartine was recovering his temper, and I waited. Then I said:

"Was that all?"

"No—there was something else. A few weeks after my great-grandfather's arrest his watch was found lying on the porch at the front door of his dwelling. It was wrapped in a sheet of letter paper bearing the name of Rupert Bartine, his only son, my grandfather. I am wearing that watch."

Bartine paused. His usually restless black eyes were staring fixedly into the grate, a point of red light in each, reflected from the glowing coals. He seemed to have forgotten me. A sudden threshing of the branches of a tree outside one of the windows, and almost at the same instant a rattle of rain against the glass, recalled him to a sense of his surroundings. A storm had risen, heralded by a single gust of wind, and in a few moments the steady plash of the water on the pavement was distinctly heard. I hardly know why I relate this incident; it seemed somehow to have a certain significance and relevancy which I am unable now to discern. It at least added an element of seriousness, almost solemnity. Bartine resumed:

"I have a singular feeling toward this watch—a kind of affection for it; I like to have it about me, though partly from its weight, and partly for a reason I shall now explain, I seldom carry it. The reason is this: Every evening when I have it with me I feel an unaccountable desire to open and consult it, even if I can think of no reason for wishing to know the time. But if I yield to it, the moment my eyes rest upon the dial I am filled with a mysterious apprehension—a sense of imminent calamity. And this is the more insupportable the nearer it is to eleven o'clock—by this watch, no matter what the actual hour may be. After the hands have registered eleven the desire to look is gone; I am entirely indifferent. Then I can consult the thing as often as I like, with no more emotion than you feel in looking at your own. Naturally I have trained myself not to look at that watch in the evening before eleven; nothing could induce me. Your insistence this evening upset me a trifle. I felt very much as I suppose an opium-eater might feel if his yearning for his special and particular kind of hell were re-enforced by opportunity and advice.

"Now that is my story, and I have told it in the interest of your trumpery science; but if on any evening hereafter you observe me wearing this damnable watch, and you have the thoughtfulness to ask me the hour, I shall beg leave to put you to the inconvenience of being knocked down."

His humor did not amuse me. I could see that in relating his delusion he was again somewhat disturbed. His concluding smile was positively ghastly, and his eyes had resumed something more than their old restlessness; they shifted hither and thither about the room with apparent aimlessness and I fancied had taken on a wild expression, such as is sometimes observed in cases of dementia. Perhaps this was my own imagination, but at any rate I was now persuaded that my friend was afflicted with a most singular and interesting monomania. Without, I trust, any abatement of my affectionate solicitude for him as a friend, I began to regard him as a patient, rich in possibilities of profitable study. Why not? Had he not described his delusion in the interest of science? Ah, poor fellow, he was doing more for science than he knew: not only his story but himself was in evidence. I should cure him if I could, of course, but first I should make a little experiment in psychology—nay, the experiment itself might be a step in his restoration.

"That is very frank and friendly of you, Bartine," I said cordially, "and I'm rather proud of your confidence. It is all very odd, certainly. Do you mind showing me the watch?"

He detached it from his waistcoat, chain and all, and passed it to me without a word. The case was of gold, very thick and strong, and singularly engraved. After closely examining the dial and observing that it was nearly twelve o'clock, I opened it at the back and was interested to observe an inner case of ivory, upon which was painted a miniature portrait in that exquisite and delicate manner which was in vogue during the eighteenth century.

"Why, bless my soul!" I exclaimed, feeling a sharp artistic delight— "how under the sun did you get that done? I thought miniature painting on ivory was a lost art."

"That," he replied, gravely smiling, "is not I; it is my excellent great-grandfather, the late Bramwell Olcott Bartine, Esquire, of Virginia. He was younger then than later—about my age, in fact. It is said to resemble me; do you think so?"

"Resemble you? I should say so! Barring the costume, which I supposed you to have assumed out of compliment to the art—or for *vraisemblance*, so to say—and the no mustache, that portrait is you in every feature, line, and expression."

No more was said at that time. Bartine took a book from the table and began reading. I heard outside the incessant plash of the rain in the street. There were occasional hurried footfalls on the sidewalks; and once a slower, heavier tread seemed to cease at my door—a policeman, I thought, seeking shelter in the doorway. The boughs of the trees tapped significantly on the window panes, as if asking for admittance. I remember it all through these years and years of a wiser, graver life.

Seeing myself unobserved, I took the old-fashioned key that dangled from the chain and quickly turned back the hands of the watch a full hour; then, closing the case, I handed Bartine his property and saw him replace it on his person.

"I think you said," I began, with assumed carelessness, "that after eleven the sight of the dial no longer affects you. As it is now nearly twelve"—looking at my own timepiece— "perhaps, if you don't resent my pursuit of proof, you will look at it now."

He smiled good-humoredly, pulled out the watch again, opened it, and instantly sprang to his feet with a cry that Heaven has not had the mercy to permit me to forget! His eyes, their blackness strikingly intensified by the pallor of his face, were fixed upon the watch, which he clutched in both hands. For some time he remained in that attitude without uttering another sound; then, in a voice that I should not have recognized as his, he said:

"Damn you! it is two minutes to eleven!"

I was not unprepared for some such outbreak, and without rising replied, calmly enough:

"I beg your pardon; I must have misread your watch in setting my own by it."

He shut the case with a sharp snap and put the watch in his pocket. He looked at me and made an attempt to smile, but his lower lip quivered and he seemed unable to close his mouth. His hands, also, were shaking, and he thrust them, clenched, into the pockets of his sack-coat. The courageous spirit was manifestly endeavoring to subdue the coward body. The effort was too great; he began to sway from side to side, as from vertigo, and before I could spring from my chair to support him his knees gave way and he pitched awkwardly forward and fell upon his face. I sprang to assist him to rise; but when John Bartine rises we shall all rise.

The post-mortem examination disclosed nothing; every organ was normal and sound. But when the body had been prepared for burial a faint dark circle was seen to have developed around the neck; at least I was so assured by several persons who said they saw it, but of my own knowledge I cannot say if that was true.

Nor can I set limitations to the law of heredity. I do not know that in the spiritual world a sentiment or emotion may not survive the heart that held it, and seek expression in a kindred life, ages removed. Surely, if I were to guess at the fate of Bramwell Olcott Bartine, I should guess that he was hanged at eleven o'clock in the evening, and that he had been allowed several hours in which to prepare for the change.

As to John Bartine, my friend, my patient for five minutes, and—Heaven forgive me!—my victim for eternity, there is no more to say. He is buried, and his watch with him—I saw to that. May God rest his soul in Paradise, and the soul of his Virginian ancestor, if, indeed, they are two souls.

The Hour-Glass
Robert Barr

Bertram Eastford had intended to pass the shop of his old friend, the curiosity dealer, into whose pockets so much of his money had gone for trinkets gathered from all quarters of the globe. He knew it was weakness on his part, to select that street when he might have taken another, but he thought it would do no harm to treat himself to one glance at the seductive window of the old curiosity shop, where the dealer was in the habit of displaying his latest acquisitions. The window was never quite the same, and it had a continued fascination for Bertram Eastford; but this time, he said to himself resolutely, he would not enter, having, as he assured himself, the strength of mind to forego this temptation. However, he reckoned without his window, for in it there was an old object newly displayed which caught his attention as effectually as a half-driven nail arrests the hem of a cloak. On the central shelf of the window stood an hour-glass, its framework of some wood as black as ebony. He stood gazing at it for a moment, then turned to the door and went inside, greeting the ancient shopman, whom he knew so well.

"I want to look at the hour-glass you have in the window," he said.

"Ah, yes," replied the curiosity dealer; "the cheap watch has driven the hour-glass out of the commercial market, and we rarely pick up a thing like that nowadays." He took the hour-glass from the shelf in the window, reversed it, and placed it on a table. The ruddy sand began to pour through into the lower receptacle in a thin, constant stream, as if it were blood that had been dried and powdered. Eastford watched the ever-increasing heap at the bottom, rising conically, changing its shape every moment, as little avalanches of the sand fell away from its heightening sides.

"There is no need for you to extol its antiquity," said Eastford, with a smile. "I knew the moment I looked at it that such glasses are rare, and you are not going to find me a cheapening customer."

"So far from over-praising it," protested the shopman, "I was about to call your attention to a defect. It is useless as a measurer of time."

185

"It doesn't record the exact hour, then?" asked Eastford.

"Well, I suppose the truth is, they were not very particular in the old days, and time was not money, as it is now. It measures the hour with great accuracy," the curio dealer went on— "that is, if you watch it; but, strangely enough, after it has run for half an hour, or thereabouts, it stops, because of some defect in the neck of the glass, or in the pulverising of the sand, and will not go again until the glass is shaken."

The hour-glass at that moment verified what the old man said. The tiny stream of sand suddenly ceased, but resumed its flow the moment its owner jarred the frame, and continued pouring without further interruption.

"That is very singular," said Eastford. "How do you account for it?"

"I imagine it is caused by some inequality in the grains of sand; probably a few atoms larger than the others come together at the neck, and so stop the percolation. It always does this, and, of course, I cannot remedy the matter because the glass is hermetically sealed."

"Well, I don't want it as a timekeeper, so we will not allow that defect to interfere with the sale. How much do you ask for it?"

The dealer named his price, and Eastford paid the amount.

"I shall send it to you this afternoon."

"Thank you," said the customer, taking his leave.

That night in his room Bertram Eastford wrote busily until a late hour. When his work was concluded, he pushed away his manuscript with a sigh of that deep contentment which comes to a man who has not wasted his day. He replenished the open fire, drew his most comfortable arm-chair in front of it, took the green shade from his lamp, thus filling the luxurious apartment with a light that was reflected from armour and from ancient weapons standing in corners and hung along the walls. He lifted the paper-covered package, cut the string that bound it, and placed the ancient hour-glass on his table, watching the thin stream of sand which his action had set running. The constant, unceasing, steady downfall seemed to hypnotise him. Its descent was as silent as the footsteps of time itself. Suddenly it stopped, as it had done in the shop, and its abrupt ceasing jarred on his tingling nerves like an unexpected break in the stillness. He could almost imagine an unseen hand clasping the thin cylinder of the glass and throttling it. He shook the bygone time-measurer and breathed again more steadily when the sand resumed its motion. Presently he took the glass from the table and examined it with some attention.

He thought at first its frame was ebony, but further inspection convinced him it was oak, blackened with age. On one round end was carved rudely two hearts overlapping, and twined about them a pair of serpents.

"Now, I wonder what that's for?" murmured Eastford to himself. "An attempt at a coat of arms, perhaps."

There was no clue to the meaning of the hieroglyphics, and Eastford, with the glass balanced on his knee, watched the sand still running, the crimson thread sparkling in the lamplight. He fancied he saw distorted reflections of faces in the convex glass, although his reason told him they were but caricatures of his own. The great bell in the tower near by, with slow solemnity, tolled twelve. He counted its measured strokes one by one, and then was startled by a decisive knock at his door. One section of his brain considered this visit untimely, another looked on it as perfectly usual, and while the two were arguing the matter out, he heard his own voice cry: "Come in."

The door opened, and the discussion between the government and the opposition in his mind ceased to consider the untimeliness of the visit, for here, in the visitor himself, stood another problem. He was a young man in military costume, his uniform being that of an officer. Eastford remembered seeing something like it on the stage, and knowing little of military affairs, thought perhaps the costume of the visitor before him indicated an officer in the Napoleonic war.

"Good evening!" said the incomer. "May I introduce myself? I am Lieutenant Sentore, of the regular army."

"You are very welcome," returned his host. "Will you be seated?"

"Thank you, no. I have but a few moments to stay. I have come for my hour-glass, if you will be good enough to let me have it."

"Your hour-glass?" ejaculated Eastford, in surprise. "I think you labour under a misapprehension. The glass belongs to me; I bought it to-day at the old curiosity shop in Finchmore Street."

"Rightful possession of the glass would appear to rest with you, technically; but taking you to be a gentleman, I venture to believe that a mere statement of my priority of claim will appeal to you, even though it might have no effect on the minds of a jury of our countrymen."

"You mean to say that the glass has been stolen from you and has been sold?"

"It has been sold undoubtedly over and over again, but never stolen, so far as I have been able to trace its history."

"If, then, the glass has been honestly purchased by its different owners, I fail to see how you can possibly establish any claim to it."

"I have already admitted that my claim is moral rather than legal," continued the visitor. "It is a long story; have I your permission to tell it?"

"I shall be delighted to listen," replied Eastford, "but before doing so I beg to renew my invitation, and ask you to occupy this easy-chair before the fire."

The officer bowed in silence, crossed the room behind Eastford, and sat down in the arm-chair, placing his sword across his knees. The stranger spread his hands before the fire, and seemed to enjoy the comforting warmth. He remained for a few moments buried in deep reflection, quite ignoring the presence of his host, who, glancing upon the hour-glass in dispute upon his knees, seeing that the sands had all run out silently reversed it and set them flowing again. This action caught the corner of the stranger's eye, and brought him to a realisation of why he was there. Drawing a heavy sigh, he began his story.

"In the year 1706 I held the post of lieutenant in that part of the British Army commanded by General Trelawny, the supreme command, of course, being in the hands of the great Marlborough."

Eastford listened to this announcement with a feeling that there was something wrong about the statement. The man sitting there was calmly talking of a time one hundred and ninety-two years past, and yet he himself could not be a day more than twenty-five years old. Somewhere entangled in this were the elements of absurdity. Eastford found himself unable to unravel them, but the more he thought of the matter, the more reasonable it began to appear, and so, hoping his visitor had not noted the look of surprise on his face, he said, quietly, casting his mind back over the history of England, and remembering what he had learned at school:—

"That was during the war of the Spanish Succession?"

"Yes: the war had then been in progress four years, and many brilliant victories had been won, the greatest of which was probably the Battle of Blenheim."

"Quite so," murmured Eastford.

"It was the English," Casper cried,
    "That put the French to rout;
"But what they killed each other for,
    "I never could make out."

The officer looked up in astonishment.

"I never heard anything like that said about the war. The reason for it was perfectly plain. We had to fight or acknowledge France to be the dictator of Europe. Still, politics have nothing to do with my story. General Trelawny and his forces were in Brabant, and were under orders to join the Duke of Marlborough's army. We were to go through the country as speedily as possible, for a great battle was expected. Trelawny's instructions were to capture certain towns and cities that lay in our way, to dismantle the fortresses, and to parole their garrisons. We could not encumber ourselves with prisoners, and so marched the garrisons out, paroled them, destroyed their arms, and bade them disperse. But, great as was our hurry, strict orders had been given to leave no strongholds in our rear untaken.

"Everything went well until we came to the town of Elsengore, which we captured without the loss of a man. The capture of the town, however, was of little avail, for in the centre of it stood a strong citadel, which we tried to take by assault, but could not. General Trelawny, a very irascible, hotheaded man, but, on the whole, a just and capable officer, impatient at this unexpected delay, offered the garrison almost any terms they desired to evacuate the castle. But, having had warning of our coming, they had provisioned the place, were well supplied with ammunition, and their commander refused to make terms with General Trelawny.

"'If you want the place,' said the Frenchman, 'come and take it.'

"General Trelawny, angered at this contemptuous treatment, flung his men again and again at the citadel, but without making the slightest impression on it.

"We were in no wise prepared for a long siege, nor had we expected stubborn resistance. Marching quickly, as was our custom heretofore, we possessed no heavy artillery, and so were at a disadvantage when attacking a fortress as strong as that of Elsengore. Meanwhile, General Trelawny sent mounted messengers by different roads to his chief giving an account of what had happened, explaining his delay in joining the main army, and asking for definite instructions. He expected that one or two, at least, of the mounted messengers sent away would reach his chief and be enabled to return. And that is exactly what happened, for one day a dusty horseman came to General Trelawny's headquarters with a brief note from Marlborough. The Commander-in-Chief said:—

"'I think the Frenchman's advice is good. We want the place; therefore, take it.'

"But he sent no heavy artillery to aid us in this task, for he could not spare his big guns, expecting, as he did, an important battle. General Trelawny having his work thus cut out for him, settled down to accomplish it as best he might. He quartered officers and men in various parts of the town, the more thoroughly to keep watch on the citizens, of whose good intentions, if the siege were prolonged, we were by no means sure.

"It fell to my lot to be lodged in the house of Burgomaster Seidelmier, of whose conduct I have no reason to complain, for he treated me well. I was given two rooms, one a large, low apartment on the first floor, and communicating directly with the outside, by means of a hall and a separate stairway. The room was lighted by a long, many-paned window, leaded and filled with diamond-shaped glass. Beyond this large drawing-room was my bedroom. I must say that I enjoyed my stay in Burgomaster Seidelmier's house none the less because he had an only daughter, a most charming girl. Our acquaintance ripened into deep friendship, and afterwards into—— but that has nothing to do with what I have to tell you. My story is of war, and not of love. Gretlich Seidelmier presented me with the hour-glass you have in your hand, and on it I carved the joined hearts entwined with our similar initials."

"So they are initials, are they?" said Eastford, glancing down at what he had mistaken for twining serpents.

"Yes," said the officer; "I was more accustomed to a sword than to an etching tool, and the letters are but rudely drawn. One evening, after dark, Gretlich and I were whispering together in the hall, when we heard the heavy tread of the general coming up the stair. The girl fled precipitately, and I, holding open the door, waited the approach of my chief. He entered and curtly asked me to close the door.

"'Lieutenant,' he said, 'it is my intention to capture the citadel tonight. Get together twenty-five of your men, and have them ready under the shadow of this house, but give no one a hint of what you intend to do with them. In one hour's time leave this place with your men as quietly as possible, and make an attack on the western entrance of the citadel. Your attack is to be but a feint and to draw off their forces to that point. Still, if any of your men succeed in gaining entrance to the fort they shall not lack reward and promotion. Have you a watch?'

"'Not one that will go, general; but I have an hourglass here.'

"'Very well, set it running. Collect your men, and exactly at the hour lead them to the west front; it is but five minutes' quick march from here. An hour and five minutes from this moment I expect you to begin the attack, and the instant you are before the western gate make as much noise as your twenty-five men are capable of, so as to lead the enemy to believe that the attack is a serious one.'

"Saying this, the general turned and made his way, heavy-footed, through the hall and down the stairway.

"I set the hour-glass running, and went at once to call my men, stationing them where I had been ordered to place them. I returned to have a word with Gretlich before I departed on what I knew was a dangerous mission. Glancing at the hour-glass, I saw that not more than a quarter of the sand had run down during my absence. I remained in the doorway, where I could keep an eye on the hour-glass, while the girl stood leaning her arm against the angle of the dark passageway, supporting her fair cheek on her open palm; and, standing thus in the darkness, she talked to me in whispers. We talked and talked, engaged in that sweet, endless conversation that murmurs in subdued tone round the world, being duplicated that moment at who knows how many places. Absorbed as I was in listening, at last there crept into my consciousness the fact that the sand in the upper bulb was not diminishing as fast as it should. This knowledge was fully in my mind for some time before I realised its fearful significance. Suddenly the dim knowledge took on actuality. I sprang from the door-lintel, saying:—

"'Good heavens, the sand in the hour-glass has stopped running!'

"I remained there motionless, all action struck from my rigid limbs, gazing at the hour-glass on the table.

"Gretlich, peering in at the doorway, looking at the hour-glass and not at me, having no suspicion of the ruin involved in the stoppage of that miniature sandstorm, said, presently:—

"'Oh, yes, I forgot to tell you it does that now and then, and so you must shake the glass.'

"She bent forward as if to do this when the leaden windows shuddered, and the house itself trembled with the sharp crash of our light cannon, followed almost immediately by the deeper detonation of the heavier guns from the citadel. The red sand in the glass began to fall again, and its liberation seemed to unfetter my paralysed limbs. Bareheaded as I was, I rushed like one frantic along the passage and down the stairs. The air was resonant with the quick-following reports of the cannon, and the long, narrow street was fitfully lit up as if by sudden flashes of summer lightning. My men were still standing where I had placed them. Giving a sharp word of command, I marched them down the street and out into the square, where I met General Trelawny coming back from his futile assault. Like myself, he was bareheaded. His military countenance was begrimed with powder-smoke, but he spoke to me with no trace of anger in his voice.

"'Lieutenant Sentore,' he said, 'disperse your men.'

"I gave the word to disband my men, and then stood at attention before him.

"'Lieutenant Sentore,' he said, in the same level voice, 'return to your quarters and consider yourself under arrest. Await my coming there.'

"I turned and obeyed his orders. It seemed incredible that the sand should still be running in the hour-glass, for ages appeared to have passed over my head since last I was in that room. I paced up and down, awaiting the coming of my chief, feeling neither fear nor regret, but rather dumb despair. In a few minutes his heavy tread was on the stair, followed by the measured tramp of a file of men. He came into the room, and with him were a sergeant and four soldiers, fully armed. The general was trembling with rage, but held strong control over himself, as was his habit on serious occasions.

"'Lieutenant Sentore,' he said, 'why were you not at your post?'"

"'The running sand in the hour-glass' (I hardly recognised my own voice on hearing it) 'stopped when but half exhausted. I did not notice its interruption until it was too late.'

"The general glanced grimly at the hour-glass. The last sands were falling through to the lower bulb. I saw that he did not believe my explanation.

"'It seems now to be in perfect working order,' he said, at last.

"He strode up to it and reversed it, watching the sand pour for a few moments, then he spoke abruptly:—

"'Lieutenant Sentore, your sword.'

"I handed my weapon to him without a word. Turning to the sergeant, he said: 'Lieutenant Sentore is sentenced to death. He has an hour for whatever preparations he cares to make. Allow him to dispose of that hour as he chooses, so long as he remains within this room and holds converse with no one whatever. When the last sands of this hour-glass are run, Lieutenant Sentore will stand at the other end of this room and meet the death merited by traitors, laggards, or cowards. Do you understand your duty, sergeant?'

"'Yes, general.'

"General Trelawny abruptly left the room, and we heard his heavy steps echoing throughout the silent house, and later, more faintly on the cobble-stones of the street. When they had died away a deep stillness set in, I standing alone at one end of the room, my eyes fixed on the hour-glass, and the sergeant with his four men, like statues at the other, also gazing at the same sinister object. The sergeant was the first to break the silence.

"'Lieutenant,' he said, 'do you wish to write anything—?'

"He stopped short, being an unready man, rarely venturing far beyond 'Yes' and 'No.'

"'I should like to communicate with one in this household,' I said, 'but the general has forbidden it, so all I ask is that you shall have my body conveyed from this room as speedily as possible after the execution.'

"'Very good, lieutenant,' answered the sergeant.

"After that, for a long time no word was spoken. I watched my life run redly through the wasp waist of the transparent glass, then suddenly the sand ceased to flow, half in the upper bulb, half in the lower.

"'It has stopped,' said the sergeant; 'I must shake the glass.'

"'Stand where you are!' I commanded, sharply. 'Your orders do not run to that.'

"The habit of obedience rooted the sergeant to the spot.

"'Send one of your men to General Trelawny,' I said, as if I had still the right to be obeyed. 'Tell him what has happened, and ask for instructions. Let your man tread lightly as he leaves the room.'

"The sergeant did not hesitate a moment, but gave the order I required of him. The soldier nearest the door tip-toed out of the house. As we all stood there the silence seeming the deeper because of the stopping of the sand, we heard the hour toll in the nearest steeple. The sergeant was visibly perturbed, and finally he said:—

"'Lieutenant, I must obey the general's orders. An hour has passed since he left here, for that clock struck as he was going down the stair. Soldiers, make ready. Present.'

"The men, like impassive machines levelled their muskets at my breast. I held up my hand.

"'Sergeant,' I said as calmly as I could, 'you are now about to exceed your instructions. Give another command at your peril. The exact words of the general were, 'When the last sands of this hour-glass are run.' I call your attention to the fact that the conditions are not fulfilled. Half of the sand remains in the upper bulb.'

"The sergeant scratched his head in perplexity, but he had no desire to kill me, and was only actuated by a soldier's wish to adhere strictly to the letter of his instructions, be the victim friend or foe. After a few moments he muttered, 'It is true,' then gave a command that put his men into their former position.

"Probably more than half an hour passed, during which time no man moved; the sergeant and his three remaining soldiers seemed afraid to breathe; then we heard the step of the general himself on the stair. I feared that this would give the needed impetus to the sand in the glass, but, when Trelawny entered, the status quo remained. The general stood looking at the suspended sand, without speaking.

"'That is what happened before, general, and that is why I was not at my place. I have committed the crime of neglect, and have thus deservedly earned my death; but I shall die the happier if my general believes I am neither a traitor nor a coward.'

"The general, still without a word, advanced to the table, slightly shook the hour-glass, and the sand began to pour again. Then he picked the glass up in his hand, examining it minutely, as if it were some strange kind of toy, turning it over and over. He glanced up at me and said, quite in his usual tone, as if nothing in particular had come between us:—

"'Remarkable thing that, Sentore, isn't it?'

"'Very,' I answered, grimly.

"He put the glass down.

"'Sergeant, take your men to quarters. Lieutenant Sentore, I return to you your sword; you can perhaps make better use of it alive than dead; I am not a man to be disobeyed, reason or no reason. Remember that, and now go to bed.'

"He left me without further word, and buckling on my sword, I proceeded straightway to disobey again.

"I had a great liking for General Trelawny. Knowing how he fumed and raged at being thus held helpless by an apparently impregnable fortress in the unimportant town of Elsengore, I had myself studied the citadel from all points, and had come to the conclusion that it might be successfully attempted, not by the great gates that opened on the square of the town, nor by the inferior west gates, but by scaling the seemingly unclimbable cliffs at the north side. The wall at the top of this precipice was low, and owing to the height of the beetling cliff, was inefficiently watched by one lone sentinel, who paced the battlements from corner tower to corner tower. I had made my plans, intending to ask the general's permission to risk this venture, but now I resolved to try it without his knowledge or consent, and thus retrieve, if I could, my failure of the foregoing part of the night.

"Taking with me a long, thin rope which I had in my room, anticipating such a trial for it, I roused five of my picked men, and silently we made our way to the foot of the northern cliff. Here, with the rope around my waist, I worked my way diagonally up along a cleft in the rock, which, like others parallel to it, marked the face of the precipice. A slip would be fatal. The loosening of a stone would give warning to the sentinel, whose slow steps I heard on the wall above me, but at last I reached a narrow ledge without accident, and standing up in the darkness, my chin was level with the top of the wall on which the sentry paced. The shelf between the bottom of the wall and the top of the cliff was perhaps three feet in width, and gave ample room for a man careful of his footing. Aided by the rope, the others, less expert climbers than myself, made their way to my side one by one, and the six of us stood on the ledge under the low wall. We were all in our stockinged feet, some of the men, in fact, not even having stockings on. As the sentinel passed, we crouching in the darkness under the wall, the most agile of our party sprang up behind him. The soldier had taken off his jacket, and tip-toeing behind the sentinel, he threw the garment over his head, tightening it with a twist that almost strangled the man. Then seizing his gun so that it would not clatter on the stones, held him thus helpless while we five climbed up beside him. Feeling under the jacket, I put my right hand firmly on the sentinel's throat, and nearly choking the breath out of him, said:—

"'Your life depends on your actions now. Will you utter a sound if I let go your throat?'

"The man shook his head vehemently, and I released my clutch.

"'Now,' I said to him, 'where is the powder stored? Answer in a whisper, and speak truly.'

"'The bulk of the powder,' he answered, 'is in the vault below the citadel.'

"'Where is the rest of it?' I whispered.

"'In the lower room of the round tower by the gate.'

"'Nonsense,' I said: 'they would never store it in a place so liable to attack.'

"'There was nowhere else to put it,' replied the sentinel, 'unless they left it in the open courtyard, which would be quite as unsafe.'

"'Is the door to the lower room in the tower bolted?'

"'There is no door,' replied the sentry, 'but a low archway. This archway has not been closed, because no cannon-balls ever come from the northern side.'

"'How much powder is there in this room?'

"'I do not know; nine or ten barrels, I think.'

"It was evident to me that the fellow, in his fear, spoke the truth. Now, the question was, how to get down from the wall into the court-yard and across that to the archway at the southern side? Cautioning the sentinel again, that if he made the slightest attempt to escape or give the alarm, instant death would be meted to him, I told him to guide us to the archway, which he did, down the stone steps that led from the northern wall into the courtyard. They seemed to keep loose watch inside, the only sentinels in the place being those on the upper walls. But the man we had captured not appearing at his corner in time, his comrade on the western side became alarmed, spoke to him, and obtaining no answer, shouted for him, then discharged his gun. Instantly the place was in an uproar. Lights flashed, and from differ-ent guard-rooms soldiers poured out. I saw across the courtyard the archway the sentinel had spoken of, and calling my men made a dash for it. The besieged garrison, not expecting an enemy within, had been rushing up the stone steps at each side to the outer wall to man the cannon they had so recently quitted, and it was some minutes before a knowledge of the real state of things came to them. These few min-utes were all we needed, but I saw there was no chance for a slow match, while if we fired the mine we probably would die under the tottering tower.

"By the time we reached the archway and discovered the powder barrels, the besieged, finding everything silent outside, came to a realisation of the true condition of affairs. We faced them with bayonets fixed, while Sept, the man who had captured the sentinel, took the hatchet he had brought with him at his girdle, flung over one of the barrels on its side, knocked in the head of it, allowing the dull black powder to pour on the cobblestones. Then filling his hat with the explosive, he came out towards us, leaving a thick trail behind him. By this time we were sorely beset, and one of our men had gone down under the fire of the enemy, who shot wildly, being baffled by the darkness, otherwise all of us had been slaughtered. I seized a musket from a comrade and shouted to the rest:—

"'Save yourselves', and to the garrison, in French, I gave the same warning; then I fired the musket into the train of powder, and the next instant found myself half stunned and bleeding at the farther end of the courtyard. The roar of the explosion and the crash of the falling tower were deafening. All Elsengore was groused by the earthquake shock, I called to my men when I could find my voice, and Sept answered from one side, and two more from another. Together we tottered across the debris-strewn courtyard. Some woodwork inside the citadel had taken fire and was burning fiercely, and this lit up the ruins and made visible the great gap in the wall at the fallen gate. Into the square below we saw the whole town pouring, soldiers and civilians alike coming from the narrow streets into the open quadrangle. I made my way, leaning on Sept, over the broken gate and down the causeway into the square, and there, foremost of all, met my general, with a cloak thrown round him, to make up for his want of coat.

"'There, general,' I gasped, 'there is your citadel, and through this gap can we march to meet Marlborough.'

"'Pray, sir, who the deuce are you?' cried the general, for my face was like that of a blackamoor.

"'I am the lieutenant who has once more disobeyed your orders, general, in the hope of retrieving a former mistake.'

"'Sentore!' he cried, rapping out an oath. 'I shall have you court-martialled, sir.'

"'I think, general,' I said, 'that I am court-martialled already,' for I thought then that the hand of death was upon me, which shows the effect of imagination, for my wounds were not serious, yet I sank down unconscious at the general's feet. He raised me in his arms as if I had been his own son, and thus carried me to my rooms. Seven years later, when the war ended, I got leave of absence and came back to Elsengore for Gretlich Seidelmier and the hour-glass."

As the lieutenant ceased speaking, Eastford thought he heard again the explosion under the tower, and started to his feet in nervous alarm, then looked at the lieutenant and laughed, while he said:—

"Lieutenant, I was startled by that noise just now, and imagined for the moment that I was in Brabant. You have made good your claim to the hour-glass, and you are welcome to it."

But as Eastford spoke, he turned his eyes towards the chair in which the lieutenant had been seated, and found it vacant. Gazing round the room, in half somnolent dismay, he saw that he was indeed alone. At his feet was the shattered hour-glass, which had fallen from his knee, its blood-red sand mingling with the colours on the carpet. Eastford said, with an air of surprise:—

"By Jove!"

The New Accelerator
H. G. WELLS

Certainly, if ever a man found a guinea when he was looking for a pin it is my good friend Professor Gibberne. I have heard before of investigators overshooting the mark, but never quite to the extent that he has done. He has really, this time at any rate, without any touch of exaggeration in the phrase, found something to revolutionise human life. And that when he was simply seeking an all-round nervous stimulant to bring languid people up to the stresses of these pushful days. I have tasted the stuff now several times, and I cannot do better than describe the effect the thing had on me. That there are astonishing experiences in store for all in search of new sensations will become apparent enough.

Professor Gibberne, as many people know, is my neighbour in Folkestone. Unless my memory plays me a trick, his portrait at various ages has already appeared in The Strand Magazine—I think late in 1899; but I am unable to look it up because I have lent that volume to some one who has never sent it back. The reader may, perhaps, recall the high forehead and the singularly long black eyebrows that give such a Mephistophelian touch to his face. He occupies one of those pleasant little detached houses in the mixed style that make the western end of the Upper Sandgate Road so interesting. His is the one with the Flemish gables and the Moorish portico, and it is in the little room with the mullioned bay window that he works when he is down here, and in which of an evening we have so often smoked and talked together. He is a mighty jester, but, besides, he likes to talk to me about his work; he is one of those men who find a help and stimulus in talking, and so I have been able to follow the conception of the New Accelerator right up from a very early stage. Of course, the greater portion of his experimental work is not done in Folkestone, but in Gower Street, in the fine new laboratory next to the hospital that he has been the first to use.

As every one knows, or at least as all intelligent people know, the special department in which Gibberne has gained so great and deserved a reputation among physiologists is the action of drugs upon the nervous system. Upon soporifics, sedatives, and anaesthetics he is, I am told, unequalled. He is also a chemist of considerable eminence, and I suppose in the subtle and complex jungle of riddles that centres about the ganglion cell and the axis fibre there are little cleared places of his making, little glades of illumination, that, until he sees fit to publish his results, are still inaccessible to every other living man. And in the last few years he has been particularly assiduous upon this question of nervous stimulants, and already, before the discovery of the New Accelerator, very successful with them. Medical science has to thank him for at least three distinct and absolutely safe invigorators of unrivalled value to practising men. In cases of exhaustion the preparation known as Gibberne's B Syrup has, I suppose, saved more lives already than any lifeboat round the coast.

"But none of these little things begin to satisfy me yet," he told me nearly a year ago. "Either they increase the central energy without affecting the nerves or they simply increase the available energy by lowering the nervous conductivity; and all of them are unequal and local in their operation. One wakes up the heart and viscera and leaves the brain stupefied, one gets at the brain champagne fashion and does nothing good for the solar plexus, and what I want—and what, if it's an earthly possibility, I mean to have—is a stimulant that stimulates all round, that wakes you up for a time from the crown of your head to the tip of your great toe, and makes you go two—or even three—to everybody else's one. Eh? That's the thing I'm after."

"It would tire a man," I said.

"Not a doubt of it. And you'd eat double or treble—and all that. But just think what the thing would mean. Imagine yourself with a little phial like this"—he held up a little bottle of green glass and marked his points with it— "and in this precious phial is the power to think twice as fast, move twice as quickly, do twice as much work in a given time as you could otherwise do."

"But is such a thing possible?"

"I believe so. If it isn't, I've wasted my time for a year. These various preparations of the hypophosphites, for example, seem to show that something of the sort ... Even if it was only one and a half times as fast it would do."

"It would do," I said.

"If you were a statesman in a corner, for example, time rushing up against you, something urgent to be done, eh?"

"He could dose his private secretary," I said.

"And gain—double time. And think if you, for example, wanted to finish a book."

"Usually," I said, "I wish I'd never begun 'em."

"Or a doctor, driven to death, wants to sit down and think out a case. Or a barrister—or a man cramming for an examination."

"Worth a guinea a drop," said I, "and more to men like that."

"And in a duel, again," said Gibberne, "where it all depends on your quickness in pulling the trigger."

"Or in fencing," I echoed.

"You see," said Gibberne, "if I get it as an all-round thing it will really do you no harm at all—except perhaps to an infinitesimal degree it brings you nearer old age. You will just have lived twice to other people's once—"

"I suppose," I meditated, "in a duel—it would be fair?"

"That's a question for the seconds," said Gibberne.

I harked back further. "And you really think such a thing *is* possible?" I said.

"As possible," said Gibberne, and glanced at something that went throbbing by the window, "as a motor-bus. As a matter of fact—"

He paused and smiled at me deeply, and tapped slowly on the edge of his desk with the green phial. "I think I know the stuff. ... Already I've got something coming." The nervous smile upon his face betrayed the gravity of his revelation. He rarely talked of his actual experimental work unless things were very near the end. "And it may be, it may be—I shouldn't be surprised—it may even do the thing at a greater rate than twice."

"It will be rather a big thing," I hazarded.

"It will be, I think, rather a big thing."

But I don't think he quite knew what a big thing it was to be, for all that.

I remember we had several talks about the stuff after that. "The New Accelerator" he called it, and his tone about it grew more confident on each occasion. Sometimes he talked nervously of unexpected physiological results its use might have, and then he would get a little unhappy; at others he was frankly mercenary, and we debated long and anxiously how the preparation might be turned to commercial account. "It's a good thing," said Gibberne, "a tremendous thing. I know I'm giving the world something, and I think it only reasonable we should expect the world to pay. The dignity of science is all very well, but I think somehow I must have the monopoly of the stuff for, say, ten years. I don't see why all the fun in life should go to the dealers in ham."

My own interest in the coming drug certainly did not wane in the time. I have always had a queer little twist towards metaphysics in my mind. I have always been given to paradoxes about space and time, and it seemed to me that Gibberne was really preparing no less than the absolute acceleration of life. Suppose a man repeatedly dosed with such a preparation: he would live an active and record life indeed, but he would be an adult at eleven, middle-aged at twenty-five, and by thirty well on the road to senile decay. It seemed to me that so far Gibberne was only going to do for any one who took his drug exactly what Nature has done for the Jews and Orientals, who are men in their teens and aged by fifty, and quicker in thought and act than we are all the time. The marvel of drugs has always been great to my mind; you can madden a man, calm a man, make him incredibly strong and alert or a helpless log, quicken this passion and allay that, all by means of drugs, and here was a new miracle to be added to this strange armoury of phials the doctors use! But Gibberne was far too eager upon his technical points to enter very keenly into my aspect of the question.

It was the 7th or 8th of August when he told me the distillation that would decide his failure or success for a time was going forward as we talked, and it was on the 10th that he told me the thing was done and the New Accelerator a tangible reality in the world. I met him as I was going up the Sandgate Hill towards Folkestone—I think I was going to get my hair cut, and he came hurrying down to meet me—I suppose he was coming to my house to tell me at once of his success. I remember that his eyes were unusually bright and his face flushed, and I noted even then the swift alacrity of his step.

"It's done," he cried, and gripped my hand, speaking very fast; "it's more than done. Come up to my house and see."

"Really?"

"Really!" he shouted. "Incredibly! Come up and see."

"And it does—twice?"

"It does more, much more. It scares me. Come up and see the stuff. Taste it! Try it! It's the most amazing stuff on earth." He gripped my arm and, walking at such a pace that he forced me into a trot, went shouting with me up the hill. A whole char-a-banc-ful of people turned and stared at us in unison after the manner of people in chars-a-banc. It was one of those hot, clear days that Folkestone sees so much of, every colour incredibly bright and every outline hard. There was a breeze, of course, but not so much breeze as sufficed under these conditions to keep me cool and dry. I panted for mercy.

"I'm not walking fast, am I?" cried Gibberne, and slackened his pace to a quick march.

"You've been taking some of this stuff," I puffed.

"No," he said. "At the utmost a drop of water that stood in a beaker from which I had washed out the last traces of the stuff. I took some last night, you know. But that is ancient history, now."

"And it goes twice?" I said, nearing his doorway in a grateful perspiration.

"It goes a thousand times, many thousand times!" cried Gibberne, with a dramatic gesture, flinging open his Early English carved oak gate.

"Phew!" said I, and followed him to the door.

"I don't know how many times it goes," he said, with his latch-key in his hand.

"And you—"

"It throws all sorts of light on nervous physiology, it kicks the theory of vision into a perfectly new shape! ... Heaven knows how many thousand times. We'll try all that after—The thing is to try the stuff now."

"Try the stuff?" I said, as we went along the passage.

"Rather," said Gibberne, turning on me in his study. "There it is in that little green phial there! Unless you happen to be afraid?"

I am a careful man by nature, and only theoretically adventurous. I was afraid. But on the other hand there is pride.

"Well," I haggled. "You say you've tried it?"

"I've tried it," he said, "and I don't look hurt by it, do I? I don't even look livery and I feel—"

I sat down. "Give me the potion," I said. "If the worst comes to the worst it will save having my hair cut, and that I think is one of the most hateful duties of a civilised man. How do you take the mixture?"

"With water," said Gibberne, whacking down a carafe.

He stood up in front of his desk and regarded me in his easy chair; his manner was suddenly affected by a touch of the Harley Street specialist. "It's rum stuff, you know," he said.

I made a gesture with my hand.

"I must warn you in the first place as soon as you've got it down to shut your eyes, and open them very cautiously in a minute or so's time. One still sees. The sense of vision is a question of length of vibration, and not of multitude of impacts; but there's a kind of shock to the retina, a nasty giddy confusion just at the time, if the eyes are open. Keep 'em shut."

"Shut," I said. "Good!"

"And the next thing is, keep still. Don't begin to whack about. You may fetch something a nasty rap if you do. Remember you will be going several thousand times faster than you ever did before, heart, lungs, muscles, brain—everything—and you will hit hard without knowing it. You won't know it, you know. You'll feel just as you do now. Only everything in the world will seem to be going ever so many thousand times slower than it ever went before. That's what makes it so deuced queer."

"Lor'," I said. "And you mean—"

"You'll see," said he, and took up a little measure. He glanced at the material on his desk. "Glasses," he said, "water. All here. Mustn't take too much for the first attempt."

The little phial glucked out its precious contents.

"Don't forget what I told you," he said, turning the contents of the measure into a glass in the manner of an Italian waiter measuring whisky. "Sit with the eyes tightly shut and in absolute stillness for two minutes," he said. "Then you will hear me speak."

He added an inch or so of water to the little dose in each glass.

"By-the-by," he said, "don't put your glass down. Keep it in your hand and rest your hand on your knee. Yes—so. And now—"

He raised his glass.

"The New Accelerator," I said.

"The New Accelerator," he answered, and we touched glasses and drank, and instantly I closed my eyes.

You know that blank non-existence into which one drops when one has taken "gas." For an indefinite interval it was like that. Then I heard Gibberne telling me to wake up, and I stirred and opened my eyes. There he stood as he had been standing, glass still in hand. It was empty, that was all the difference.

"Well?" said I.

"Nothing out of the way?"

"Nothing. A slight feeling of exhilaration, perhaps. Nothing more."

"Sounds?"

"Things are still," I said. "By Jove! yes! They are still. Except the sort of faint pat, patter, like rain falling on different things. What is it?"

"Analysed sounds," I think he said, but I am not sure. He glanced at the window. "Have you ever seen a curtain before a window fixed in that way before?"

I followed his eyes, and there was the end of the curtain, frozen, as it were, corner high, in the act of flapping briskly in the breeze.

"No," said I; "that's odd."

"And here," he said, and opened the hand that held the glass. Naturally I winced, expecting the glass to smash. But so far from smashing it did not even seem to stir; it hung in mid-air—motionless.

"Roughly speaking," said Gibberne, "an object in these latitudes falls 16 feet in the first second. This glass is falling 16 feet in a second now. Only, you see, it hasn't been falling yet for the hundredth part of a second. That gives you some idea of the pace of my Accelerator."

And he waved his hand round and round, over and under the slowly sinking glass. Finally, he took it by the bottom, pulled it down, and placed it very carefully on the table. "Eh?" he said to me, and laughed.

"That seems all right," I said, and began very gingerly to raise myself from my chair. I felt perfectly well, very light and comfortable, and quite confident in my mind. I was going fast all over. My heart, for example, was beating a thousand times a second, but that caused me no discomfort at all. I looked out of the window. An immovable cyclist, head down and with a frozen puff of dust behind his driving-wheel, scorched to overtake a galloping char-a-banc that did not stir. I gaped in amazement at this incredible spectacle. "Gibberne," I cried, "how long will this confounded stuff last?"

"Heaven knows!" he answered. "Last time I took it I went to bed and slept it off. I tell you, I was frightened. It must have lasted some minutes, I think—it seemed like hours. But after a bit it slows down rather suddenly, I believe."

I was proud to observe that I did not feel frightened—I suppose because there were two of us. "Why shouldn't we go out?" I asked.

"Why not?"

"They'll see us."

"Not they. Goodness, no! Why, we shall be going a thousand times faster than the quickest conjuring trick that was ever done. Come along! Which way shall we go? Window, or door?"

And out by the window we went.

Assuredly of all the strange experiences that I have ever had, or imagined, or read of other people having or imagining, that little raid I made with Gibberne on the Folkestone Leas, under the influence of the New Accelerator, was the strangest and maddest of all. We went out by his gate into the road, and there we made a minute examination of the statuesque passing traffic. The tops of the wheels and some of the legs of the horses of this char-a-banc, the end of the whip-lash and the lower jaw of the conductor—who was just beginning to yawn— were perceptibly in motion, but all the rest of the lumbering conveyance seemed still. And quite noiseless except for a faint rattling that came from one man's throat! And as parts of this frozen edifice there were a driver, you know, and a conductor, and eleven people! The effect as we walked about the thing began by being madly queer, and ended by being disagreeable. There they were, people like ourselves and yet not like ourselves, frozen in careless attitudes, caught in mid-gesture. A girl and a man smiled at one another, a leering smile that threatened to last for evermore; a woman in a floppy capelline rested her arm on the rail and stared at Gibberne's house with the unwinking stare of eternity; a man stroked his moustache like a figure of wax, and another stretched a tiresome stiff hand with extended fingers towards his loosened hat. We stared at them, we laughed at them, we made faces at them, and then a sort of disgust of them came upon us, and we turned away and walked round in front of the cyclist towards the Leas.

"Goodness!" cried Gibberne, suddenly; "look there!"

He pointed, and there at the tip of his finger and sliding down the air with wings flapping slowly and at the speed of an exceptionally languid snail—was a bee.

And so we came out upon the Leas. There the thing seemed madder than ever. The band was playing in the upper stand, though all the sound it made for us was a low-pitched, wheezy rattle, a sort of prolonged last sigh that passed at times into a sound like the slow, muffled ticking of some monstrous clock. Frozen people stood erect, strange, silent, self-conscious-looking dummies hung unstably in mid-stride, promenading upon the grass. I passed close to a little poodle dog suspended in the act of leaping, and watched the slow movement of his legs as he sank to earth. "Lord, look here!" cried Gibberne, and we halted for a moment before a magnificent person in white faint-striped flannels, white shoes, and a Panama hat, who turned back to wink at two gaily dressed ladies he had passed. A wink, studied with such leisurely deliberation as we could afford, is an unattractive thing. It loses any quality of alert gaiety, and one remarks that the winking eye does not completely close, that under its drooping lid appears the lower edge of an eyeball and a little line of white. "Heaven give me memory," said I, "and I will never wink again."

"Or smile," said Gibberne, with his eye on the lady's answering teeth.

"It's infernally hot, somehow," said I. "Let's go slower."

"Oh, come along!" said Gibberne.

We picked our way among the bath-chairs in the path. Many of the people sitting in the chairs seemed almost natural in their passive poses, but the contorted scarlet of the bandsmen was not a restful thing to see. A purple-faced little gentleman was frozen in the midst of a violent struggle to refold his newspaper against the wind; there were many evidences that all these people in their sluggish way were exposed to a considerable breeze, a breeze that had no existence so far as our sensations went. We came out and walked a little way from the crowd, and turned and regarded it. To see all that multitude changed, to a picture, smitten rigid, as it were, into the semblance of realistic wax, was impossibly wonderful. It was absurd, of course; but it filled me with an irrational, an exultant sense of superior advantage. Consider the wonder of it! All that I had said, and thought, and done since the stuff had begun to work in my veins had happened, so far as those people, so far as the world in general went, in the twinkling of an eye. "The New Accelerator—" I began, but Gibberne interrupted me.

"There's that infernal old woman!" he said.

"What old woman?"

"Lives next door to me," said Gibberne. "Has a lapdog that yaps. Gods! The temptation is strong!"

There is something very boyish and impulsive about Gibberne at times. Before I could expostulate with him he had dashed forward, snatched the unfortunate animal out of visible existence, and was running violently with it towards the cliff of the Leas. It was most extraordinary. The little brute, you know, didn't bark or wriggle or make the slightest sign of vitality. It kept quite stiffly in an attitude of somnolent repose, and Gibberne held it by the neck. It was like running about with a dog of wood. "Gibberne," I cried, "put it down!" Then I said something else. "If you run like that, Gibberne," I cried, "you'll set your clothes on fire. Your linen trousers are going brown as it is!"

He clapped his hand on his thigh and stood hesitating on the verge. "Gibberne," I cried, coming up, "put it down. This heat is too much! It's our running so! Two or three miles a second! Friction of the air!"

"What?" he said, glancing at the dog.

"Friction of the air," I shouted. "Friction of the air. Going too fast. Like meteorites and things. Too hot. And, Gibberne! Gibberne! I'm all over pricking and a sort of perspiration. You can see people stirring slightly. I believe the stuff's working off! Put that dog down."

"Eh?" he said.

"It's working off," I repeated. "We're too hot and the stuff's working off! I'm wet through."

He stared at me. Then at the band, the wheezy rattle of whose performance was certainly going faster. Then with a tremendous sweep of the arm he hurled the dog away from him and it went spinning upward, still inanimate, and hung at last over the grouped parasols of a knot of chattering people. Gibberne was gripping my elbow. "By Jove!" he cried. "I believe—it is! A sort of hot pricking and—yes. That man's moving his pocket-handkerchief! Perceptibly. We must get out of this sharp."

But we could not get out of it sharply enough. Luckily, perhaps! For we might have run, and if we had run we should, I believe, have burst into flames. Almost certainly we should have burst into flames! You know we had neither of us thought of that. ... But before we could even begin to run the action of the drug had ceased. It was the business of a minute fraction of a second. The effect of the New Accelerator passed like the drawing of a curtain, vanished in the movement of a hand. I heard Gibberne's voice in infinite alarm. "Sit down," he said, and flop, down upon the turf at the edge of the Leas I sat—scorching as I sat. There is a patch of burnt grass there still where I sat down.

The whole stagnation seemed to wake up as I did so, the disarticu-
lated vibration of the band rushed together into a blast of music, the
promenaders put their feet down and walked their ways, the papers and
flags began flapping, smiles passed into words, the winker finished
his wink and went on his way complacently, and all the seated people
moved and spoke.

The whole world had come alive again, was going as fast as we
were, or rather we were going no faster than the rest of the world. It
was like slowing down as one comes into a railway station. Everything seemed to spin round for a second or two, I had the most transient feeling of nausea, and that was all. And the little dog which had
seemed to hang for a moment when the force of Gibberne's arm was
expended fell with a swift acceleration clean through a lady's parasol!

That was the saving of us. Unless it was for one corpulent old
gentleman in a bath-chair, who certainly did start at the sight of us
and afterwards regarded us at intervals with a darkly suspicious eye,
and, finally, I believe, said something to his nurse about us, I doubt if
a solitary person remarked our sudden appearance among them. Plop!
We must have appeared abruptly. We ceased to smoulder almost at
once, though the turf beneath me was uncomfortably hot. The attention of every one—including even the Amusements' Association band,
which on this occasion, for the only time in its history, got out of
tune—was arrested by the amazing fact, and the still more amazing
yapping and uproar caused by the fact that a respectable, over-fed
lap-dog sleeping quietly to the east of the bandstand should suddenly
fall through the parasol of a lady on the west—in a slightly singed
condition due to the extreme velocity of its movements through the
air. In these absurd days, too, when we are all trying to be as psychic,
and silly, and superstitious as possible! People got up and trod on
other people, chairs were overturned, the Leas policeman ran. How
the matter settled itself I do not know—we were much too anxious to
disentangle ourselves from the affair and get out of range of the eye
of the old gentleman in the bath-chair to make minute inquiries. As
soon as we were sufficiently cool and sufficiently recovered from our
giddiness and nausea and confusion of mind to do so we stood up
and, skirting the crowd, directed our steps back along the road below
the Metropole towards Gibberne's house. But amidst the din I heard
very distinctly the gentleman who had been sitting beside the lady of
the ruptured sunshade using quite unjustifiable threats and language
to one of those chair-attendants who have "Inspector" written on their
caps. "If you didn't throw the dog," he said, "who did?"

The sudden return of movement and familiar noises, and our natural
anxiety about ourselves (our clothes were still dreadfully hot, and the

fronts of the thighs of Gibberne's white trousers were scorched a
drabbish brown), prevented the minute observations I should have
liked to make on all these things. Indeed, I really made no observations of any scientific value on that return. The bee, of course, had
gone. I looked for that cyclist, but he was already out of sight as we
came into the Upper Sandgate Road or hidden from us by traffic; the
char-a-banc, however, with its people now all alive and stirring, was
clattering along at a spanking pace almost abreast of the nearer
church.

We noted, however, that the window-sill on which we had stepped
in getting out of the house was slightly singed, and that the impressions of our feet on the gravel of the path were unusually deep.

So it was I had my first experience of the New Accelerator. Practi-
cally we had been running about and saying and doing all sorts of
things in the space of a second or so of time. We had lived half an
hour while the band had played, perhaps, two bars. But the effect it
had upon us was that the whole world had stopped for our convenient inspection. Considering all things, and particularly considering our rashness in venturing out of the house, the experience might
certainly have been much more disagreeable than it was. It showed,
no doubt, that Gibberne has still much to learn before his preparation is a manageable convenience, but its practicability it certainly
demonstrated beyond all cavil.

Since that adventure he has been steadily bringing its use under
control, and I have several times, and without the slightest bad result,
taken measured doses under his direction; though I must confess I
have not yet ventured abroad again while under its influence. I may
mention, for example, that this story has been written at one sitting
and without interruption, except for the nibbling of some chocolate,
by its means. I began at 6.25, and my watch is now very nearly at the
minute past the half-hour. The convenience of securing a long, uninter-
rupted spell of work in the midst of a day full of engagements cannot
be exaggerated. Gibberne is now working at the quantitative handling
of his preparation, with especial reference to its distinctive effects
upon different types of constitution. He then hopes to find a Retarder
with which to dilute its present rather excessive potency. The Retarder
will, of course, have the reverse effect to the Accelerator; used alone
it should enable the patient to spread a few seconds over many hours of
ordinary time,—and so to maintain an apathetic inaction, a glacier-
like absence of alacrity, amidst the most animated or irritating surroundings. The two things together must necessarily work an entire
revolution in civilised existence. It is the beginning of our escape from
that Time Garment of which Carlyle speaks. While this Accelerator

will enable us to concentrate ourselves with tremendous impact upon any moment or occasion that demands our utmost sense and vigour, the Retarder will enable us to pass in passive tranquillity through infinite hardship and tedium. Perhaps I am a little optimistic about the Retarder, which has indeed still to be discovered, but about the Accelerator there is no possible sort of doubt whatever. Its appearance upon the market in a convenient, controllable, and assimilable form is a matter of the next few months. It will be obtainable of all chemists and druggists, in small green bottles, at a high but, considering its extraordinary qualities, by no means excessive price. Gibberne's Nervous Accelerator it will be called, and he hopes to be able to supply it in three strengths: one in 200, one in 900, and one in 2000, distinguished by yellow, pink, and white labels respectively.

No doubt its use renders a great number of very extraordinary things possible; for, of course, the most remarkable and, possibly, even criminal proceedings may be effected with impunity by thus dodging, as it were, into the interstices of time. Like all potent preparations it will be liable to abuse. We have, however, discussed this aspect of the question very thoroughly, and we have decided that this is purely a matter of medical jurisprudence and altogether outside our province. We shall manufacture and sell the Accelerator, and, as for the consequences—we shall see.

"Wireless"

Rudyard Kipling

"It's a funny thing, this Marconi business, isn't it?" said Mr. Shaynor, coughing heavily. "Nothing seems to make any difference, by what they tell me—storms, hills, or anything; but if that's true we shall know before morning."

"Of course it's true," I answered, stepping behind the counter. "Where's old Mr. Cashell?"

"He's had to go to bed on account of his influenza. He said you'd very likely drop in."

"Where's his nephew?"

"Inside, getting the things ready. He told me that the last time they experimented they put the pole on the roof of one of the big hotels here, and the batteries electrified all the water-supply, and"—he giggled— "the ladies got shocks when they took their baths."

"I never heard of that."

"The hotel wouldn't exactly advertise it, would it? Just now, by what Mr. Cashell tells me, they're trying to signal from here to Poole, and they're using stronger batteries than ever. But, you see, he being the guvnor's nephew and all that (and it will be in the papers too), it doesn't matter how they electrify things in this house. Are you going to watch?"

"Very much. I've never seen this game. Aren't you going to bed?"

"We don't close till ten on Saturdays. There's a good deal of influenza in town, too, and there'll be a dozen prescriptions coming in before morning. I generally sleep in the chair here. It's warmer than jumping out of bed every time. Bitter cold, isn't it?"

"Freezing hard. I'm sorry your cough's worse."

"Thank you. I don't mind cold so much. It's this wind that fair cuts me to pieces." He coughed again hard and hackingly, as an old lady came in for ammoniated quinine. "We've just run out of it in bottles, madam," said Mr. Shaynor, returning to the professional tone, "but if you will wait two minutes, I'll make it up for you, madam."

I had used the shop for some time, and my acquaintance with the proprietor had ripened into friendship. It was Mr. Cashell who revealed to me the purpose and power of Apothecaries' Hall what time a fellow-chemist had made an error in a prescription of mine, had lied to cover his sloth, and when error and lie were brought home to him had written vain letters.

"A disgrace to our profession," said the thin, mild-eyed man, hotly, after studying the evidence. "You couldn't do a better service to the profession than report him to Apothecaries' Hall."

I did so, not knowing what djinns I should evoke; and the result was such an apology as one might make who had spent a night on the rack.

I conceived great respect for Apothecaries' Hall, and esteem for Mr. Cashell, a zealous craftsman who magnified his calling. Until Mr. Shaynor came down from the North his assistants had by no means agreed with Mr. Cashell. "They forget," said he, "that, first and foremost, the compounder is a medicine-man. On him depends the physician's reputation. He holds it literally in the hollow of his hand, Sir."

Mr. Shaynor's manners had not, perhaps, the polish of the grocery and Italian warehouse next door, but he knew and loved his dispensary work in every detail. For relaxation he seemed to go no farther afield than the romance of drugs—their discovery, preparation, packing, and export—but it led him to the ends of the earth, and on this subject, and the Pharmaceutical Formulary, and Nicholas Culpepper, most confident of physicians, we met.

Little by little I grew to know something of his beginnings and his hopes—of his mother, who had been a school-teacher in one of the northern counties, and of his red-headed father, a small job-master at Kirby Moors, who died when he was a child; of the examinations he had passed and of their exceeding and increasing difficulty; of his dreams of a shop in London; of his hate for the price-cutting Co-operative stores; and, most interesting, of his mental attitude towards customers.

"There's a way you get into," he told me, "of serving them carefully, and I hope, politely, without stopping your own thinking. I've been reading Christy's *New Commercial Plants* all this autumn, and that needs keeping your mind on it, I can tell you. So long as it isn't a prescription, of course, I can carry as much as half a page of Christy in my head, and at the same time I could sell out all that window twice over, and not a penny wrong at the end. As to prescriptions, I think I could make up the general run of 'em in my sleep, almost."

For reasons of my own, I was deeply interested in Marconi experiments at their outset in England; and it was of a piece with Mr. Cashell's unvarying thoughtfulness that, when his nephew the electrician appropriated the house for a long-range installation, he should, as I have said, invite me to see the result.

The old lady went away with her medicine, and Mr. Shaynor and I stamped on the tiled floor behind the counter to keep ourselves warm. The shop, by the light of the many electrics, looked like a Paris-diamond mine, for Mr. Cashell believed in all the ritual of his craft. Three superb glass jars—red, green, and blue—of the sort that led Rosamond to parting with her shoes—blazed in the broad plate-glass windows, and there was a confused smell of orris, Kodak films, vulcanite, tooth-powder, sachets, and almond-cream in the air. Mr. Shaynor fed the dispensary stove, and we sucked cayenne-pepper jujubes and men-thol lozenges. The brutal east wind had cleared the streets, and the few passers-by were muffled to their puckered eyes. In the Italian warehouse next door some gay feathered birds and game, hung upon hooks, sagged to the wind across the left edge of our window-frame.

"They ought to take these poultry in—all knocked about like that," said Mr. Shaynor. "Doesn't it make you feel fair perishing? See that old hare! The wind's nearly blowing the fur off him."

I saw the belly-fur of the dead beast blown apart in ridges and streaks as the wind caught it, showing bluish skin underneath. "Bitter cold," said Mr. Shaynor, shuddering. "Fancy going out on a night like this! Oh, here's young Mr. Cashell."

The door of the inner office behind the dispensary opened, and an energetic, spade-bearded man stepped forth, rubbing his hands.

"I want a bit of tin-foil, Shaynor," he said. "Good-evening. My uncle told me you might be coming." This to me, as I began the first of a hundred questions.

"I've everything in order," he replied. "We're only waiting until Poole calls us up. Excuse me a minute. You can come in whenever you like—but I'd better be with the instruments. Give me that tin-foil. Thanks."

While we were talking, a girl—evidently no customer—had come into the shop, and the face and bearing of Mr. Shaynor changed. She leaned confidently across the counter.

"But I can't," I heard him whisper uneasily—the flush on his cheek was dull red, and his eyes shone like a drugged moth's. "I can't. I tell you I'm alone in the place."

"No, you aren't. Who's *that?* Let him look after it for half an hour. A brisk walk will do you good. Ah, come now, John."

"But he isn't—"

"I don't care. I want you to; we'll only go round by St. Agnes'. If you don't—"

He crossed to where I stood in the shadow of the dispensary counter, and began some sort of broken apology about a lady-friend.

"Yes," she interrupted. "You take the shop for half an hour—to oblige *me*, won't you?" She had a singularly rich and promising voice that well matched her outline.

"All right," I said. "I'll do it—but you'd better wrap yourself up, Mr. Shaynor."

"Oh, a brisk walk ought to help me. We're only going round by the church." I heard him cough grievously as they went out together.

I refilled the stove, and, after reckless expenditure of Mr. Cashell's coal, drove some warmth into the shop. I explored many of the glass-knobbed drawers that lined the walls, tasted some disconcerting drugs, and, by the aid of a few cardamoms, ground ginger, chloric-ether, and dilute alcohol, manufactured a new and wildish drink, of which I bore a glassful to young Mr. Cashell, busy in the back office. He laughed shortly when I told him that Mr. Shaynor had stepped out—but a frail coil of wire held all his attention, and he had no word for me bewildered among the batteries and rods. The noise of the sea on the beach began to make itself heard as the traffic in the street ceased. Then briefly, but very lucidly, he gave me the names and uses of the mechanism that crowded the tables and the floor.

"When do you expect to get the message from Poole?" I demanded, sipping my liquor out of a graduated glass.

"About midnight, if everything is in order. We've got our installation-pole fixed to the roof of the house. I shouldn't advise you to turn on a tap or anything to-night. We've connected up with the plumbing, and all the water will be electrified." He repeated to me the history of the agitated ladies at the hotel at the time of the first installation.

"But what *is* it?" I asked. "Electricity is out of my beat altogether."

"Ah, if you knew *that* you'd know something nobody knows. It's just It—what we call Electricity, but the magic—the manifestations—the Hertzian waves—are all revealed by this. The coherer, we call it."

He picked up a glass tube not much thicker than a thermometer, in which, almost touching, were two tiny silver plugs, and between them an infinitesimal pinch of metallic dust. "That's all," he said, proudly, as though himself responsible for the wonder. "That is the thing that will reveal to us the Powers—whatever the Powers may be—at work—through space—a long distance away."

Just then Mr. Shaynor returned alone and stood coughing his heart out on the mat.

"Serves you right for being such a fool," said young Mr. Cashell, as annoyed as myself at the interruption. "Never mind—we've all the night before us to see wonders."

Shaynor clutched the counter, his handkerchief to his lips. When he brought it away I saw two bright red stains.

"I—I've got a bit of a rasped throat from smoking cigarettes," he panted. "I think I'll try a cubeb."

"Better take some of this. I've been compounding while you've been away." I handed him the brew.

"'Twon't make me drunk, will it? I'm almost a teetotaller. My word! That's grateful and comforting."

He set down the empty glass to cough afresh.

"Brr! But it was cold out there! I shouldn't care to be lying in my grave a night like this. Don't you ever have a sore throat from smoking?" He pocketed the handkerchief after a furtive peep.

"Oh, yes, sometimes," I replied, wondering, while I spoke, into what agonies of terror I should fall if ever I saw those bright-red danger-signals under my nose. Young Mr. Cashell among the batteries coughed slightly to show that he was quite ready to continue his scientific explanations, but I was thinking still of the girl with the rich voice and the significantly cut mouth, at whose command I had taken charge of the shop. It flashed across me that she distantly resembled the seductive shape on a gold-framed toilet-water advertisement whose charms were unholily heightened by the glare from the red bottle in the window. Turning to make sure, I saw Mr. Shaynor's eyes bent in the same direction, and by instinct recognised that the flamboyant thing was to him a shrine. "What do you take for your—cough?" I asked.

"Well, I'm the wrong side of the counter to believe much in patent medicines. But there are asthma cigarettes and there are pastilles. To tell you the truth, if you don't object to the smell, which is very like incense, I believe, though I'm not a Roman Catholic, Blaudett's Cathedral Pastilles relieve me as much as anything."

"Let's try." I had never raided a chemist's shop before, so I was thorough. We unearthed the pastilles—brown, gummy cones of benzoin—and set them alight under the toilet-water advertisement, where they fumed in thin blue spirals.

"Of course," said Mr. Shaynor, to my question, "what one uses in the shop for one's self comes out of one's pocket. Why, stock-taking in our business is nearly the same as with jewellers—and I can't say more than that. But one gets them"—he pointed to the pastille-box— "at trade prices." Evidently the censing of the gay, seven-tinted wench with the teeth was an established ritual which cost something.

"And when do we shut up shop?"

"We stay like this all night. The guv—old Mr. Cashell—doesn't believe in locks and shutters as compared with electric light. Besides, it brings trade. I'll just sit here in the chair by the stove and write a letter, if you don't mind. Electricity isn't my prescription."

The energetic young Mr. Cashell snorted within, and Shaynor settled himself up in his chair over which he had thrown a staring red, black, and yellow Austrian jute blanket, rather like a table-cover. I cast about, amid patent-medicine pamphlets, for something to read, but finding little, returned to the manufacture of the new drink. The Italian warehouse took down its game and went to bed. Across the street blank shutters flung back the gaslight in cold smears; the dried pavement seemed to rough up in goose-flesh under the scouring of the savage wind, and we could hear, long ere he passed, the policeman flapping his arms to keep himself warm. Within, the flavours of cardamoms and chloric-ether disputed those of the pastilles and a score of drugs and perfume and soap scents. Our electric lights, set low down in the windows before the tun-bellied Rosamond jars, flung inward three monstrous daubs of red, blue, and green, that broke into kaleidoscopic lights on the faceted knobs of the drug-drawers, the cut-glass scent flagons, and the bulbs of the sparklet bottles. They flushed the white-tiled floor in gorgeous patches; splashed along the nickel-silver counter-rails, and turned the polished mahogany counter-panels to the likeness of intricate grained marbles—slabs of porphyry and malachite. Mr. Shaynor unlocked a drawer, and ere he began to write, took out a meagre bundle of letters. From my place by the stove, I could see the scalloped edges of the paper with a flaring monogram m the corner and could even smell the reek of chypre. At each page he turned toward the toilet-water lady of the advertisement and devoured her with over-luminous eyes. He had drawn the Austrian blanket over his shoulders, and among those warring lights he looked more than ever the incarnation of a drugged moth—a tiger-moth as I thought.

He put his letter into an envelope, stamped it with stiff mechanical movements, and dropped it in the drawer. Then I became aware of the silence of a great city asleep—the silence that underlay the even voice of the breakers along the sea-front—a thick, tingling quiet of warm life stilled down for its appointed time, and unconsciously I moved about the glittering shop as one moves in a sick-room. Young Mr. Cashell was adjusting some wire that crackled from time to time with the tense, knuckle-stretching sound of the electric spark. Upstairs, where a door shut and opened swiftly, I could hear his uncle coughing abed.

"Here," I said, when the drink was properly warmed, "take some of this, Mr. Shaynor."

He jerked in his chair with a start and a wrench, and held out his hand for the glass. The mixture, of a rich port-wine colour, frothed at the top.

"It looks," he said, suddenly, "it looks—those bubbles—like a string of pearls winking at you—rather like the pearls round that young lady's

neck." He turned again to the advertisement where the female in the
dove-coloured corset had seen fit to put on all her pearls before she
cleaned her teeth.

"Not bad, is it?" I said.

"Eh?"

He rolled his eyes heavily full on me, and, as I stared, I beheld all
meaning and consciousness die out of the swiftly dilating pupils. His
figure lost its stark rigidity, softened into the chair, and, chin on chest,
hands dropped before him, he rested open-eyed, absolutely still.

"I'm afraid I've rather cooked Shaynor's goose," I said, bearing
the fresh drink to young Mr. Cashell. "Perhaps it was the chloric-
ether."

"Oh, he's all right." The spade-bearded man glanced at him piti-
ingly. "Consumptives go off in those sort of dozes very often. It's exhaustion ... I don't wonder. I daresay the liquor will do him good. It's grand
stuff." He finished his share appreciatively. "well, as I was saying—
before he interrupted—about this little coherer. The pinch of dust,
you see, is nickelfilings. The Hertzian waves, you see, come out of
space from the station that despatches 'em, and all these little particles are attracted together—cohere, we call it—for just so long as
the current passes through them. Now, its important to remember
that the current is an induced current. There are a good many kinds
of induction—"

"Yes, but what *is* induction?"

"That's rather hard to explain untechnically. But the long and the
short of it is that when a current of electricity passes through a wire
there's a lot of magnetism present round that wire; and if you put
another wire parallel to, and within what we call its magnetic field—
why, then the second wire will also become charged with electricity."

"On its own account?"

"On its own account."

"Then let's see if I've got it correctly. Miles off, at Poole, or wherever it is—"

"It will be anywhere in ten years."

"You've got a charged wire—"

"Charged with Hertzian waves which vibrate, say two hundred and
thirty million times a second." Mr. Cashell snaked his forefinger rapidly through the air.

"All right—a charged wire at Poole, giving out these waves into
space. Then this wire of yours sticking out into space—on the roof of
the house—in some mysterious way gets charged with those waves
from Poole—"

"Or anywhere—it only happens to be Poole to-night."

"And those waves set the coherer at work, just like an ordinary telegraph-office ticker?"

"No! That's where so many people make the mistake. The Hertzian waves wouldn't be strong enough to work a great heavy Morse instrument like ours. They can only just make that dust cohere, and while it coheres (a little while for a dot and a longer while for a dash) the current from this battery—the home battery"—he laid his hand on the thing— "can get through to the Morse printing-machine to record the dot or dash. Let me make it clearer. Do you know anything about steam?"

"Very little. But go on."

"Well, the coherer is like a steam-valve. Any child can open a valve and start a steamer's engines, because a turn of the hand lets in the main steam, doesn't it? Now, this home battery here ready to print is the main steam. The coherer is the valve, always ready to be turned on. The Hertzian wave is the child's hand that turns it."

"I see. That's marvellous."

"Marvellous, isn't it? And, remember, we're only at the beginning. There's nothing we shan't be able to do in ten years. I want to live— my God, how I want to live, and see it develop!" He looked through the door at Shaynor breathing lightly in his chair. "Poor beast! And he wants to keep company with Fanny Brand."

"Fanny *who?*" I said, for the name struck an obscurely familiar chord in my brain—something connected with a stained handkerchief, and the word "arterial."

"Fanny Brand—the girl you kept shop for." He laughed. "That's all I know about her, and for the life of me I can't see what Shaynor sees in her, or she in him."

"*Can't* you see what he sees in her?" I insisted.

"Oh, yes, if *that's* what you mean. She's a great, big, fat lump of a girl, and so on. I suppose that's why he's so crazy after her. She isn't his sort. Well, it doesn't matter. My uncle says he's bound to die before the year's out. Your drink's given him a good sleep, at any rate." Young Mr. Cashell could not catch Mr. Shaynor's face, which was half turned to the advertisement.

I stoked the stove anew, for the room was growing cold, and lighted another pastille. Mr. Shaynor in his chair, never moving, looked through and over me with eyes as wide and lustreless as those of a dead hare.

"Poole's late," said young Mr. Cashell, when I stepped back. "I'll just send them a call."

He pressed a key in the semi-darkness, and with a rending crackle there leaped between two brass knobs a spark, streams of sparks, and sparks again.

"Grand, isn't it? *That's* the Power—our unknown Power—kicking and fighting to be let loose," said young Mr. Cashell. "There she goes—kick—kick—kick into space. I never get over the strangeness of it when I work a sending-machine—waves going into space, you know. T.R. is our call. Poole ought to answer with L.L.L."

We waited two, three, five minutes. In that silence, of which the boom of the tide was an orderly part, I caught the clear "*kiss—kiss—kiss*" of the halliards on the roof, as they were blown against the installation-pole.

"Poole is not ready. I'll stay here and call you when he is."

I returned to the shop, and set down my glass an a marble slab with a careless clink. As I did so, Shaynor rose to his feet, his eyes fixed once more on the advertisement, where the young woman bathed in the light from the red jar simpered pinkly over her pearls. His lips moved without cessation. I stepped nearer to listen. "And threw—and threw—and threw," he repeated; his face all sharp with some inexplicable agony.

I moved forward astonished. But it was then he found words—delivered roundly and clearly. These:

AND THREW WARM GULES ON MADELEINE'S YOUNG BREAST.

The trouble passed off his countenance, and he returned lightly to his place, rubbing his hands.

It had never occurred to me, though we had many times discussed reading and prize-competitions as a diversion, that Mr. Shaynor ever read Keats, or could quote him at all appositely. There was, after all, a certain stained-glass effect of light on the high bosom of the highly-polished picture which might, by stretch of fancy, suggest, as a vile chromo recalls some incomparable canvas, the line he had spoken. Night, my drink, and solitude were evidently turning Mr. Shaynor into a poet. He sat down again and wrote swiftly on his villainous note-paper, his lips quivering.

I shut the door into the inner office and moved up behind him. He made no sign that he saw or heard. I looked over his shoulder, and read, amid half-formed words, sentences, and wild scratches:—

——VERY COLD IT WAS. VERY COLD
THE HARE—THE HARE—THE HARE—
THE BIRDS——

He raised his head sharply, and frowned toward the blank shutters of the poulterer's shop where they jutted out against our window. Then one clear line came:—

The hare, in spite of fur, was very cold.

The head, moving machine-like, turned right to the advertisement where the Blaudett's Cathedral pastille reeked abominably. He grunted, and went on:—

Incense in a censer——
Before her darling picture framed in gold—
Maiden's picture—angel's portrait—

"Hsh!" said Mr. Cashell guardedly from the inner office, as though in the presence of spirits. "There's something coming through from somewhere; but it isn't Poole." I heard the crackle of sparks as he depressed the keys of the transmitter. In my own brain, too, something crackled, or it might have been the hair on my head. Then I heard my own voice, in a harsh whisper: "Mr. Cashell, there is something coming through here, too. Leave me alone till I tell you."

"But I thought you'd come to see this wonderful thing—Sir," indignantly at the end.

"Leave me alone till I tell you. Be quiet."

I watched—I waited. Under the blue-veined hand—the dry hand of the consumptive—came away clear, without erasure:—

And my weak spirit fails
To think how the dead must freeze—

he shivered as he wrote—

Beneath the churchyard mould.

Then he stopped, laid the pen down, and leaned back.

For an instant, that was half an eternity, the shop spun before me in a rainbow-tinted whirl, in and through which my own soul most dispassionately considered my own soul as that fought with an over-mastering fear. Then I smelt the strong smell of cigarettes from Mr. Shaynor's clothing, and heard, as though it had been the rending of trumpets, the rattle of his breathing. I was still in my place of observation, much as one would watch a rifle-shot at the butts, half-bent, hands on my knees, and head within a few inches of the black, red, and yellow blanket of his shoulder. I was whispering encouragement, evidently to my other self, sounding sentences, such as men pronounce in dreams.

"If he has read Keats, it proves nothing. If he hasn't—like causes *must* beget like effects. There is no escape from this law. *You* ought to be grateful that you know "St. Agnes' Eve" without the book; because, given the circumstances, such as Fanny Brand, who is the key of the enigma, and approximately represents the latitude and longitude of Fanny Brawne; allowing also for the bright red colour of the arterial blood upon the handkerchief, which was just what you were puzzling over in the shop just now; and counting the effect of the professional environment, here almost perfectly duplicated—the result is logical and inevitable. As inevitable as induction."

Still, the other half of my soul refused to be comforted. It was cowering in some minute and inadequate corner—at an immense distance.

Hereafter, I found myself one person again, my hands still gripping my knees, and my eyes glued on the page before Mr. Shaynor. As dreamers accept and explain the upheaval of landscapes and the resurrection of the dead, with excerpts from the evening hymn or the multiplication-table, so I had accepted the facts, whatever they might be, that I should witness, and had devised a theory, sane and plausible to my mind, that explained them all. Nay, I was even in advance of my facts, walking hurriedly before them, assured that they would fit my theory. And all that I now recall of that epoch-making theory are the lofty words: "If he has read Keats it's the chloric-ether. If he hasn't, it's the identical bacillus, or Hertzian wave of tuberculosis, *plus* Fanny Brand and the professional status which, in conjunction with the main-stream of subconscious thought common to all mankind, has thrown up temporarily an induced Keats."

Mr. Shaynor returned to his work, erasing and rewriting as before with swiftness. Two or three blank pages he tossed aside. Then he wrote, muttering:

THE LITTLE SMOKE OF A CANDLE THAT GOES OUT.

"No," he muttered. "Little smoke—little smoke—little smoke. What else?" He thrust his chin forward toward the advertisement, whereunder the last of the Blaudett's Cathedral pastilles fumed in its holder. "Ah!" Then with relief:—

THE LITTLE SMOKE THAT DIES IN MOONLIGHT COLD.

Evidently he was snared by the rhymes of his first verse, for he wrote and rewrote "gold—cold—mould" many times. Again he sought inspiration from the advertisement, and set down, without erasure, the line I had overheard:—

AND THREW WARM GULES ON MADELEINE'S YOUNG BREAST.

As I remembered the original it is "fair"—a trite word—instead of "young," and I found myself nodding approval, though I admitted that the attempt to reproduce "Its little smoke in pallid moonlight died" was a failure.

Followed without a break ten or fifteen lines of bald prose—the naked soul's confession of its physical yearning for its beloved—unclean as we count uncleanliness; unwholesome, but human exceedingly; the raw material, so it seemed to me in that hour and in that place, whence Keats wove the twenty-sixth, seventh, and eighth stanzas of his poem. Shame I had none in overseeing this revelation; and my fear had gone with the smoke of the pastille.

"That's it," I murmured. "That's how it's blocked out. Go on! Ink it in, man. Ink it in!"

Mr. Shaynor returned to broken verse wherein "loveliness" was made to rhyme with a desire to look upon "her empty dress." He picked up a fold of the gay, soft blanket, spread it over one hand, caressed it with infinite tenderness, thought, muttered, traced some snatches which I could not decipher, shut his eyes drowsily, shook his head, and dropped the stuff. Here I found myself at fault, for I could not then see (as I do now) in what manner a red, black, and yellow Austrian blanket coloured his dreams.

In a few minutes he laid aside his pen, and, chin on hand, considered the shop with thoughtful and intelligent eyes. He threw down the blanket, rose, passed along a line of drug-drawers, and read the names on the labels aloud. Returning, he took from his desk Christy's *New Commercial Plants* and the old Culpepper that I had given him, opened and laid them side by side with a clerky air, all trace of passion gone from his face, read first in one and then in the other, and paused with pen behind his ear.

"What wonder of Heaven's coming now?" I thought.

"Manna—manna—manna," he said at last, under wrinkled brows. "That's what I wanted. Good! Now then! Now then! Good! Good! Oh, by God, that's good!" His voice rose and he spoke rightly and fully without a falter:—

Candied apple, quince and plum and gourd,
With jellies smoother than the creamy curd,
And lucent syrops tinct with cinnamon;
Manna and dates in argosy transferred
From Fez; and spiced dainties, every one
From silken Samarcand to cedared Lebanon.

He repeated it once more, using "blander" for "smoother" in the second line; then wrote it down without erasure, but this time (my

set eyes missed no stroke of any word) he substituted "soother" for
his atrocious second thought, so that it came away under his hand as
it is written in the book—as it is written in the book.

A wind went shouting down the street, and on the heels of the
wind followed a spurt and rattle of rain.

After a smiling pause—and good right had he to smile—he began
anew, always tossing the last sheet over his shoulder:—

THE SHARP RAIN FALLING ON THE WINDOW-PANE.
RATTLING SLEET—THE WIND-BLOWN SLEET.

Then prose: "It is very cold of mornings when the wind brings
rain and sleet with it. I heard the sleet on the window-pane outside,
and thought of you, my darling. I am always thinking of you. I wish
we could both run away like two lovers into the storm and get that little
cottage by the sea which we are always thinking about, my own dear
darling. We could sit and watch the sea beneath our windows. It would
be a fairyland all of our own—a fairy sea—a fairy sea ..."

He stopped, raised his head, and listened. The steady drone of
the Channel along the sea-front that had borne us company so long
leaped up a note to the sudden fuller surge that signals the change
from ebb to flood. It beat in like the change of step throughout an army—
this renewed pulse of the sea—and filled our ears till they, accepting
it, marked it no longer.

A FAIRYLAND FOR YOU AND ME
ACROSS THE FOAM-BEYOND ...
A MAGIC FOAM, A PERILOUS SEA.

He grunted again with effort and bit his underlip. My throat dried,
but I dared not gulp to moisten it lest I should break the spell that
was drawing him nearer and nearer to the highwater mark but two of the
sons of Adam have reached. Remember that in all the millions permitted
there are no more than five—five little lines—of which one can say: "These
are the pure Magic. These are the clear Vision. The rest is only poetry."
And Mr. Shaynor was playing hot and cold with two of them!

I vowed no unconscious thought of mine should influence the
blindfold soul, and pinned myself desperately to the other three, repeating and re-repeating:—

A SAVAGE PLACE! AS HOLY AND ENCHANTED
AS E'ER BENEATH A WANING MOON WAS HAUNTED
BY WOMAN WAILING FOR HER DEMON-LOVER.

But though I believed my brain thus occupied, my every sense hung upon the writing under the dry, bony hand, all brown-fingered with chemicals and cigarette-smoke.

OUR WINDOWS FRONTING ON THE DANGEROUS FOAM,

(he wrote, after long, irresolute snatches), and then—

OUR OPEN CASEMENTS FACING DESOLATE SEAS
FORLORN—FORLORN—

Here again his face grew peaked and anxious with that sense of loss I had first seen when the Power snatched him. But this time the agony was tenfold keener. As I watched it mounted like mercury in the tube. It lighted his face from within till I thought the visibly scourged soul must leap forth naked between his jaws, unable to endure. A drop of sweat trickled from my forehead down my nose and splashed on the back of my hand.

OUR WINDOWS FACING ON THE DESOLATE SEAS
AND PEARLY FOAM OF MAGIC FAIRYLAND—

"Not yet—not yet," he muttered, "wait a minute. *Please* wait a minute. I shall get it then—

OUR MAGIC WINDOWS FRONTING ON THE SEA,
THE DANGEROUS FOAM OF DESOLATE SEAS ...
FOR AYE.

Ouh, my God!"
From head to heel he shook—shook from the marrow of his bones outwards—then leaped to his feet with raised arms, and slid the chair screeching across the tiled floor where it struck the drawers behind and fell with ajar. Mechanically, I stooped to recover it.

As I rose, Mr. Shaynor was stretching and yawning at leisure.

"I've had a bit of a doze," he said. "How did I come to knock the chair over? You look rather—"

"The chair startled me," I answered. "It was so sudden in this quiet."

Young Mr. Cashell behind his shut door was offendedly silent.

"I suppose I must have been dreaming," said Mr. Shaynor.

"I suppose you must," I said. "Talking of dreams—I—I noticed you writing—before—"

He flushed consciously.

"I meant to ask you if you've ever read anything written by a man called Keats."

"Oh! I haven't much time to read poetry, and I can't say that I remember the name exactly. Is he a popular writer?"

"Middling. I thought you might know him because he's the only poet who was ever a druggist. And he's rather what's called the lover's poet."

"Indeed. I must dip into him. What did he write about?"

"A lot of things. Here's a sample that may interest you."

Then and there, carefully, I repeated the verse he had twice spoken and once written not ten minutes ago.

"Ah! Anybody could see he was a druggist from that line about the tinctures and syrups. It's a fine tribute to our profession."

"I don't know," said young Mr. Cashell, with icy politeness, opening the door one half-inch, "if you still happen to be interested in our trifling experiments. But, should such be the case—"

I drew him aside, whispering, "Shaynor seemed going off into some sort of fit when I spoke to you just now. I thought, even at the risk of being rude, it wouldn't do to take you off your instruments just as the call was coming through. Don't you see?"

"Granted—granted as soon as asked," he said, unbending. "I *did* think it a shade odd at the time. So that was why he knocked the chair down?"

"I hope I haven't missed anything," I said.

"I'm afraid I can't say that, but you're just in time for the end of a rather curious performance. You can come in too, Mr. Shaynor. Listen, while I read it off."

The Morse instrument was ticking furiously. Mr. Cashell interpreted: "'*K.K.V. Can make nothing of your signals.*'" A pause. "'*M.M.V. M.M.V. Signals unintelligible. Purpose anchor Sundown Bay. Examine instruments to-morrow.*' Do you know what that means? It's a couple of men-o'-war working Marconi signals off the Isle of Wight. They are trying to talk to each other. Neither can read the other's messages, but all their messages are being taken in by our receiver here. They've been going on for ever so long. I wish you could have heard it."

"How wonderful!" I said. "Do you mean we're overhearing Portsmouth ships trying to talk to each other—that we're eavesdropping across half South England?"

"Just that. Their transmitters are all right, but their receivers are out of order, so they only get a dot here and a dash there. Nothing clear."

"Why is that?"

"God knows—and Science will know tomorrow. Perhaps the induction is faulty; perhaps the receivers aren't tuned to receive just the number of vibrations per second that the transmitter sends. Only a word here and there. Just enough to tantalise."

Again the Morse sprang to life.

"That's one of 'em complaining now. Listen *"Disheartening—most disheartening."* It's quite pathetic. Have you ever seen a spiritualistic stance? It reminds me of that sometimes—odds and ends of messages coming out of nowhere—a word here and there—no good at all."

"But mediums are all impostors," said Mr. Shaynor, in the doorway, lighting an asthma-cigarette. "They only do it for the money they can make. I've seen 'em."

"Here's Poole, at last—clear as a bell. L.L.L. *Now* we shan't be long." Mr. Cashell rattled the keys merrily. "Anything you'd like to tell 'em?"

"No, I don't think so," I said. "I'll go home and get to bed. I'm feeling a little tired."

Phantas

OLIVER ONIONS

For, barring all pother,
With this, or the other,
Still Britons are Lords of the Main.
The Chapter of Admirals

I

As Abel Keeling lay on the galleon's deck, held from rolling down
it only by his own weight and the sun-blackened hand that lay outstretched upon the planks, his gaze wandered, but ever returned to
the bell that hung, jammed with the dangerous heel-over of the vessel, in
the small ornamental belfry immediately abaft the mainmast. The bell
was of cast bronze, with half-obliterated bosses upon it that had been
the heads of cherubs; but wind and salt spray had given it a thick
incrustation of bright, beautiful, lichenous green. It was this colour
that Abel Keeling's eyes liked.

For wherever else on the galleon his eyes rested they found only
whiteness—the whiteness of extreme eld. There were slightly varying
degrees in her whiteness; here she was of a white that glistened like
salt-granules, there of a greyish chalky white, and again her whiteness had the yellowish cast of decay; but everywhere it was the mild,
disquieting whiteness of materials out of which the life had departed.
Her cordage was bleached as old straw is bleached, and half her ropes
kept their shape little more firmly than the ash of a string keeps its
shape after the fire has passed; her pallid timbers were white and clean
as bones found in sand; and even the wild frankincense with which
(for lack of tar, at her last touching of land) she had been pitched,
had dried to a pale hard gum that sparkled like quartz in her open
seams. The sun was yet so pale a buckler of silver through the still
white mists that not a cord or timber cast a shadow; and only Abel
Keeling's face and hands were black, carked and cinder-black from
exposure to his pitiless rays.

226

The galleon was the *Mary of the Tower*, and she had a frightful list to starboard. So canted was she that her mainyard dipped one of its steel sickles into the glassy water, and, had her foremast remained, or more than the broken stump of her bonaventure mizzen, she must have turned over completely. Many days ago they had stripped the mainyard of its course, and had passed the sail under the *Mary*'s bottom, in the hope that it would stop the leak. This it had partly done as long as the galleon had continued to glide one way; then, without coming about, she had begun to glide the other, the ropes had parted, and she had dragged the sail after her, leaving a broad tarnish on the silver sea.

For it was broadside that the galleon glided, almost imperceptibly, ever sucking down. She glided as if a loadstone drew her, and, at first, Abel Keeling had thought it was a loadstone, pulling at her iron, drawing her through the pearly mists that lay like face-cloths to the water and hid at a short distance the tarnish left by the sail. But later he had known that it was no loadstone drawing at her iron. The motion was due—must be due—to the absolute deadness of the calm in that silent, sinister, three-miles-broad waterway. With the eye of his mind he saw that loadstone now as he lay against a gun-truck, all but toppling down the deck. Soon that would happen again which had happened for five days past. He would hear again the chattering of monkeys and the screaming of parrots, the mat of green and yellow weeds would creep in towards the Mary over the quicksilver sea, once more the sheer wall of rock would rise, and the men would run ...

But no; the men would not run this time to drop the fenders. There were no men left to do so, unless Bligh was still alive. Perhaps Bligh was still alive. He had walked half-way down the quarter-deck steps a little before the sudden nightfall of the day before, had then fallen and lain for a minute (dead, Abel Keeling had supposed, watching him from his place by the gun-truck), and had then got up again and tottered forward to the forecastle, his tall figure swaying and his long arms waving. Abel Keeling had not seen him since. Most likely, he had died in the forecastle during the night. If he had not been dead he would have come aft again for water ...

At the remembrance of the water Abel Keeling lifted his head. The strands of lean muscle about his emaciated mouth worked, and he made a little pressure of his sun-blackened hand on the deck, as if to verify its steepness and his own balance. The mainmast was some seven or eight yards away ... He put one stiff leg under him and began, seated as he was, to make shuffling movements down the slope.

To the mainmast, near the belfry, was affixed his contrivance for catching water. It consisted of a collar of rope set lower at one side than at the other (but that had been before the mast had steeved so many degrees away from the zenith), and tallowed beneath. The mists lingered later in that gully of a strait than they did on the open ocean, and the collar of rope served as a collector for the dews that condensed on the mast. The drops fell into a small earthen pipkin placed on the deck beneath it.

Abel Keeling reached the pipkin and looked into it. It was nearly a third full of fresh water. Good. If Bligh, the mate, was dead, so much the more water for Abel Keeling, master of the *Mary of the Tower*. He dipped two fingers into the pipkin and put them into his mouth. This he did several times. He did not dare to raise the pipkin to his black and broken lips for dread of a remembered agony, he could not have told how many days ago, when a devil had whispered to him, and he had gulped down the contents of the pipkin in the morning, and for the rest of the day had gone waterless ... Again he moistened his fingers and sucked them; then he lay sprawling against the mast, idly watching the drops of water as they fell.

It was odd how the drops formed. Slowly they collected at the edge of the tallowed collar, trembled in their fullness for an instant, and fell, another beginning the process instantly. It amused Abel Keeling to watch them. Why (he wondered) were all the drops the same size? What cause and compulsion did they obey that they never varied, and what frail tenuity held the little globules intact? It must be due to some Cause ... He remembered that the aromatic gum of the wild frankincense with which they had parcelled the seams had hung on the buckets in great sluggish gouts, obedient to a different compulsion; oil was different again, and so were juices and balsams. Only quicksilver (perhaps the heavy and motionless sea put him in mind of quicksilver) seemed obedient to no law ... Why was it so?

Bligh, of course, would have had his explanation: it was the Hand of God. That sufficed for Bligh, who had gone forward the evening before, and whom Abel Keeling now seemed vaguely and as at a distance to remember as the deep-voiced fanatic who had sung his hymns as, man by man, he had committed the bodies of the ship's company to the deep. Bligh was that sort of man; accepted things without question; was content to take things as they were and be ready with the fenders when the wall of rock rose out of the opalescent mists. Bligh, too, like the waterdrops, had his Law, that was his and nobody else's ...

There floated down from some rotten rope up aloft a flake of scurf, that settled in the pipkin. Abel Keeling watched it dully as it settled towards the pipkin's rim. When presently he again dipped his fingers into the vessel the water ran into a little vortex, drawing the flake with it. The water settled again; and again the minute flake determined towards the rim and adhered there, as if the rim had power to draw it ...

It was exactly so that the galleon was gliding towards the wall of rock, the yellow and green weeds, and the monkeys and parrots. Put out into mid-water again (while there had been men to put her out) she had glided to the other wall. One force drew the chip in the pipkin and the ship over the tranced sea. It was the Hand of God, said Bligh ...

Abel Keeling, his mind now noting minute things and now clouded with torpor, did not at first hear a voice that was quakingly lifted up over by the forecastle—a voice that drew nearer, to an accompaniment of swirling water.

"O Thou, that Jonas in the fish
    Three days didst keep from pain,
Which was a figure of Thy death
    And rising up again—"

It was Bligh, singing one of his hymns:

"O Thou, that Noah keptst from flood
    And Abram, day by day,
As he along through Egypt passed
    Didst guide him in the way—"

The voice ceased, leaving the pious period uncompleted. Bligh was alive, at any rate ...

Abel Keeling resumed his fitful musing.

Yes, that was the Law of Bligh's life, to call things the Hand of God; but Abel Keeling's Law was different; no better, no worse, only different. The Hand of God, that drew chips and galleons, must work by some method; and Abel Keeling's eyes were dully on the pipkin again as if he sought the method there ...

Then conscious thought left him for a space, and when he resumed it was without obvious connection.

Oars, of course, were the thing. With oars, men could laugh at calms. Oars, that only pinnaces and galliasses now used, had had their advantages. But oars (which was to say a method, for you could say if you liked that the Hand of God grasped the oar-loom, as the Breath of God filled the sail)—oars were antiquated, belonged to the past, and meant a throwing-over of all that was good and new and a return to fine lines, a battle-formation abreast to give effect to the shock of the ram, and a day or two at sea and then to port again for provisions. Oars ... no. Abel Keeling was one of the new men, the men who swore by the line-ahead, the broadside fire of sakers and demi-cannon, and weeks and months without a landfall. Perhaps one day the wits of such

men as he would devise a craft, not oar-driven (because oars could not
penetrate into the remote seas of the world)—not sail-driven (because
men who trusted to sails found themselves in an airless, three-mile
strait, suspended motionless between cloud and water, ever gliding
to a wall of rock)—but a ship ... a ship ...

> "To Noah and his sons with him
>   God spake, and thus said He:
> A covenant set I up with you
>   And your posterity—"

It was Bligh again, wandering somewhere in the waist. Abel
Keeling's mind was once more a blank. Then slowly, slowly, as the water
drops collected on the collar of rope, his thought took shape again.

A galliasse? No, not a galliasse. The galliasse made shift to be two
things, and was neither. This ship, that the hand of man should one
day make for the Hand of God to manage, should be a ship that should
take and conserve the force of the wind, take it and store it as she
stored her victuals; at rest when she wished, going ahead when she
wished; turning the forces both of calm and storm against themselves.
For, of course, her force must be wind—stored wind—a bag of the
winds, as the children's tale had it—wind probably directed upon the
water astern, driving it away and urging forward the ship, acting by
reaction. She would have a wind-chamber, into which wind would be
pumped with pumps ... Bligh would call that equally the Hand of God,
this driving-force of the ship of the future that Abel Keeling dimly
foreshadowed as he lay between the mainmast and the belfry, turning his eyes now and then from ashy white timbers to the vivid green
bronze-rust of the bell above him ...

Bligh's face, liver-coloured with the sun and ravaged from inwards
by the faith that consumed him, appeared at the head of the quarter-
deck steps. His voice beat uncontrolledly out.

> "And in the earth here is no place
>   Of refuge to be found,
> Nor in the deep and water-course
>   That passeth under ground—"

II

Bligh's eyes were lidded, as if in contemplation of his inner ecstasy.
His head was thrown back, and his brows worked up and down
tormentedly. His wide mouth remained open as his hymn was suddenly

interrupted on the long-drawn note. From somewhere in the shim-
mering mists the note was taken up, and there drummed and rang
and reverberated through the strait a windy, hoarse, and dismal bel-
low, alarming and sustained. A tremor rang through Bligh. Moving like a
sightless man, he stumbled forward from the head of the quarter-deck
steps, and Abel Keeling was aware of his gaunt figure behind him,
taller for the steepness of the deck. As that vast empty sound died
away, Bligh laughed in his mania.

"Lord, hath the grave's wide mouth a tongue to praise Thee? Lo,
again—"

Again the cavernous sound possessed the air, louder and nearer.
Through it came another sound, a slow throb, throb—throb, throb—
Again the sounds ceased.

"Even Leviathan lifteth up his voice in praise!" Bligh sobbed.

Abel Keeling did not raise his head. There had returned to him
the memory of that day when, before the morning mists had lifted
from the strait, he had emptied the pipkin of the water that was the
allowance until night should fall again. During that agony of thirst
he had seen shapes and heard sounds with other than his mortal eyes
and ears, and even in the moments that had alternated with his lightness, when he had known these to be hallucinations, they had come
again. He had heard the bells on a Sunday in his own Kentish home,
the calling of children at play, the unconcerned singing of men at their
daily labour, and the laughter and gossip of the women as they had
spread the linen on the hedge or distributed bread upon the platters.
These voices had rung in his brain, interrupted now and then by the
groans of Bligh and of two other men who had been alive then. Some
of the voices he had heard had been silent on earth this many a long
year, but Abel Keeling, thirst-tortured, had heard them, even as he
was now hearing that vacant moaning with the intermittent throbbing that filled the strait with alarm ...

"Praise Him, praise Him, praise Him!" Bligh was calling deliriously.

Then a bell seemed to sound in Abel Keeling's ears, and, as if something in the mechanism of his brain had slipped, another picture rose
in his fancy—the scene when the *Mary of the Tower* had put out, to a
bravery of swinging bells and shrill fifes and valiant trumpets. She
had not been a leper-white galleon then. The scroll-work on her prow
had twinkled with gilding; her belfry and stern-galleries and elabo-
rate lanterns had flashed in the sun with gold; and her fighting-tops and
the war-pavesse about her waist had been gay with painted coats and
scutcheons. To her sails had been stitched gaudy ramping lions of scarlet
say, and from her mainyard, now dipping in the water, had hung the broad
two-tailed pennant with the Virgin and Child embroidered upon it ...

Then suddenly a voice about him seemed to be saying, *"And a half-seven—and a half-seven—"* and in a twink the picture in Abel Keeling's brain changed again. He was at home again, instructing his son, young Abel, in the casting of the lead from the skiff they had pulled out of the harbour.

"And a half-seven!" the boy seemed to be calling.

Abel Keeling's blackened lips muttered: "Excellently well cast, Abel, excellently well cast!"

"And a half-seven—and a half-seven—seven—seven—"

"Ah," Abel Keeling murmured, "that last was not a clear cast—give me the line—thus it should go ... ay, so ... Soon you shall sail the seas with me in the *Mary of the Tower*. You are already perfect in the stars and the motions of the planets; to-morrow I will instruct you in the use of the backstaff ..."

For a minute or two he continued to mutter; then he dozed. When again he came to semi-consciousness it was once more to the sound of bells, at first faint, then louder, and finally becoming a noisy clamour immediately above his head. It was Bligh. Bligh, in a fresh attack of delirium, had seized the bell-lanyard and was ringing the bell insanely. The cord broke in his fingers, but he thrust at the bell with his hand, and again called aloud.

"Upon an harp and an instrument of ten strings ... let Heaven and Earth praise Thy Name! ..."

He continued to call aloud, and to beat on the bronze-rusted bell.

"Ship ahoy! What ship's that?"

One would have said that a veritable hail had come out of the mists; but Abel Keeling knew those hails that came out of the mists. They came from ships which were not there.

"Ay, ay, keep a good look-out, and have a care to your lode-manage," he muttered again to his son ...

But, as sometimes a sleeper sits up in his dream, or rises from his couch and walks, so all of a sudden Abel Keeling found himself on his hands and knees on the deck, looking back over his shoulder. In some deep-seated region of his consciousness he was dimly aware that the cant of the deck had become more perilous, but his brain received the intelligence and forgot it again. He was looking out into the bright and baffling mists. The buckler of the sun was of a more ardent silver; the sea below it was lost in brilliant evaporation; and between them, suspended in the haze, no more substantial than the vague darknesses that float before dazzled eyes, a pyramidal phantom-shape hung. Abel Keeling passed his hand over his eyes, but when he removed it the shape was still there, gliding slowly towards the Mary's quarter. Its form changed as he watched it. The spirit-grey shape that had been a

pyramid seemed to dissolve into four upright members, slightly graduated in tallness, that nearest the Mary's stern the tallest and that to
the left the lowest. It might have been the shadow of the gigantic set
of reed-pipes on which that vacant mournful note had been sounded.

And as he looked, with fooled eyes, again his ears became fooled:
*"Ahoy there! What ship's that? Are you a ship? ... Here, give me
that trumpet—"* Then a metallic barking. *"Ahoy there! What the devil
are you? Didn't you ring a bell? Ring it again, or blow a blast or
something, and go dead slow!"*

All this came, as it were, indistinctly, and through a sort of high
singing in Abel Keeling's own ears. Then he fancied a short bewildered
laugh, followed by a colloquy from somewhere between sea and sky.

*"Here, Ward, just pinch me, will you? Tell me what you see there.
I want to know if I'm awake."*

"See where?"

*"There, on the starboard bow. (Stop that ventilating fan; I can't
hear myself think.) See anything? Don't tell me it's that damned
Dutchman—don't pitch me that old Vanderdecken tale—give me an
easy one first, something about a sea-serpent ... You did hear that
bell, didn't you?"*

"Shut up a minute—listen—"

Again Bligh's voice was lifted up.

"This is the cov'nant that I make:
    From henceforth nevermore
Will I again the world destroy
    With water, as before."

Bligh's voice died away again in Abel Keeling's ears.

"Oh—my—fat—Aunt—Julia!" the voice that seemed to come from
between sea and sky sounded again. Then it spoke more loudly. *"I
say,"* it began with careful politeness, *"if you are a ship, do you mind
telling us where the masquerade is to be? Our wireless is out of order,
and we hadn't heard of it ... Oh, you do see it, Ward, don't you? ...
Please, please tell us what the hell you are!"*

Again Abel Keeling had moved as a sleepwalker moves. He had
raised himself up by the belfry timbers, and Bligh had sunk in a heap
on the deck. Abel Keeling's movement overturned the pipkin, which
raced the little trickle of its contents down the deck and lodged where
the still and brimming sea made, as it were, a chain with the carved
balustrade of the quarter-deck—one link a still gleaming edge, then a
dark baluster, and then another gleaming link. For one moment only
Abel Keeling found himself noticing that that which had driven Bligh

aft had been the rising of the water in the waist as the galleon settled by the head—the waist was now entirely submerged; then once more he was absorbed in his dream, its voices, and its shape in the mist, which had again taken the form of a pyramid before his eyeballs.

"*Of course,*" a voice seemed to be complaining anew, and still through that confused dinning in Abel Keeling's ears, "*we can't turn a four-inch on it ... And, of course, Ward, I don't believe in 'em. D'you hear, Ward? I don't believe in 'em, I say ... Shall we call down to old A. B.? This might interest His Scientific Skippership ...*"

"*Oh, lower a boat and pull out to it—into it—over it—through it—*"

"*Look at our chaps crowded on the barbette yonder. They've seen it. Better not give an order you know won't be obeyed ...*"

Abel Keeling, cramped against the antique belfry, had begun to find his dream interesting. For, though he did not know her build, that mirage was the shape of a ship. No doubt it was projected from his brooding on ships of half an hour before; and that was odd ... But perhaps, after all, it was not very odd. He knew that she did not really exist; only the appearance of her existed; but things had to exist like that before they really existed. Before the *Mary of the Tower* had existed she had been a shape in some man's imagination; before that, some dreamer had dreamed the form of a ship with oars; and before that, far away in the dawn and infancy of the world, some seer had seen in a vision the raft before man had ventured to push out over the water on his two planks. And since this shape that rode before Abel Keeling's eyes was a shape in his, Abel Keeling's dream, he, Abel Keeling, was the master of it. His own brooding brain had contrived her, and she was launched upon the illimitable ocean of his own mind ...

"And I will not unmindful be
    Of this, My covenant, passed
Twixt Me and you and every flesh
    Whiles that the world should last,"

sang Bligh, rapt ...

But as a dreamer, even in his dream, will scratch upon the wall by his couch some key or word to put him in mind of his vision on the morrow when it has left him, so Abel Keeling found himself seeking some sign to be a proof to those to whom no vision is vouchsafed. Even Bligh sought that—could not be silent in his bliss, but lay on the deck there, uttering great passionate Amens and praising his Maker, as he said, upon an harp and an instrument of ten strings. So with Abel Keeling. It would be the Amen of his life to have praised God, not upon a harp, but upon a ship that should carry her own power, that should store wind or its equivalent as she stored her victuals, that should be something wrested from the chaos of uninvention and ordered and disciplined and subordinated to Abel Keeling's will ... And there she was, that ship-shaped thing of spirit-grey, with the four pipes that resembled a phantom organ now broadside and of equal length. And the ghost-crew of that ship were speaking again ...

The interrupted silver chain by the quarterdeck balustrade had now become continuous, and the balusters made a herring-bone over their own motionless reflections. The spilt water from the pipkin had dried, and the pipkin was not to be seen. Abel Keeling stood beside the mast, erect as God made man to go. With his leathery hand he smote upon the bell. He waited for the space of a minute, and then cried:

"Ahoy! ... Ship ahoy! ... What ship's that?"

III

We are not conscious in a dream that we are playing a game the beginning and end of which are in ourselves. In this dream of Abel Keeling's a voice replied:

"*Hallo, it's found its tongue ... Ahoy there! What are you?*"

Loudly and in a clear voice Abel Keeling called: "Are you a ship?"

With a nervous giggle the answer came:

"*We are a ship, aren't we, Ward? I hardly feel sure ... Yes, of course, we're a ship. No question about us. The question is what the dickens you are.*"

Not all the words these voices used were intelligible to Abel Keeling, and he knew not what it was in the tone of these last words that reminded him of the honour due to the *Mary of the Tower*. Blister-white and at the end of her life as she was, Abel Keeling was still jealous of her dignity; the voice had a youngish ring; and it was not fitting that young chins should be wagged about his galleon. He spoke curtly.

"You that spoke—are you the master of that ship?"

"*Officer of the watch,*" the words floated back; "*the captain's below.*"

"Then send for him. It is with masters that masters hold speech," Abel Keeling replied.

He could see the two shapes, flat and without relief, standing on a high narrow structure with rails. One of them gave a low whistle, and seemed to be fanning his face; but the other rumbled something into a sort of funnel. Presently the two shapes became three. There was a murmuring, as of a consultation, and then suddenly a new voice spoke. At its thrill and tone a sudden tremor ran through Abel Keeling's frame. He wondered what response it was that that voice found in the forgotten recesses of his memory ...

"*Ahoy!*" seemed to call this new yet faintly remembered voice. "*What's all this about? Listen. We're His Majesty's destroyer* SEAPINK, *out of Devonport last October, and nothing particular the matter with us. Now who are you?*"

"The *Mary of the Tower*, out of the Port of Rye on the day of Saint Anne, and only two men—"

A gasp interrupted him.

"*Out of* WHERE?" that voice that so strangely moved Abel Keeling said unsteadily, while Bligh broke into groans of renewed rapture.

"Out of the Port of Rye, in the County of Sussex ... nay, give ear, else I cannot make you hear me while this man's spirit and flesh wrestle so together! ... Ahoy! Are you gone?" For the voices had become a low murmur, and the ship-shape had faded before Abel Keeling's eyes. Again and again he called. He wished to be informed of the disposition and economy of the wind-chamber ...

"The wind-chamber!" he called, in an agony lest the knowledge almost within his grasp should be lost. "I would know about the wind-chamber ..."

Like an echo, there came back the words, uncomprehendingly uttered, "*The wind-chamber? ...*"

"... That driveth the vessel—perchance 'tis not wind—a steel bow that is bent also conserveth force—the force you store, to move at will through calm and storm ..."

"*Can you make out what it's driving at?*"

"*Oh, we shall all wake up in a minute ...*"

"*Quiet, I have it; the engines; it wants to know about our engines. It'll be wanting to see our papers presently. Rye Port! ... Well, no harm in humouring it; let's see what it can make of this. Ahoy there!*" came the voice to Abel Keeling, a little more strongly, as if a shifting wind carried it, and speaking faster and faster as it went on. "*Not wind, but steam; d'you hear? Steam, steam. Steam, in eight Yarrow water-tube boilers. S-t-e-a-m, steam. Got it? And we've twin-screw triple expansion engines, indicated horse-power four thousand, and we can do 430 revolutions per minute; savvy? Is there anything your phantomhood would like to know about our armament? ...*"

Abel Keeling was muttering fretfully to himself. It annoyed him that words in his own vision should have no meaning for him. How did words come to him in a dream that he had no knowledge of when wide awake? The SEAPINK—that was the name of this ship; but a pink was long and narrow, low-carged and square-built aft ...

"*And as for our armament,*" the voice with the tones that so profoundly troubled Abel Keeling's memory continued, "*we've two revolving Whitehead torpedo-tubes, three six-pounders on the upper deck, and that's a twelve-pounder forward there by the conning-tower. I forgot to mention that we're nickel steel, with a coal capacity of sixty tons in most damnably placed bunkers, and that thirty and a quarter knots is about our top. Care to come aboard?"*

But the voice was speaking still more rapidly and feverishly, as if to fill a silence with no matter what, and the shape that was uttering it was straining forward anxiously over the rail.

"Ugh! But I'm glad this happened in the daylight," another voice was muttering.

"I wish I was sure it was happening at all ... Poor old spook!"

"I suppose it would keep its feet if her deck was quite vertical. Think she'll go down, or just melt?"

"Kind of go down ... without wash ..."

"Listen—here's the other one now—"

For Bligh was singing again:

"For, Lord, Thou know'st our nature such
    If we great things obtain,
And in the getting of the same
    Do feel no grief or pain,

"We little do esteem thereof;
    But, hardly brought to pass,
A thousand times we do esteem
    More than the other was."

"But oh, look—look—look at the other! ... Oh, I say, wasn't he a grand old boy! Look!"

For, transfiguring Abel Keeling's form as a prophet's form is transfigured in the instant of his rapture, flooding his brain with the white eureka-light of perfect knowledge, that for which he and his dream had been at a standstill had come. He knew her, this ship of the future, as if God's Finger had bitten her lines into his brain. He knew her as those already sinking into the grave know things, miraculously, completely, accepting Life's impossibilities with a nodded "Of course." From the ardent mouths of her eight furnaces to the last drip from her lubricators, from her bed-plates to the breeches of her quick-firers, he knew her—read her gauges, thumbed her bearings, gave the ranges from her range-finders, and lived the life he lived who was in command of her. And he would not forget on the morrow, as he had forgotten on many morrows, for at last he had seen the water about his feet, and knew that there would be no morrow for him in this world ...

And even in that moment, with but a sand or two to run in his glass, indomitable, insatiable, dreaming dream on dream, he could not die until he knew more. He had two questions to ask, and a master-question; and but a moment remained. Sharply his voice rang out.

"Ho, there! ... This ancient ship, the *Mary of the Tower*, cannot steam thirty and a quarter knots, but yet she can sail the waters. What more does your ship? Can she soar above them, as the fowls of the air soar?"

"Lord, he thinks we're an aeroplane! ... No, she can't ..."

"And can you dive, even as the fishes of the deep?"

"No ... Those are submarines ... we aren't a submarine ..."

But Abel Keeling waited for no more. He gave an exulting chuckle.

"Oho, oho—thirty knots, and but on the face of the waters—no more than that? Oho! ... Now my ship, the ship I see as a mother sees full-grown the child she has but conceived—my ship, I say—oho!—my ship shall ... Below there—trip that gun!"

The cry came suddenly and alertly, as a muffled sound came from below and an ominous tremor shook the galleon.

"By Jove, her guns are breaking loose below—that's her finish—"

"Trip that gun, and double-breech the others!" Abel Keeling's voice rang out, as if there had been any to obey him. He had braced himself within the belfry frame; and then in the middle of the next order his voice suddenly failed him. His ship-shape, that for the moment he had forgotten, rode once more before his eyes. This was the end, and his master-question, apprehension for the answer to which was now torturing his face and well-nigh bursting his heart, was still unasked.

"Ho—he that spoke with me—the master," he cried in a voice that ran high, "is he there?"

"Yes, yes!" came the other voice across the water, sick with suspense. *"Oh, be quick!"*

There was a moment in which hoarse cries from many voices, a heavy thud and rumble on wood, and a crash of timbers and a gurgle and a splash were indescribably mingled; the gun under which Abel Keeling had lain had snapped her rotten breechings and plunged down the deck, carrying Bligh's unconscious form with it. The deck came up vertical, and for one instant longer Abel Keeling clung to the belfry.

"I cannot see your face," he screamed, "but meseems your voice is a voice I know. WHAT IS YOUR NAME?"

In a torn sob the answer came across the water:

"Keeling—Abel Keeling ... Oh, my God!"

And Abel Keeling's cry of triumph, that mounted to a victorious "Huzza!" was lost in the downward plunge of the *Mary of the Tower*, that left the strait empty save for the sun's fiery blaze and the last smoke-like evaporation of the mists.

Accessory Before The Fact

ALGERNON BLACKWOOD

At the moorland cross-roads Martin stood examining the sign-post for several minutes in some bewilderment. The names on the four arms were not what he expected, distances were not given, and his map, he concluded with impatience, must be hopelessly out of date. Spreading it against the post, he stooped to study it more closely. The wind blew the corners flapping against his face.

The small print was almost indecipherable in the fading light. It appeared, however—as well as he could make out—that two miles back he must have taken the wrong turning.

He remembered that turning. The path had looked inviting; he had hesitated a moment, then followed it, caught by the usual lure of walkers that it "might prove a short cut." The short-cut snare is old as human nature. For some minutes he studied the sign-post and the map alternately.

Dusk was falling, and his knapsack had grown heavy. He could not make the two guides tally, however, and a feeling of uncertainty crept over his mind. He felt oddly baffled, frustrated. His thought grew thick. Decision was most difficult. "I'm muddled," he thought; "I must be tired," as at length he chose the most likely arm. "Sooner or later it will bring me to an inn, though not the one I intended." He accepted his walker's luck, and started briskly. The arm read, "Over Litacy Hill" in small, fine letters that danced and shifted every time he looked at them; but the name was not discoverable on the map. It was, however, inviting like the short cut. A similar impulse again directed his choice. Only this time it seemed more insistent, almost urgent.

And he became aware, then, of the exceeding loneliness of the country about him. The road for a hundred yards went straight, then curved like a white river running into space; the deep blue-green of heather lined the banks, spreading upwards through the twilight; and occasional small pines stood solitary here and there, all unexplained. The curious adjective, having made its appearance, haunted him. So many things that afternoon were similarly—unexplained: the short cut, the darkened map, the names on the sign-post, his own erratic impulses, and the growing strange confusion that crept upon his spirit. The entire country-side needed explanation, though perhaps "interpretation" was the truer word. Those little lonely trees had made him see it. Why had he lost his way so easily? Why did he suffer vague impressions to influence his direction? Why was he here—exactly here? And why did he go now "over Litacy Hill"? Then, by a green field that shone like a thought of daylight amid the darkness of the moor, he saw a figure lying in the grass. It was a blot upon the landscape, a mere huddled patch of dirty rags, yet with a certain horrid picturesqueness too; and his mind—though his German was of the schoolroom order—at once picked out the German equivalents as against the English. Lump and Lumpen flashed across his brain most oddly. They seemed in that moment right, and so expressive, almost like onomatopoeic words, if that were possible of sight. Neither "rags" nor "rascal" would have fitted what he saw. The adequate description was in German.

Here was a clue tossed up by the part of him that did not reason. But it seems he missed it.

And the next minute the tramp rose to a sitting posture and asked the time of evening. In German he asked it. And Martin, answering without a second's hesitation, gave it, also in German, "halb sieben"—half-past six. The instinctive guess was accurate. A glance at his watch when he looked a moment later proved it. He heard the man say, with the covert insolence of tramps, "T'ank you; much opliged." For Martin had not shown his watch—another intuition subconsciously obeyed.

He quickened his pace along that lonely road, a curious jumble of thoughts and feelings surging through him. He had somehow known the question would come, and come in German.

Yet it flustered and dismayed him. Another thing had also flustered and dismayed him. He had expected it in the same queer fashion: it was right. For when the ragged brown thing rose to ask the question, a part of it remained lying on the grass—another brown, dirty thing. There were two tramps. And he saw both faces clearly. Behind the untidy beards, and below the old slouch hats, he caught the look of unpleasant, clever faces that watched him closely while he passed.

The eyes followed him. For a second he looked straight into those eyes, so that he could not fail to know them. And he understood, quite horridly, that both faces were too sleek, refined, and cunning for those of ordinary tramps. The men were not really tramps at all. They were disguised.

"How covertly they watched me!" was his thought, as he hurried along the darkening road, aware in dead earnestness now of the loneliness and desolation of the moorland all about him.

Uneasy and distressed, he increased his pace. Midway in thinking what an unnecessarily clanking noise his nailed boots made upon the hard white road, there came upon him with a rush together the company of these things that haunted him as "unexplained." They brought a single definite message: That all this business was not really meant for him at all, and hence his confusion and bewilderment; that he had intruded into someone else's scenery, and was trespassing upon another's map of life. By some wrong inner turning he had interpolated his person into a group of foreign forces which operated in the little world of someone else.

Unwittingly, somewhere, he had crossed the threshold, and now was fairly in—a trespasser, an eavesdropper, a Peeping Torn. He was listening, peeping; overhearing things he had no right to know, because they were intended for another. Like a ship at sea he was intercepting wireless messages he could not properly interpret, because his Receiver was not accurately tuned to their reception. And more—these messages were warnings!

Then fear dropped upon him like the night. He was caught in a net of delicate, deep forces he could not manage, knowing neither their origin nor purpose. He had walked into some huge psychic trap elaborately planned and baited, yet calculated for another than himself. Something had lured him in, something in the landscape, the time of day, his mood. Owing to some undiscovered weakness in himself he had been easily caught. His fear slipped easily into terror.

What happened next happened with such speed and concentration that it all seemed crammed into a moment. At once and in a heap it happened. It was quite inevitable. Down the white road to meet him a man came swaying from side to side in drunkenness quite obviously feigned—a tramp; and while Martin made room for him to pass, the lurch changed in a second to attack, and the fellow was upon him. The blow was sudden and terrific, yet even while it fell Martin was aware that behind him rushed a second man, who caught his legs from under him and bore him with a thud and crash to the ground. Blows rained then; he saw a gleam of something shining; a sudden deadly nausea plunged him into utter weakness where resistance was impossible.

Something of fire entered his throat, and from his mouth poured a thick sweet thing that choked him. The world sank far away into darkness. ... Yet through all the horror and confusion ran the trail of two clear thoughts: he realised that the first tramp had sneaked at a fast double through the heather and so come down to meet him; and that something heavy was torn from fastenings that clipped it tight and close beneath his clothes against his body. ...

Abruptly then the darkness lifted, passed utterly away. He found himself peering into the map against the signpost. The wind was flapping the corners against his cheek, and he was poring over names that now he saw quite clear. Upon the arms of the sign-post above were those he had expected to find, and the map recorded them quite faithfully. All was accurate again and as it should be. He read the name of the village he had meant to make—it was plainly visible in the dusk, two miles the distance given. Bewildered, shaken, unable to think of anything, he stuffed the map into his pocket unfolded, and hurried forward like a man who has just wakened from an awful dream that had compressed into a single second all the detailed misery of some prolonged, oppressive nightmare.

He broke into a steady trot that soon became a run; the perspiration poured from him; his legs felt weak, and his breath was difficult to manage. He was only conscious of the overpowering desire to get away as fast as possible from the sign-post at the cross-roads where the dreadful vision had flashed upon him. For Martin, accountant on a holiday, had never dreamed of any world of psychic possibilities. The entire thing was torture. It was worse than a "cooked" balance of the books that some conspiracy of clerks and directors proved at his innocent door. He raced as though the country-side ran crying at his heels. And always still ran with him the incredible conviction that none of this was really meant for himself at all. He had overheard the secrets of another. He had taken the warning for another into himself, and so altered its direction. He had thereby prevented its right delivery. It all shocked him beyond words. It dislocated the machinery of his just and accurate soul. The warning was intended for another, who could not—would not—now receive it.

The physical exertion, however, brought at length a more comfortable reaction and some measure of composure. With the lights in sight, he slowed down and entered the village at a reasonable pace. The inn was reached, a bedroom inspected and engaged, and supper ordered with the solid comfort of a large Bass to satisfy an unholy thirst and complete the restoration of balance. The unusual sensations largely passed away, and the odd feeling that anything in his simple, wholesome world required explanation was no longer present. Still with a vague uneasiness about him, though actual fear quite gone, he went into the bar to smoke an after-supper pipe and chat with the natives, as his pleasure was upon a holiday, and so saw two men leaning upon the counter at the far end with their backs towards him. He saw their faces instantly in the glass, and the pipe nearly slipped from between his teeth. Clean-shaven, sleek, clever faces—and he caught a word or two as they talked over their drinks—German words. Well dressed they were, both men, with nothing about them calling for particular attention; they might have been two tourists holiday-making like himself in tweeds and walking-boots. And they presently paid for their drinks and went out. He never saw them face to face at all; but the sweat broke out afresh all over him, a feverish rush of heat and ice together ran about his body; beyond question he recognised the two tramps, this time not disguised—not yet disguised.

He remained in his corner without moving, puffing violently at an extinguished pipe, gripped helplessly by the return of that first vile terror. It came again to him with an absolute clarity of certainty that it was not with himself they had to do, these men, and, further, that he had no right in the world to interfere. He had no *locus standi* at all; it would be immoral ... even if the opportunity came. And the opportunity, he felt, would come. He had been an eavesdropper, and had come upon private information of a secret kind that he had no right to make use of, even that good might come—even to save life. He sat on in his corner, terrified and silent, waiting for the thing that should happen next.

But night came without explanation. Nothing happened. He slept soundly. There was no other guest at the inn but an elderly man, apparently a tourist like himself. He wore gold-rimmed glasses, and in the morning Martin overheard him asking the landlord what direction he should take for Litacy Hill. His teeth began then to chatter and a weakness came into his knees. "You turn to the left at the cross-roads," Martin broke in before the landlord could reply; "you'll see the sign-post about two miles from here, and after that it's a matter of four miles more." How in the world did he know, flashed horribly through him. "I'm going that way myself," he was saying next; "I'll go with you for a bit—if you don't mind!" The words came out impulsively and ill-considered; of their own accord they came. For his own direction was exactly opposite.

He did not want the man to go alone. The stranger, however, easily evaded his offer of companionship. He thanked him with the remark that he was starting later in the day. ... They were standing, all three, beside the horse-trough in front of the inn, when at that very moment a tramp, slouching along the road, looked up and asked the time of day. And it was the man with the gold-rimmed glasses who told him.

"T'ank you; much opliged," the tramp replied, passing on with his slow, slouching gait, while the landlord, a talkative fellow, proceeded to remark upon the number of Germans that lived in England and were ready to swell the Teutonic invasion which he, for his part, deemed imminent.

But Martin heard it not. Before he had gone a mile upon his way he went into the woods to fight his conscience all alone. His feebleness, his cowardice, were surely criminal. Real anguish tortured him. A dozen times he decided to go back upon his steps, and a dozen times the singular authority that whispered he had no right to interfere prevented him. How could he act upon knowledge gained by eavesdropping? How interfere in the private business of another's hidden life merely because he had overheard, as at the telephone, its secret dangers? Some inner confusion prevented straight thinking altogether. The stranger would merely think him mad. He had no "fact" to go upon. ... He smothered a hundred impulses ... and finally went on his way with a shaking, troubled heart.

The last two days of his holiday were ruined by doubts and questions and alarms—all justified later when he read of the murder of a tourist upon Litacy Hill. The man wore gold-rimmed glasses, and carried in a belt about his person a large sum of money. His throat was cut.

And the police were hard upon the trail of a mysterious pair of tramps, said to be—Germans.

Enoch Soames:
A Memory of the Eighteen-Nineties
Max Beerbohm

When a book about the literature of the eighteen-nineties was given by Mr. Holbrook Jackson to the world, I looked eagerly in the index for Soames, Enoch. It was as I feared: he was not there. But everybody else was. Many writers whom I had quite forgotten, or remembered but faintly, lived again for me, they and their work, in Mr. Holbrook Jackson's pages. The book was as thorough as it was brilliantly written. And thus the omission found by me was an all the deadlier record of poor Soames's failure to impress himself on his decade.

I dare say I am the only person who noticed the omission. Soames had failed so piteously as all that! Nor is there a counterpoise in the thought that if he had had some measure of success he might have passed, like those others, out of my mind, to return only at the historian's beck. It is true that had his gifts, such as they were, been acknowledged in his lifetime, he would never have made the bargain I saw him make—that strange bargain whose results have kept him always in the foreground of my memory. But it is from those very results that the full piteousness of him glares out.

Not my compassion, however, impels me to write of him. For his sake, poor fellow, I should be inclined to keep my pen out of the ink. It is ill to deride the dead. And how can I write about Enoch Soames without making him ridiculous? Or, rather, how am I to hush up the horrid fact that he *was* ridiculous? I shall not be able to do that. Yet, sooner or later, write about him I must. You will see in due course that I have no option. And I may as well get the thing done now.

In the summer term of '93 a bolt from the blue flashed down on Oxford. It drove deep; it hurtlingly embedded itself in the soil. Dons and undergraduates stood around, rather pale, discussing nothing but it. Whence came it, this meteorite? From Paris. Its name? Will Rothenstein. Its aim? To do a series of twenty-four portraits in lithograph. These were to be published from the Bodley Head, London.

The matter was urgent. Already the warden of A, and the master of B, and the Regius Professor of C had meekly "sat." Dignified and doddering old men who had never consented to sit to any one could not withtand this dynamic little stranger. He did not sue; he invited: he did not invite; he commanded. He was twenty-one years old. He wore spectacles that flashed more than any other pair ever seen. He was a wit. He was brimful of ideas. He knew Whistler. He knew Daudet and the Goncourts. He knew every one in Paris. He knew them all by heart. He was Paris in Oxford. It was whispered that, so soon as he had polished off his selection of dons, he was going to include a few undergraduates. It was a proud day for me when I—I was included. I liked Rothenstein not less than I feared him; and there arose between us a friendship that has grown ever warmer, and been more and more valued by me, with every passing year.

At the end of term he settled in, or, rather, meteoritically into, London. It was to him I owed my first knowledge of that forever-enchanting little world-in-itself, Chelsea, and my first acquaintance with Walter Sickert and other August elders who dwelt there. It was Rothenstein that took me to see, in Cambridge Street, Pimlico, a young man whose drawings were already famous among the few—Aubrey Beardsley by name. With Rothenstein I paid my first visit to the Bodley Head. By him I was inducted into another haunt of intellect and daring, the domino-room of the Cafe Royal.

There, on that October evening—there, in that exuberant vista of gilding and crimson velvet set amidst all those opposing mirrors and upholding caryatids, with fumes of tobacco ever rising to the painted and pagan ceiling, and with the hum of presumably cynical conversation broken into so sharply now and again by the clatter of dominoes shuffled on marble tables, I drew a deep breath and, "This indeed," said I to myself, "is life!" (Forgive me that theory. Remember the waging of even the South African War was not yet.)

It was the hour before dinner. We drank vermuth. Those who knew Rothenstein were pointing him out to those who knew him only by name. Men were constantly coming in through the swing-doors and wandering slowly up and down in search of vacant tables or of tables occupied by friends. One of these rovers interested me because I was sure he wanted to catch Rothenstein's eye. He had twice passed our table, with a hesitating look; but Rothenstein, in the thick of a disquisition on Puvis de Chavannes, had not seen him. He was a stooping, shambling person, rather tall, very pale, with longish and brownish hair. He had a thin, vague beard, or, rather, he had a chin on which a large number of hairs weakly curled and clustered to cover its retreat. He was an odd-looking person; but in the nineties odd apparitions were more frequent, I think, than they are now. The young writers of that era—and I was sure this man was a writer—strove earnestly to be distinct in aspect. This man had striven unsuccessfully. He wore a soft black hat of clerical kind, but of Bohemian intention, and a gray waterproof cape which, perhaps because it was waterproof, failed to be romantic. I decided that "dim" was the *mot juste* for him. I had already essayed to write, and was immensely keen on the mot juste, that Holy Grail of the period.

The dim man was now again approaching our table, and this time he made up his mind to pause in front of it.

"You don't remember me," he said in a toneless voice.

Rothenstein brightly focused him.

"Yes, I do," he replied after a moment, with pride rather than effusion—pride in a retentive memory. "Edwin Soames."

"Enoch Soames," said Enoch.

"Enoch Soames," repeated Rothenstein in a tone implying that it was enough to have hit on the surname. "We met in Paris a few times when you were living there. We met at the Cafe Groche."

"And I came to your studio once."

"Oh, yes; I was sorry I was out."

"But you were in. You showed me some of your paintings, you know. I hear you're in Chelsea now."

"Yes."

I almost wondered that Mr. Soames did not, after this monosyllable, pass along. He stood patiently there, rather like a dumb animal, rather like a donkey looking over a gate. A sad figure, his. It occurred to me that "hungry" was perhaps the *mot juste* for him; but—hungry for what? He looked as if he had little appetite for anything. I was sorry for him; and Rothenstein, though he had not invited him to Chelsea, did ask him to sit down and have something to drink.

Seated, he was more self-assertive. He flung back the wings of his cape with a gesture which, had not those wings been waterproof, might have seemed to hurl defiance at things in general. And he ordered an absinthe. "Je me tiens toujours fidele," he told Rothenstein, "a la sorciere glauque."

"It is bad for you," said Rothenstein, dryly.

"Nothing is bad for one," answered Soames. "Dans ce monde il n'y a ni bien ni mal."

"Nothing good and nothing bad? How do you mean?"

"I explained it all in the preface to 'Negations.'"

"'Negations'?"

"Yes, I gave you a copy of it."

"Oh, yes, of course. But, did you explain, for instance, that there was no such thing as bad or good grammar?"

"N-no," said Soames. "Of course in art there is the good and the evil. But in life—no." He was rolling a cigarette. He had weak, white hands, not well washed, and with finger-tips much stained with nicotine. "In life there are illusions of good and evil, but"—his voice trailed away to a murmur in which the words "vieux jeu" and "rococo" were faintly audible. I think he felt he was not doing himself justice, and feared that Rothenstein was going to point out fallacies. Anyhow, he cleared his throat and said, "Parlons d'autre chose."

It occurs to you that he was a fool? It didn't to me. I was young, and had not the clarity of judgment that Rothenstein already had. Soames was quite five or six years older than either of us. Also—he had written a book. It was wonderful to have written a book.

If Rothenstein had not been there, I should have revered Soames. Even as it was, I respected him. And I was very near indeed to reverence when he said he had another book coming out soon. I asked if I might ask what kind of book it was to be.

"My poems," he answered. Rothenstein asked if this was to be the title of the book. The poet meditated on this suggestion, but said he rather thought of giving the book no title at all. "If a book is good in itself—" he murmured, and waved his cigarette.

Rothenstein objected that absence of title might be bad for the sale of a book.

"If," he urged, "I went into a bookseller's and said simply, 'Have you got?' or, 'Have you a copy of?' how would they know what I wanted?"

"Oh, of course I should have my name on the cover," Soames answered earnestly. "And I rather want," he added, looking hard at Rothenstein, "to have a drawing of myself as frontispiece." Rothenstein admitted that this was a capital idea, and mentioned that he was going into the country and would be there for some time. He then looked at his watch, exclaimed at the hour, paid the waiter, and went away with me to dinner. Soames remained at his post of fidelity to the glaucous witch.

"Why were you so determined not to draw him?" I asked.

"Draw him? Him? How can one draw a man who doesn't exist?"

"He is dim," I admitted. But my *mot juste* fell flat. Rothenstein repeated that Soames was non-existent.

Still, Soames had written a book. I asked if Rothenstein had read

"Negations." He said he had looked into it, "but," he added crisply, "I don't profess to know anything about writing." A reservation very characteristic of the period! Painters would not then allow that any one outside their own order had a right to any opinion about painting. This law (graven on the tablets brought down by Whistler from the summit of Fuji-yama) imposed certain limitations. If other arts than painting were not utterly unintelligible to all but the men who practiced them, the law tottered—the Monroe Doctrine, as it were, did not hold good. Therefore no painter would offer an opinion of a book without warning you at any rate that his opinion was worthless. No one is a better judge of literature than Rothenstein; but it wouldn't have done to tell him so in those days, and I knew that I must form an unaided judgment of "Negations."

Not to buy a book of which I had met the author face to face would have been for me in those days an impossible act of self-denial. When I returned to Oxford for the Christmas term I had duly secured "Negations." I used to keep it lying carelessly on the table in my room, and whenever a friend took it up and asked what it was about, I would say: "Oh, it's rather a remarkable book. It's by a man whom I know." Just "what it was about" I never was able to say. Head or tail was just what I hadn't made of that slim, green volume. I found in the preface no clue to the labyrinth of contents, and in that labyrinth nothing to explain the preface.

LEAN NEAR TO LIFE. LEAN VERY NEAR—NEARER.

LIFE IS WEB AND THEREIN NOR WARP NOR WOOF IS, BUT WEB ONLY.

IT IS FOR THIS I AM CATHOLICK IN CHURCH AND IN THOUGHT, YET DO LET SWIFT MOOD WEAVE THERE WHAT THE SHUTTLE OF MOOD WILLS.

These were the opening phrases of the preface, but those which followed were less easy to understand. Then came "Stark: A Conte," about a midinette who, so far as I could gather, murdered, or was about to murder, a mannequin. It was rather like a story by Catulle Mendes in which the translator had either skipped or cut out every alternate sentence. Next, a dialogue between Pan and St. Ursula, lacking, I rather thought, in "snap." Next, some aphorisms (entitled "Aphorismata" [spelled in Greek]). Throughout, in fact, there was a great variety of form, and the forms had evidently been wrought with much care. It was rather the substance that eluded me. Was there, I wondered, any substance at all? It did not occur to me: suppose Enoch Soames was a fool! Up cropped a rival hypothesis: suppose *I* was! I inclined to give Soames the benefit of the doubt. I had read "L'Apres-midi d'un faune" without extracting a glimmer of meaning; yet Mallarme, of course, was a master. How was I to know that Soames wasn't another? There was a sort of music in his prose, not indeed, arresting, but perhaps, I thought, haunting, and laden, perhaps, with meanings as deep as Mallarme's own. I awaited his poems with an open mind.

And I looked forward to them with positive impatience after I had had a second meeting with him. This was on an evening in January. Going into the aforesaid domino-room, I had passed a table at which sat a pale man with an open book before him. He had looked from his book to me, and I looked back over my shoulder with a vague sense that I ought to have recognized him. I returned to pay my respects. After exchanging a few words, I said with a glance to the open book, "I see I am interrupting you," and was about to pass on, but, "I prefer," Soames replied in his toneless voice, "to be interrupted," and I obeyed his gesture that I should sit down.

I asked him if he often read here.

"Yes; things of this kind I read here," he answered, indicating the title of his book— "The Poems of Shelley."

"Anything that you really"—and I was going to say "admire?" But I cautiously left my sentence unfinished, and was glad that I had done so, for he said with unwonted emphasis, "Anything second-rate."

I had read little of Shelley, but, "Of course," I murmured, "he's very uneven."

"I should have thought evenness was just what was wrong with him. A deadly evenness. That's why I read him here. The noise of this place breaks the rhythm. He's tolerable here." Soames took up the book and glanced through the pages. He laughed. Soames's laugh was a short, single, and mirthless sound from the throat, unaccompanied by any movement of the face or brightening of the eyes. "What a period!" he uttered, laying the book down. And, "What a country!" he added.

I asked rather nervously if he didn't think Keats had more or less held his own against the drawbacks of time and place. He admitted that there were "passages in Keats," but did not specify them. Of "the older men," as he called them, he seemed to like only Milton. "Milton," he said, "wasn't sentimental." Also, "Milton had a dark insight." And again, "I can always read Milton in the reading-room."

"The reading-room?"

"Of the British Museum. I go there every day."

"You do? I've only been there once. I'm afraid I found it rather a depressing place. It—it seemed to sap one's vitality."

"It does. That's why I go there. The lower one's vitality, the more sensitive one is to great art. I live near the museum. I have rooms in Dyott Street."

"And you go round to the reading-room to read Milton?"

"Usually Milton." He looked at me. "It was Milton," he certificatively added, "who converted me to diabolism."

"Diabolism? Oh, yes? Really?" said I, with that vague discomfort and that intense desire to be polite which one feels when a man speaks of his own religion. "You—worship the devil?"

Soames shook his head.

"It's not exactly worship," he qualified, sipping his absinthe. "It's more a matter of trusting and encouraging."

"I see, yes. I had rather gathered from the preface to 'Negations' that you were a—a Catholic."

"Je l'etais a cette epoque. In fact, I still am. I am a Catholic diabolist."

But this profession he made in an almost cursory tone. I could see that what was upmost in his mind was the fact that I had read "Negations." His pale eyes had for the first time gleamed. I felt as one who is about to be examined viva voce on the very subject in which he is shakiest. I hastily asked him how soon his poems were to be published.

"Next week," he told me.

"And are they to be published without a title?"

"No. I found a title at last. But I sha'n't tell you what it is," as though I had been so impertinent as to inquire. "I am not sure that it wholly satisfies me. But it is the best I can find. It suggests something of the quality of the poems—strange growths, natural and wild, yet exquisite," he added, "and many-hued, and full of poisons."

I asked him what he thought of Baudelaire. He uttered the snort that was his laugh, and, "Baudelaire," he said, "was a bourgeois malgre lui." France had had only one poet—Villon; "and two thirds of Villon were sheer journalism." Verlaine was "an epicier malgre lui." Altogether, rather to my surprise, he rated French literature lower than English. There were "passages" in Villiers de l'Isle-Adam. But, "I," he summed up, "owe nothing to France." He nodded at me. "You'll see," he predicted.

I did not, when the time came, quite see that. I thought the author of "Fungoids" did, unconsciously of course, owe something to the young Parisian decadents or to the young English ones who owed something to *them*. I still think so. The little book, bought by me in Oxford, lies before me as I write. Its pale-gray buckram cover and silver lettering have not worn well. Nor have its contents. Through these, with a melancholy interest, I have again been looking. They are not much. But at the time of their publication I had a vague suspicion that they *might* be. I suppose it is my capacity for faith, not poor Soames's work, that is weaker than it once was.

To A Young Woman
Thou Art, Who Hast Not Been!

Pale tunes irresolute
And traceries of old sounds
Blown from a rotted flute
Mingle with noise of cymbals rouged with
rust, Nor not strange forms and epicene
Lie bleeding in the dust,
Being wounded with wounds.
For this it is
That in thy counterpart
Of age-long mockeries
Thou Hast Not Been Nor Art!

There seemed to me a certain inconsistency as between the first and last lines of this. I tried, with bent brows, to resolve the discord. But I did not take my failure as wholly incompatible with a meaning in Soames's mind. Might it not rather indicate the depth of his meaning? As for the craftsmanship, "rouged with rust' seemed to me a fine stroke, and "nor not" instead of "and" had a curious felicity. I wondered who the "young woman" was and what she had made of it all. I sadly suspect that Soames could not have made more of it than she. Yet even now, if one doesn't try to make any sense at all of the poem, and reads it just for the sound, there is a certain grace of cadence. Soames was an artist, in so far as he was anything, poor fellow!

It seemed to me, when first I read "Fungoids," that, oddly enough, the diabolistic side of him was the best. Diabolism seemed to be a cheerful, even a wholesome influence in his life.

Nocturne

Round and round the shutter'd Square
I strolled with the Devil's arm in mine.
No sound but the scrape of his hoofs was there
And the ring of his laughter and mine.
        We had drunk black wine.

I scream'd, "I will race you, Master!"
"What matter," he shriek'd, "to-night
Which of us runs the faster?

There is nothing to fear to-night
In the foul moon's light!"

Then I look'd him in the eyes
And I laugh'd full shrill at the lie he told
And the gnawing fear he would fain disguise.
It was true, what I'd time and again been told:
He was old—old.

There was, I felt, quite a swing about that first stanza—a joyous and rollicking note of comradeship. The second was slightly hysterical, perhaps. But I liked the third, it was so bracingly unorthodox, even according to the tenets of Soames's peculiar sect in the faith. Not much "trusting and encouraging" here! Soames triumphantly exposing the devil as a liar, and laughing "full shrill," cut a quite heartening figure, I thought, then! Now, in the light of what befell, none of his other poems depresses me so much as "Nocturne."

I looked out for what the metropolitan reviewers would have to say. They seemed to fall into two classes: those who had little to say and those who had nothing. The second class was the larger, and the words of the first were cold; insomuch that

Strikes a note of modernity. ... These tripping numbers.—
"The Preston Telegraph."

was the only lure offered in advertisements by Soames's publisher. I had hoped that when next I met the poet I could congratulate him on having made a stir, for I fancied he was not so sure of his intrinsic greatness as he seemed. I was but able to say, rather coarsely, when next I did see him, that I hoped "Fungoids" was "selling splendidly." He looked at me across his glass of absinthe and asked if I had bought a copy. His publisher had told him that three had been sold. I laughed, as at a jest.

"You don't suppose I *care*, do you?" he said, with something like a snarl. I disclaimed the notion. He added that he was not a tradesman. I said mildly that I wasn't, either, and murmured that an artist who gave truly new and great things to the world had always to wait long for recognition. He said he cared not a sou for recognition. I agreed that the act of creation was its own reward.

His moroseness might have alienated me if I had regarded myself as a nobody. But ah! hadn't both John Lane and Aubrey Beardsley suggested that I should write an essay for the great new venture that

was afoot— "The Yellow Book"? And hadn't Henry Harland, as editor, accepted my essay? And wasn't it to be in the very first number?
At Oxford I was still *in statu pupillari*. In London I regarded myself
as very much indeed a graduate now—one whom no Soames could
ruffle. Partly to show off, partly in sheer good-will, I told Soames he
ought to contribute to "The Yellow Book." He uttered from the throat
a sound of scorn for that publication.

Nevertheless, I did, a day or two later, tentatively ask Harland if
he knew anything of the work of a man called Enoch Soames. Harland
paused in the midst of his characteristic stride around the room, threw
up his hands toward the ceiling, and groaned aloud: he had often met
"that absurd creature" in Paris, and this very morning had received
some poems in manuscript from him.

"Has he *no* talent?" I asked.

"He has an income. He's all right." Harland was the most joyous
of men and most generous of critics, and he hated to talk of anything
about which he couldn't be enthusiastic. So I dropped the subject of
Soames. The news that Soames had an income did take the edge off
solicitude. I learned afterward that he was the son of an unsuccessful
and deceased bookseller in Preston, but had inherited an annuity of
three hundred pounds from a married aunt, and had no surviving relatives of any kind. Materially, then, he was "all right." But there was
still a spiritual pathos about him, sharpened for me now by the possibility that even the praises of "The Preston Telegraph" might not have
been forthcoming had he not been the son of a Preston man He had a
sort of weak doggedness which I could not but admire. Neither he
nor his work received the slightest encouragement; but he persisted
in behaving as a personage: always he kept his dingy little flag flying.
Wherever congregated the jeunes feroces of the arts, in whatever Soho
restaurant they had just discovered, in whatever music-hall they were
most frequently, there was Soames in the midst of them, or, rather,
on the fringe of them, a dim, but inevitable, figure. He never sought
to propitiate his fellow-writers, never bated a jot of his arrogance
about his own work or of his contempt for theirs. To the painters he
was respectful, even humble; but for the poets and prosaists of "The
Yellow Book" and later of "The Savoy" he had never a word but of
scorn. He wasn't resented. It didn't occur to anybody that he or his
Catholic diabolism mattered. When, in the autumn of '96, he brought
out (at his own expense, this time) a third book, his last book, nobody said a word for or against it. I meant, but forgot, to buy it. I
never saw it, and am ashamed to say I don't even remember what it
was called. But I did, at the time of its publication, say to Rothenstein
that I thought poor old Soames was really a rather tragic figure, and

that I believed he would literally die for want of recognition. Rothenstein scoffed. He said I was trying to get credit for a kind heart which I didn't possess; and perhaps this was so. But at the private view of the New English Art Club, a few weeks later, I beheld a pastel portrait of "Enoch Soames, Esq." It was very like him, and very like Rothenstein to have done it. Soames was standing near it, in his soft hat and his waterproof cape, all through the afternoon. Anybody who knew him would have recognized the portrait at a glance, but nobody who didn't know him would have recognized the portrait from its by-stander: it "existed" so much more than he; it was bound to. Also, it had not that expression of faint happiness which on that day was dis-cernible, yes, in Soames's countenance. Fame had breathed on him. Twice again in the course of the month I went to the New English, and on both occasions Soames himself was on view there. Looking back, I regard the close of that exhibition as having been virtually the close of his career. He had felt the breath of Fame against his cheek— so late, for such a little while; and at its withdrawal he gave in, gave up, gave out. He, who had never looked strong or well, looked ghastly now—a shadow of the shade he had once been. He still frequented the domino-room, but having lost all wish to excite curiosity, he no longer read books there. "You read only at the museum now?" I asked, with attempted cheerfulness. He said he never went there now. "No absinthe there," he muttered. It was the sort of thing that in old days he would have said for effect; but it carried conviction now. Absinthe, erst but a point in the "personality" he had striven so hard to build up, was solace and necessity now. He no longer called it "la sorciere glauque." He had shed away all his French phrases. He had become a plain, unvarnished Preston man.

Failure, if it be a plain, unvarnished, complete failure, and even though it be a squalid failure, has always a certain dignity. I avoided Soames because he made me feel rather vulgar. John Lane had pub-lished, by this time, two little books of mine, and they had had a pleas-ant little success of esteem. I was a—slight, but definite— "personality." Frank Harris had engaged me to kick up my heels in "The Saturday Re-view," Alfred Harmsworth was letting me do likewise in "The Daily Mail." I was just what Soames wasn't. And he shamed my gloss. Had I known that he really and firmly believed in the greatness of what he as an artist had achieved, I might not have shunned him. No man who hasn't lost his vanity can be held to have altogether failed. Soames's dignity was an illusion of mine. One day, in the first week of June, 1897, that illu-sion went. But on the evening of that day Soames went, too.

I had been out most of the morning and, as it was too late to reach home in time for luncheon, I sought the Vingtieme. This little place—

Restaurant du Vingtieme Siecle, to give it its full title—had been discovered in '96 by the poets and prosaists, but had now been more or
less abandoned in favor of some later find. I don't think it lived long
enough to justify its name; but at that time there it still was, in Greek
Street, a few doors from Soho Square, and almost opposite to that
house where, in the first years of the century, a little girl, and with
her a boy named De Quincey, made nightly encampment in darkness
and hunger among dust and rats and old legal parchments. The
Vingtieme was but a small whitewashed room, leading out into the
street at one end and into a kitchen at the other. The proprietor and
cook was a Frenchman, known to us as Monsieur Vingtieme; the waiters
were his two daughters, Rose and Berthe; and the food, according to faith,
was good. The tables were so narrow and were set so close together
that there was space for twelve of them, six jutting from each wall.

Only the two nearest to the door, as I went in, were occupied. On
one side sat a tall, flashy, rather Mephistophelian man whom I had
seen from time to time in the domino-room and elsewhere. On the
other side sat Soames. They made a queer contrast in that sunlit room,
Soames sitting haggard in that hat and cape, which nowhere at any
season had I seen him doff, and this other, this keenly vital man, at
sight of whom I more than ever wondered whether he were a diamond
merchant, a conjurer, or the head of a private detective agency. I was
sure Soames didn't want my company; but I asked, as it would have
seemed brutal not to, whether I might join him, and took the chair
opposite to his. He was smoking a cigarette, with an untasted salmi
of something on his plate and a half-empty bottle of Sauterne before him,
and he was quite silent. I said that the preparations for the Jubilee
made London impossible. (I rather liked them, really.) I professed a
wish to go right away till the whole thing was over. In vain did I at-
tune myself to his gloom. He seemed not to hear me or even to see
me. I felt that his behavior made me ridiculous in the eyes of the other
man. The gangway between the two rows of tables at the Vingtieme
was hardly more than two feet wide (Rose and Berthe, in their minis-
trations, had always to edge past each other, quarreling in whispers
as they did so), and any one at the table abreast of yours was virtually
at yours. I thought our neighbor was amused at my failure to interest
Soames, and so, as I could not explain to him that my insistence was
merely charitable, I became silent. Without turning my head, I had
him well within my range of vision. I hoped I looked less vulgar than
he in contrast with Soames. I was sure he was not an Englishman,
but what *was* his nationality? Though his jet-black hair was en brosse,
I did not think he was French. To Berthe, who waited on him, he spoke
French fluently, but with a hardly native idiom and accent. I gathered

that this was his first visit to the Vingtieme; but Berthe was offhand in her manner to him: he had not made a good impression. His eyes were handsome, but, like the Vingtieme's tables, too narrow and set too close together. His nose was predatory, and the points of his mustache, waxed up behind his nostrils, gave a fixity to his smile. Decidedly, he was sinister. And my sense of discomfort in his presence was intensified by the scarlet waistcoat which tightly, and so unseasonably in June, sheathed his ample chest. This waistcoat wasn't wrong merely because of the heat, either. It was somehow all wrong in itself. It wouldn't have done on Christmas morning. It would have struck a jarring note at the first night of "Hernani." I was trying to account for its wrongness when Soames suddenly and strangely broke silence. "A hundred years hence!" he murmured, as in a trance.

"We shall not be here," I briskly, but fatuously, added.

"We shall not be here. No," he droned, "but the museum will still be just where it is. And the reading-room just where it is. And people will be able to go and read there." He inhaled sharply, and a spasm as of actual pain contorted his features.

I wondered what train of thought poor Soames had been following. He did not enlighten me when he said, after a long pause, "You think I haven't minded."

"Minded what, Soames?"

"Neglect. Failure."

"*Failure?*" I said heartily. "Failure?" I repeated vaguely. "Neglect—yes, perhaps; but that's quite another matter. Of course you haven't been—appreciated. But what, then? Any artist who—who gives—" What I wanted to say was,

"Any artist who gives truly new and great things to the world has always to wait long for recognition"; but the flattery would not out: in the face of his misery—a misery so genuine and so unmasked—my lips would not say the words.

And then he said them for me. I flushed. "That's what you were going to say, isn't it?" he asked.

"How did you know?"

"It's what you said to me three years ago, when 'Fungoids' was published." I flushed the more. I need not have flushed at all. "It's the only important thing I ever heard you say," he continued. "And I've never forgotten it. It's a true thing. It's a horrible truth. But—d'you remember what I answered? I said, 'I don't care a sou for recognition.' And you believed me. You've gone on believing I'm above that sort of thing. You're shallow. What should *you* know of the feelings of a man like me? You imagine that a great artist's faith in himself and in the verdict of posterity is enough to keep him happy. You've never guessed at the bitterness and loneliness, the"—his voice broke; but presently he resumed, speaking with a force that I had never known in him. "Posterity! What use is it to *me*? A dead man doesn't know that people are visiting his grave, visiting his birth-place, putting up tablets to him, unveiling statues of him. A dead man can't read the books that are written about him. A hundred years hence! Think of it! If I could come back to life *then*—just for a few hours—and go to the reading-room and *read*! Or, better still, if I could be projected now, at this moment, into that future, into that reading-room, just for this one after-noon! I'd sell myself body and soul to the devil for that! Think of the pages and pages in the catalogue: 'Soames, Enoch' endlessly—endless editions, commentaries, prolegomena, biographies"— But here he was interrupted by a sudden loud crack of the chair at the next table. Our neighbor had half risen from his place. He was leaning toward us, apologetically intrusive.

"Excuse—permit me," he said softly. "I have been unable not to hear. Might I take a liberty? In this little restaurant-sans-façon—might I, as the phrase is, cut in?"

I could but signify our acquiescence. Berthe had appeared at the kitchen door, thinking the stranger wanted his bill. He waved her away with his cigar, and in another moment had seated himself beside me, commanding a full view of Soames.

"Though not an Englishman," he explained, "I know my London well, Mr. Soames. Your name and fame—Mr. Beerbohm's, too—very known to me. Your point is, who am *I*?" He glanced quickly over his shoulder, and in a lowered voice said, "I am the devil."

I couldn't help it; I laughed. I tried not to, I knew there was nothing to laugh at, my rudeness shamed me; but—I laughed with increasing volume. The devil's quiet dignity, the surprise and disgust of his raised eyebrows, did but the more dissolve me. I rocked to and fro; I lay back aching; I behaved deplorably.

"I am a gentleman, and," he said with intense emphasis, "I thought I was in the company of GENTLEMEN."

"Don't!" I gasped faintly. "Oh, don't!"

"Curious, nicht wahr?" I heard him say to Soames. "There is a type of person to whom the very mention of my name is—oh, so awfully— funny! In your theaters the dullest comedien needs only to say 'The devil!' and right away they give him 'the loud laugh what speaks the vacant mind.' Is it not so?"

I had now just breath enough to offer my apologies. He accepted them, but coldly, and re-addressed himself to Soames.

"I am a man of business," he said, "and always I would put things through 'right now,' as they say in the States. You are a poet. Les affaires—you detest them. So be it. But with me you will deal, eh? What you have said just now gives me furiously to hope."

Soames had not moved except to light a fresh cigarette. He sat crouched forward, with his elbows squared on the table, and his head just above the level of his hands, staring up at the devil.

"Go on," he nodded. I had no remnant of laughter in me now.

"It will be the more pleasant, our little deal," the devil went on, "because you are—I mistake not?—a diabolist."

"A Catholic diabolist," said Soames.

The devil accepted the reservation genially.

"You wish," he resumed, "to visit now—this afternoon as-ever-is—the reading-room of the British Museum, yes? But of a hundred years hence, yes? Parfaitement. Time—an illusion. Past and future—they are as ever present as the present, or at any rate only what you call 'just round the corner.' I switch you on to any date. I project you—pouf! You wish to be in the reading-room just as it will be on the afternoon of June 3, 1997? You wish to find yourself standing in that room, just past the swing-doors, this very minute, yes? And to stay there till closing-time? Am I right?"

Soames nodded.

The devil looked at his watch. "Ten past two," he said. "Closing-time in summer same then as now—seven o'clock. That will give you almost five hours. At seven o'clock—pouf!—you find yourself again here, sitting at this table. I am dining to-night dans le monde—dans le higlif. That concludes my present visit to your great city. I come and fetch you here, Mr. Soames, on my way home."

"Home?" I echoed.

"Be it never so humble!" said the devil, lightly.

"All right," said Soames.

"Soames!" I entreated. But my friend moved not a muscle.

The devil had made as though to stretch forth his hand across the table, but he paused in his gesture.

"A hundred years hence, as now," he smiled, "no smoking allowed in the reading-room. You would better therefore—"

Soames removed the cigarette from his mouth and dropped it into his glass of Sauterne.

"Soames!" again I cried. "Can't you"—but the devil had now stretched forth his hand across the table. He brought it slowly down on the table-cloth. Soames's chair was empty. His cigarette floated sodden in his wine-glass. There was no other trace of him.

For a few moments the devil let his hand rest where it lay, gazing at me out of the corners of his eyes, vulgarly triumphant.

A shudder shook me. With an effort I controlled myself and rose from my chair. "Very clever," I said condescendingly. "But— 'The Time Machine' is a delightful book, don't you think? So entirely original!"

"You are pleased to sneer," said the devil, who had also risen, "but it is one thing to write about an impossible machine; it is a quite other thing to be a supernatural power." All the same, I had scored.

Berthe had come forth at the sound of our rising. I explained to her that Mr. Soames had been called away, and that both he and I would be dining here. It was not until I was out in the open air that I began to feel giddy. I have but the haziest recollection of what I did, where I wandered, in the glaring sunshine of that endless afternoon. I remember the sound of carpenters' hammers all along Piccadilly and the bare chaotic look of the half-erected "stands." Was it in the Green Park or in Kensington Gardens or *where* was it that I sat on a chair beneath a tree, trying to read an evening paper? There was a phrase in the leading article that went on repeating itself in my fagged mind: "Little is hidden from this August Lady full of the garnered wisdom of sixty years of Sovereignty." I remember wildly conceiving a letter (to reach Windsor by an express messenger told to await answer): "Madam: Well knowing that your Majesty is full of the garnered wisdom of sixty years of Sovereignty, I venture to ask your advice in the following delicate matter. Mr. Enoch Soames, whose poems you may or may not know—" Was there *no* way of helping him, saving him? A bargain was a bargain, and I was the last man to aid or abet any one in wriggling out of a reasonable obligation. I wouldn't have lifted a little finger to save Faust. But poor Soames! Doomed to pay without respite an eternal price for nothing but a fruitless search and a bitter disillusioning.

Odd and uncanny it seemed to me that he, Soames, in the flesh, in the waterproof cape, was at this moment living in the last decade of the next century, poring over books not yet written, and seeing and seen by men not yet born. Uncannier and odder still that to-night and evermore he would be in hell. Assuredly, truth was stranger than fiction.

Endless that afternoon was. Almost I wished I had gone with Soames, not, indeed, to stay in the reading-room, but to sally forth for a brisk sight-seeing walk around a new London. I wandered restlessly out of the park I had sat in. Vainly I tried to imagine myself an ardent tourist from the eighteenth century. Intolerable was the strain of the slow-passing and empty minutes. Long before seven o'clock I was back at the Vingtieme.

I sat there just where I had sat for luncheon. Air came in listlessly through the open door behind me. Now and again Rose or Berthe appeared for a moment. I had told them I would not order any dinner till Mr. Soames came. A hurdy-gurdy began to play, abruptly drowning the noise of a quarrel between some Frenchmen farther up the street.

Whenever the tune was changed I heard the quarrel still raging. I had bought another evening paper on my way. I unfolded it. My eyes gazed ever away from it to the clock over the kitchen door.

Five minutes now to the hour! I remembered that clocks in restaurants are kept five minutes fast. I concentrated my eyes on the paper. I vowed I would not look away from it again. I held it upright, at its full width, close to my face, so that I had no view of anything but it. Rather a tremulous sheet? Only because of the draft, I told myself.

My arms gradually became stiff; they ached; but I could not drop them—now. I had a suspicion, I had a certainty. Well, what, then? What else had I come for? Yet I held tight that barrier of newspaper. Only the sound of Berthe's brisk footstep from the kitchen enabled me, forced me, to drop it, and to utter:

"What shall we have to eat, Soames?"

"Il est souffrant, ce pauvre Monsieur Soames?" asked Berthe.

"He's only—tired." I asked her to get some wine—Burgundy—and whatever food might be ready. Soames sat crouched forward against the table exactly as when last I had seen him. It was as though he had never moved—he who had moved so unimaginably far. Once or twice in the afternoon it had for an instant occurred to me that perhaps his journey was not to be fruitless, that perhaps we had all been wrong in our estimate of the works of Enoch Soames. That we had been horribly right was horribly clear from the look of him. But, "Don't be discouraged," I falteringly said. "Perhaps it's only that you—didn't leave enough time. Two, three centuries hence, perhaps—"

"Yes," his voice came; "I've thought of that."

"And now—now for the more immediate future! Where are you going to hide? How would it be if you caught the Paris express from Charing Cross? Almost an hour to spare. Don't go on to Paris. Stop at Calais. Live in Calais. He'd never think of looking for you in Calais."

"It's like my luck," he said, "to spend my last hours on earth with an ass." But I was not offended. "And a treacherous ass," he strangely added, tossing across to me a crumpled bit of paper which he had been holding in his hand. I glanced at the writing on it—some sort of gibberish, apparently. I laid it impatiently aside.

"Come, Soames, pull yourself together! This isn't a mere matter of life or death. It's a question of eternal torment, mind you! You don't mean to say you're going to wait limply here till the devil comes to fetch you."

"I can't do anything else. I've no choice."

"Come! This is 'trusting and encouraging' with a vengeance! This is diabolism run mad!" I filled his glass with wine. "Surely, now that you've *seen* the brute—"

"It's no good abusing him."

"You must admit there's nothing Miltonic about him, Soames."

"I don't say he's not rather different from what I expected."

"He's a vulgarian, he's a swell mobs-man, he's the sort of man who hangs about the corridors of trains going to the Riviera and steals ladies' jewel-cases. Imagine eternal torment presided over by *him*!"

"You don't suppose I look forward to it, do you?"

"Then why not slip quietly out of the way?"

Again and again I filled his glass, and always, mechanically, he emptied it; but the wine kindled no spark of enterprise in him. He did not eat, and I myself ate hardly at all. I did not in my heart believe that any dash for freedom could save him. The chase would be swift, the capture certain. But better anything than this passive, meek, miserable waiting. I told Soames that for the honor of the human race he ought to make some show of resistance. He asked what the human race had ever done for him. "Besides," he said, "can't you understand that I'm in his power? You saw him touch me, didn't you? There's an end of it. I've no will. I'm sealed."

I made a gesture of despair. He went on repeating the word "sealed." I began to realize that the wine had clouded his brain. No wonder! Foodless he had gone into futurity, foodless he still was. I urged him to eat, at any rate, some bread. It was maddening to think that he, who had so much to tell, might tell nothing. "How was it all," I asked, "yonder? Come, tell me your adventures!"

"They'd make first-rate 'copy,' wouldn't they?"

"I'm awfully sorry for you, Soames, and I make all possible allowances; but what earthly right have you to insinuate that I should make 'copy,' as you call it, out of you?"

The poor fellow pressed his hands to his forehead.

"I don't know," he said. "I had some reason, I know. I'll try to remember. He sat plunged in thought.

"That's right. Try to remember everything. Eat a little more bread. What did the reading-room look like?"

"Much as usual," he at length muttered.

"Many people there?"

"Usual sort of number."

"What did they look like?"

Soames tried to visualize them.

"They all," he presently remembered, "looked very like one another."

My mind took a fearsome leap.

"All dressed in sanitary woolen?"

"Yes, I think so. Grayish-yellowish stuff."

"A sort of uniform?" He nodded. "With a number on it perhaps—a number on a large disk of metal strapped round the left arm? D. K. F.

78,910—that sort of thing?" It was even so. "And all of them, men and women alike, looking very well cared for? Very Utopian, and smelling rather strongly of carbolic, and all of them quite hairless?" I was right every time. Soames was only not sure whether the men and women were hairless or shorn. "I hadn't time to look at them very closely," he explained.

"No, of course not. But—"

"They stared at *me*, I can tell you. I attracted a great deal of attention." At last he had done that! "I think I rather scared them. They moved away whenever I came near. They followed me about, at a distance, wherever I went. The men at the round desk in the middle seemed to have a sort of panic whenever I went to make inquiries."

"What did you do when you arrived?"

Well, he had gone straight to the catalogue, of course,—to the S volumes,—and had stood long before SN-SOF, unable to take this volume out of the shelf because his heart was beating so. At first, he said, he wasn't disappointed; he only thought there was some new arrangement. He went to the middle desk and asked where the catalogue of twentieth-century books was kept. He gathered that there was still only one catalogue. Again he looked up his name, stared at the three little pasted slips he had known so well. Then he went and sat down for a long time.

"And then," he droned, "I looked up the 'Dictionary of National Biography,' and some encyclopedias. I went back to the middle desk and asked what was the best modern book on late nineteenth-century literature. They told me Mr. T. K. Nupton's book was considered the best. I looked it up in the catalogue and filled in a form for it. It was brought to me. My name wasn't in the index, but—yes!" he said with a sudden change of tone, "that's what I'd forgotten. Where's that bit of paper? Give it me back."

I, too, had forgotten that cryptic screed. I found it fallen on the floor, and handed it to him.

He smoothed it out, nodding and smiling at me disagreeably.

"I found myself glancing through Nupton's book," he resumed. "Not very easy reading. Some sort of phonetic spelling. All the modern books I saw were phonetic."

"Then I don't want to hear any more, Soames, please."

"The proper names seemed all to be spelt in the old way. But for that I mightn't have noticed my own name."

"Your own name? Really? Soames, I'm *very* glad."

"And yours."

"No!"

"I thought I should find you waiting here to-night, so I took the trouble to copy out the passage. Read it."

I snatched the paper. Soames's handwriting was characteristically dim. It and the noisome spelling and my excitement made me all the slower to grasp what T. K. Nupton was driving at.

The document lies before me at this moment. Strange that the words I here copy out for you were copied out for me by poor Soames just eighty-two years hence!

From page 234 of "Inglish Littracher 1890-1900" bi T. K. Nupton, publishd bi th Stait, 1992.

Fr egzarmpl, a riter ov th time, naimed Max Beerbohm, hoo woz stil alive in th twentith senchri, rote a stauri in wich e pautraid an immajnari karrakter kauld "Enoch Soames"—a thurd-rait poit hoo beleevz imself a grate jeneus an maix a bargin with th Devvl in auder ter no wot posterriti thinx ov im! It iz a sumwot labud sattire, but not without vallu az show-ing hou seriusli the yung men ov th aiteen-ninetiz took themselvz. Nou that th littreri profeshn haz bin auganized az a departmnt of publik servis, our riters hav found their levvl an hav lernt ter doo their duti without thort ov th morro. "Th laibrer iz werthi ov hiz hire" an that iz aul. Thank hevvn we hav no Enoch Soameses amung us to-dai!

I found that by murmuring the words aloud (a device which I com-mend to my reader) I was able to master them little by little. The clearer they became, the greater was my bewilderment, my distress and horror. The whole thing was a nightmare. Afar, the great grisly background of what was in store for the poor dear art of letters; here, at the table, fixing on me a gaze that made me hot all over, the poor fellow whom—whom evidently—but no: whatever down-grade my character might take in coming years, I should never be such a brute as to—

Again I examined the screed. "Immajnari." But here Soames was, no more imaginary, alas! than I. And "labud"—what on earth was that? (To this day I have never made out that word.) "It's all very—baffling," I at length stammered.

Soames said nothing, but cruelly did not cease to look at me.

"Are you sure," I temporized, "quite sure you copied the thing out correctly?"

"Quite."

"Well, then, it's this wretched Nupton who must have made—must be going to make—some idiotic mistake. Look here Soames, you know me better than to suppose that I—After all, the name Max Beerbohm is not at all an uncommon one, and there must be several Enoch

Soameses running around, or, rather, Enoch Soames is a name that might occur to any one writing a story. And I don't write stories; I'm an essayist, an observer, a recorder. I admit that it's an extraordinary coincidence. But you must see—"

"I see the whole thing," said Soames, quietly. And he added, with a touch of his old manner, but with more dignity than I had ever known in him, "Parlons d'autre chose."

I accepted that suggestion very promptly. I returned straight to the more immediate future. I spent most of the long evening in renewed appeals to Soames to come away and seek refuge somewhere. I remember saying at last that if indeed I was destined to write about him, the supposed "stauri" had better have at least a happy ending. Soames repeated those last three words in a tone of intense scorn.

"In life and in art," he said, "all that matters is an *inevitable* ending."

"But," I urged more hopefully than I felt, "an ending that can be avoided *isn't* inevitable."

"You aren't an artist," he rasped. "And you're so hopelessly not an artist that, so far from being able to imagine a thing and make it seem true, you're going to make even a true thing seem as if you'd made it up. You're a miserable bungler. And it's like my luck."

I protested that the miserable bungler was not I, was not going to be I, but T. K. Nupton; and we had a rather heated argument, in the thick of which it suddenly seemed to me that Soames saw he was in the wrong: he had quite physically cowered. But I wondered why— and now I guessed with a cold throb just why—he stared so past me. The bringer of that "inevitable ending" filled the doorway.

I managed to turn in my chair and to say, not without a semblance of lightness, "Aha, come in!" Dread was indeed rather blunted in me by his looking so absurdly like a villain in a melodrama. The sheen of his tilted hat and of his shirt-front, the repeated twists he was giving to his mustache, and most of all the magnificence of his sneer, gave token that he was there only to be foiled.

He was at our table in a stride. "I am sorry," he sneered witheringly, "to break up your pleasant party, but—"

"You don't; you complete it," I assured him. "Mr. Soames and I want to have a little talk with you. Won't you sit? Mr. Soames got nothing, frankly nothing, by his journey this afternoon. We don't wish to say that the whole thing was a swindle, a common swindle. On the contrary, we believe you meant well. But of course the bargain, such as it was, is off."

The devil gave no verbal answer. He merely looked at Soames and pointed with rigid forefinger to the door. Soames was wretchedly rising from his chair when, with a desperate, quick gesture, I swept together two dinner-knives that were on the table, and laid their blades across each other. The devil stepped sharp back against the table behind him, averting his face and shuddering.

"You are not superstitious!" he hissed.

"Not at all," I smiled.

"Soames," he said as to an underling, but without turning his face, "put those knives straight!"

With an inhibitive gesture to my friend, "Mr. Soames," I said emphatically to the devil, "is a Catholic diabolist"; but my poor friend did the devil's bidding, not mine; and now, with his master's eyes again fixed on him, he arose, he shuffled past me. I tried to speak. It was he that spoke. "Try," was the prayer he threw back at me as the devil pushed him roughly out through the door— "*Try* to make them know that I did exist!"

In another instant I, too, was through that door. I stood staring all ways, up the street, across it, down it. There was moonlight and lamplight, but there was not Soames nor that other.

Dazed, I stood there. Dazed, I turned back at length into the little room, and I suppose I paid Berthe or Rose for my dinner and luncheon and for Soames's; I hope so, for I never went to the Vingtieme again. Ever since that night I have avoided Greek Street altogether. And for years I did not set foot even in Soho Square, because on that same night it was there that I paced and loitered, long and long, with some such dull sense of hope as a man has in not straying far from the place where he has lost something. "Round and round the shutter'd Square"—that line came back to me on my lonely beat, and with it the whole stanza, ringing in my brain and bearing in on me how tragically different from the happy scene imagined by him was the poet's actual experience of that prince in whom of all princes we should put not our trust!

But strange how the mind of an essayist, be it never so stricken, roves and ranges! I remember pausing before a wide door-step and wondering if perchance it was on this very one that the young De Quincey lay ill and faint while poor Ann flew as fast as her feet would carry her to Oxford Street, the "stony-hearted stepmother" of them both, and came back bearing that "glass of port wine and spices" but for which he might, so he thought, actually have died. Was this the very door-step that the old De Quincey used to revisit in homage? I pondered Ann's fate, the cause of her sudden vanishing from the ken of her boy friend; and presently I blamed myself for letting the past override the present. Poor vanished Soames!

And for myself, too, I began to be troubled. What had I better do? Would there be a hue and cry— "Mysterious Disappearance of an Author," and all that? He had last been seen lunching and dining in my company. Hadn't I better get a hansom and drive straight to Scotland Yard? They would think I was a lunatic. After all, I reassured myself, London was a very large place, and one very dim figure might easily drop out of it unobserved, now especially, in the blinding glare of the near Jubilee. Better say nothing at all, I thought.

And I was right. Soames's disappearance made no stir at all. He was utterly forgotten before any one, so far as I am aware, noticed that he was no longer hanging around. Now and again some poet or prosaist may have said to another, "What has become of that man Soames?" but I never heard any such question asked. As for his landlady in Dyott Street, no doubt he had paid her weekly, and what possessions he may have had in his rooms were enough to save her from fretting. The solicitor through whom he was paid his annuity may be presumed to have made inquiries, but no echo of these resounded. There was something rather ghastly to me in the general unconsciousness that Soames had existed, and more than once I caught myself wondering whether Nupton, that babe unborn, were going to be right in thinking him a figment of my brain.

In that extract from Nupton's repulsive book there is one point which perhaps puzzles you. How is it that the author, though I have here mentioned him by name and have quoted the exact words he is going to write, is not going to grasp the obvious corollary that I have invented nothing? The answer can be only this: Nupton will not have read the later passages of this memoir. Such lack of thoroughness is a serious fault in any one who undertakes to do scholar's work. And I hope these words will meet the eye of some contemporary rival to Nupton and be the undoing of Nupton.

I like to think that some time between 1992 and 1997 somebody will have looked up this memoir, and will have forced on the world his inevitable and startling conclusions. And I have reason for believing that this will be so. You realize that the reading-room into which Soames was projected by the devil was in all respects precisely as it will be on the afternoon of June 3, 1997. You realize, therefore, that on that afternoon, when it comes round, there the selfsame crowd will be, and there Soames will be, punctually, he and they doing precisely what they did before. Recall now Soames's account of the sensation he made. You may say that the mere difference of his costume was enough to make him sensational in that uniformed crowd. You wouldn't say so if you had ever seen him, and I assure you that in no period would Soames be anything but dim. The fact that people are going to stare at him and follow him around and seem afraid of him, can be explained only on the hypothesis that they will somehow have been prepared for his ghostly visitation. They will have been awfully waiting to see whether he really would come. And when he does come the effect will of course be—awful.

An authentic, guaranteed, proved ghost, but; only a ghost, alas! Only that. In his first visit Soames was a creature of flesh and blood, whereas the creatures among whom he was projected were but ghosts, I take it—solid, palpable, vocal, but unconscious and automatic ghosts, in a building that was itself an illusion. Next time that building and those creatures will be real. It is of Soames that there will be but the semblance. I wish I could think him destined to revisit the world actually, physically, consciously. I wish he had this one brief escape, this one small treat, to look forward to. I never forget him for long. He is where he is and forever. The more rigid moralists among you may say he has only himself to blame. For my part, I think he has been very hardly used. It is well that vanity should be chastened; and Enoch Soames's vanity was, I admit, above the average, and called for special treatment. But there was no need for vindictiveness. You say he contracted to pay the price he is paying. Yes; but I maintain that he was induced to do so by fraud. Well informed in all things, the devil must have known that my friend would gain nothing by his visit to futurity. The whole thing was a very shabby trick. The more I think of it, the more detestable the devil seems to me.

Of him I have caught sight several times, here and there, since that day at the Vingtieme. Only once, however, have I seen him at close quarters. This was a couple of years ago, in Paris. I was walking one afternoon along the rue d'Antin, and I saw him advancing from the opposite direction, overdressed as ever, and swinging an ebony cane and altogether behaving as though the whole pavement belonged to him. At thought of Enoch Soames and the myriads of other sufferers eternally in this brute's dominion, a great cold wrath filled me, and I drew myself up to my full height. But—well, one is so used to nodding and smiling in the street to anybody whom one knows that the action becomes almost independent of oneself; to prevent it requires a very sharp effort and great presence of mind. I was miserably aware, as I passed the devil, that I nodded and smiled to him. And my shame was the deeper and hotter because he, if you please, stared straight at me with the utmost haughtiness.

To be cut, deliberately cut, by *him!* I was, I still am, furious at having had that happen to me.

Coachwhip Publications

CoachwhipBooks.com

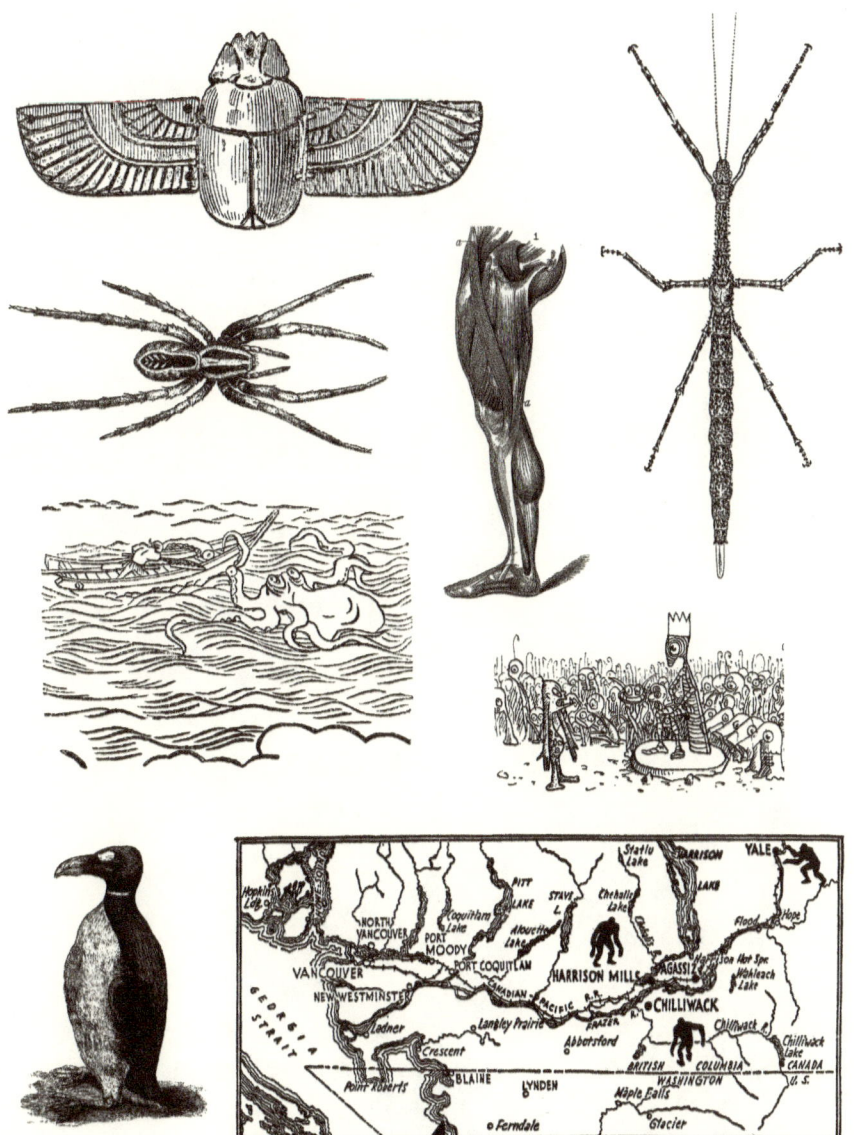